Brooke's Bliss

Other Books by Lexi Blake

ROMANTIC SUSPENSE

Masters and Mercenaries
The Dom Who Loved Me
The Men With The Golden Cuffs
A Dom is Forever
On Her Master's Secret Service
Sanctum: A Masters and Mercenaries Novella
Love and Let Die
Unconditional: A Masters and Mercenaries Novella
Dungeon Royale
Dungeon Games: A Masters and Mercenaries Novella
A View to a Thrill
Cherished: A Masters and Mercenaries Novella
You Only Love Twice
Luscious: Masters and Mercenaries~Topped
Adored: A Masters and Mercenaries Novella
Master No
Just One Taste: Masters and Mercenaries~Topped 2
From Sanctum with Love
Devoted: A Masters and Mercenaries Novella
Dominance Never Dies
Submission is Not Enough
Master Bits and Mercenary Bites~The Secret Recipes of Topped
Perfectly Paired: Masters and Mercenaries~Topped 3
For His Eyes Only
Arranged: A Masters and Mercenaries Novella
Love Another Day
At Your Service: Masters and Mercenaries~Topped 4
Master Bits and Mercenary Bites~Girls Night
Nobody Does It Better
Close Cover
Protected: A Masters and Mercenaries Novella
Enchanted: A Masters and Mercenaries Novella
Charmed: A Masters and Mercenaries Novella
Taggart Family Values
Treasured: A Masters and Mercenaries Novella
Delighted: A Masters and Mercenaries Novella
Tempted: A Masters and Mercenaries Novella

Masters and Mercenaries: The Forgotten
Lost Hearts (Memento Mori)
Lost and Found
Lost in You
Long Lost
No Love Lost

Masters and Mercenaries: Reloaded
Submission Impossible
The Dom Identity
The Man from Sanctum
No Time to Lie
The Dom Who Came in from the Cold

Masters and Mercenaries: New Recruits
Love the Way You Spy
Live, Love, Spy
Sweet Little Spies
The Bodyguard and the Bombshell: A Masters and Mercenaries New Recruits Novella
No More Spies
Spy With Me
Love and Let Spy, Coming March 24, 2026

Butterfly Bayou
Butterfly Bayou
Bayou Baby
Bayou Dreaming
Bayou Beauty
Bayou Sweetheart
Bayou Beloved

Park Avenue Promise
Start Us Up
My Royal Showmance
Built to Last

Lawless
Ruthless
Satisfaction
Revenge

Courting Justice
Order of Protection
Evidence of Desire

Masters Of Ménage (by Shayla Black and Lexi Blake)
Their Virgin Captive
Their Virgin's Secret
Their Virgin Concubine
Their Virgin Princess
Their Virgin Hostage
Their Virgin Secretary
Their Virgin Mistress

The Perfect Gentlemen (by Shayla Black and Lexi Blake)
Scandal Never Sleeps
Seduction in Session
Big Easy Temptation
Smoke and Sin
At the Pleasure of the President

URBAN FANTASY

Thieves
Steal the Light
Steal the Day
Steal the Moon
Steal the Sun
Steal the Night
Ripper
Addict
Sleeper
Outcast
Stealing Summer
The Rebel Queen
The Rebel Guardian
The Rebel Witch
The Rebel Seer

LEXI BLAKE WRITING AS SOPHIE OAK

Texas Sirens
Small Town Siren
Siren in the City
Siren Enslaved
Siren Beloved
Siren in Waiting
Siren in Bloom
Siren Unleashed
Siren Reborn
The Accidental Siren
The Reluctant Siren

Nights in Bliss, Colorado
Three to Ride
Two to Love
One to Keep
Lost in Bliss
Found in Bliss
Pure Bliss
Chasing Bliss
Once Upon a Time in Bliss
Back in Bliss
Sirens in Bliss
Happily Ever After in Bliss
Far from Bliss
Unexpected Bliss
Wild Bliss
Brooke's Bliss

A Faery Story
Bound
Beast
Beauty

Standalone
Away From Me
Snowed In

Brooke's Bliss

Nights in Bliss, Colorado, Book 15

Lexi Blake
writing as
Sophie Oak

Brooke's Bliss
Nights in Bliss, Colorado Book 15

Published by DLZ Entertainment LLC

Edited by Chloe Vale
ISBN: 978-1-963890-20-4

Sign up for Lexi Blake's newsletter
and be entered to win a $25 gift certificate
to the bookseller of your choice.

Join us for news, fun, and exclusive content
including free Thieves short stories.

There's a new contest every month!

Go to www.LexiBlake.net to subscribe.

Acknowledgments

For everyone who's been with me on this journey. I wish you all Bliss.

Prologue

Wyoming

Shane Kent pulled the gloves off his hands as he walked into the barn. Despite the heavy, warm material, his fingers still felt stiff. There wasn't much that could keep a Wyoming winter from freezing a man's bones.

Why did it seem warmer in Colorado? He knew on an intellectual level that it wasn't, but the time he'd spent at Stef Talbot's always seemed so much warmer. Likely since in the first couple of years they'd known the man he'd been more than happy to share his lovers with them. Stef Talbot was Bay's mentor when it came to art, but he'd been an excellent tutor at other things for Shane.

Since the man had married, he'd been happy to sponsor them at a couple of clubs, but he was far more private. Now a good deal of the warmth Shane felt came from Stef's wife, Jennifer, and his parents, Sebastian and Stella. Oh, most people would call Stella Benoit-Talbot Stef's stepmom, but she was his mother in every way but biology.

Biology meant nothing, and Shane knew it. Not that he'd been as lucky as Stef.

Don't expect me to give a damn about you, you piece of shit.

Shane took a long breath and tried to let the memory go. He'd been five, maybe. Perhaps a bit older, but his stepmom never let him forget that while he and Bay shared a dad, Shane was the product of her husband's affair.

He shook off the snow. The barn was quiet at this time of night. He should have headed to the bunkhouse where Bay was undoubtedly sitting on his bed sketching while the young cowpokes played cards and drank until they passed out.

They were getting far too old for this shit.

The last piece of work Stef sold for Bay had brought in five thousand dollars.

Which they immediately had to put into buying a new truck since the craptastic one they'd been driving for ten plus years finally died.

They couldn't get ahead no matter what they did.

They were never going to get that sweet wife and house and family that actually gave a damn. They were going to be the old men of whatever ranch they happened to be working at. Always changing. Best he could hope for was to find a place where they felt comfortable and work until they died.

He was almost certain it wouldn't be Kingman Ranch.

There was something wrong here. Something felt off. Off? He was almost certain Kale Kingman ran this ranch in fairly criminal ways and didn't mind getting rid of what he considered baggage.

"We have a problem."

Shane went still at the sound of the ranch foreman talking quietly. The voice floated down from the upper level where they kept a lot of the feed and equipment they needed for the ranch. Kingman was a top-of-the-line ranch with three big barns. This was the biggest and was equipped with what was essentially an elevator so they could move heavier stock up and down from the storage spaces.

There was a horse barn with every comfort he could imagine.

And there was that barn no one was supposed to go into.

"We always have a problem," another voice said. Andy Mills. He was the foreman's right hand. Andy and Dennis were the epitome of older career cowboys. Dennis lived in his own place next to the bunkhouse, while Andy had the only private room in the building that housed the ten ranch hands who lived on property. There were more who commuted in, but the hands who lived here were considered the inner circle.

Well, except for him and Bay. They'd been told they were in a probationary period and would be so for the first year. After that they would consider making them real Kingman men.

At the time he thought they'd watched too much *Yellowstone.*

He was starting to wonder if the dudes who made *Yellowstone* had gotten the idea from Kale Kingman.

"It's the new guys," Dennis said, and then his voice went too low to hear.

Shane froze, and it had nothing to do with the sub-zero temperatures outside. He stood stock-still, trying hard not to even breathe. He'd thought about sneaking out or calling up to let them know he was here.

But he and his brother were "the new guys."

Bay didn't see the problems, but then Bay saw the world through his weird-ass artist eyes and often missed the reality of situations. While he was trying to capture the essence of a place, Shane was having to make sure that place didn't eat them alive.

He wished he could flip his stepmom off and let her know her precious baby boy was only alive because the bastard saved him.

But she was dead and no longer cared. And it wasn't like she'd been great to Bay either. She was drunk most of the time, and when she wasn't taking her rage out on Shane, she was weeping to Bay about how terrible her life was and how it was up to him to fix things, and why did he have to spend so much time with that bastard?

"Are you sure?" Andy's voice could be heard.

"Yeah. I don't think the idiot knows." Dennis's voice came and went, with Shane catching maybe half of it. "…witness. You know… about witnesses."

Witness? First, who was the idiot? It could be either of them. It wasn't like Dennis thought much of anyone. They were all dumbasses. The only smart one was Meli. She'd been the only woman in the bunkhouse, and she'd packed up and left one day, saying she decided to go home. He had no idea why she'd left, but he was kind of jealous of her.

What would he have witnessed?

He thought briefly about the glint of metal in the boxes he moved from the back of Dennis's truck. He'd been helping out, lifting the heavy box so Dennis wouldn't have to. He hadn't meant for the cover to slip slightly so he saw that hint of gray, smelled the scent of gun oil.

Was that what he meant by witnessed?

Those guns could be for anything. It was a ranch. Of course they had guns.

He'd gotten the impression they weren't rifles.

"We need to make a run," Dennis said with some finality.

Andy sighed. "Seriously? You honestly think that dumbass…"

Shame washed through him. How many times had he been told how dumb he was?

Well, he wasn't so dumb he didn't realize what making a run meant. He'd heard the rumors. His damn ears worked, and the other hands talked. Oh, he'd thought it was all gossip meant to bring some drama to an otherwise dull existence, but he was putting it all together now.

One of the things that Kale Kingman liked when hiring his hands was no real strong family ties. At least in the men who lived on property. He'd heard one of the hands who commuted ask why he couldn't move out here and Dennis had told him maybe when his momma passed on he could live here.

It seemed like nothing more than a cruel taunt at the time.

What if it was something more?

"I ain't taking them out tonight. I suppose we have to do both of them," Andy said with a long-suffering sigh. "It's too fucking cold. You want to… Maybe you should think about waiting 'til spring."

Dennis snorted. "Tomorrow's soon enough." The sound of boots moving across the wooden floors above crackled through the barn. He was walking to the stairs. "Tell 'em you're taking them into town. Don't make a mess."

"Damn it, they're good," Andy said.

"One of them is, but unfortunately, I don't think he's going to stay on after his brother disappears. It's precisely why I advised Kale to not hire fucking brothers," Dennis shot back. "Tomorrow."

Shane slipped out of the barn, his gut in knots.

He'd fucked it up again, and this time it could cost Bay his life.

He moved through the snow, circling around the barn so it would look like he was coming in from the north field where he'd been repairing a fence. He prayed his face didn't give away the panic he felt.

* * * *

Bailey Kent stared at his brother. "What do you mean they're..."

Shane slapped a hand over his mouth, his eyes going wide. "Shhh. I don't care if it seems like everyone is sleeping. You know this place has ears on at all times."

It was two in the morning, and his brother had been acting completely weird since he'd come back in from the north field. He'd been weird through dinner and hadn't wanted to play cards with the others. He'd barely touched his beer, and Shane was coming to love his beer more and more. It kind of worried him how much beer his brother could go through lately, but Shane not even finishing one was concerning.

He was pretty sure his brother wasn't going on a health kick. He had his "it's all about to fall apart" face on. He'd had that expression on his face way too often the last couple of years.

Not that anyone else seemed to notice, but then that might be because Shane didn't have a ton of facial expressions. He was a stoic dude. Still, Bay couldn't remember a time when he wasn't close to his brother, so he could tell. He could sometimes feel when Shane was in turmoil.

They were only half brothers, but they almost never mentioned that to people. When some folks they met thought they were twins, they never corrected them. Just because they hadn't shared a womb didn't mean they didn't share everything else.

"We need to get out of here," Shane said in a whisper. He was kneeling beside Bay's bed. Bay always took the lower bunk and Shane took the top. Like when they were kids and he made Shane sleep on the top bunk so it was harder for his mom to come in drunk off her ass and start beating on him. She was short, and Shane had learned to sleep close to the wall.

Bay blinked, trying to wake up. It looked like he was going to need all of his faculties to deal with whatever had Shane's panties in a wad. "We should talk about this in the morning."

They had so much work to do and it would be cold as hell, and all he wanted to do was go back to sleep because sometimes when he dreamed he saw her.

"We are leaving tonight." Even at a whisper he could hear the finality in Shane's tone. That was his "we're going to do my will" voice.

Bay bit back a groan and started to slide out of bed as quietly as possible. It didn't take long to pack since they lived like college kids in a freaking dorm. It should take longer for a nearly thirty-year-old man to pack all of his belongings. A couple pairs of jeans, underwear, and socks. His cell phone that only worked half the time when they could afford service.

He slid the most important thing in his pack and picked it up. His sketchbook. He didn't have access to clay out here, and no one would let him use the welding materials for anything but work, so drawing was his only refuge.

He followed Shane out into the frigid night after slipping on his coat and exiting the bunkhouse as quietly as possible.

The truth of the matter was he didn't like Kingman Ranch. There was a heaviness to the place that seeped into his work. It wasn't like Bliss, where everything had an aura of beauty around it. He had an entire sketchpad devoted to Bliss. Over the years they'd been several times, and every visit yielded work. At first they'd been erotic sketches of the lovers he and Shane shared, and portraits of Stef Talbot in his element. Those early works had been lush and blatantly sexual, as if that was the only thing on his mind at the time.

Except for one. One sketch of the most beautiful woman he'd ever seen. The one who sometimes haunted his dreams. Golden brown hair and blue eyes, the wind had caressed her like a lover, blowing her hair across her cheeks as she'd turned toward him. Time felt like it stopped in that moment, but it hadn't. Years had passed, but he could still call up the vision.

He'd seen her so long ago at one of those festivals that seemed to happen once a month in Bliss.

Lately when he visited Talbot, he found himself sketching things like the old couple at Stella's Café who held hands while they drank their coffee. A new mom with her baby and two husbands watching them with a glow in their eyes he worried he would never understand.

A mangy dog who wagged that tail like the world was a wonderful place.

He found none of that here. Everything at this ranch was coated in a darkness he hadn't been able to explain to his brother.

Looked like he'd figured it out himself.

He followed Shane as they moved toward the long driveway where all the trucks were parked. Most of the hands didn't have their own trucks, but Shane wouldn't let them be without a car. Hence them spending everything they had on that old piece of crap they were driving now. "All right, we're out. Want to tell me why we're skulking away without a last paycheck?" A thought occurred to him. "Damn it, Shane. Tell me you didn't sleep with one of Kingman's daughters."

It wouldn't be the first time Shane's libido got them in trouble, though usually he talked Bay into joining whichever forbidden fruit he was pursuing that month. Not that he would touch one of the Kingman girls. They were lovely and colder than the Wyoming winter they were currently walking through.

Snow clung to Shane's hair as they made it to the truck and tossed their paltry possessions in the back. "No. I think they're running guns, and I accidently saw a shipment. I overheard Dennis and Andy talking about taking me out tomorrow. They were going to kill you, too."

Fuck. He stood there watching his brother climb into the cab.

This was serious, and they were in trouble. Or Shane was way overreacting. That was the likeliest reason. Leaving wouldn't cause too much trouble except for the lack of a paycheck. It was two weeks until Christmas. Not a lot of people were hiring at this time of year. He hopped in beside his brother and closed the door as quietly as he could.

Shane started the truck but left the lights off. He turned Bay's way. "You're not going to fight me? Tell me I'm overreacting?"

Bay shrugged. "I never liked this place anyway. But, Shane, we have to work. It's not like we have a place to stay. We got enough cash for a couple of nights at a cheap motel, but that's about it. I don't know what you heard, but I do know something's not right here. It's like that time that we stayed at the artist commune and it turned out to be a cult. I get those vibes, but with less tofu and more violence."

Shane huffed out a groan. "Damn, but we're dumb." He started to pull the truck around the drive, going slowly so the sound of tires on gravel didn't wake up anyone in the bunkhouse. Across the way, the lights were off at the foreman's house. His brother had been smart and waited until he was sure everyone would be asleep since they had to move the herd early the next morning. "We have to get out of Wyoming. We should head south. There's probably work in Texas."

Bay had to be careful about this. "That sounds good." He watched the big house as they drove by. There were a few lights on, but Kingman's house was far enough away he wasn't worried they would hear them. "Maybe we can stop at Stef's. I've got a couple of ideas I'd like to work on, and you know he said we could use the guesthouse whenever I needed a break."

Stef Talbot had "discovered" him as an artist, and the man had been an excellent mentor. Oh, Bay knew Stef viewed him as something of an enigma, but he was still kind to them, offering them room and board and a space in his studio to work.

Shane sighed. "And what would I do? I assume we're staying for Christmas. I can't sit on my ass and watch you sculpt and paint."

Shane didn't understand him either, but it didn't matter. Shane was…more than his brother. He was the odd other half of his soul. He couldn't function without Shane. Didn't even want to try. It had driven his mother crazy, but even from an early age he'd recognized the importance of Shane. "We'll find something. It's a couple of weeks. Nothing more. I'm sure there's some seasonal jobs we can do. I just…I need to work for a while."

It had been building for months, the need to spend days with his hands in clay or chipping away at wood or marble to find the treasure hidden underneath, the one only his eyes could see until he uncovered it.

"All right then. But only until we're back on our feet," Shane said.

Bay nodded.

When they made it to the highway, Shane turned on the lights and headed south.

To Bliss.

* * * *

Manhattan, NY
Five months later

Brooke Harper sat on the sofa and sniffled. "I can't believe it."

Her roommate sat across from her, and Brooke realized there was not an ounce of sympathy in her eyes. It might be the colored contacts that somehow hid the empathy, but Brooke doubted it. Ami had never been empathetic, but shouldn't this be the one case where the sisterhood stuck together?

"I don't see why not." Nope, not an ounce of sympathy. "You called human resources on your boss. You told them he stole your designs and presented them as his own."

Yes, that summed up the situation neatly. "He did."

Ami sighed, a world-weary sound that matched her ennui aesthetic. "They all do. I told you it's how it works. If you wanted things to be fair, you should have picked another industry."

"He got a massive bonus for my work," Brooke pointed out.

Her boss led the design team at House of Bianchi, an up-and-coming design firm. They'd gotten their first big buy from Macy's, and it was all from Brooke's fall leisurewear line. She'd been deeply influenced by her trip home for the holidays a few months before. She had designed some skiwear and sweaters and whole outfits inspired by the horse ranch her brothers and sister-in-law ran. Cowboy chic, she'd called it. She kept it on her laptop because she hadn't thought it was ready yet.

Mark Hallway hadn't cared. He'd explained that the laptop was the company's, and so were her designs. She hadn't even known he'd stolen them, changed a couple of the fabrics and patterns, and put his name on them until one morning two weeks before. The company had a big presentation of the fall line with the announcement that they'd made the Macy's sale and were close to inking distribution deals with several European store lines. She'd sat in stunned silence, not moving even when they'd brought the champagne out.

That champagne should have been for her.

Keep your mouth shut and I'll make sure you get to go to Milan this year.

If only that had been all he told her to do.

It was some *Devil Wears Prada* bullshit, and she wasn't taking it.

Not that it seemed like she had much of a choice now. The human resources lady had pointed out all the places in her contract that stated plainly any designs belonged to the company. It was on the laptop they provided for her, and clearly she'd done much of the design work during office hours, so it belonged to the House of Bianchi. The woman had been somewhat sympathetic but clear. Mark was more important than she was. He was influential, and she was nobody. She had only been working at Bianchi for a couple of years, and all she had under her belt were some accessories for lesser lines.

Ami shrugged. "Everyone knows when you're a junior designer you keep your mouth shut and do your job."

"No." She wasn't completely naïve. "Everyone knows the boss will take most of the credit for the work, but the designer's name should be somewhere. He should have given me some credit and introduced me to the owners. Instead, he told me I was lucky he thought I had something worth putting his name on and maybe if I…"

She didn't even want to say it. She could still feel the humiliation, the opening in the pit of her stomach. She'd felt so small in that moment, like nothing she did would ever matter. Like if she wanted to move up she would have to pay for it with her body, and that would take something from her soul.

Ami's lips quirked up. "Not gay, huh? They're the worst. So did he offer you a promotion if you let him in your panties?"

He'd told her if she gave him a blow job then and there, that he'd think about mentioning her helping him with the designs in the *Vogue* interview he was doing at the end of the week.

She'd walked right out and headed to HR. She'd filed two reports and been told they would take the situation seriously.

She should have known it would all go wrong when Mark walked by her smirking.

A week later she'd been called in and fired. The reason given was that she wasn't fitting in with the company's culture, and it was causing people on her team to feel uncomfortable. They'd brought up all the times she talked about her brothers and the fact that they were both married to the same woman. She'd never hidden that her brothers were in an unconventional relationship, and everyone joked about it. She kept a picture of her brothers and their wife Rachel and their three kids on her desk. Her niece and nephews. She missed them. Her colleagues always asked for stories about them and the quirky town she'd grown up in where threesomes were a thing.

Then they used it when she became inconvenient.

She'd walked out with her head held high, vowing legal vengeance. "I intend to make sure everyone knows what kind of a boss he is. I'll sue the hell out of the company and him personally."

Ami winced. "You might want to think that through. You're already going to have a tough time finding another job. You don't accuse a man like Mark Hallway without receipts, and I'm not talking about him stealing your designs. No one will give a shit that he took credit for your clothes. You're nobody. He's… Well, he's been a top designer for twenty years. Bianchi was lucky to get him."

"He's been a top designer by stealing ideas." Brooke couldn't believe what she was hearing. No one would listen to her. They acted like it was the fifties and Me Too never happened. "And he acted unprofessionally. He tried to force me into a sexual relationship."

Ami's eyes rolled, and she took a sip of her kombucha. "Brooke, if you wanted to be pure and shit you should have picked another industry. You should have stayed in that rural, backwater town and like answered phones and stuff. This is the big leagues. It's not fair, but that's the price we pay. Do you know how many photographers I've had to handle? I've had to make some decisions I'm not necessarily proud of, but that's what you do. You never were cut out for this life, and this proves it. The first time something goes wrong, you're whining and crying."

Ami was a model. She did catalog work right now but was absolutely certain her big break was coming. At twenty-five. She was also highly judgmental of everything Brooke did. From her clothes to the way she talked, Ami had always made fun of her. But she owned this rent-controlled apartment, passed to her from her mother.

How was she going to pay rent? Even with the controlled rent,

"That's not what the papers will say when they pick up the story," Ami pointed out. "I can imagine the memes now. Didn't you say there were a bunch of relationships like that in that town? I hope they're ready for reporters."

Her gut sank.

Ami wasn't wrong. It would be a juicy story, and reporters would come out of the woodwork. They would take everything in the most salacious manner. She had a sudden vision of her brothers surrounded by reporters and Rachel getting requests for talk show appearances. Mel would decide the reporters were aliens and lose his shit, and Caleb would have to tranq him in the middle of town square.

Chaos. It would be chaos when so many people came to Bliss to find peace and acceptance.

"There it is." Ami sat back, one beautifully done brow arching. "I knew you could figure it out. You've fucked yourself over by being an uptight bitch."

"Excuse me?"

Ami stood. "Look, I get it. All of it sucks, but did you think of anyone else? I have a real shot at working with Bianchi this fall. I'm not going to be able to do that if my out-of-touch renter is suing everyone and making a nuisance of herself. Your best bet is to find something as fast as you can. I would look to places that do uniforms or maybe the big box retailers. You're done in high fashion, and that means I have to be done with you. I think I have to give you thirty days or something, but consider yourself on a clock."

Ami walked out, and Brooke sat in stunned silence.

How was this her life? She bragged about how well things were going a few months ago when she went home for the holidays. She'd talked with Rachel about work and living in New York. She'd brought her sister-in-law and Callie some accessory samples. Rachel had been so thrilled with the custom diaper bag Brooke had made her, and Callie loved her sandals.

They thought she was doing well, were so proud of her, and she was putting them all in danger.

She should have stayed in Bliss. She'd thought briefly about not going back to New York. She was lonely. She worked long hours and hadn't found many friends she trusted. Ami was awful. It wasn't like she had anything going there. Brooke hadn't been on a date in over a year.

We could go to Stella's or Trio if you like.

She closed her eyes and could see those two dumbass, hot-as-hell cowboys standing out in the snow, asking her to go out with them.

Why had she turned them down? She'd been leaving the next day, and she knew damn well her brothers kind of had a problem with them. Something about them hitting on Rachel when she first came to town. It didn't matter. She'd said no and closed the door on that opportunity.

All her opportunities were getting lost.

Her cell buzzed, and she thought about ignoring it.

Bestest SIL in the World

Rachel. She was pregnant again. What if something went wrong? She picked up and ran her finger across the screen. "Hey, what's going on? Is everything okay?"

It felt like she was living through a slow-moving Armageddon and everything was falling apart. What if her family was caught in it, too?

A low chuckle came over the line. "Of course. I mean it's as okay as it can be when I've got three kids under the age of seven and one on the way. Did I mention your brother finally got that vasectomy? I swear Max is the biggest damn baby in the world. He claims Caleb made the whole thing extra snippy. What is that supposed to mean? Doc is a professional. He's only going to snip as much as is required to ensure we don't have baby number five."

Brooke wasn't so sure about that. Her brother Max and the town's doc, Caleb Burke, had a long history between them. If Caleb could justify a couple of extra stitches, he might. "I'm glad he finally got it done. So what's up?"

She wanted to cry it all out and tell Rachel everything. Over the years Rach had become the big sister she never had. But she didn't want to put any more pressure on her. Finding out the reason they gave for her getting fired would do exactly that.

"Well, I wanted to let you know that we're having a baby boom here in Bliss, and we've decided to do a big shower for me and Hope Glen and Nell."

"Nell's pregnant? Again? The last time I talked to her she was one and done. Something about keeping the population down." Nell Flanders had come into town as Brooke was finishing high school. She'd never been particularly close to her, but she seemed like a nice woman.

"Yeah, Henry got the snip, too," Rachel admitted. "He handled it so much better than Max, although he did make sure the bag of frozen peas he held to his balls were organic. Anyway, I know you're busy so I wanted to let you know there's no pressure for you to come. It's kind of a last-minute thing. We're putting it together for two weeks from now. You've been to every one of mine, and I don't need anything. It's more about celebrating Hope, but she didn't want to do it alone. I want you to know…"

"I'll come. I can help." She took that invite like a damn lifeline. "I can come out in a couple of days and help you plan and set everything up. I have a lot of ideas."

She had no ideas beyond getting the hell out of Manhattan and clearing her head. She could figure things out. Talk to Gemma privately about her options.

Breathe. She might be able to breathe.

"Uhm, I thought you would have to work," Rachel pointed out.

What she wasn't ready to do was let her brothers know she'd fucked up so brutally. "I have a bunch of paid time off. I finished a big campaign a few days ago, and I was thinking about taking a vacation."

"Sweetie, you should do that," Rachel replied. "Don't get me wrong. I'll take any excuse to get you home. Your brothers recently finished the guesthouse. It's darling, but it needs some interior design. But you're young and should have fun. If you come home, you're going to have kids hanging all over you."

Paige and Ethan and Eli. They loved their Auntie Brooke. They wanted her to play with them and talk to them and have ice cream with them. They wanted her around. "I can babysit. I want to come home, Rachel. It's been…a lot lately. Christmas wasn't enough time for me. It was too busy."

"It's always busy in Bliss," Rachel admitted. "But I would love to have you home for a couple of weeks. I could use some help, but I don't want…"

The idea that she could feel needed gave her some hope. She could take a couple of weeks and clear her head. She could figure out what to do next. "I want to come home for a while, Rachel. I need to come home."

There was a slight hesitation, and she knew damn well Rachel suspected something. Brooke breathed a sigh of relief when her sister-in-law continued. "Well, then I'll make sure the tiny house is ready for you. I'll use stuff from our place, and we can go shopping while you're here. I would love your eye for design. I know it's a guesthouse for you, but I would love for it to be nice."

She could make something pretty. She could do something that helped her family. "That sounds perfect."

She packed her bags that night. She was surprised at how little there was. Everything here was Ami's. She'd moved from dorms in Denver to a small place she shared with a bunch of students who were in her grad class at Parsons. Then she'd gotten the job with Bianchi and moved in with Ami.

She'd never had her own place. Never had her own dishes or furniture. Never picked out curtains. Her whole adult life had been about preparing for the job, getting the job, doing the job.

Who was she without her work?

It was time to go home.

Chapter One

Bliss, CO

Brooke waved to Logan Warner, who sat in the driver's seat of the Navigator. They hadn't been forced to do anything so ordinary as fly into the small airfield in Alamosa. Nope. Seth Stark's "cabin" came with its own landing strip and small hangar.

And Nell and Poppy protesting at the end of it.

It was good to be home.

"Tell your brothers hi for me and that we hope they'll come out and meet our little monster," Logan said with a smile. Logan had dropped off Seth, Georgia, and their son at the big cabin they kept here in Bliss and given Brooke a ride into town. He was planning on slipping into The Trading Post and surprising his moms.

"I will, and thanks so much, Logan." Logan was only a year older than she was and he had a kid. A whole kid. Wesley Stark-Warner was the cutest baby. After her niece and nephews, of course. Wes was a cuddly six-month-old who looked at the world through curious eyes.

She'd held him and wished she could find wonder in the every day the way that baby did.

The Navigator rolled away, and Brooke stepped into Stella's

Café and thought about the fact that just this morning she had been in Manhattan. It had taken less than twenty-four hours to leave her entire life behind. She'd even packed what little she had in case she decided not to come back. She'd stuffed her suitcase as full as possible and started searching the Internet for the cheapest flight she could find, thinking it could be days before she could get home.

"Brooke," a familiar voice called out.

She turned and saw her brothers sitting near the window in a corner booth at the front of the café. Their booth. When she'd been a kid, they would always try to get that particular booth because you could see all of the people walking down the sidewalk. Stella's was in the heart of Bliss's downtown. Which consisted of about two blocks. Doc's office was on one end and the "downtown" ended with the sheriff's station on the other. In between were a bunch of stores and restaurants. Stella's and Trio and The Bear Creek Lounge. The Trading Post was across the street, and she'd noticed the Bee Bliss Store. The honey farm had been selling their wares for decades, but someone had given the place a glow up.

Home. She was home, and even though a couple of things had changed, what hadn't was this feeling.

Her heart filled. She'd been numb the last couple of weeks, but seeing her brothers made those walls quake. The numb part was going to end at some point, and she was not looking forward to it. Not at all.

But not now. It wasn't happening now. She plastered a smile on her face and strode over, rolling her big suitcase along the black and white laminated floors. Nothing changed in Stella's except the special. When things got worn, Stella found a way to restore them, from the red leather seats to the shiny countertops, Stella's looked the way it had when Brooke was a kid.

A wave of comfort sank into her skin for a moment. This was her home. These were her brothers. They would understand. They would help her.

Then she remembered all the ways they'd helped her before. Like giving up their twenties to raise her, pouring all their money into her education. They'd spent their party time, college time, young adult era, working—Max on the horse ranch they'd grown up on, and

Rye had taken a job as a county deputy and later was elected sheriff. All so she could have a good life, be successful.

She put them in danger by joking about them.

"Hey, how was the flight? I heard Seth took the big jet this time," Rye said, scooting out of the booth and opening his arms for a hug.

She breathed her brother in. He smelled like pine and fabric softener. Home. She was not going to cry.

She stepped back, settling the big case beside the booth and sliding in across from them. Max hadn't gotten up but she didn't mind because he had a baby sleeping on his shoulder. Her newest nephew. Eli Harper was almost a year old, and he was the sweetest chunk of humanity. "It was great. I was so lucky Georgia called."

Max snorted, his hand on his son's back. "You weren't lucky. Rach called Georgia and demanded she take you with them. She knew damn well Seth, Georgia, and Logan were coming home this weekend and staying for a few weeks. She also knew you hadn't taken a lot of personal time in the last couple of years beyond quick trips, and she knew that company of yours takes time off this month to send a big part of the team to Milan."

Brooke felt her jaw drop. "Rachel said she was inviting me out of courtesy."

Rye's head shook. "Nah. She planned this whole thing to make it as easy for you to come home as possible. Now she thought you would be coming in for the shower. She meant to talk you into a week if you weren't going to Milan."

That ticket to Milan had been far too expensive. "I'm not part of that team, and we do slow way down when they're gone. We're encouraged to take time off now."

Not untrue. They were between fall and spring. She supposed most of the vacations she'd taken in the last few years had been around this time. Had her sister-in-law been plotting and planning? To get her home?

"Yeah, see, you look at Rach and see nothing more than a gorgeous woman," Max began.

Brooke shook her head. "No, I do not."

She was well aware Rachel Harper was a force of nature. Her sister-in-law was the single most competent woman she'd ever met.

"But there's more to her than beauty." Max was good at ignoring anything and anyone when he wanted to make a point. That he didn't need to make. Her brother was incredibly dramatic for a cowboy. They tended to be known for their stoicism, but not Max Harper. He was a rebel. "There's a ruthless will to that woman that will not be denied."

"His balls just met up with her ruthless streak," Rye quipped.

Oh, she loved her brothers, but she was with her sister on this one. "Four kids in seven years, Max. Four. If she had taken your balls herself and hung them like a trophy on the wall, I would have helped her design the case for them."

Max shrank back a little. "I think Rachel might be a bad influence on you, sister."

Rye grinned. "Nah, she's taught Brooke how to stand up for herself. And don't tell her you taught her how to do that. You taught her to knee a dick if one got too close to her."

She hadn't had one get close to her in forever. Not since she'd broken it off with that guy from down the hall when she found out exactly how many friends with benefits he had.

"Well, she had to protect herself because she was so pretty," Max argued. "Still is, and that is one thing I need to talk to you about."

Rye sighed as though they'd already had this argument. "They're out on the G. I scarcely think they're going to try to run our sister down. She told them a polite no at Christmas. Stef swears they're good kids."

A flash of heat went through Brooke. "Are you talking about the Kent brothers?"

They were the only cowboys who hit on her at Christmastime, and it wasn't some sleazy thing. Bay had asked nicely if she would join them for a drink at Trio or to have some dinner or lunch while she was in town. His brother had stood behind him, watching her with hooded eyes like she was a treat and he was sure he would be denied.

Now that she thought about it, only their words had been polite. Everything else about their demeanor had reminded her of a couple of hungry predators desperate to eat her up. She'd stood there in the beautifully decorated town hall with all the happy families around her. The wholesome atmosphere should have had her backing away, and yet all she could think about was how nice it would be if they made a meal of her. She'd had a vision of one of them feeding her his cock while the other ate her pussy like a starving man.

And she'd said no. That woman in her vision wasn't the woman who took Manhattan. She was too old to run around having wild nights with cowboys. By the time her mother was her age she'd had two kids and been married for a long time. To a dick, but married.

She'd told herself that *no* came from a place of logic and reason. She was leaving, so it would be nothing more than a one-night stand. They didn't have a place in her life, and it was so obvious they were looking for something more. They needed. She'd felt it, and it called to her and… Damn it. She'd said no because she felt something for them and it scared her.

Max growled. "Little fuckers called me old."

"They called you vintage," Rye corrected.

"They asked me if I remember when JR was shot." Max's jaw tightened. "I wasn't born then. I don't even think our momma was born then."

So the Kent brothers were having fun with hers. She wondered if they knew she was their sister. Likely not. They probably thought she was a tourist having fun for the night. Or a relative visiting, which she had been. That feeling she got from them had probably been nothing more than her own projection. She read way too many romance novels. "Mom was born, but she would have been a baby. So the Kent brothers are back in town? I know they were here for the holidays, but I assumed they would go back to whatever ranch they were working. I think the older one mentioned they were between jobs and would be working again after the new year."

"They decided to hang around," Max said with a frown. "Stef talked to Jamie and McNamara, and now they are living and working on the G."

They were here? Not here here. But here in town. Not in town since the Circle G was absolutely outside of town, but here.

Her brain was threatening to fritz. Lack of sleep. That was it. It wasn't her libido turning on and thinking about how well those cowboys could handle her.

"Are you talking about Shane and Bay?" Stella stood at the end of the booth. She was dressed in blinged-out jeans, a Western shirt, and some serious diamond jewelry that Brooke would suspect was lab created, but Stella's hubs was the CEO of Talbot Industries, so those puppies were real. The cowboy hat on her head, though, had almost certainly come from The Trading Post. The café owner was a study in contrasts. A bit like the town itself.

"I'm talking about those two assholes who better not sniff around my sister like they sniffed around my wife," Max said as primly as a six-foot two-inch cowboy could be. "My sister is a good girl. She's saving herself for marriage, and it won't be with two lowly cow-pokes."

Brooke looked to Rye. "He's joking, right?"

Rye winced. "Just let him live in a haze of delusion. It does him good. He's going to find you a husband, and we'll pay the family your bride price in well-trained horses. And maybe the barn cat. She's good at what she does."

Stella's grin told Brooke she was thrilled with the drama. She filled the coffee cup in front of Brooke, despite the fact that it was afternoon. "I'm going to be honest. I thought those two boys would hit the ground running when they got here. I've told all the younger women around to be on the lookout, if you know what I mean."

Max used his free hand to point Stella's way. "See, that is a public service."

Brooke didn't think that was what Stella meant, but she wasn't getting her brother spun up again. They hadn't even gotten to pay for her lunch yet.

"Oh, I was telling them where to go if they had an itch to scratch." Stella never had minded spinning Max up. She seemed to think it was a fun game.

Max's frown went even frownier. "Well, Doc better run a blood panel on those two because I'm pretty sure they've already run through half of Southern Colorado. I'm glad Trev's baby girl is too young for them to try anything on."

"She's just a kid," Brooke pointed out, though she knew it wouldn't do any good. When Max got going, he did not stop.

"I wouldn't put anything past them. They might take one look at little Miranda and think she's the way to riches." Max nodded like he'd finally figured out their evil plans. "That's what they're doing. Looking for a meal ticket."

Stella's eyes rolled. "Well, then they are the dumbest cons in the history of time since Stef offered to set them up wherever they liked so Bay can work as an artist. He offered them their own cabin. They turned him down."

Max gestured Stella's way like she'd just made his point. "Because they are holding out for more, and they are going to take one look at my rich, successful baby sister and think they can mooch off her for the rest of their lives."

She shook her head. "Not rich. They would not fit into the tiny thing I call an apartment."

Max plowed on. "They'll probably want her to introduce them to all her artsy fartsy friends in New York City."

Another head shake. "They're mostly fartsy, and they're poorer than I am."

Not that she had many friends. The people she'd thought were her friends were the same people who turned on her and went along with the *let's get rid of the chick who doesn't like having her work stolen and won't blow a dude to keep her job* plan.

She looked to Stella, determined to change the topic. She wasn't going to think about those two men. She was here to take a breath and figure out her next steps. "Could I get a burger? Georgia's on a health kick because Logan's cholesterol came back out of range. You should have seen Seth trying to choke down his beet salad. Surprisingly, Logan was cool with it."

"That boy's been eating beets since he could have solid food," Stella admitted. "And yes, I'll get you a juicy burger, baby girl. It's good to have you back. Are you in town for the weekend?"

"I'm here for a couple of weeks. The company I work for takes a sabbatical this time of year when the owners all head to Milan." Not an untruth, but not the whole truth. She had four weeks before she was getting kicked out of her apartment. Unless she found a job, which she wasn't going to do here in Bliss. Deep breath. Two weeks. She was taking two weeks to figure out what she wanted to do. She gave Stella what she hoped was a confident smile. "I'm here to help

Rachel with the party and to finish up the guesthouse. Although I'm wondering if the guesthouse isn't really the doghouse. How many times have you had to sleep there, Max?"

Max shrugged. "It's comfy if I do say so myself. But I did not sleep out there because my wife was angry. She prefers I sleep on the couch so she can wake me up and yell at me some more. The tiny house is for guests and those times when I need to be close to the mares. We've got two who are going to foal in a couple of months. I'll sleep out there when we're getting close, and it's got a place for Noah, too, so Animal Doc and I can switch off if the birth gets difficult."

"It's a cute place." Rye sat back. "I'm afraid all of our bedrooms are taken now, so if we're going to have our sister spend time with us and not sleep in Paige's room, we needed some space."

Her niece's room used to be hers. She'd grown up there, the space morphing from pink and princesses to rock star posters and some black paint from her goth phase. The first time she'd seen that room as a little girl's, she'd gotten teary because she'd known she would never be the daughter of the family again. It was Paige's place now, and she was so happy to be her aunt.

"I'm sure I'll love it," Brooke said, trying not to sniffle. It would be good to have a space for herself.

She might have to live in that tiny house and work here at Stella's for the rest of her life and pretend she was doing something important.

"Hey, if you want to stay in the big house, I'll make room," Rye said, looking at her with sympathetic eyes. "We held off on using that fourth bedroom for as long as we could. I probably should have squeezed my office into the living room."

Absolutely not. "Rye, I don't live there. I'm happy Paige has my room. I've shown her all my hidey-holes, and when she's a teen I'm going to teach her how to sneak out the west window."

"What?" Max's head came up.

Stella laughed. "Oh, I remember the days. I'll be back with lunch. Let me know if I need to heat up a bottle for Eli." She leaned toward Brooke, whispering conspiratorially. "We keep a bottle warmer in the kitchen now since we are in a baby boom. They are coming up everywhere, and soon we'll have three more."

"Four because the Stark-Warner clan is in town, and they're staying for a month or two while Logan's on summer break." She had lunch with Georgia once a month or so, but they lived on the Upper East Side and she was down close to Battery Park. And everyone was busy. So busy. She never had time to do anything because she was busy making her boss look good.

"Teeny and Marie are going to spoil that baby rotten," Stella announced and winked as she walked away.

Brooke slid out of the booth. "I'm going to wash my hands before we have lunch. Thanks for that, by the way. And for the ride out to the house. I've heard that the Farley brothers have started up their own ride share service."

Rye shook his head. "Why their parents let them fix up an old limo, I have no idea. It's a menace, but at least they drive like old ladies. The new schoolteacher used them so they wouldn't feel bad. It took forty-five minutes to get from school to her sister's house. In the valley."

Well, she liked a nice drive so she wouldn't complain. "I've already put the app on my phone."

"Let me know if you need to go somewhere," Max offered, though she didn't want her brother driving her around.

She turned and walked to the bathroom, taking a long breath. She had time, but she needed to figure out how she was going to tell them she didn't have a job anymore.

Keep it together, Brooke. It's a couple of weeks at home, and Gemma will help you come up with something.

"Brooke Harper?"

She looked over, and a familiar face was at the sink. Cleo Rhea. She'd been one of the forty-seven students in Brooke's graduating class. Brooke hadn't been particularly close to her, but she'd liked working with her on theater projects. She felt a smile slide over her face. "Cleo, what are you doing here? The last thing I heard you were working the LA theater scene."

Cleo was a thin young woman with a long blue bob and a nose ring. She was clearly in her witchy phase as she wore a flowy white skirt and a T-shirt that said *Theater is Magic*. The white contrasted to her gorgeous dark skin. She gave Brooke a hug and stepped back to look her over. "And I heard you were taking over the fashion scene in New York."

Brooke sighed and shook her head. "I'm working at a house but definitely won't be taking over anytime soon. I'm in town for my sister-in-law's baby shower."

Cleo laughed. "I can't believe how many kids your brothers have now. It's kind of crazy. Everyone's got babies. I heard Stef and Jen are trying for another one, and Nell is pregnant again. I think I should protest her. After all those lectures…"

Brooke had to laugh because she remembered those lectures, too. "I think she would probably get teary and say she'd done the right thing." Brooke sobered. "I think it was an oops, from what Rachel told me. We should probably let it go. I assure you those kids will grow up with the smallest carbon footprint possible."

Cleo settled her bag over her shoulder. "I'm directing the drama at the rep theater this year."

The Bliss Repertory Theater had been around since shortly after the town was established. They ran three shows in rotation all summer long. A comedy. A drama. A musical.

Her brothers would take her to every show during the summers. Max would almost always fall asleep, and she was certain Rye hadn't loved them all—not a big theater person—but they never failed. Her heart squeezed with the memories.

Cleo's expression had taken on a distinctly thoughtful air. She looked down at her watch. "Hey, you could be the answer to my prayers. How long are you here?"

Forever. A few days. It could be anything. "At least a couple of weeks. I'm kind of on a sabbatical."

If by sabbatical she meant fired and blackballed across the industry…

"I've got a rehearsal in a couple of minutes, but I would love to talk to you about something. Any chance you could have a drink with me? The cast is celebrating a birthday tonight at Hell on Wheels. We would love to see you."

What else was she doing? Brooding. She could do that any time. Railing at fate. Also something she could put off in favor of drinking too much and making some truly bad decisions. If she'd said Trio, it might have been an easy no. Zane Hollister ran Trio, and despite the fact that he hadn't been around when she was a child, he kind of acted like an overprotective uncle. Sawyer Hathaway, who owned and ran Hell on Wheels, *had* been around for her childhood. He wouldn't let anything happen to her, but he also wouldn't call her brothers if she ended up crying in the bathroom.

"Yeah, that sounds great. I would love to meet the cast. It's been a long time since I got to enjoy a season," she said.

Cleo smiled brightly, an air of odd relief about her. "Excellent. Drinks are totally on me. We're going to meet around nine. Come with an open mind. It's good to see you."

And she was gone.

Why did she need an open mind?

It was a mystery and one she could solve.

She washed her hands and took a long breath. Smile.

Everything was fine.

* * * *

Shane sat back and tried not to give away the fact that his whole body had gone on full alert the minute that girl walked into the café hauling that big old suitcase behind her.

Really big suitcase. The last time she'd been in town she'd used a carry-on.

It was creepy stalker shit that he knew that, but he couldn't help it. He'd been looking for any excuse to get close to her, and he had been prepared to carry whatever luggage she had.

Thanks so much. That's so sweet of you, but I'm leaving for home in a couple of days. I need to spend as much time with my family as possible.

And yet he'd caught her watching them. Even after she'd turned them down at the Christmas party. When she'd danced with him, he hadn't felt like she was trying to stay away from him. Her body had brushed against his, and they'd had a magical moment when she looked up and her mouth had opened slightly and he'd almost kissed her.

Brooke Harper didn't look toward the back of the café. Her whole attention was on her brothers, who sat on the other side.

"What exactly are we going to do until they finish up?" Bay had his back to the door. "I can't drink anymore coffee, and if I stuff another piece of pie in, Trev is going to make a joke about me being tubby. You know not all of us have ex-NFL quarterback metabolisms."

Trev McNamara was actually the best boss they'd ever had. Well, he and his partner were. The Circle G was run by Trev McNamara and James Glen. Trev had bought into the ranch years back after his NFL career had ended in scandal and he'd moved from Texas to Colorado, bringing along his wife, Beth, and partner, Bo O'Malley. Bo preferred working the ranch to dealing with the business side of things. Bo was great, but Shane wouldn't call him a boss.

When the Harper brothers had walked in and taken a place near the big windows, he'd known he would try to wait them out. Or at least sneak by without Max Harper starting something. Bay couldn't help but take the bait every single time. Now he had a different reason. Now he wanted to sit here and watch her.

She was smiling, but it wasn't her goddess of the world smile. There was a tightness to her whole body that gave her away. He'd made a careful study of the woman who would fit so perfectly between him and his brother. He was starting to think she might be the only woman in the world for them.

And wasn't it the story of his life that she didn't want to want them.

The chemistry was there. She was curious. She watched them both but she was…scared? Disappointed in her own needs? Disgusted that she was attracted to a couple of lowly cowboys? One he could fix. The second he could possibly turn around.

He was deeply worried it was the third, and he couldn't make himself more respectable.

Bay, he could talk up. Bay was a real artist. He was quirky. Bay was Stef Talbot's student.

Shane was just his bastard brother.

"I know you think it's a funny rivalry, but the Harper brothers are cornerstones of this town." His brother rarely thought about anything but his art. He was brilliantly talented but could be short sighted when it came to…well, anything else. "If we irritate him and he wants us gone, he can do it."

Bay sat back with a long sigh. "Somehow I think Stef would have something to say about it. He's happy with the work I've been doing. He's planning a whole… What did he call it?"

"Showing." Sometimes Shane was sure he listened to Talbot more than his brother did. Sometimes he was sure he knew more about the damn art world than the actual artist. "He and Jennifer are going to do a showing at the end of the summer, and they're inviting a bunch of people they know who have influence in that world. He thinks you'll be able to make some serious sales."

Bay nodded. "See. There's no way he's going to pick Max over his star pupil."

Short sighted. "Max, who he views as his brother. Max, who's the godfather to his son. That Max?"

Stef Talbot didn't have any blood siblings, but he considered the friend group he'd grown up with to be his family. Max and Rye Harper and Callie Hollister-Wright were his siblings, and he would never turn his back on them. Rachel Harper was Jennifer's best friend. The billionaire did not need to make money off of them. It was pure kindness that he was doing all this work for Bay.

Bay sighed. "Fine, but I don't think you understand. I know he seems like we annoy him, but Max enjoys being annoyed. He's one of those guys. He likes the banter. Especially now that he's married with all those kids. It reminds him of when he was young and could fuck around with people."

Shane worried the "banter" reminded Max that they were assholes who'd hit on his wife before they got married.

And now he wanted to hit on the guy's sister again.

She laughed at something her brothers said but he still didn't buy it.

None of her socials had mentioned she was coming to Bliss. In fact, she'd talked about spending the whole summer in Manhattan working on what she called her fall line.

So why was she here?

"They're awful. I don't understand how we're supposed to deal with half-done costumes? Are they going to be ready? We've only got six weeks before we open," one of the women was saying in the booth in front of them. There were four people, and they'd been here even longer than he and Bay. Three women and one man, and they were obviously in some kind of crisis.

But he had a crisis of his own.

She was here, and it might be their last shot.

Were they even ready to make a go of it with any woman? Much less the one he was pretty sure was the right one? What the hell did they have to offer her? It wasn't like they owned much of anything.

Bay held up his hands, obviously giving up the argument. "Fine. But when I'm polite to the man, you'll see what I mean. We have a relationship, Max and I, and this will tilt that fucker, and you might not like where we land." He took a long breath. "I don't think we should be held hostage here so my presence doesn't offend the prince of Bliss County. Besides, don't you think our waitress is going to get antsy? We are literally taking up a table she could be earning another tip from. Especially since you're a miserly bastard."

He wasn't. They didn't have a lot of money, but he tipped. He simply didn't throw down wads of cash the way Stef did. He tried. The whole money thing was in his lap, like most of their existence.

"Shane, I'm sorry." Bay frowned, his eyes softening. "I shouldn't have used that word."

He had to think about it for a second, and then he waved his brother off. "It's fine. I am what I am. It doesn't bother me. Also, you didn't mean it that way. You know your mother was surprisingly old fashioned for a woman of her age."

He'd been called it all by his stepmom's family. Bastard. By blow—he still wasn't sure what that meant. Illegitimate. Base born.

That was Shane Kent. First of his name. Ruiner of Marriages. Mistakenly Born.

Someone should have worn a condom.

"My mom was a mean woman who couldn't find it in her heart to be kind to a kid who had nothing to do with the circumstances of his birth," Bay corrected.

"No, but my momma could have handled it better."

His mother had gotten sick of waiting for her married lover to leave his wife and marry her.

"I'm sorry all the same. I'll be nice to Max, but we have to think about the fact that we'll be late if we don't leave soon," Bay pointed out. "Some of those supplies we picked up are for the work this afternoon. Bo is planning on mowing the back field, and we need to get those parts in or he's going to have a hard time with it."

He'd thought he might be able to get through this without telling Bay who was sitting in a booth across the café, but they were tight on time. He glanced over and she wasn't there. Her big suitcase was by the table, and it looked like Max and Rye were in serious conversation, though Max also had a now-awake kid trying to stuff his fist in his father's mouth.

Damn, but he wanted that life.

He shoved the thought aside. The key takeaway was that Brooke was gone and they could sneak out and walk right by. Easy peasy. They didn't have to engage. She likely wasn't staying for long and would be back to her high-powered job in New York, surrounded by men with affluence and money who came from good families.

"We should go. I'm being ridiculous. Like they'll even notice." He pulled out the cash and set it on the table. And then pulled a few more dollars out. He didn't mean to be tight with money but money was always tight.

The woman from the booth in front of him strode back, a huge smile on her face. "I have a solution. I ran into Brooke Harper. She's literally got a degree from Parsons, and she's in town for a couple of weeks. She's coming to the party at Hell on Wheels tonight, and we're going to make her part of the team. She's fabulous, so everyone is expected to treat her like the queen she is."

The group got up, all chattering about the party tonight.

The party Brooke Harper was attending.

Bay stopped, his eyes catching Shane's. "She's here? She's not supposed to be in town. I haven't heard anything about her coming to town."

They both listened to town gossip whenever they could. Strangely, Bo was the helpful one. The man was always willing to talk about what he heard. She'd turned them down once, but asking her again as long as they were polite and not aggressive was fine. They'd discussed it endlessly. She hadn't told them she didn't want to see them. She'd explained she needed to spend time with her family.

He knew it was an excuse, but he was taking it.

"She walked in fifteen minutes ago with a big-ass suitcase, and despite the smile she gave her brothers, I don't buy it. She's had some trouble," Shane explained. He leaned over and let his voice go low. "And now we know where she's going to be tonight. A bar."

A public place. Where they could be as well.

He kind of wished he'd heard when that party was supposed to start.

Bay's lips curled up as though he was thinking the whole plan through. "And we have tomorrow off."

Shane held up a hand. "She'll probably turn us down, and we need to be ready for that."

Bay looked back, and Brooke was sliding into the booth. He stared for a moment, and there was a determined look on his face. "I'm ready for anything. I want a shot with her. I haven't been able to get that girl out of my head for years. It's always been the wrong time."

"Let's hope it's the right time now," Shane said.

Bay nodded and stood, putting his hat on his head and turning toward the exit with a resolute expression on his face. "Then I should probably start being polite to her family."

They were always polite to Rachel Harper, and mostly to Rye. Max would be a new experience.

Brooke looked up as they approached the table, and her eyes went wide. Not scared wide. Nope. Her eyes were like a kid in a candy store, and she was wondering how much she could eat before someone stopped her. Her breath seemed to catch, and she bit her bottom lip.

"Miss Brooke," Shane said with a tip of his hat. "Good to see you again. Mr. Harper. Mr. Harper."

Max turned like a hawk scenting prey. Oddly, so did that baby boy in his arms. Father and son both stared at them with narrowed eyes. "You two. What are you doing here?"

"We came into town to pick up some parts for the mower. We're clearing the back field for hay," Bay explained, and didn't even say a damn thing about how Max could use a haircut or how he should understand because he was so old he could probably use a few new parts, too.

Max frowned. "Yeah, it's getting to be that time. You boys should head back to the G."

Shane nodded his way. "Will do. Miss Brooke."

"Just Brooke," she said in a breathy tone, and then she seemed to realize how she'd sounded. She shook off the sex-kitten voice and sounded more normal. "It's nice to see you, Shane. And Bay."

Rye Harper sipped his coke and looked from his sister then back to them. "Shane, could you tell Trev we got Beth's saddle in? I'll bring it out for our session tomorrow."

The boss's wife had ordered a custom saddle for her riding lessons. She'd driven her husbands a little insane by requesting the Harper brothers teach her instead of one of them. Rye Harper had been coming out for a couple of weeks, teaching her how to ride and take care of her gentle mare.

"Will do, sir. Have a nice day, Brooke. It's good to see you in our town again," Shane said.

"Hey, what do you mean by our town?" Max asked, and Shane could have sworn the baby nodded as though he wanted to know, too. The kid was the spitting image of his dads, with golden brown hair and serious eyes. "You boys are going to be out of here by summer, right?"

Bay simply tipped his hat Brooke's way, giving her a slight smile. "Y'all have a nice afternoon."

"And what the hell did he mean with that bullshit mister stuff," Max was saying as they started out the door.

"I do believe we call that a polite hello," Rye replied with a chuckle.

"Those two assholes are planning something," Max declared.

His brother looked back as he walked through the door. "Told you."

Shane wasn't listening. He was aware that Brooke watched them. The whole way.

They had their shot, and they were going to take it.

Chapter Two

Brooke sat back in the somewhat broke-down limo. It was more of a town car. Roomy, but certainly nothing like the limos she sometimes got to ride in when she was following the boss around. Before Mark had taken over, she'd worked for a nice woman who had been a true mentor to her. She'd treated Brooke like someone she was teaching, and that meant taking her to a lot of meetings and letting her share in the experiences.

Mark had shut that shit down and told her that her place was in the office making sure things worked well for him. He'd shrank her role to that of barista and errand girl, but hadn't minded stealing her designs.

"Air okay for you, Miss?" Bobby asked from the driver's seat. The seventeen-year-old had shown up exactly where she'd asked him to and had been politely on time.

She'd wanted to avoid her brothers knowing she was spending her first night home at a bar they would consider disreputable. Even though she knew when they were younger they'd spent plenty of time at Hell on Wheels.

"Bobby, you know my name is Brooke." She knew her brothers made fun of this service the twin genius menaces of Bliss were providing, but she kind of liked it. They'd tricked out the sucker. Oh, on the outside there were a couple of dents, and the bumper was obviously from another car, but inside they'd put some lumbar pillows and installed LED lights. There was a tray with bottles of water and snack cakes straight from The Trading Post. No one in NYC would ever think to stock up on snack cakes.

They were delicious.

"I am keeping a professional distance, madam customer," Bobby said as he turned onto the highway that would lead them up to Hell on Wheels.

She sighed. She knew how to get the kid to talk. "I already tipped you on the app."

Yeah, they had their own app, and she was certain they'd programmed it themselves. The Farley brothers were known for two things—shenanigans and their ridiculously high IQs.

He took off the cap he was wearing. Flat cap. Also known as a newsboy. This one was oddly elegant, done in herringbone. He wore slacks and a button-down, but she'd noticed he hadn't traded his sneakers for loafers. "Cool, because I have so many questions."

"No." She was the one who had tipped. "I have questions. It's been six months since I got some real gossip because my sister-in-law is surprisingly not as forthcoming as one would think, and Callie's been busy. I heard Sawyer is living with someone now. Two someones."

He nodded, their eyes meeting in the rearview mirror. "Yeah, and she's the coolest teacher in the world. Ms. Sabrina Leal. And Wyatt's cool, too. I think he likes it here. Especially since the kids stopped kicking him in the shins after he asked Ms. Leal to marry him. Sawyer did, too. Wyatt's running the business part of the bar now. I got a lot of advice from him on how to keep the books for our business, and I helped him with the math on his taxes. He said he thought we were clever to see a need in the community and fill it. Though I guess there wasn't much need since you're the first ride we've had in a week. Turns out most tourists rent cars."

Of course they did since the nearest major airport was three hours away. "I met her at the Christmas party. So you like her? I know Sawyer seems difficult, but he's a nice guy down deep."

Bobby got serious. As serious as Bobby ever got. "He couldn't possibly do better than Ms. Leal. She's…she's the best. Will and I thought we would have to skip college, but Ms. Leal helped us get all the right paperwork and she found teachers online to help us with the advanced mathematics and science we need to get into a good program."

She'd always thought those boys belonged in the Ivies. "Tell me you're going to MIT."

A grin flashed. "I think we'll do our doctorates there, but we're starting at Yale. I still can't believe we got into Yale. I've never been east of Kansas."

Oh, if she hadn't had a good impression of Sabrina Leal before, she had one now. "I'm happy for you, Bobby. You will love it, and the best part is how nice it feels to come home."

She picked up another snack cake. See, she never got sugar back in New York. Everyone was on a diet, so she thought she should be on one. Which sucked because it wasn't like she was the model.

"Do you like to come home?" Bobby asked.

"I do. I love seeing my brothers and Rachel and the kids."

"They have a lot of kids."

She nodded. "I think this is the last, though. Both of my brothers got the snip."

Though she was worried about them. They'd seemed disconnected tonight at dinner. Like they were going through the motions. They'd passed the kids around and everyone had done their part, but there had been a fundamental lack of the sexual chemistry that had always defined them. Even Max had seemed physically disconnected.

Of course Rachel had been pregnant four of the last seven years, so there was that.

"I know. Max told everyone horror stories about it. Do you really think Doc did it without any pain killers? Max said it was like a loose tooth. Doc wrapped a string around his balls and tied them to the door and then slammed it shut. I don't think it's supposed to work that way. I think that's a castration. Does he still actually have balls? Or is it smooth down there?"

She rolled her eyes and vowed to get that rumor out there. Her brother more than deserved to be thought of as Bliss's Ken doll. "Doc Burke is a professional, and we're lucky to have him. I assure you he used all of the latest techniques."

Bobby was quiet for a moment, and she noted that there was a package marked beet treats. So Mel had weighed in on the new business. He'd probably advised the kids to test any unknown traveler. "I would have come up to the house, you know. I'm a real good driver. I've been driving my dad's truck since I was fourteen, and mostly Sheriff turned the other way. I'm sure he breathed a sigh of relief when we got our driver's licenses. Did you not want them to know you left? Is this what they would call a clandestine meeting?"

"No." She wasn't sure why she hadn't asked her brothers for a ride. Or to borrow the car. They would have been happy to let her drive the extra SUV they kept in a garage, but she wanted to keep her options open.

Was she thinking about picking up a guy at the bar?

Had she been thinking about it from the moment she'd seen those brothers standing there like two man cupcakes she wanted to swallow whole?

It wouldn't be the Kent brothers. It probably wouldn't be anyone at all, and she definitely wouldn't be taking him home with her since she currently resided in a 300-square-foot tiny home not far from the big house where her family was likely getting ready for bed.

"Let's just say I wanted some privacy. Not that I'm planning anything," she replied. "I want to keep my options open, and if my brothers know I'm out, they'll wait up. By the way, can I schedule a ride back?"

"Uh, I have a curfew."

She snorted. Definitely not in New York anymore. "I'm meeting some friends. I'm sure they can take me back. So everything is the same here?"

"Besides all the babies and the school and the new store and the new deputies? One of them is Ms. Leal's sister and she's living with the new guys." He huffed. "There's actually a lot of new stuff when you think about it."

"Anything to worry about?" She'd discovered the Farley brothers knew more than a lot of the adults around town imagined, and they were willing to talk. Those boys loved to gossip, and they had ears everywhere. Literally. They'd created a device that amplified sound and had gotten caught eavesdropping from afar many times.

Just last Christmas she'd found out Rachel was pissed off at her brothers for forgetting her birthday. Luckily in advance. Rachel had complained to Callie and Nell that her husbands hadn't planned anything for her birthday, and Bobby had gone into detail about how Rachel's pregnancy hormones were making her a little on the murdery side. Brooke had thought maybe her brothers were just planning a surprise.

And then she remembered they ran a business and had three kids under seven, with one on the way.

Yeah, she'd saved the day that time. Max and Rye had time to put together a surprise party and give their wife a signed set of her favorite romance novels.

So she checked in.

The idea of that family breaking down wrecked her. She counted on coming home to happy families so she could at least believe happily ever after could happen.

"So Jen wants another baby, but Stef isn't sure he can handle her being pregnant again. He had this whole like heartfelt conversation with your brother about it. Rye. Not Max."

This was what she was here for. What no one understood was that she often played fairy godmother. Quietly. From behind the scenes. "What did Rye say?"

"That Jen was strong, and he needed to man up. It was one thing to not want another kid, but he shouldn't hold Jen back if it was about his own fear." Bobby nodded as though he agreed. "It was a real nice conversation. Nell is worried that she's added to the world's overpopulation, but Henry tells her this baby is going to be the sweetest, kindest girl in the whole world, and that she's a gift."

"Oh, that's sweet." She was happy little Poppy was getting a sister. Though she supposed Poppy wasn't so little anymore. Nell still hauled her around, but the kid was definitely a full-sized toddler.

"Also, Max is real upset about his bloodwork, but Rye's cholesterol was actually worse than his, so they are both on diets and they both sneak in wings at Trio. If you need pocket change, they can be blackmailed."

"Good to know." She sighed and asked the question she truly

wanted the answer to. The question that had been running through her brain since the minute she'd seen them in the diner. Probably before, if she was honest with herself. "What have you heard about the Kent brothers?"

"Bay and Shane? They're real quiet. They keep to themselves a lot, but they seem nice. When Will and I first started the business, we got a flat." Bobby frowned. "We're better with engines. Anyway, they were on their way into town and stopped and taught us how to change the tire. Bay said the inside could use some work. He's the one who told us rich people who need drivers like amenities. He suggested the snacks and that the LED lights would make it feel like a club."

That was kind of them. It didn't answer her question. "My brothers told me they've been friendly."

"I wouldn't call them unfriendly. They're like most cowboys," Bobby explained in a cheerful tone. "They come out to the town parties, though. Usually with the group of hands from the G. They always offer to help out. I like them. Especially how they whip Max up in a frenzy." He sobered. "Sorry. I bet you don't like that part."

Her brother could handle himself and usually deserved it. But he wasn't answering her question, and she should probably know that a seventeen-year-old boy who'd spent his whole life with his nose in a book wouldn't get the subtleties. "Bobby, are they dating anyone? According to my brothers they've been active, if you know what I mean."

"I do not. I mean, they seem fit, and I suspect they get a lot of exercise out at the G."

She bit back a groan. "Max calls them walking STIs and said Doc better have upped his orders for penicillin."

"Why would he order penicillin? Doxycycline is the recommended antibiotic for most sexually transmitted infections," Bobby replied.

"I don't want to know how you know that, do I?"

He grinned, and she wondered if she'd ever been that young. "It was a Jeopardy question. I'm going to be a master one day. But now I understand. You like them."

"I don't like them. I don't know them." She liked how they looked. She was on the fence about how they made her feel. In one way it was good to have a little bit of a libido again.

It was bad that it was the only thing she could think about. Those men and their big hands and broad shoulders and the way they looked at her like they would eat her alive and she would thank them for it.

"All right. I've listened in a bit and I think they used to visit that guesthouse at Stef's often. I'm not supposed to know about it. My mom says it's like a reading room or something, but I think it's probably a weird sex thing. She prays for Stef a lot."

No one ever said he wasn't smart. "It's definitely a weird sex thing. So they go there often?"

Bobby shrugged. "They spend time out at Stef's, but from what I've heard through the grapevine, Bay spends time in the studio working on art stuff and Shane plays Xbox. He even invited me and Will to play with him this weekend because they have time off and Bay wants to work. Stef has weird treats. If he's there someone brings us a plate of all these meats and fancy cheeses. If Jen's in charge she tosses us a couple of bags of chips, and once she made us pizza rolls. I like it when Jen's in charge."

She would never turn down a nice charcuterie, but she could see how it wouldn't be the hungry teens favorite since she was sure those cheeses weren't anything so ordinary as cheddar. Stef would bring out the stinky cheeses. She wondered how Bay and Shane reacted to those. She would bet those cowboys were more chips and meat stick guys. "So there are no rumors about them having a girlfriend?"

"Nope. And Mel certified them alien free when they took the jobs on the G. He gave them the pamphlet about what to look out for if they don't want to end up as an incubator for an alien species."

She bet that had gone well. It was something to hold onto. If they were awful to someone as kind as Mel, she could easily shove down her libido. "Did they laugh in his face?"

Bobby's head shook. "No. They thanked him and promised to be careful. Shane went out to one of Mel's alien towers because Stef thought the ladder was rusty. Hale did the actual welding part, but Van was working so Shane offered to be an extra set of hands."

So they weren't assholes.

It didn't matter. She wasn't going to be here for long. She had a meeting with Gemma tomorrow and would have a better handle on what to do, and in a couple of weeks she would hopefully be right back to her old life.

Did she want her old life?

"I like them," Bobby admitted. "But I do worry they're in some kind of trouble. Though it seems to have passed."

"What else do you know?"

Up ahead she could see the lights of the neon sign that pointed customers to Hell on Wheels. It was an odd bar, set in amongst the old pines and aspens. It was a place her brothers had told her she shouldn't come to because nothing good ever happened at Hell on Wheels after…well, ever. She would bet they didn't want her coming here because Sawyer's fry cook wasn't married to Rachel's best friend.

"I don't because they're not talking, but from what I can tell they left their old jobs at Kingman Ranch quickly, and right about Christmas. That's when they showed up on Stef's doorstep, and he got them on at the G. But I happen to know Jamie and Trev weren't looking for new hands."

So they needed work, and Stef made it happen. "That's a big ranch. Kingman, that is. I wonder…" She sighed. Kale Kingman had three lovely daughters. She bet she knew what happened. But she wasn't about to go into that with Bobby. He was pulling up to the bar. She grabbed her bag. And a packet of peanut butter crackers. She'd tipped well. "Well, thanks so much for the ride. I'll give you a five-star rating."

"Any time, Brooke." He winced as he corrected himself. "I mean except for when we're in school or if it's too late or when we're in church. I told Mom I thought God would want us to save money for college, but she said if God wanted us to go to college, there would be one in Bliss. She's in denial."

Brooke leaned forward. "Bobby, you know you have to go. You and Will…you're too smart to stay here. It doesn't mean you can't come back. It doesn't mean you don't love your parents and your home. It simply means that there's a big world out there, and you owe it to yourself to chase your dreams. I know that your parents might not want you to leave."

Bobby put the car in park and turned in his seat. "They think we should stay and help with the house. Maybe get jobs at one of the ranches or in town. But I want to study physics. So does Will. We want to know what makes the stars work. My mom said I should leave everything to God, but why can't she see that science is just a way to understand God?"

She reached out and took his hand. "Sweetie, you can love your parents and follow your own road. I know it's going to be hard to leave them, and they might be angry, but you owe yourself more. If you need help with money…"

"Miss Leal helped us sign up for the SAT last year and we scored almost perfect. She doesn't think we'll have problems with scholarships, and she's helping us apply for them. My mom doesn't even know we're National Merit Scholars."

She felt so much for him. How many of her friends had been weighed down by guilt for wanting to leave their small towns? Some parents viewed it as a betrayal. "You stick with Miss Leal and know if anything goes wrong, we'll bully Seth Stark into paying for all of it. We won't even have to. I'll go to Georgia, and she'll be happy to start a scholarship fund. You're going to do great things, Bobby Farley."

He gave her a watery smile. "Thanks, Brooke. That means a lot coming from you. Everyone's real proud of you."

She had to force that smile to stay on her face. She sniffled and gave him one last squeeze. "Thanks. Now let's talk about what a real limo driver should do."

He gasped. "Shit…I mean, uh, shoot. I'm supposed to open your door." He unhooked his seat belt and then glanced back. "Oh, I think he's got it."

She turned and the door was opening, and there was a big cowboy standing there. Bay Kent. He looked down at her with seriously gorgeous eyes and held out a hand.

"Miss Brooke," he said in that low, slow drawl that seemed to have a direct line to all her pink parts.

They were here. Right here.

Dark hair that peeked out from under his Stetson, and emerald eyes that seemed to glow in the low light. Shane stood behind him, and in the shadows. She wondered which one was older. She didn't know how they'd grown up or what got them into ranching. Or how Bay discovered art and what moved Shane, but she suddenly wanted to, and that was so dangerous.

It was right there on the tip of her tongue to yell at Bobby to drive and fast.

Why was it dangerous? It wasn't like she was going to fall in love. She'd never been in love before. She'd kind of given up on the idea.

So why was her heart racing? Oh, yeah, it had been a while. They were gorgeous men, and hadn't she kind of always wanted to know what it would feel like to have two men pleasuring her?

She took Bay's hand and let him help her out. Bay stepped back and glanced inside, with its pillows and LED lights and snack trays.

He leaned over and gave Bobby a thumbs-up. "Looks good in here, Bobby. I like the lights. Very cosmopolitan."

It wasn't, but it didn't have to be.

Shane tipped his hat. "Miss Brooke."

"Just Brooke." His stare practically singed her. "I should go inside. I'm meeting some friends. Thanks for the chivalry."

She turned and walked inside and felt their eyes on her every step of the way.

It was going to be a long night.

* * * *

Bay watched her from across the bar. She was in the back by the new pool table where they now had what the barkeep called a party room.

He'd been coming to Hell on Wheels off and on for years. It was a place he felt comfortable in because it was an old-school, no-frills bar where at any moment a fight could break out. Not that he wanted to fight. If he broke a few fingers he wouldn't be able to draw or sculpt, and then where would he be?

Still, he'd been surprised at the changes Sawyer taking on a girlfriend and a partner had wrought. The fire hadn't helped.

There were blinds now instead of the threadbare shades that covered the windows, and where once there had been three kinds of glasses—beer, wine, and rocks—there were martini glasses and different kinds of wine glasses. And apparently now there were wines beyond red, white, and pink. He should know because Brooke had commented on being able to order a Sauvignon Blanc.

Damn, she looked good, but Shane was right. There was something dark in that girl's eyes.

"She's in some kind of trouble." He took a long sip of beer.

"Told you." Shane sat beside him. "I'm wondering why she decided to order a ride. I can't imagine her brothers wouldn't let her borrow a car. They have several. Unless she didn't want them to know where she was going."

"Why would… You think she's looking for someone?" Bay asked, not taking his eyes off her. Brooke Harper was made of delicate lines and generous curves. She was a study in contrasts. She was solid, with hips and breasts and a healthy figure, but there was a fragility to the woman, too. He tried so hard to capture it in drawings, and more importantly, the sculptures he felt the desperate need to make. Like an impulse he couldn't control.

Stef Talbot supplying him with materials, letting him experiment with things like marble that he would never be able to afford, was a godsend. If the man hadn't been so good-hearted, he could have pulled some seriously Mephistophelean shit with him.

He wondered if Brooke would be impressed with his proper use of a literary figure. He wondered if she would be surprised by how much he and Shane read. Not that they were well educated. They'd barely made it through high school, but part of that had been the chaos after their parents had died.

They'd never had a real chance at college. The rodeo had been their salvation.

The question now was how long they kept doing what they were doing. How long until they put down roots and tried to build something that might have a chance at lasting?

"I think she's looking at us," Shane said, his voice going low.

There weren't a ton of customers on a Thursday night. There were a few people in the booths, but the majority of patrons this evening seemed to be at the private party. "I wonder how they know each other."

"Cleo and Brooke went to school together." Sawyer Hathaway was polishing glasses at the end of the bar. He was a huge, kind of brutal-looking man who only softened up with his girl and partner and tight-knit group of friends.

Bay wished they had a group like Sawyer seemed to have in Lucy and Ty and River. The four had gone to school together and grown up alongside one another, and still held those ties through adulthood.

Shane was his only tie to anyone, really.

"Where did they go?" Shane seemed way more comfortable with the big guy. "I know they recently built a school here. Was there another one?"

Sawyer huffed out a laugh and replaced the glass. "Oh, we didn't have a school here in Bliss when I was growing up. We got our asses on a bus and drove forty-five minutes to Del Norte to go to school. Rain or shine or blizzard, we all went."

"You went to school with Brooke?" Bay wasn't much of a talker, but he couldn't help but ask.

Sawyer's dark eyes narrowed. "You two interested in Brooke?"

"Yes." They said it at the same time.

Neither of them liked to prevaricate.

Would she be impressed that he knew how to properly use the word prevaricate? She'd seemed interested in Bobby Farley's education. He didn't think a real limo would be so easy to listen in on, but he wasn't going to complain.

For a moment he thought they'd made a mistake. Sawyer studied them like he was planning to throw them out on their asses. "Aren't you two the little assholes who hit on Rachel Harper before she married the twins in an attempt to force them to buy her at Stef's auction?"

Not their proudest moment. "We were doing it as a favor for a friend. That friend being Stef."

"We respect Mrs. Harper and her marriage very much," Shane tried.

A brow arched over Sawyer's eyes. "Do you? Would you do it again?"

"Absolutely not," Shane began.

"Oh, yeah." Bay might not always pick up on social cues, but he felt like Sawyer might be his people. "Max is an asshole. I would do it again in a heartbeat, but my brother thinks we probably shouldn't flirt with Brooke's sister-in-law since we're into her. Miss Rachel is nice and lovely, but it was always Brooke."

A smile broke out over Sawyer's face. "You are going to drive Max crazy. I approve."

He wasn't sure what Sawyer's approval meant, but he was willing to use it to test some boundaries. "So you grew up with Brooke?"

"I was a few years older," Sawyer said, relaxing against the bar. "I always kind of felt for her. Not that I have feelings, per se, but it must have been hard on Brooke since she was the only kid in town. Ty lived in Bliss. River was closer to Creede. Lucy and I lived on this side of the mountain, but honestly, even if we had been in the valley, she was years younger than us. She was a freshman when we were in our senior year. All of her friends were at school, and she was alone during the summers."

He didn't like the thought of that. He and Shane had been alone a lot since his mom didn't like having anyone in her home. But they'd had each other. He looked toward the party room. Brooke seemed like the life of the party. She was laughing at something a ridiculously handsome guy said. He studied the man for a moment and then relaxed. That dude was gay. He'd been in the art world long enough to recognize the signs. Well dressed, perfectly groomed, and he was not looking at her chest. Also, he'd briefly held hands with another guy as he passed him a glass of wine. "She looks like she has friends now."

Sawyer glanced behind him. "Oh, I think she's about to discover her old friend Cleo is in a bit of a bind. Wyatt overheard them talking about how the costume designer for this season up and quit two days ago because she fell in love with… It was either a squatcher or the big guy himself. Wyatt needs to learn to listen better if he's going to gossip."

Shane sat forward. "That sounds like she's hanging around for a while."

"I heard she was here for a couple of weeks. She's on some kind of sabbatical with that job of hers, but I'm not so sure that's going to work out." Sawyer nodded to his waitress and started pouring out a beer. "I've seen her a couple of times since she started there. She and Lucy have gotten to be good friends since she graduated from college. River, too. It's funny how that small age gap that meant she was left out of most things as a kid doesn't mean that much now. We're all on the same playing field, if you know what I mean. I think those three get along because they're invested in their careers."

"Why do you think it's not going to work out?" Bay asked, trying to keep Sawyer on track since for a dude who didn't talk much, he was chatty as hell this evening. Normally he preferred companionable silence, but they were talking about the one thing he liked to hear. Brooke Harper.

Sawyer passed the waitress the glass and began filling another. "She doesn't seem like she's happy. Even when she's here she's always calling back to the office. From what Lucy can tell she doesn't have friends in New York. She works all the time, and she doesn't feel like she's getting anywhere. If I was a betting man, she's stuck and doesn't know how to get out."

"So no boyfriend?" Shane asked.

They had come to that conclusion back at Christmastime, but it had been months and she could have met someone.

"Not that she's mentioned to the girls," Sawyer replied, finishing up the order, and then his whole face lit up. "Hey there, Teach."

Sabrina Leal slapped her bag on the bar and hauled herself onto the stool next to Shane. She was a pretty woman in a yellow dress and a matching cardigan, her dark hair in a bun. She was the quintessential schoolteacher, if one forgave the whole engaged to two men thing. "Wedding planning with my sister is going to drive me insane. I need tequila."

Sawyer winked her way. "I told you. We should go to Vegas."

"No Vegas." Wyatt had walked in after Sabrina. He gave Bay and his brother a wave. "Hello, Bay. Shane. You two doing okay?"

"If we went to Vegas, you wouldn't have to wear a tux," Sawyer insisted. "I kinda thought we would be able to outvote Teach here since I can't imagine Van or Hale in a monkey suit."

"I think a tuxedo is appropriate, and so does Van." Wyatt managed to sound oddly prim for a dude who used to run with one percenters. "It's Elisa who thinks she should be able to get married in her deputy uniform."

Sabrina laughed at the idea. "She's joking. I mean not about wearing a frilly dress, but about the polyester uniform as wedding wear. My sister is not as into elegance as I am."

"She called her bougie," Wyatt explained.

"Well, you know there's a dress designer in town right now. Like a real New York City, works-for-a-design-house designer," Shane pointed out.

Oh, his brother was smart. If Sawyer was right and she wasn't happy in the city, maybe working some Bliss jobs would show her how nice it was here.

The city was a problem. He'd never felt comfortable in a city as big and cramped as New York. It wasn't like Stef hadn't tried. Somehow when he got surrounded by all that concrete and metal, he couldn't breathe, much less work. He found his peace in the simple things. The mountains and pines. Soft grass under his feet. The sound of the river rushing by.

But he would try it if it meant being close to her.

Of course, it would be way better if she decided to stay here in Bliss.

"Seriously?" Sabrina had perked up. "Because Alamosa is the closest place with an actual wedding shop, and it doesn't have much. Teeny can order a lot of what we want, but I want some work done on my dress. It's the right silhouette but it needs some…oomph, if you know what I mean."

He did not, but he was going with it. "You should ask Brooke."

"She works for Bianchi," Shane added.

"Seriously?" Sabrina asked. "I met her, and she said she did something in design. I didn't realize it was fashion. I've heard of Bianchi. I've wanted a pair of their palazzo pants for years."

"She designed the navy ones from this spring's collection," Bay offered.

"How the hell would you know that?" a very familiar voice asked. Brooke.

He winced and looked at his brother. "She's right behind me, isn't she?"

Shane nodded.

"I seem like a creepy stalker now. Don't I?" It was good to know what he was going into. If he turned around. He could pretend she wasn't there. The stool turned, so if she moved, he could move, too. He could keep turning, and at some point he would get a chance to run, and he could live in the woods for the rest of his life.

"He's good at recognizing what I like to call artistic tells," Shane began. "You showed us some of your sketches. Bay is an artist. He recognized your style."

Thank the universe for Shane. His brother was so much cooler under pressure than he was. Shane didn't regularly think about running into the woods and becoming one of those dudes who got misidentified as a Sasquatch, though apparently there was love for them out there too, if the runaway costume designer was any indication.

Did Brooke have a thing for Bigfoot?

He turned since his brother had given such an excellent non-stalkery explanation. "That's right. You talked about working real hard on those pants. You said you thought they were coming back in style and wanted to put your own flair to them."

She stared for a minute as though trying to figure something out. "It was my first big addition to a line. I did some T-shirts and accessories. The palazzo pants were well received."

"Because they were awesome," Sabrina said with a grin.

Brooke flushed, a pink tone hitting her skin, and he wondered if she blushed like that all over her body. If her skin would be that sweet shade of pink when he got her naked and spanked her pretty ass.

And that was a mistake because his jeans weren't all that forgiving.

"Thanks," Brooke said. "I love a good pair of leggings, but there are days when I need the freedom of those pants. It's good to see you again, Sabrina. I hear congratulations are in order."

Sabrina practically glowed as she showed off the one-carat ring her men had bought her. They'd asked her to marry them on New Year's Eve right here in the bar.

"Yes, and I hope you'll be able to come," Sabrina said as Brooke inspected the ring.

There was a lot of talk about venues and parties and stuff. He was watching Brooke. So was his brother. Wyatt moved behind the bar and talked to his partner. Likely about them, because they were probably back to desperate stalker vibes.

Brooke ordered her second glass of wine and thanked Sawyer. She promised Sabrina she would help her with the wedding dress and then nodded Bay and Shane's way.

And left.

"Now she thinks you're a complete weirdo," Sawyer said with a cheeriness that Bay had never associated with the big guy.

Yep. That chance was probably blown.

Chapter Three

Shane watched the party as they started to break up.

He and Bay had moved to a booth when it became apparent Brooke was staying for a while.

"It's her and Cleo and three others left. The drunk girl who sang karaoke without a machine, one guy, and another I suspect is his boyfriend." Shane had made a study of the people around Brooke tonight. She'd been hit on more than once by random dudes, but she'd given them polite but firm nos. Surprisingly enough, he and Bay had been left alone all night. At one point a couple of women had walked in and looked Shane and his brother over like they were an all-you-can-eat sex buffet and they had some excellent coupons. He'd prepared several excuses, including he was married and he didn't like women. The last thing he'd needed was to have Brooke think they were open to anyone but her.

Then they'd come back from the bathroom, looked him over like he was dirty, and walked out.

He didn't smell or anything. He looked good. It didn't matter. He knew why he was here, and he was close to meeting that goal.

He also knew something else. "I'm fairly certain they came in Cleo's car. It's tiny. I don't think they'll all fit."

It was late, almost closing time. The last time he'd gone to the restroom, he'd taken a tour of the parking lot and the only cars remaining were Sawyer's Jeep, their truck, and that tiny Fiat that wouldn't fit more than four people.

The Farley brothers weren't allowed out after ten, since apparently that was when the devil showed up, so Brooke was going to need a ride.

Was she thinking she would get one from Cleo? Or was she planning to call her brothers at almost two in the morning? Did she think they were so bad for her she wouldn't even accept a ride from them?

He intended to correct that impression tonight. By being a gentleman. He intended to show her how good they could be for her.

And how are you going to do that? His inner voice kept creeping in. *What good are you going to do her? You got no real money. You don't have a house. You barely have a car, and you can't even consider going after her yourself because you learned long ago that you're half a man and always will be.*

He took the last sip of beer, the one he'd been saving. He wasn't listening to that crap tonight.

"Hey, guys. It's last call," Sawyer announced from the bar in a booming voice. "I close in twenty, and I mean to be up that mountain about two minutes after. You don't have to go home but you..."

Shane knew the next words. "Can't stay here."

How many nights had he and Bay stayed at the bar until they heard those words because it was better than wherever they happened to be staying? His rodeo days had definitely been spent that way. Cheap motel room. Closest dive bar. Rinse. Repeat.

How many women had they gone home with? Oh, he'd told himself it was for sex, but it was also to stay out of that room they shared. Whether it was a motel or a bunkhouse, he was constantly reminded that there was no home for him.

No one wants you. Your father only took you in because his pastor knew about you and it would make us look bad if we let you go into the system.

Sometimes he wished she had.

But then that would have left Bay alone with her. He suspected if he hadn't been his stepmother's whipping boy, she would have turned all that anger and regret on her son. In some ways, he thought having him around had spared Bay a lot of pain.

Sawyer walked up and grabbed their empty glasses with a frown. "You two are disappointments."

Not anything he hadn't heard before. "Yeah, we get that a lot."

"You've been here for hours and you've nursed two whole beers. I don't do this for my health. I need serious drinkers, and that's not the two of you." Sawyer glanced back at the only other table left. "You stay for her?"

Was this the moment when Sawyer took away their big chance with her? "We thought we should hang around. She's going to need a ride. Unless you think they can strap one of them to the top of a Fiat. I suppose she could call someone, but I thought we should make sure she gets home okay."

"So you kept the drinking to a minimum." Sawyer stared at him as though he could see through to his damn soul. Or he was deciding how to kill him in the cleanest fashion. He'd heard the big guy didn't like a mess. He finally nodded. "Okay. I need you to know that I'm watching you. If she doesn't get home all right or if you take advantage of her, I'll kill you. Deal?"

"Could we talk about the word advantage?" Bay asked. "It could mean different things to different people."

"How much has she had to drink?" Shane got right to the point. "I saw her drink two glasses of wine and some water."

"She had a glass of champagne about an hour ago, but since she's been drinking club soda, and she split a BLT with Cleo, who is also sober," Sawyer explained. "I can't say the same for the rest. They look wasted, but then they're actors, so I'm not surprised. I think the only class of employed people who can drink actors under the table are teachers, but I totally don't blame them. I've seen what those kids can do." He looked over and Cleo and the group were walking up. "Can you handle them okay? I can get Wyatt to come down and drive some of you home while I close."

Cleo held a hand up. "I am a director, Sawyer. I am used to corralling a bunch of artists and getting them where they need to be. Besides, we're all staying out at the Movie Motel. Val is in my room, and the boys have the one next to us."

Brooke winced. "Are you still driving the Fiat?"

Cleo nodded. "Yeah, but Val can sit on Dave's lap. We can squeeze in."

Bay held up a hand. "Uhm, be careful about that. The sheriff is on a rampage, and by rampage I mean he's writing tickets right and left because he needs a new chair and he wants one of those massagers. The last one broke, and I do not want to know how. I got a ticket for jaywalking, which apparently is a real thing, and I got a lecture on protecting my vertebrae because they go bad or something."

Shane had never been happier to report a sighting of a law enforcement professional. "One of the deputies is parked at the base of the mountain."

Cleo sighed. "Maybe we're going to need that ride, Sawyer."

"I am not making Wyatt come down here and drive me home. He's probably already in bed." Brooke looked to Sawyer. "Can they drive safely or should I take their truck and run?"

And that was why they'd sat here nursing beers when they should have been getting drunk off their asses and proving what cowboys they were.

He didn't want to be a cowboy tonight. He wanted to serve her in some way.

He was making himself nauseous. If his brother said those words to him, he would punch him and ask him if Doc took his dick like he'd taken Max Harper's balls.

But it was still true. He wanted to take her home and make sure she got in okay, and he would ask if she wanted to have lunch with them. He would be polite. He would take it slow.

"They've been nursing two whole beers all night," Sawyer confirmed. "They've done nothing but stare at you like the creepers they are."

Asshole. He felt his skin flush and hoped he hadn't gone totally red.

Brooke's lips curled up as if she had them right where she wanted them. Not a hint of fear or disgust in her eyes. Nope. She looked like a cat who knew she was going to get all the cream she wanted.

And didn't that make his cock tighten.

"But then you spent most of the night telling the two single women in here that they have chlamydia," Sawyer continued. "Think I didn't hear that? So like get a room. You're all capable of consent and to drive. Spare the rest of us and get it out of your systems."

Cleo laughed. "I missed you, Sawyer. You are every bit the asshole you were in high school. Never change, my friend. Let's go. Brooke, I'll see you at the theater tomorrow." She looked Shane and Bay over before turning back to Brooke. "Don't do anything I wouldn't do. But you should know I would do a lot."

She winked and gave Brooke a hug.

"I don't have chlamydia." Bay leaned over and whispered as though there weren't a bunch of people watching him. "Do you? You didn't say anything."

Shane slid out of the booth. "No one has chlamydia. She's being a territorial chick. She didn't want those women hitting on us. She wanted to keep her options open."

"Did not," Brooke protested. "I was being mean. You're not nice to my brother."

Sawyer snorted. "Then everyone has chlamydia, Brooke. Girl, don't do this. Say what you want, take it, and get it out of your system. No one will think less of you."

Shane didn't like how that sounded. He didn't want to be out of her system. He hadn't known he was in it. Shouldn't he have enjoyed that more?

Brooke frowned and crossed her arms under her breasts, which only made them more prominent. "Well, let's go then. We need to take the back way onto the property. The lights could wake the kids up, and I don't want to be the reason three kids climb into my brothers' bed tonight."

She started walking for the door.

Bay looked at him as he slid out of the booth. "It's a good thing she thinks we have an STI?"

His brother could miss the point from time to time. It was the whole genius-artist thing. Sometimes he checked to make sure Bay still had both his ears. He'd decided if he had one job in life it was to ensure Bay went to his grave with both ears intact. "No. She didn't want those women hitting on us. Now we need to treat her like a lady.

Go and open the door for her. We should have some interesting conversation because I'm fairly certain she views us as two himbo cowpokes without a brain to share between us. Show her we're smarter than she thinks."

Bay nodded and rushed to get to the door.

"This is going to be fun," Sawyer said with a grin that lit up his usually grim expression.

He wasn't sure what the guy meant by that since they were going to see the lady home and ensure her safety and that was all. They had about fifteen minutes to convince her they would be fun to spend time with. A lunch. Then dinner maybe. Or drinks first and that could slide into dinner if she wanted.

The point was he was going to give her all the space she needed before he mentioned he would like to tie her up, spank her ass, and fuck her until she couldn't see straight.

Time. They were taking it this go around.

Bay held the door open for Cleo and her group and finally Brooke. He smiled at her. His brother could look fairly grim most of the time, but he had a smile that women flocked to. "Did you know ninety percent of koalas have chlamydia?"

Yep. They saw that *aw, shucks* smile of Bay's and were interested, and then the fucker opened his mouth.

Brooke stopped and stared at Bay. "No, they don't."

Oh, she shouldn't challenge Bay's trivia knowledge when it came to animals. When they were kids, he had a monthly shipment of cards he kept in a well-organized box. Each contained animal facts. Shane would quiz him. "I'm pretty sure they do. What I am unsure of is why we are bringing that unimportant fact up now."

Sawyer slapped the bar he was laughing so hard.

Brooke frowned Shane's way. "I am fairly certain it's important to the koala bears. The sweet, cuddly bears."

Bay shook his head. "Yeah, they're more than cuddly. They're kind of nature's pervs. Like if Stef before Jen had been a bear, he would have been a koala."

Brooke went still, and Shane worried for a moment Bay had offended her. Then her lips curled up and she laughed, the sound ringing through the almost empty bar.

She looked back at Sawyer, sobering slightly. "You won't feel the need to call my brothers if you think I'm doing something dumb, will you?"

Sawyer shrugged. "I don't even like your brothers. Make some mistakes. Have fun. Soon some dumbass will show up on your doorstep and he won't leave, and then there's a dog and a glorious angel who yells at you when you do stupid shit and you're getting married." He sighed, a soft sound. "Yeah, that's the good part."

Brooke put a hand on Bay's shirt and went up on her toes. She planted a kiss right on his lips. "You're weird, Kent. I like weird." She stepped back. "Let's get this show on the road. I'd like to have a couple of orgasms before dawn, boys."

Wait. What?

Bay stood there like a statue.

Shane looked to Sawyer. "We aren't planning anything for tonight. No taking advantage. We are driving her home and making sure she's safe, and hopefully making a date for another time. We're not interested in a quick roll with her."

Sawyer winced. "Yeah, but I think she's interested in a quick roll with the two of you."

"Uh, she kissed me," Bay pointed out needlessly.

Shane never thought he would panic at the thought of a woman wanting to go to bed with them, but here he was. "We can save this. We can tell her we should take it slow."

Sawyer huffed. "Have you ever told a woman who wants sex you should take it slow? She's not going to hear 'hey, I'd like to date you.' She's going to hear one thing and that's 'you don't find me attractive.' Something's bugging that girl, and she needs affirmation. She can get it from the two of you or she'll find it somewhere else, and it won't be a self-help course, no matter how much Alexi keeps trying to push that off on everyone. You are in a pickle, guys. Take the fruit or the fruit will likely ignore you the next time you see it."

Shit. This was not his plan.

"Uhm, I think the fruit might steal our truck if we don't get out there." Bay started out the door. "Hey, Brooke. You don't have to break in. I have a key."

Shane followed his brother and heard the door close and lock behind him.

So there would be no more help from that source.

Brooke waved as Cleo drove off in her clown car. He had no idea how those boys managed to get their bodies in the back. Those were some flexible motherfuckers.

Brooke turned to him as he joined them. She sent him a challenging look, her chin coming up and arrogance in her expression. "So, you want to take me back to your place and have your way with me?"

Shit. Sawyer was right. She was on the edge tonight, and if they turned her down, she would go one of two ways. She would either freeze up and cut herself off from something she needed out of shame, or she would tell them to fuck off and find it somewhere else.

It was right there in the tight set of her jaw, the way her eyes seemed to blaze with willpower. Something happened and she needed control. At least in the way of getting what she wanted, which was to feel good for a night.

Not the way he'd planned, but the good news was so very little of his life had gone to plan. He was good at thinking on his feet. She wanted a man to treat her like a fucking goddess? He could do that. She probably thought she could enjoy them and toss them out, but that wasn't how it had to go.

She liked that Bay was weird.

They'd been playing this all wrong. Every time they approached Brooke Harper they put on a show of being normal. Not damaged. They were attractive cowboys who could show a girl a good time. That's how he'd played it at first. When that hadn't worked, he'd decided to try being the nice guy who never got in bar fights and who'd probably come from parents who loved him. The all-American classic boyfriend.

What if she liked damaged? What if she was that woman who wanted something real, even if it wasn't perfect. Oh, she might think she wanted the type A, love 'em and leave 'em cowboy, but she was about to get something different.

Bay loomed over her but held his hands back as though he wasn't sure if he should touch her or try to stick to the original no sex because we're courting the lady plan.

They were still courting the lady, but the evening was definitely going to include sex.

"Uhm, we can't take you back to our place because our place doesn't exist," Bay replied.

This was a problem, but one they could solve. Besides, the woman seemed to like to get hit with some honesty. It wasn't like she didn't know they weren't exactly undercover billionaires. "What he means is we're living out at the G. We're in the bunkhouse, and what I'm planning on doing to you would overeducate the nineteen-year-olds we're sharing that house with."

Even in the low light from the neon sign above, he could see how she flushed.

"Movie Motel," Bay spat out. "We can go there. I have cash."

She winced at the thought. "Gene is the single worst gossip there is."

Damn it. If only he had invested in camping gear. He could save this. Somehow. "The lodge."

Way more expensive but also private. He could make it happen.

She sighed. "Fine. Back to plan A. I'm staying on my brothers' property, but in a guesthouse. They can't see it from the main house. You'll just have to get out early."

He wasn't planning on leaving at all. He was planning on… Could one squat a relationship? If he stayed, would she get used to him? He could be helpful. He was already planning on how to feed her in the morning. Bacon. Eggs. Pancakes. The key was to use real butter and real milk.

Sometimes the way to a woman's heart was through her stomach and proving he could be a competent member of the household.

Also, "early" was relative.

He moved in, unwilling to give her another second to think about it. He thrust his fingers into all that brown and gold hair that he wanted to tangle himself in. She was so fucking gorgeous. "Anything you want, baby. Look at me. How do you want me to play this? You want straight sex?"

She bit her bottom lip. "I want it however you like, Kent."

He tightened his hold, giving her hair a twist. "Shane. My name is Shane and his is Bay. We're two separate people, and you will refer to us as such."

Her eyes flared but then her tongue ran along that lip she'd nipped. "Shane. You've spent time in Stef's playroom, haven't you? You like to top a woman."

He needed to. Not like in everyday life, but in this way. He needed to feel in control. Needed. Wanted. Welcome. "I can handle you, Brooke. Don't ever think I can't. Whatever you need, I can take it."

She seemed to stop for a moment, almost like she was going to get emotional on him, and he'd meant what he'd said. He could handle her emotions. He wanted them. He was already half in love with her, but she didn't need to know that right now. Then her expression smoothed out, and he knew she planned to brazen her way through it. She went on her toes again, her mouth close to his. "All I need from you is a couple of mind-blowing orgasms, Shane Kent. Do you think you can handle that?"

She needed so much more, and he planned on figuring out what had happened to put her in this place where she needed validation. But he was going with it for the night. "I can."

He lowered his lips to hers and kissed her for the first time, using his hold on her to control the kiss. After a moment's play at her lips, he swiped his tongue across them, demanding entry. Her mouth opened and he pressed inside, sliding his tongue along hers, his whole body coming alive.

He felt Bay move in behind her. He swept her hair aside, avoiding Shane's hand with the expertise of long practice, and kissed her neck while his hands came up to cup her breasts.

"Not in the parking lot," Sawyer shouted as he started toward his Jeep.

Asshole.

Shane broke the kiss and was thrilled to see Brooke had lost her devil-may-care expression and seemed a bit drugged.

Good. Her very nearness drugged him. He pulled his keys out. "Get in. It's time we got you home."

She didn't have to know he kind of wanted her to be his home.

When he pulled out of the parking lot, he vowed it would be a night she never forgot.

* * * *

Brooke sat in between the two hottest guys she'd ever met and wished she'd had more champagne. More wine. Maybe a couple of margaritas, but no, she'd had to stay in control. The minute she realized Cleo was talking about a job, she'd decided to be an adult. She didn't even have the comfort of being totally smashed.

But they'd waited for her. They'd been at the bar, and now that she thought about it, they'd walked out of Stella's this morning behind Cleo.

"Did you hear I was going to be at Hell on Wheels tonight and showed up so you could be hanging around in case I needed a ride?"

They had already passed the deputy at the bottom of the mountain. She thought it was the new guy who was all of twenty-one and definitely not asleep since he had someone pulled over. She hadn't recognized the car, so some tourist was getting the full-on "sheriff needs a chair" ticket.

"That depends," Shane said.

"Depends?" They were different than she'd thought. All she honestly knew about them was that Stef liked them and Max hated them. Rye was somewhat indifferent, though probably leaned toward Max since he constantly reminded Rye that they'd hit on Rachel.

"It depends on whether you think that behavior is a red flag or the kind of flag that makes you feel like a desirable woman since two men plotted and planned to be right here," Shane replied.

Well, put that way… "I'm only here for a couple of weeks. I'm just…stressed."

Sure. That was sexy.

They were weirder than she thought they would be. Somehow in her head they were like a lot of the guys she met when she came home. Concerned with partying and rodeoing their way through life. A girl in every town. They weren't serious and wouldn't ever be about a woman.

And that was exactly how she wanted it.

She was a conquest. But then they were stress relief. It was good. No one would get hurt because there weren't feelings involved. They wouldn't have any, and she wouldn't let herself have any.

Except when Shane kissed her, it felt like something more. It felt like the ground moving under her feet, the world shifting in a significant way.

It scared her but she wasn't going to let that stop her since Bay's kiss hadn't been the same.

"I'm stressed, too," Bay said quietly.

"Is there something going on out at the G? The cows giving you hell?" she teased.

"He's got an exhibit coming up, and Stef's bringing out his wealthy art critic friends," Shane replied. "Not that it matters because his worth is not tied to some guy from LA liking what he does."

She'd forgotten he was an artist. She would blow that off since everyone thought they were an artist, but there was the problem of Stef Talbot being his mentor. If Stef was behind him, he was good.

Which meant he wasn't a simple, gorgeous cowboy walking around like sex on a stick.

Nope. That's what he was tonight, and they only had tonight. Besides, the kiss she'd shared with Shane hadn't really been that good. It felt that way because it had been a while. She wouldn't respond to Bay the way she had to him.

But she kind of wanted to find out.

She unbuckled the belt around her hips. Their truck was old school, so it didn't protest her lack of seatbelt as she moved and placed herself on Bay's lap.

"Oh, damn," he breathed, but his hands went to her hips. "This is not how I thought the night would go."

She stared at him. He was a work of art. With sensual lips and a straight jawline and green eyes that seemed to sparkle in the low light. She took off his hat and tossed it in the small back seat before running her hands over his hair.

He was hers for the night, and she was going to enjoy him.

Them. Both of them. Her treat for the night.

"How did you think it would go?" She whispered the question, her lips almost touching his. "Did you think I would ignore my creepy stalkers?"

"Well," he whispered back, "I kind of hoped you wouldn't

consider me creepy or a stalker. How about you think of me as an interested party?"

"What are you interested in, Bay?" she asked, feeling her whole body tighten as his hands started to move on her.

"You," Bay replied, his eyes on her lips. "I'm interested in you, Brooke Harper."

Dangerous words, but she didn't care at this point. He was doing exactly what she needed him to do. Making her feel like she was important, like someone wanted her.

Cleo had done that, too. Her old friend had asked her to come in and look at the costumes for the season that opened in six weeks. She'd agreed to it since it wasn't like she had anything better to do, but being a basic seamstress for a rural theater hadn't exactly brought her spirits up.

This was. The way they looked at her. Like she was the most gorgeous woman on the planet. She realized this was all a part of their routine, but it worked.

"Good, because I'm interested in you, too…" She was about to call him Kent. She'd planned on calling both of them Kent, but Shane had stopped her from putting that careful distance between them. Damn Dom. She knew one when she met one. It wasn't like she hadn't understood what happened in Stef Talbot's playroom. She'd just thought they'd gone because of the kinky sex. He'd been serious with that question.

Did she want vanilla sex? It was all she'd ever had, and honestly, there hadn't been much of that in the first place.

It didn't matter since they had one night, and she intended to make it last.

But first she was going to kiss Bay again and remind herself that they weren't perfect since the connection she'd felt to Shane hadn't been in that first kiss with Bay. It had been a little awkward, like the man himself. It was good because the last thing she needed was to find wild chemistry with both of them when she wasn't going to keep them.

She stared at him for a moment, memorizing the stark lines of his face and how his jaw tightened as he stared back at her. It wasn't the only part of his body that reacted. She could feel his cock under her, and it took everything she had not to rub herself against him. She leaned over and kissed him.

His lips were soft and warm and the kiss was nice, but it didn't stir her the way Shane had.

It was okay. They were a team, and if she didn't fall for them both, she was completely safe.

"Bay, I think it's safe to say you're off the leash," Shane said quietly. "It's okay. She'll tell you if it's too much."

Too much? She wasn't sure how it would be too much since Bay seemed reluctant to really touch her.

The words seemed to do something to Bailey Kent. His gaze narrowed, and he seemed to go from kind of goofy hot guy who knew way too much about the sexual practices of koala bears to a predator. She could practically feel the heat coming off him. His hands tightened on her hips and then one moved up her back to grip the nape of her neck.

"Do you have any idea what I want to do to you, girl?" Bay asked, his voice far deeper than it had been before.

It did something for her. Was this the real Bay? "Tell me."

One hand found its way from her hip to under the shirt she was wearing. She shivered as she felt his fingertips running along her skin, moving up to cup her breast.

"I'm going to put my mouth on you. Everywhere, Brooke. I'll kiss your lips and taste your tongue. I'll work my way down, but only after I'm sure you're going to be a very good girl for me. Will you be my good girl, Brooke? Understand this isn't a question I would ask anywhere but the bedroom. I know you're a strong, independent woman who can handle her own shit and probably deal with all mine, too, but when my mouth is on you, when my cock is in you, you are my good girl."

Oh, that should not work on her but it did. Who the hell was he? He was goofy and weird and gorgeous, and now he was also good with the dirty talk. "I can be good."

If she thought he would want her to submit to him—because she was absolutely certain that's what they were talking about, thanks, Uncle Stef—she would…well she would probably still spend the night with them, but she felt better that he wasn't some twenty-four seven, do-my-will guy.

His thumb brushed over her nipple, and even with the bra between them she could feel both get hard and needy. "You can and you will, or you'll face our discipline, sweetheart. Have you ever had that gorgeous ass spanked?"

She felt her whole body tighten at the thought, but she was feeling sassy. "How do you know it's gorgeous? It might be terrible."

She nearly yelped when he twisted her nipple. It didn't hurt exactly, simply caught her attention.

"Brattery will be punished, baby. I know it's gorgeous because every single fucking thing about you is gorgeous, and I won't hear anything else. Do I make myself plain, Brooke? I will not hear anything bad about you. Not from the people around us, and definitely not from you."

"He's got a thing about it," Shane explained quietly. "There are reasons, but this isn't a therapy session. And there's zero doubt in my mind that your ass is going to be beautiful. You know how beautiful you are."

"Well, I'm feeling kind of sexy right now." And off kilter since she'd never contemplated how the tiny sting of getting a nipple tweaked would make her wet and hot and ready for sex. Right here. Right now. Going fifty miles an hour down the highway and she wanted to ride Bailey Kent's cock.

His cock seemed to swell against her. She felt the hard ridge under her pussy. "When we get back to your place, you will strip for us, and we'll show you how fucking sexy you are. We'll put our hands everywhere. There's not going to be an inch of your skin left unworshipped. Tell me something, Brooke. Do you want this?"

He pressed his pelvis up, and a wave of sensation jolted through her as he rubbed against her clit.

Why did she wear jeans? Skirts. Skirts were better. Skirts could be pulled up and panties down, and then she would have him.

Had she ever wanted a man more than she wanted to breathe? How had she thought for a second they didn't have a connection? There was a live wire running between them, and she couldn't help but pick it up and let the electricity flow through her.

"Yes." She didn't even recognize the breathy sounds coming

from her mouth. "I'll be honest. I really want you. I want an orgasm, and I want it from you."

His hips moved again, and her eyes nearly crossed. It felt so good.

"Then take one," he urged, his hands back on her hips. He got his pelvis in the perfect place. "Ride me. I want to watch you come. I want to know how to make you scream. I want to make you crave my cock the way I crave you."

"You are a bossy man," she whispered as her hips rolled.

"You have no idea, and you haven't really met my brother yet," Bay whispered as his hands shifted to her backside. He squeezed her. "He's going to want to fuck you here."

She would have protested but she was rubbing herself against his dick, the pleasure building and building and it didn't matter that they were on the road that would lead to the house she grew up in. She looked at Shane, whose jaw was tight, hands carefully gripping the wheel. "You have to go around the back way."

"I am, baby," Shane promised, his eyes still on the road as though he didn't trust himself to watch them. "I've delivered hay to your brothers before. I know which way the help comes in."

She didn't like the sound of that, but she wasn't thinking straight. All that mattered was the fact that she was riding Bailey Kent like the stallion he was, and it felt so good. It felt like control and power and something she might not have felt before.

She leaned back against the dashboard, hips moving in time with his. One big hand came up and traced the line of her jaw. Then his thumb came out and ran along her bottom lip and she couldn't help it. She licked him, sucking his thumb into her mouth and giving him a nip.

He hissed, but it wasn't a bad sound. It was the sound of a man who wanted more. More of her.

She wanted more, too. She wanted this night. Needed it. These men made her feel. Oh, it would be rough in the morning when they were gone and she realized this was how they worked as a team, but she would take it tonight.

A cry spilled from her throat as she came. Sparks went through her system making her whole body sing, and she slumped forward, letting her arms go around Bay.

Who was not boring. Who was not a typical party cowboy, and that made him infinitely more dangerous than he'd been before.

It didn't matter.

She breathed him in. He smelled like soap and leather and a bit of beer.

She should get some beer so it was in her fridge for…

Nope. Not going there. She started to come out of it. Maybe she should say goodnight and send them on their way.

"I'm going to eat your pussy like it's my fucking goal in life, girl," Bay whispered. "I'll tie you down so you can't squirm when I give you orgasm after orgasm. You'll start to wonder if there was a time when my tongue wasn't inside you, and that's when I'll give you my cock. For real. That was an appetizer."

Or she could not.

The truck rolled to a stop, and she realized she was home.

Or an approximation of it.

She looked over and Shane put the truck in park and killed the engine and then leaned over and kissed her.

"I'm going to play with your ass," he vowed. "And give you my cock, too. We won't let you sleep until dawn."

It was an offer she wasn't going to refuse.

Chapter Four

Bailey barely looked at the house.

All that mattered was getting Brooke inside it and getting her naked.

He'd damn near come in his jeans like a teenaged boy when he'd watched her take her pleasure. She'd been bold and strong, riding him like it was her right.

She was the one. Oh, she didn't know it yet, and she might end up railing against fate because he was pretty sure they weren't good bets, but it was still true.

"They put you in here? Is it a storage shed?" Shane stood outside the door.

Bay didn't care. He would do her in the parking lot at this point. Maybe they should think about getting a camper for the truck.

She was so fucking gorgeous. And he was off the leash.

He tugged on her hand before she could reply and drew her back, gripping her neck and slipping his tongue in her mouth the minute she softened and opened for him. He let his tongue find hers as her arms wound around him.

This. This was what he needed. This was what they needed.

"Let her open the door, Bay. We don't want to wake up those horses." Shane had to be the voice of reason.

He pulled back, but he needed to make a few things plain. He shoved his hands in all that soft hair of hers and forced her to look up at him. The moonlight caressed her face like a lover, bringing out all her glowy beauty. "Little brother is more prim and proper than I am. If I had my way, I'd put you on the hood of the truck and fuck you right there."

The sweetest grin lit her face, and she turned slightly Shane's way. "Thanks for being prim, Shane. Also, now I at least know the birth order. How many minutes apart?"

So she bought the whole twins thing. He shouldn't get into it, but he would answer any question she had as long as she was naked in the next few minutes. "I don't know the exact number, but something like a hundred and fifty thousand."

"We're not twins, baby. We're half brothers," Shane said, holding out a hand. "I'm our dad's affair kid. There's three months and a couple of days between us. Give me the keys."

"There aren't keys. It's open. My brothers lose keys, and they want Paige to be able to get in," she replied, her gaze going from one to the other. "How did you find each other?"

Shane's head shook. "We can talk when we get inside and you're naked. If you wanted a historical rundown, you shouldn't have mentioned multiple orgasms."

He opened the door.

"We're getting a lock if you're staying here," Shane announced. "Anyone could walk in."

"There's no one out here," she protested. "It's not like the city."

She was naïve. Bay picked her up because he wasn't going to argue with her. "Like nothing bad ever happens in Bliss."

He could run down a list of shitty things that happened here. Russian mobsters. Serial killers. An odd amount of corporations trying to kill for profit, according to Nell. Feminist aliens who wanted to show men how hard pregnancy was. The list went on and on.

He carried her into the…very small house.

There was a tiny kitchen and a couch and table. There was a set of stairs that led to… He wasn't sure.

"Where is the bed?" Bay asked. "What is this?"

"It's a tiny house." Brooke frowned, and he set her on her feet.

"My brothers said it was for foaling or when they have to stay up late with the horses, but I think it might be my spinster house."

"Your brothers think you're a spinster?" Shane asked.

"What's a spinster?" Bay was confused.

"It's an old timey word for a woman of a certain age who remains unmarried," Shane replied. "You would know it if you hadn't fallen asleep during all of *Bridgerton*."

Brooke's expression lit up again. She did seem to love when they were weird. "You watched *Bridgerton*?"

"When we were working at this ranch in New Mexico, the lady who ran the ranch invited all the hands to watch with her. She was lonely. She was young when her husband died, and she was focused on the ranch, so she didn't have a lot of friends," Bay explained. "Shane and I were the only ones who took her up on it."

"Dumbasses. She made all these little cakes and sandwiches. It was delicious," Shane continued. "And you know what? I liked the story. After we moved to a ranch in Texas, I snuck into the owner's man cave real late at night to watch season two."

Asshole. "He blamed his daughter for that. He lost his shit when they upset his algorithm and instead of John Wick, his watch nexts became a bunch of period dramas and Taylor Swift concerts."

"Well, who do you think I watched it with, brother?" Shane taunted.

He pointed his brother's way. "I knew you were fucking her. Liar."

"If you wanted some, you should have been interested in Anthony and Kate," Shane shot back.

Brooke got between them, the most amused look on her face. "Thanks. I now know which brother I can role-play with. Shouldn't one of you be ripping my clothes off now?"

Shane pointed his way. "Don't you dare. That shirt is her design from last season, and she'll be pissed in the morning."

Brooke's jaw dropped. "How do you… I don't care. Welcome to my spinster home. Please let me do dirty, nasty things before I hit my crone stage."

He would have to deal with his brother later. Not that there was anything to really deal with. It wasn't like they hadn't had sex on their own before, though it proved the relationship wasn't important to Shane because he would never have dated on his own.

Brooke was another story. Months of plotting and planning, and here they were.

Longer, when he thought about it since he'd been sketching her for years. Wondering about her. Longing for what she represented.

She should be a disappointment. She was a little mean and was probably using them for sex, but it made him more determined than ever to have her. And since she responded so well to her lover taking charge, that seemed like a fine plan.

"Take off the shirt," he commanded. "Take it all off, and then we're going to see how you taste."

A shudder went through her and her hands went to the bottom of her shirt. She pulled it over her head and tossed it to the couch that looked like it was Barbie-doll sized.

He hoped the bed was bigger.

She had a bed, right? No one would set their spinster sister up with a house and leave out the bed, right?

He let the thought go because she took off her bra, and he got his first good look at her tits.

Breasts. He was going to be a gentleman.

So it would be her breasts he intended to suck on and nip and cup and press together so he could tongue her nipples one after the other. Gorgeous breasts. They would be a perfect handful, and they were tipped with pretty nipples that tightened under his gaze.

"All of it, Brooke." Shane stood beside him, both watching her. "He said all of it."

"That doesn't feel fair," she said, though her hands were already on the fly of her jeans. She toed out of her shoes and worked the button.

Shane pulled his T-shirt over his head and tossed it alongside hers.

"Fair doesn't matter here. You either trust us to give you what you need or…" Bay actually didn't want to go there.

"Or we make you trust us." Shane always saved him. "Damn, you're gorgeous, girl. We need to make this spinster house your slutty house."

Brooke grinned. "Yeah, that's what I was thinking, too. And I realize you two are going to be a handful, so before you get so deep into top space I can't get you back, I have a request."

He was almost there. He could be bossy when it came to sex, but he felt over the top with her. Caveman like. Still, he could hold off for a couple of minutes. "What is it?"

She stood there like a goddess in a small temple. She bit her bottom lip, and her eyes went hot. "I want to suck your cocks."

Yep, he was going to go off.

Bay took a long breath. It wasn't a request he would refuse. He nodded. "Get on your knees, baby."

Shane was out of his clothes in superhero time. He was already stroking his cock as Bay held out a hand. She placed hers in his, but before she could start to settle down, he brought it to his lips, turning it over so he could kiss her palm.

"You're in charge of this part, but you're mine after."

She nodded. "I'm yours after." She stared into his eyes. "You should know it's been a while for me. A long while. I don't have… uhm, I mean I don't carry around…"

His bold girl was suddenly shy, and he realized what she was talking about. "We have condoms. Baby, we really did overhear the clown car girl talking about where you would be tonight and followed you there. You should know we only intended to take you home. But we're not so dumb that we're not prepared in case you wanted…well, this."

"Bay, this is all I can have right now."

Again, he wasn't going to argue with her. He would show her they could have something special. "Then we should make it count."

He kissed her again and let his hands find her breasts. So soft. So responsive, since her nipples were hard pebbles against his palm.

When he broke off the kiss, she gave him a mysterious smile and dropped to her knees with his help.

She was precious, and he didn't want her banging her knees. They needed carpet instead of the hardwoods.

And then her hand was on the fly of his jeans, and he wasn't thinking about decorating anymore.

She was a fucking goddess. He'd dreamed of seeing her this way, but she was so much more. He supposed in a lot of ways he'd viewed her as a perfect woman. He was rapidly learning that his version of perfect included a sassy mouth and a bad attitude at times. And that impish grin she got when she knew her own power.

He wanted to see that grin on her face way more often.

He took a long breath as she wrapped a hand around his cock and heard Shane do the same.

She wasn't bothering to hesitate. She didn't need alcohol to drop her inhibitions about sleeping with two men. She didn't seem to have any inhibitions when it came to this. She loved her brothers and didn't have a single problem with their relationship.

Was she looking for that kind of relationship?

Brooke stroked him, her fist tightening slightly as she leaned over and ran her tongue over his cockhead.

The sensation sizzled through his body. "I know this is going to surprise you, but it's been a while for us. Well, me at least since apparently Shane has been using costume dramas to get laid."

His brother groaned because Brooke was tonguing him now. "That was two years ago, but he's right. It's been a long time for us. At least six months."

She frowned up at him. "Are you telling me you haven't had sex since you started working at the G?"

He growled and reached for her hair, tugging it slightly from the base of her neck. "I answer nothing if you're not playing. If you want a Q&A, we can sit down and talk."

"Bossy," she complained but she sucked his cockhead behind her lips. Her tongue worried the underhead and threatened to make him lose it.

He concentrated on the question she'd asked. It was that or animal facts, and he'd already gotten in trouble with those once tonight. "No. We've worked, and sometimes we come into town, but we haven't found a girlfriend."

"We haven't found anyone we wanted. Not this way," Shane corrected. "Anyone but you. As we tried to show you last Christmas."

"I wasn't…" Her words hummed along his skin, making his eyes threaten to roll to the back of his head. "…in a good place. I'm still not. Guys, I'm not dating material, but I wouldn't hate enjoying this while I'm here."

He bit back a groan as she ran that tongue all over his dick. Every lick made his body pulse with anticipation. Her words should give him pause, but all he could feel was pleasure. They could sort the rest out later. Sex could bind her to them. He would bet she was like a lot of women and if they were intimate often enough, her heart would get involved.

"I can handle that," Bay replied. Lied. Well, it wasn't a lie since he fully intended to handle it because it was becoming more and more obvious that Sawyer was right and all was not well in Brooke's castle in the city. Something was up, and he was going to get to the bottom of it. But for now, he had set them on a good footing. She didn't seem to mind his need for control. "Cup my balls, Brooke. I want to feel your hands on me."

His spine tingled when she obeyed him. He glanced down and caught sight of her watching him.

Powerful. This made her feel powerful. She didn't know it yet, but he could make her feel like the goddess she was.

"Finish him off, Brooke," Shane commanded, his voice hoarse. "Finish him and then we'll figure out a way to make that loft bed work. I want inside you."

He did, too, but they would have to take turns until they got her pretty asshole ready for them. He twisted her hair and pushed his pelvis forward. "You heard him. We're going to take you upstairs and fuck you all night."

He hoped the bed wasn't a twin.

She settled in, and he watched as Shane moved behind her. He knelt down, and his hand disappeared between her legs.

"That's right, baby," Shane urged. "Keep going and I'll keep doing what I'm doing. When you swallow him down, I'm going to eat that pussy of yours and then you're going to take my cock like the good girl you are. You're going to take all of it. You're going to spread yourself wide and wrap your legs around me and show me all your sweet spots."

Oh, he was going to learn all of them. They would explore her body and become experts at making her scream, and then they would show her how much they could add to her life. But she didn't want to hear that right now. So he used words she could appreciate. "And then when you think you can't handle another second of pleasure, you'll take me, too."

She groaned around his cock and then seemed determined. She sucked him until he couldn't see straight, and he felt his spine stiffen as he emptied himself into her mouth.

She whimpered even as she swallowed him down, not missing a drop.

When he stepped back, he could see why. Shane had his thumb on her clit as he fucked her with two fingers. Her body bowed back, giving him full access, knees splayed wide. Her breasts bounced, and even though he'd just spent himself, his cock stirred again.

She came on a breathy moan.

It was time to show her how much more they could give her.

* * * *

Shane sucked his fingers in his mouth and bit back a sigh. Her arousal was a tangy taste on his tongue, and he knew he was already addicted to her.

His second thought was that this place was small, and he was going to have to get creative.

He didn't have his kit. He hadn't been that optimistic. He'd kind of thought he would have to ease her into kink, but she was right there with them, her eyes wide and curious and now sleepy from the two orgasms they'd given her, but they'd been little things. He could do so much better.

"That was fantastic," she said with a slightly loopy grin. "I think I might be super kinky."

He knew she was kinky. He needed to show her that it was safe to be exactly who she was. He got the feeling she was hiding so much.

"I'm going to need for you to grip the rails of the ladder." Shane could see how the ladder that apparently led to her bed could be useful. Though it would be hard to carry her to bed. They were going to have to figure something out. Hopefully they didn't hang off that tiny bed.

Though it would mean they had to cuddle.

"Like this?" She moved to the ladder and pulled it out so it was on an incline. The whole place seemed well designed for function in such a small space. He oddly didn't feel overwhelmed by the living area. It was smaller when the ladder was out. She leaned over and gripped the rails and looked like his every wet dream. Her hair was around her shoulders, the tips brushing her nipples like they were playing hide and seek with him. Her pussy glistened with her arousal, and there was still lust in her eyes.

"No, baby. He wants you like this." Bay turned her, positioning her, bringing her legs back and arms down so her backside was in the air.

Pretty ass. Shane moved in, putting a hand on her hip and moving it across the globes. It was time to start preparing her for more than just tonight. He couldn't tempt her the way he thought he would—with soft words and promises of courtly dates. She didn't want that. But he could show her what she did want. "You think this is only for tonight, right, Brooke?"

"It's all I have," she replied quietly, some of the sweet lust in her tone fleeing.

He wasn't doing it to bring her down. She had so much more to give. "No. I think you have several nights. You're not going back to New York for a couple of weeks. I can't do everything I want to you tonight. We can't have you the way we want."

Her head turned slightly, and there was a hitch to her breath. "Together. Both of you."

It wasn't a question. She knew what they wanted, and it was clear she was curious. "Both of us. But unless you can tell me you have experience and this place is stocked with lube, that can't happen tonight."

He put a hand on one of her cheeks, caressing her there.

"Oh." She breathed the word out, and her hips rolled like she sought his affection with her every move. "No experience. Despite my family history, I've never had two men, and the few boyfriends I've had were fairly vanilla. I've never tried any of this before. It feels like you're going to spank me."

"I would like that very much." He wanted to do everything to her. All the glorious, filthy things he'd ever had go through his mind, he wanted to explore with her. "But you see how putting such a short time on this is restricting. I need to work a plug into that little asshole of yours. I need to play with it. I need to teach it so it opens to my cock and lets me in because it knows how much pleasure I'm going to bring you."

"I can't be your girlfriend." She said the words, but he felt the hesitation.

"Let us in at night," Bay whispered. "If you can't stand to be seen with us during the day, let us in at night."

She stood and turned to him. "It's not that."

And gave him the perfect excuse to spank her.

"Did I tell you to move, Brooke?"

She stopped, her eyes going wide. "But I…"

"If I only get one night with you, I want you to play my way." He had zero intentions of this being one night. He wanted all the nights she was here. It was the days he would have to negotiate. "And that means when you're naked and I've given you an orgasm, you obey me."

For a moment she looked like she was going to argue with him, and then she turned and settled back into her position. "I was only trying to say it's not that I'm embarrassed. It's just that you and my brothers do not get along. After all, you went after their wife."

Ah, there she was. He'd been waiting for the sassy girl to show up. She'd been sidelined by orgasms, but she would find her way, no doubt. "That was a job from Stef Talbot, baby. If you want to rail at someone, rail at him. We had just met the man, and he was helping with Bay's art career. Not that there's much of one."

"I have a showing at the end of summer," Bay argued.

He had zero head for business, and that was okay. Shane had a point to make. "I'm going to spank you, Brooke. If it's too much, tell me and I'll find another way to get my point across."

"I just…" she began.

And he slapped her ass. A light tap, but it brought her up on her toes and had breath huffing from her. "We gave your brothers some hell at the request of Stef, and it did what he intended for it to do." Another smack. This time to her right cheek. "It got them to move and make a claim on Rachel, and now they're happy. Well, some of them are happy, and one of them seems to be in a perpetual state of pregnancy, like a lot of the women around here. Is it in the water?" One more smack and her hands tightened on the railing.

"I don't know, but I'll stick to coffee while I'm here, Shane," she replied as her head dropped. "It hurts."

He laid a hand on her cheek. It was barely pink. "I don't have to."

"But I like it. It hurts and then it doesn't," she explained. "It goes straight to my pussy. How is this making me so hot?"

Because she'd likely never spent any real time on sex. He doubted there was much sexual education from her brothers, and then she'd been an ambitious college kid. "Have you ever spent hours and hours on sex, Brooke? Have you ever had a couple of men who did nothing but worship your body until you were spent and couldn't move, so you fell asleep with them still inside you?"

"I'm not a virgin," she argued.

Another smack and then another. Bay took the left cheek and he the right. "Not what I asked. Also, I don't care about virginity. I lost mine so long ago I barely remember it as anything but a fond memory, so I don't care about how many men you've had. I care about the quality of the sex you've had."

"Well, I would have said good before tonight," she admitted.

So he was right and no one had spent real time on her before. She'd had boys who wanted to get off, who took as little time as they needed and didn't truly understand what intimacy meant.

He would have been one of those men if it hadn't been for Stef Talbot. Stef taught them to take sex seriously. That it wasn't simply a bodily function. That it could be so much more even if the actual relationship didn't last for more than a night. Even if it was merely a stop on the way to he and his brother finding the woman who could give them what they needed.

"Tell me I have more time. Tell me we can explore this thing between us while you're here," Shane demanded.

He spanked her again, trading off smacks with his brother. She started to cry, but she didn't tell them to stop. He put a hand up, halting his brother. They didn't know her the way they needed to. If he had his way, he would get to know her every tell, to be able to read her body language as well as he knew his own. But for now, they had to talk. He thrust a hand into her hair and tilted her head up to him.

"Is it too much?" Shane asked.

She nodded but then released the ladder, and her arms wrapped around him. "Not you. It's everything. Please, Shane, make me forget anything but you. We can have the nights together. I want you both. I want to know."

All thoughts of controlling this scene fled. She needed, and he was going to give her everything he had.

He picked her up and turned, looking for a proper place to put her because they weren't going to make it to a bed. The need was too urgent. He set her on top of the small bistro-style table, his heart thudding in his chest. Emotion rode him high because he realized this might be the first time he could truly give something to a woman. Something beyond an orgasm. She needed him. Them.

She gasped as he spread her legs and went down on his knees. Bay moved his big body to the opposite side of the table and got his hands on her breasts. He stared down at her like he could memorize her and capture this moment in whatever material he had. Paint or clay or marble. It wouldn't matter. All that would matter was how gorgeous she was in this moment.

And her pussy was gorgeous too. Pink and wet and pouting. Begging for his attention. She was so damn wet and ready for them. That taste he'd gotten had been nothing more than an appetizer.

He leaned toward her, breathing and taking in the scent of her arousal before he put his mouth on her.

Brooke's whole body bowed, and she let out a shout as he tongued her clitoris. He held her legs open for his feast while his brother took her arms, and they made her vulnerable to them.

She tasted like heaven, her creamy essence coating his tongue and filling all of his senses. He speared her with a long thrust of his tongue while he placed his thumb on the jewel of her clit. She was giving him all her secrets now. She couldn't hold back when she was like this. She couldn't hide from him. He wouldn't allow it.

He fucked her with his tongue until she screamed out his name and then he couldn't hold back a second longer. His cock had been aching since the moment he'd seen her earlier today, and he couldn't take more. He got to his feet.

"Shane." Bay was obviously the one who was thinking tonight because he tossed a condom Shane's way, then went back to kissing her forehead and telling her how hot she was and how much he wanted to fuck her.

It was everything he wanted. Brooke accepting both him and his brother. Opening herself up for both of them, wanting them.

He stroked his cock and moved between her legs, lining himself up. "I want to do this every night. I want all your nights, Brooke. Every night you're in Bliss."

She gasped as he thrust inside her. Pure sensation washed over him, and he watched her body tighten. Bay was kneeling beside her, kissing her cheek and whispering in her ear. Her hands came out and found the sides of his chest, running her nails over his skin and making his breath hitch.

"Tell me how she feels," Bay demanded in a guttural tone.

"She feels so fucking good." He pulled his cock out almost all the way and then pressed back in until he couldn't go further. He gripped her hips, holding her there. He fucked her hard, not holding back because if there was one thing he'd learned it was that she could handle him. He took his time, watching her, noting when her eyes flared and when her nails bit into his skin in the sexiest way. He learned her sweet spots and found the perfect rhythm.

He moved and bit back a groan when she tightened around him and pulled him into the wave of her orgasm.

He poured himself into her, and a sense of peace suffused his whole body.

He leaned over and kissed her. "More than a night, Brooke. We need more than one night."

"More than one night, but we should keep it quiet. I don't want to upset my brothers," she whispered.

Shane wasn't sure there was any way to keep it quiet, and honestly, he didn't want to think about the whys that backed up that request. He didn't want to be another dirty secret, but he wasn't thinking about it tonight. He had her concession, and he was going to take it.

Bay suddenly looked like an eager puppy. "My turn."

Bay kissed her and Shane moved back, watching as she wrapped herself around Bay without a single second's hesitation.

It was going to be okay. They could make this work.

He stood back and watched. It was a good thing he enjoyed a show.

Chapter Five

Brooke came awake to the sound of a familiar voice. At first she was fairly certain she was dreaming. She'd almost definitely dreamed the whole of the night before since she wasn't the girl who boldly walked up to two men in a bar and invited them home with her. No. She was careful and cautious. She always did the right thing.

So hearing Bay's voice was certainly a dream because that would be a bad choice, and she didn't make those.

Her brothers gave up way too much of their lives for her to make poor choices.

"Hey, keep it down, kid. She's asleep," he was saying.

She was asleep, and the bed was strangely comfy. Way more comfy than the mattress in her tiny bedroom in Manhattan. It was also warmer. Or it had been when she was dreaming about them, about them spanking her and fucking her and eating her pussy and sliding into bed beside her, despite the fact that it was tight up here. She'd dreamed that Shane had hit his head on the ceiling, and she'd opened her eyes and watched that fine ass of his moving toward the ladder.

"She's my auntie and I came to see her, and she don't have no boyfriend," another familiar voice said.

Nightmare. Nightmare. That was her niece. Paige was invading her dreams.

Another shushing sound came from Bay. "Don't wake her up. She had a long night. And I'm her friend."

"No, you're the one Daddy calls an asshole of epic proportions. I don't know what that means but it's bad. Papa says you're just another cowboy numbskull. Does that mean something's wrong with your brain? I don't think my auntie is friends with people with bad brains."

"Okay, that's actually very ableist," Bay said, obviously under his breath. "And rude. Not everyone thinks the same way. Hey, what are you doing? Oww. That's my shin."

Shit and balls. She sat straight up and realized last night was real and she had slept with two men her brothers hated, and at least one of them was still here. Why was he still here? And why was her stomach growling? Probably the smells coming from downstairs. She glanced at the clock, and it was way later than she'd planned. She was having lunch with Gemma in a couple of hours. The Kent brothers were supposed to slip out after she was asleep.

She peeked out of the tiny window, pushing back the blinds. The truck was gone.

Why was Bay here?

"You're in my auntie's house, and I don't think you have permission. I think you're a serial killer and you're here for her Lucky Charms," Paige announced, and there was another grunting sound.

Brooke rolled out of bed and wrapped a fluffy robe around her body. "Paige. Sweetie, what are you doing here?"

She stopped at the top of the ladder. It was awkward how she had to get down. Of course the only thing more awkward was the scene playing out in front of her. From her place in the loft she could see the living area. The place where they'd shed all their clothes and started the raucous sexscapades from the night before. Shane had tossed the condom wrappers on the ground, and if Paige found one, she would have a lot of explaining to do.

The living room was spotless with the exception of her clothes from the night before carefully folded and put on the table that sat beside the couch.

Paige was in full-on rage-killer mode, but it was okay since Bay had figured out she was barely seven and could be held back with a single hand. Bay had his big palm on her head, and Paige seemed to be trying to break free by running in place as fast as she could and flailing her arms.

Bay looked up, and the expression on his face would have made her laugh if the situation wasn't so dire.

Paige would totally talk.

She had to bribe her niece. Or blackmail her… What did she have on Paige?

Brooke started to scramble down, praying the robe was long enough. Actually, it made her wonder where the fluffy robe had come from since it was explained to her that only Max and Rye ever slept out here. And yet she'd found the pink robe when she'd stored her own clothes.

Max did have some sensitive skin.

She pushed it aside as she got to the floor and faced her niece. "Paige, stop trying to kick Bay in the shins."

Her niece was heartbreakingly adorable, with golden brown hair and eyes that looked like her mother's. The rage was kind of her momma's, too. But that smile she gave Brooke when she stopped her running in place was all her brothers'. "I already got him once, Auntie Brooke. My momma watches lots of stuff about cereal killers, and I ain't allowed to watch those shows, but I can protect you. What kind do you have here? I like Lucky Charms."

Bay's head fell back, and he laughed and looked utterly delicious standing in the too-small living room wearing nothing but his jeans. Also, the whole place smelled like bacon, and that did something for her, too. "I love this kid. She's weird."

"I am not. I am normal," Paige declared. "Also, it's okay to be weird. Charlie and Zander are real weird, but they're my best friends, and I ain't going to listen to anyone talk bad about them."

Brooke dropped down to her knees. She'd overheard this discussion last night at dinner. Everyone was supposed to help improve Paige's grammar since she'd spent all of her formative years with cowboys. "How would Ms. Leal feel about that sentence?"

She'd learned that Ms. Leal—who could do a shot of tequila with the best of them—was considered an actual saint in the Harper house.

Brooke was surprised there wasn't a halo-around-her-head, eyes-tilted-toward-heaven portrait of Sabrina hung in a prominent place in their house.

Paige's nose wrinkled. "They're my best friends, and I do not want to listen to anyone speak poorly of them. See, I can say it right. I just don't want to."

"You give 'em hell, baby girl."

Brooke let out a yelp and fell on her ass because she was not expecting that voice. She stopped and stared at Bay, who gave her a weak smile.

"Your brother's here," Bay explained in a whisper. "He showed up as Shane was finishing breakfast. We were about to wake you up, but then he took all the bacon and the kid thinks I'm going to eat all the cereal because she has not gotten to the portion of her education where she learns about homophones."

"What?" her brother asked.

She turned, and he was sitting at her tiny bistro table. Well, his, technically, but it was supposed to be her haven while she was here. "Two words that sound alike but have different meanings. Is Rachel on a true crime kick? Good, because it will teach her where to bury your body. You are not supposed to eat that bacon, Mr. Cholesterol."

Max sat back, his eyes narrowing. "Well, Missy, I don't think you were supposed to have guests overnight."

Bay had gone stiff beside her. "I did not realize that was a rule, Mr. Harper."

Max frowned. "Don't you Mr. Harper me, you little shit. That makes me sound like a dad."

He was so annoying. She pointed to Paige, who had gone back to her previous occupation of whirling dervish being held back by a masculine hand. Bay was good with her. He proved he could multitask. And that he was willing to kiss ass. Which was not cool.

How many cowboys would properly point out how to use the word homophone? He was so weird, and yet it did something for her. Something he hadn't done when she'd viewed him as a frat boy version of a cowboy. She didn't bother to look at the man she'd spent the night with. Well, one of them. She chose to put all her feminine rage into the stare she sent her brother's way. "You don't apologize to him, Bay. I need Shane here because my brother is acting like we're in Regency England, and I might have ruined my chances for an advantageous marriage."

"Wait." Max looked confused for a moment and then slightly outraged. "You were planning on marrying them? Girl, what is going through your head?" There was a knock from the outside and without missing a beat, Max picked up a piece of what looked like beautifully cooked bacon and then shoved it out the open window. It disappeared, and Max kept going. "I did not send you to that godawful expensive school so you could marry two down-on-their-luck cowpokes."

"There is no marriage," Bay said as he sighed and held back Paige, who seemed to think this was the most fun a kid ever had.

It was annoying, and somewhere deep inside she knew what she was about to say next was more about all the shit she'd been through in the last couple of weeks than it was a mad desire to walk down the aisle. She was so sick of being told what to do and what was and wasn't cool and what to eat if she wanted people to take her seriously and how to wear her damn hair, and it was too much.

She kind of wanted to burn it all down. Or at least have someone look at her like she wasn't the most pathetic thing to walk the earth.

How often had her brothers called her practically an angel? Who never did anything wrong. Who didn't seem to have an interest in boys, and wasn't that a good thing. She was so into her studies. So ambitious, and she was going to do all the right things to succeed in life.

Well, she'd done them, and this was what she got.

She crossed her arms under her breasts and turned to Bay. "That's not what you said last night."

There was a pause as even Paige seemed to realize something was wrong. And then another knock on the window.

"Not right now, Rye." Max had gone pale. "Our baby sister is pulling the worst practical joke of all time."

So Rye was sneaking bacon, too. She walked the whole four steps it took to get to the door and threw it open. "You might as well join us. Or are you the lookout? You know when you tell your wife, who's given you four kids in seven years, that you're going to take your diet seriously and then you run all over town hiding the fact that you're eating fried everything, it's cheating."

Sometimes their antics got to her because she felt for Rachel. She knew her brothers were playing around but Rachel was worried, and this would make her feel like her worry was foolish.

Rye's eyes had widened. He was the brother who never got caught because all he ever had to do was stand behind Max and people forgot he could be annoying, too. "What the hell is going on, Brooke?"

This was when Bay ran. He was probably panicking and wondering why the hell Shane wasn't back because it looked like his getaway would have to be on foot.

This was how she paid back all the men who annoyed her, and maybe that wasn't fair because she'd had a nice night with Bay and Shane, but none of this would have happened if they had done what they were supposed to do and gone home early this morning. Then she wouldn't be dealing with her brothers being nosy and waking her up way too early. And thinking less of her because she had perfectly human needs.

This was stupid. She should own up to her dumbass mistake. It wasn't like they'd never had a wild night.

Of course, they probably hadn't done it on their sibling's property, where their three and an almost kid were hanging around and asking tons of questions.

"Mr. Harper." Bay greeted her other brother.

She was sure he was about to tell him how this had all been a mistake.

"This is a huge misunderstanding," Bay began, proving her right. And then his arm curled around her shoulders, and he stood beside her. "We didn't plan to tell you this way but then you annoyed my baby here, and she can only handle so much. You see we've been talking online for months."

Max's eyes were narrow, and he still had a damn piece of bacon in his hand. "You have? Brooke didn't mention it."

Because it hadn't happened. Well, she supposed they had watched her online since they knew way more about her business than they should.

"Auntie Brooke is getting married?" Paige's eyes lit up. "I can be the flower girl. I'm better at it than I was for the last one. I won't even eat the rose petals. They didn't taste good but Charlie said they did, and so I made him eat some, too."

"Violently and in front of the entire congregation," Rye added. "Honestly, I'm surprised Georgia decided to have kids after she saw what this one can do."

Max waved it off. "He deserved it for trying to poison my baby girl. I don't trust those boys. They look too much like Zane."

They didn't. As they grew up, the twins looked so much like Nate Wright it hurt, but she wasn't pointing that out. She was too floored that Bay's arm was around her. Like he belonged there.

"We haven't decided on how big the wedding's going to be," Bay hedged, and she realized he was giving her space. Good. He was allowing room for them to get out of whatever this thing was she'd managed to get them all into. "We might elope. We're not getting any younger, but Max would understand that… I'm sorry, sir. I shouldn't have made a joke about your advanced age."

She kind of liked it when Bay was an asshole.

Max finished chewing his bacon and eyed Bay like he was the enemy he was about to take out. "You little… If your brother wasn't so good with bacon, I would kill you myself." He frowned Rye's way. "It was good bacon."

"Why do you want to kill him, Daddy?" Paige had her hands on her hips, staring up at her most annoying father. "He's going to be my uncle. You told me I couldn't kill family even when Ethan breaks my toys."

"And that also means she shouldn't kick me in the shins." Bay seemed way too pleased with himself.

Paige looked up at him like he'd said something terrible. "Then how will you know if I like you or not?"

"I could ask," Bay offered.

Rye chuckled and put a hand on Paige's head. "Baby girl, your aunt is playing a joke on us. Your Aunt Brooke is a good girl. She doesn't do this kind of thing. This is a practical joke and one your daddy and I probably deserve richly after all the pranks we pulled on her as a kid."

Good girl. She'd been Bay and Shane's good girl the night before, and it had felt fabulous.

"She's pulling your daddy's leg, and he's taking the bait," Rye explained with a certainty that rankled. "Brooke is concentrating on her career. She's smart and would never cause a scandal."

A scandal? Where was she? This was Bliss. Sleeping with two men at once was a tradition, not a freaking scandal.

They thought of her as some sexless work machine who smiled and never caused any trouble and never had a moment's real heartache. They had never really seen her. Never knew who she was at her heart. She was in a box, and she was supposed to stay in it or it would be a scandal.

They had basically been her dads, and she'd never once rebelled.

And why was it a scandal that she had sexual needs? She wound an arm around Bay's lean waist, the feel of warm skin bringing her some power. "Scandal? I'll tell you what a scandal is, Rye. It's getting fired from my job because I wouldn't sleep with the boss after he stole my designs and coming home with my tail between my legs because I'm going to have wasted six years of school, and the only thing that made me feel slightly better happened on that table last night." She nodded Max's way. "Yes, that one, and I am not talking about sharing late-night pizza rolls. That was not the snack those boys enjoyed at that table. You know, Max, the one you were just sitting at."

"Babe," Bay breathed.

Max had gone pale. "But we bought that table so you could have a place to eat breakfast."

She stepped away from Bay, eyeing her brother. "I thought you built this place so you had a sleeping station when you're up late."

Paige frowned at her fathers. "I thought we built this place because you said Auntie Brooke would need it one day 'cause she's going to end up all alone and without a job 'cause fashion designer ain't a real job and it's all falling apart, but then you knew it would. Shouldn't you have told Auntie Brooke? She seems real surprised."

"Paige," Rye said with a long-suffering sigh.

"Sorry," Paige said with a wince. "I forgot. It's because being a fashion designer isn't a real job. It sure cost a lot though. That's what Daddy says. I think it *is* a job. I don't think these jeans made themselves. That's what Mama says."

"This is my spinster house." How dare they? And how had they known?

"Babe, we should talk," Bay said quietly. "Like away from your parents. I mean brothers."

He'd been right the first time. It definitely felt like she was sitting in front of a set of dads who had way overstepped. "When did it go in? This house. How long has it been here?"

Rye actually looked a bit shaken at this point. "After Christmas."

After she'd talked to Rachel about being lonely. After she'd told a couple of people around town how hard it was to feel like she wasn't going anywhere. She might have mentioned to one of her friends that she was worried her boss didn't like her and was keeping her from taking the lead on projects. She'd been a little drunk, talking to Lucy and River, who had great relationships and were doing well in the workplace. Lucy and River had it all together. River had the cutest dog, and Brooke wasn't even allowed to have a cat because Ami was allergic. But then she was allergic to everything, including acting like a decent human being. She was pretty sure she'd told River and Lucy that, too.

Had her friends… Nope. She knew exactly who it was, or rather she could narrow it down to a group since she'd been sitting at the bar at Trio. Neither Lucy nor River would have gone to her brothers, but nothing in the world would have stopped Callie Hollister-Wright if she thought Brooke was in trouble.

They had called the week after it all fell apart. The very day she got fired.

"Who's paying the PI?" It was the only explanation.

"PI?" Bay asked. "As in private investigator? Why would your brothers hire a PI?"

She ignored him because she knew exactly why they would. They were deeply nosy and way overprotective. The question was how since they were also completely miserly when it came to money.

"I think it's Uncle Stef." Paige was the only one who seemed to be enjoying this altercation. She sat down in the chair Max had recently occupied and took a piece of toast for herself. "They talk about you a lot, and there's that big guy who seems real mean but he's actually nice. Big Tag is what they call him. His kids are cool. I like the girls."

She felt her jaw clench. "You hired McKay-Taggart to follow me?"

"No," Max said with the calm assurance of a man who knew how to lie.

Rye stayed quiet because he wasn't as good a liar as his twin.

Now that she thought about it, there was only one person who would tell her the truth. She could march right over to the big house and tell her sister-in-law everything. Including how her husbands ate her bacon.

Her pregnant sister-in-law. Who was under an enormous amount of stress. Who didn't need more.

She wasn't about to cry in front of them. It was obvious they thought she was a pathetic girl they had to watch over because she couldn't take care of herself.

Rye's jaw went tight, and she watched as he moved into stern-dad mode. "Brooke, go get dressed. We'll have this discussion at the big house and we'll talk about some of your more reckless choices."

There it was.

What she'd always been afraid of.

"Bay, I think it's time you got on with whatever it is you need to do with your day," Max said with a frown.

She felt like she was fifteen and caught doing something terrible, and here she was alone in front of the two men she'd tried so hard to make proud all of her life.

She'd screwed it all up, and now they would find out she'd possibly screwed them over in the process.

Except she wouldn't. She would let it all go if it meant protecting them, and they never had to know.

She was alone, and if she pissed her brothers off enough, they might decide they didn't need her drama.

"I'm not going anywhere," Bay said in a deep, no-nonsense tone. "Look, I wish Shane was here because he's way better at this part than I am."

"There is no part, son," Rye began.

Bay held up a hand. "Don't. I am not your son, and don't use that word on my brother. This is the part where I explain to you that I'm taking Brooke out of here. I can do that in a civilized way by waiting for Shane to return and packing her up in our truck. Or I can have her get dressed and I'll carry her out of here, but what I will not do is allow you to make her feel like shit when she's already going through a tough time."

"That is not what we're trying to do," Rye argued.

Bay pulled her hand into his and brought it to his lips. There was such certainty in his eyes. Like he could handle this. He wanted to handle this. "Go get dressed. We'll find a place to stay. You and me and Shane. I got some money saved. We'll check into the motel until we find a cabin to rent."

"Okay." The word was out of her mouth before she could think about the wisdom behind them. Was she going to play house with Bay and Shane? It would annoy the hell out of her brothers. They'd been watching her. She knew they'd done it because they were worried, but they hadn't even asked her before they'd started spying.

Yes, that was why she was doing this. It wasn't about the way they made her feel the night before.

What was she doing? She should tell Bay this was all a mistake. She could apologize to her brothers and promise not to cause any more trouble. They weren't monsters. They were good brothers. They were just… It wasn't fair that they would spy on her and not give her any space to figure things out on her own.

They still viewed her as a child, and maybe they always would. They were her safety net.

"I can take you out myself if you don't go," Max promised.

She stepped in front of Bay. No one in all of her years had been willing to take her brothers on for her. Her dating life had been almost non-existent when she lived here in Bliss, but the two guys who had asked her out had told her they couldn't handle her brothers.

What if Bay could?

"You are not going to touch him," Brooke vowed. "We'll be out of here as soon as I can pack up."

"That is not what we're saying…" Rye began.

Paige watched the whole awful scene play out with wide eyes. "Momma's going to be real mad."

Max moved to stand by his brother, and she prepared herself for the worst. "You need some space, little sister?"

Something eased inside her. "I do. I thought I could get it here, but I can't."

Rye looked to Max, and they seemed to have one of those psychic conversations they had all the time. She often wondered what it felt like to have someone who always knew what you were thinking. Always was connected to.

Bay's hand came down on her shoulder, silent proof that he was there.

It was supposed to be a crazy one-night stand. He was supposed to be disposable, a conquest of sorts. Evidence that she could go wild from time to time. He wasn't supposed to make her feel…safe.

"Go talk to Marie," Max advised. "Or Stella. I don't know if anyone's staying in the apartment above the café right now. I think the Texas crew's cabins are all open. She'll give you a discount."

"But I don't want my auntie to leave," Paige protested. "Momma don't want her to leave neither."

"Paige," Brooke admonished.

Paige shrugged and sighed. "Momma doesn't want her to leave either."

Rye picked her up. "Your aunt will be back. She needs some time."

"Like a time out? I don't like those." Paige wrapped her arms around her dad's shoulders. "I don't think we should put Aunt Brooke in a time out."

Oh, but she could use one.

"She's not in trouble," Rye said, his expression grim. He looked over at Brooke, his eyes on the hand on her shoulder. "Take the Jeep."

"I'm not taking the Jeep. You might need it. I'll be fine. We'll wait for Shane." It was weird for things to be so awkward. This was her home, and it suddenly felt like it wasn't.

Rye started to argue.

Max held up a hand. "She'll figure it out, and if she needs us, she'll call." He turned to Brooke. "I'm a phone call away. Maybe when you feel comfortable we can have a family dinner."

"We'll be there," Bay offered.

Oh, that seemed like a bad idea.

Max looked like a man who'd caught something in his well-laid trap. "Excellent. Then we'll discuss setting it up later. We'll make sure the kids are all in bed so we can have a nice long get-to-know-you session since you're apparently getting married."

"Max," she began.

"Oh, no, sister. We're rolling with it for now." He winked her way. "Honestly, I've always worried that you never push back. This is a good bit of rebellion since I'll do anything you need me to do so you don't make the horrible mistake of marrying beneath you."

Rye seemed to pick up on Max's vibes. "Yes, I think a nice formal dinner would be a good way to welcome those boys to the family. Suits and ties?"

"Absolutely," Max agreed.

"Wait. What?" Bay suddenly didn't sound so sure of himself. "I thought we were running away."

She sighed because they couldn't. As upset with them as she was, they were her brothers, and she had walked right into their trap.

* * * *

Shane wondered if this was a trap of some sort.

He stood in the middle of The Trading Post, the basket in his hand filled with two pounds of bacon and another dozen eggs because it looked like the Harper brothers could eat. He was still surprised Brooke hadn't woken up when they invaded this morning. She'd managed to sleep through Max's interrogation as he downed the bacon. Shane had taken it as a good excuse to avoid Paige Harper's cowboy boots. He hoped Bay's shins survived the experience.

Oddly, though, it wasn't the Harper brothers he thought might be the trap. Nope. It was the twenty-something young lady in barely-there jean shorts, a crop top, and a cowboy hat covering her blonde hair. She was pretty, but he wasn't interested.

Despite the fact that he was a somewhat attractive young man, he didn't actually get hit on often.

Was she hitting on him? Or simply lost in the weirdness that was

The Trading Post. It wasn't a regular grocery store. It was an all-purpose store that sold almost everything but feed and heavy equipment. Marie had put that thought out there and found herself on the receiving end of an aggressive prayer circle led by Pastor Dennis of the befittingly named Feed Store Church. So The Trading Post only offered everything else and stayed far from what Marie called the feed racket.

Maybe Miss Forgot That Shirts Usually Had Bottom Halves was confused and looking for direction.

"I'm having such a hard time," she confessed. "My sister sent me to get bacon, but I don't cook. Is that a good brand?"

It was *a* brand. He wasn't sure which brand since it was marked with a generic label that simply said bacon. And one of them had an obviously hand-done sticker that said a pig died for your breakfast. Yeah, Nell was definitely here.

The blonde had cornered him in the cold section. It wasn't like there weren't other people in the store she could have asked, including some incredibly competent-looking women. Laura Kincaid-Briggs was shopping with her daughter following her around with her own tiny cart. He'd noticed Gemma Wells talking to Teeny when he walked in, and Nell Flanders was protesting right outside. Though he suspected she wouldn't help the young woman find bacon.

Nell might protest him if she knew what he was buying. He should get some fruit, too. To cover up the bacon.

"Uhm, hello," she said, sounding the slightest bit aggrieved.

He didn't usually hear that tone in a woman's voice until he'd done something weird or his brother started talking about the mating habits of obscure sea creatures. She'd asked about the bacon. "It's the cheapest they have."

Honesty. It mostly repelled everyone. Especially women looking for a date.

Would it repel Brooke? He was worried he was going to drive back and find Bay walking along the highway because her brothers had kicked him out. Brooke could wake up and realize all the mistakes she'd made the night before.

Her green eyes went wide. "Oh. I suppose that's good. You're frugal." She picked up two pounds and put it in her basket. "I don't even like my sister, so why would I get her the good stuff? We're staying in a cabin down by the river. We're here for a couple of days while my brother-in-law goes rafting. Do you live here?"

"No. I think only Teeny and Marie live here since Logan moved out, but that was years ago. And they technically live in the valley. I think the only thing that lives here is the lowest prices in the valley, but they're also the only store in the valley, so I wouldn't make too much of it."

She snorted. "No, silly. I meant here in this town. It's called Bliss, right?"

He was such an idiot. He spent too much time with his way-too-literal brother. "Oh, no. I don't technically live in town. I work on a ranch, and it's a couple miles outside, though Bliss is the closest town."

She smiled brightly and moved in closer. "Really? So you're a cowboy?"

"I'm a ranch hand by profession," he replied.

"Tell me something, Shane. Have you ever rodeoed? I have a real thing for rodeo cowboys." Her voice had gone low and husky.

He tried to take a step back but ran into the dairy case. "Uhm, I did some calf roping in my time. Solo and on a couple of teams. I rode bulls until I realized I didn't want to have arthritis in every bone in my body. You know that's rough on a man, and there's no real need to do it. Like calf roping is necessary at times. Personally, I say if that bull doesn't want to be ridden, we should respect his boundaries."

She stared at him for a moment like he'd said something dumb, but he'd actually thought about this. There was a reason to ride a bronc. It was part of training and eventually helped both rider and horse, as he was sure Brooke's brother would explain in better detail. No one rode a damn bull into town or out on the range. So it seemed kind of mean. Huh, he bet Nell would approve.

He still wasn't giving up his bacon.

"Hmm, I guess I didn't think of it that way," she replied. "So you're living out on this ranch? There must be a bunch around here."

"Not really. There are a couple of small ranches, but only one big one. It's called the G. It's run by some real nice folks. The Glen-Bennetts and the McNamara-O'Malleys. They treat all their hands like family."

"Yeah, I've heard some rumors about why everyone seems to have hyphenated names out here." Her smile became seductive. At least he thought those were the vibes she was sending off. "Tell me something, cowboy. Do you have a brother?"

Yep. He was feeling cornered. This was not about where the cheese could be found. What did he do? He glanced around but Laura had turned down the aisle with baking mixes and spices. Little Sierra snuck a box of cookies into her cart and did not care that he might be dealing with real-life sexual harassment. The bell jingled at the front of the store, and he wondered who'd walked in and if they might be willing to help a brother out.

Where were all the horny dudes when a girl needed one? Not that he wasn't horny. It had been a real challenge to slip out of that bed and not wake Brooke up. She'd been curled around him with Bay at her back. She'd been so stunning in the early morning light, with her hair caressing her cheeks and her skin all warm and inviting.

They never slept with a woman. They were always up and out before dawn so no one saw them.

That was what Brooke had wanted, too. At least she'd intimated that was what she wanted.

Would she think the same if it was only Bay in her bed? Bay was the talented one, the legitimate one. Bay's birth hadn't ever been described as an affront to the natural order of things. He still didn't understand how it wasn't natural to have a baby when two people screwed like bunnies without protection. No matter their marital status.

"Uhm, yes, ma'am. I do have a brother. His name is Bay, and he is waiting back at our girlfriend's place for this bacon." There. That was how he got away. He had a girlfriend. Well, she didn't know it, but he was going to behave like a good boyfriend, and that meant chucking her right out there any time a strange woman came onto him.

"Girlfriend?" She looked at him skeptically. "I don't know many cowhands who can keep a girlfriend. Not that you're not good for a girl. No offense. Just you're not usually boyfriend material. Does she live with you? Are you screwing the rancher's daughter?"

"Uhm, Miranda is five. Brooke has her own place out on the Harper Stables." It was time to move on. "And I need to get back there. I'm making her some breakfast."

"Mr. Kent, what are you making? I like breakfast," a soft voice said.

He glanced down and saw something way scarier than the sexually aggressive chick.

Poppy Flanders. She was three or four, and she obviously had inherited her parents' intelligence and their deep belief in protesting anything they felt harmed the environment or impugned on the rights of the humans and creatures they shared that same earth with.

He gave the girl a smile and tried to hide his basket. "Hey there, Poppy. Where's your momma?"

"I'm right here." Nell walked up, a hand on her belly. She was wearing a sunny yellow dress that showed off how close she was to giving Poppy a sibling. She looked at the other woman and then back to Shane. "Can I help you, Miss? Shane here is in a hurry to get back to his fiancée."

Shane nodded and then stopped. "What?"

Nell gave him a smile. "You probably should check your messages. Apparently Max and Rye went by Brooke's tiny house, and now you're getting married. It's okay. Happens all the time here in Bliss."

"I thought she was only a girlfriend," the young woman said with a frown.

He pulled his cell out and sure enough, there was a message from Brooke's phone.

Hey, you're kind of needed back here. Forget about breakfast. I need help moving out and finding a place to stay, and also apparently we're doing this fake fiancé thing because I lost it with my brothers, so if you don't mind… Also, I could use some of Teeny's muffins if she has any left.

There were a bunch of emojis. A couple of hearts. Some prayer hands. A muffin. Oh, and a bagel. He should get some bagels, too.

What had happened?

And how did she know his name? The half-dressed chick. Not Brooke. He'd made certain Brooke knew his name.

The young woman looking for bacon had clearly called him Shane, and they hadn't exchanged names. He looked back up and she was gone.

"Where did she go?" Shane asked, glancing around.

Nell frowned. "Oh, I'm sorry. I thought you had the look of a man who didn't know how to get himself out of an uncomfortable position. If I was wrong, I apologize. I thought with the news…"

"Why was he talking to that lady if he's supposed to marry Paige's aunt?" Poppy asked.

The Flanders women could do judgment.

"Look, I'm not sure how we ended up engaged, but I'm happy about it, though you should know Brooke's not going to be. Not now. However, I will use this time to prove we can be good for her," Shane announced.

Nell's expression went bright. "Oh, I would bet Max and Rye caught her with your brother and they were obnoxious, and she decided to show them. It's a good start. Good trope. I approve of everything except the odd woman hitting on you."

"I didn't realize she was hitting on me." He heard the bell jingle again and knew it was her. She was gone. "She knew my name."

"Everyone does," Nell agreed. "You're settling in nicely. Did I thank you for helping Henry with the fencing? I never thought we would fence in any of our property, but it's safer for the goats we're rescuing. I think the idea of a home for abused and abandoned animals is so beautiful."

Those goats wouldn't have to worry about being milked or used for anything but emotional support. "It was an honor. I'm glad they'll have somewhere to go, and I would like to volunteer if you need help."

"That's wonderful. I think it'll bring the whole community together."

He let go of the odd woman who'd hit on him. He'd probably told her his name. Or she'd heard Teeny call it out as he'd walked in. But he had questions. "How did you know I was fake engaged before I did?"

Nell waved a hand. "Oh, it's the Bliss grapevine. Rachel called me and Callie the minute Max and Rye got back and Paige told her everything that happened. Also, you should tell Bay that he should ice his shin. Paige kicks harder than you would think."

"I'm not supposed to kick people. I'm supposed to use my words," Poppy said with a nod. "Words are powerful."

Okay, he might like Poppy better than Paige. "Did Paige tell Rachel that I had to leave the comfort of my fake near-marital bed because her husbands ate all the bacon?"

Nell frowned. "Yes, I do believe that was brought up as well."

Poppy's eyes shimmered with tears as she looked up at him. Like she was straight out of a Dickens novel, and he was the evil villain who would throw her to the wolves. "Did you kill the poor pig yourself, Mr. Shane?"

Nope. He was back to preferring Paige. He also slipped the basket behind him, dropping it on top of the aforementioned bacon. "I was going to grab Brooke some muffins. No more bacon."

Nell bit back a laugh and put a hand on her daughter's head. "Sorry. She's passionate about animals. And you should know Rachel is deeply upset that Brooke is leaving. I'm think she was counting on Brooke babysitting a couple of times while she's here. So where are you planning to stay? There are some cabins open for rent. That is if you intend to work after you get married."

He didn't think the getting married thing was actually happening. At least not anytime soon, but he was confused. "Why would I stop working?"

Nell's eyes narrowed. "Well, it's a question a lot of women get asked. Do you think only a woman is capable of handling the home and children?"

Yep. There were traps everywhere today. "No, ma'am. I think we're all going to work, and I'll check into the cabins."

How much would it cost? Bay would just tell her they had some money saved up. He wouldn't think about the fact that they'd had to replace all four tires, and that had eaten into their savings. Which was never much. He would have to figure something out.

"Oh, I don't think that will be necessary." Beth McNamara-O'Malley pushed her cart up to join them. She had a car seat locked into the cart, and it looked like Tanner was taking a nap. The G was flush with kiddos, and Shane kind of liked it. Miranda and Kade kept every adult on their toes, and Tanner would get there. Hope Glen-Bennett was about to have her first. It made a man think. "I heard the good news, Shane."

Did everyone know? Was there a flashing sign somewhere? "Uh, I don't think it's real, ma'am."

Beth shrugged. "It's Bliss real. That's all that counts, and why don't y'all move into the foreman's house? I'm going to warn you, the basement is our play space, but Trev doesn't mind sharing. I need you to know it'll be used at least once a week. But it's got a separate entrance. You'll be comfy there. I'll call and have Bo air it out. And get it ready for Brooke. I should get flowers. Make it sparkle a little."

"Rachel is going to be upset," Nell said under her breath.

"You snooze you lose. I promise my husbands aren't going to do anything to piss Brooke off. I heard she likes snickerdoodles. I think I'll make some this afternoon," Beth mused as she started to walk toward the baking aisle. "See you at home, Shane. We'll get someone to move your stuff over. It'll be good to have a threesome in the foreman's house."

The foreman's house was real nice. It was three bedrooms and a kitchen and a bath and a half. Way bigger than the tiny house.

And they would have a playroom.

"That is trouble," Nell said with a shake of her head.

He was missing something essential, but all that mattered was he had good news. "Thanks for the save, Mrs. Flanders. See you soon. Bye, Poppy."

"You forgot your basket," Poppy pointed out.

Nope. Not going there. "That's not mine. I'm a muffinterian now. Y'all have a nice day."

He grabbed the requested muffins and bagels and cream cheese, paid, and managed to not look guilty at all as Marie complained about someone leaving a whole basket in the meat section.

It was all looking up until he got to his truck and the door was open.

He knew he'd closed it.

He sighed and was happy when the fucker started up. Maybe it had been some kids or something, or maybe he actually hadn't shut it tight. Mel swore Sasquatches liked to get into unlocked cars.

It didn't matter. It wasn't like he had anything to steal.

He pointed the truck toward Harper Stables and let go of everything except his good news. For once the world was looking up.

Chapter Six

"So you're moving in with the new guys out on the G?" Gemma asked after handing the server the elegant menus.

Brooke sat in the smaller of the two restaurants at the Elk Creek Lodge. She was happy Gemma had chosen the lodge over Stella's since she was sure the Bliss grapevine had been working overtime. Obviously since Gemma already knew. "I suppose I am. It's better than the house my brothers built for me. I bet they bugged it or something."

Gemma winced. "So you found out about the PI?"

"Does everyone know?"

The blonde shrugged as though saying *well, it is Bliss*. "I think it's only your brothers' friend circle, which happens to include my boss. You know for a manly dude, Nate is a gossipy motherfucker. I swear Callie called and he walked right out to fill in me and Elisa. He called Cam, too. Anyway, that's why I changed our lunch location. If you walk into Stella's right now, you're going to have a lot of questions to answer. If it helps at all, I know Max and Rye were worried about you."

"Then they should have talked to me."

"That can be hard for guys. Speaking of, where are yours?"

They weren't hers. They were pretending to be hers so she could save the smallest amount of face. "They dropped me off and then they're heading back to the G for the day. We're staying in the foreman's house. Bo is pretty much the foreman, so he doesn't need it. All the hands they have right now are single, so they're out in the bunkhouse."

Gemma's eyes lit with mirth. "Yeah, I've visited the foreman's house a couple of times when my dommiest guy gets a hankering to tie me up." She winced. "Sorry. That's too much information. I'm trying to curb that."

Brooke leaned in. The last thing she needed was a Gemma who didn't tell it like it was. Gemma was brutally honest, and she needed that right now. No coddling. "Don't. I actually have questions, and I can't exactly ask my sister-in-law. I'm pretty sure they spend a lot of time in Stef's playroom."

Gemma chuckled. "Oh, yes. They have definitely played around with all the lifestyles." And then she went a bit red. "Again with the sorry."

Brooke felt her jaw tense. "I'm not a child."

Gemma studied her for a moment as though reassessing the situation. "No, you're not, but they treat you like one. I'm actually sorry for that part, not the rest. I guess I've spent years hearing about how sweet and innocent you are, but sometimes the word *innocence* is just a way to marginalize us."

"As Britney would say, not that innocent, and I have questions."

Gemma grinned brightly. "Then consider me your BDSM auntie. Although you should know Jesse and Cade are more on the D/s side. So are you asking specific questions about the lifestyle or do you want to know what I know about the Kent brothers?"

Brooke let out a deep breath. At least one person got what she needed. "All of the things, but start with what you know."

"They've played a lot both in Stef's private playroom and in a couple of the clubs Stef belongs to. Stef has been Bay's…sponsor, I suppose…for a long time. I don't even know how they met, but Stef believes Bay is an incredibly talented artist, and I've seen his work and know he's right. If that boy wanted to, he could make a lot of money as an artist."

"I don't think he would like how he would have to do it." She'd spent all of a night and half a day with the man and she already knew he wouldn't be able to handle all the bullshit that would come with cracking the artistic world. "He would never be able to kiss ass the way he would need to."

Gemma nodded. "I agree, but I don't think becoming the center of an artistic world is a goal of Bay's. I think he's that artist who actually loves art and working. I actually find him kind of fascinating. Shane as well. They've got that 'broken parts that make a whole' kind of vibe."

She got that, too. In that fashion they reminded her of her brothers. Shane and Bay needed each other in a way a lot of siblings didn't, but they hadn't exactly exchanged life histories.

And should they? She wasn't going to stay, and they would never be able to live in the city. So why was she pursuing this? Why was she pretending she was engaged? It was so dumb.

"Does that scare you?" Gemma asked.

"Not really. There are so many other things that scare me."

Gemma leaned in. "Like how you reacted to them? On a sexual level? Was it the first time you played around with Dominance and submission?"

"Yes." It felt better to talk about this part. This part was way more about her than them. "I liked it. I felt freer than I've ever felt in my life, and I started the whole thing to make myself feel better. It was supposed to be a little sex with some completely hot but inappropriate cowboys, and now I'm somehow living with them and I can't stop thinking about last night. It was more than I bargained for."

"What did you like about it?" Gemma asked softly, and there was not an ounce of judgment in the question.

How to explain it? "I didn't have to think about anything except what they were doing to me. I…it's like my brain shut down, and it's always going. Always. For the time I was with them I didn't think about how my life is falling apart or how everything's my fault. It's almost like a break from life because for once I wasn't in control. Shouldn't that scare me?"

Gemma's head shook. "Only if the partners you're submitting to aren't worthy of trust, and I don't think that's the case with Shane and Bay. You know Beth and Hope are my girls. We have our girl gangs in Bliss. Like Rachel and Callie and Jen. Or Laura and Holly and

Nell. It's me and Hope and Beth, which means I spend a lot of time out on the G. I sometimes wonder what my younger self would say if I told her one day a cattle ranch will be where you spend your free time."

Because Gemma had started out as a big-time lawyer in New York after breaking "free" from her unorthodox childhood.

They had a lot in common. "So you know Shane and Bay?"

She nodded. "They're helpful, and my guys like them. Jesse's helped them keep that junker truck of theirs running, and Shane and Bay helped us re-chink the cabin last month. I know they have a somewhat difficult relationship with your brothers over something that happened many years ago."

"Stef pulled some shit and dragged in Shane and Bay, and naturally everything played out exactly the way Stef wanted."

"Yeah, that's how things seem to go. And naturally Max can't give it up," Gemma returned. "But I think he also likes having someone to complain about. I know Max seems like an asshole, but he's a great guy and he doesn't hold a hard grudge. Which is why I'm more afraid of Rye."

So someone else truly saw her brothers. "Rye is quieter, but he's the one who thinks about real revenge. Max can be brought around. Rye still thinks I'm eight and need him to protect me."

"And that's a problem if you really like these guys."

Did she? Yeah. She kind of did. "I'm going back to New York."

Gemma seemed to think about that. "Okay. That's where your home is now. But you know not all relationships have to last forever. You can have a wonderful time and be loving and caring and not get married to the man or men. As long as all your cards are on the table, it's okay. But I kind of got the impression there's something not so great happening back in the city."

How far did this go? "What have you heard? I suppose if my fake engagement is out there, then the fact that I'm no longer employed is probably out there, too."

"That's how the rumor mill works," Gemma agreed, "though I don't think anyone knows exactly what happened. Since you're sitting here with me, I assume there are legal implications. What did some asshole boss do and why is it going to break my heart to tell you how to handle it?"

Tears pricked her eyes. "He stole my designs, but I was told he can legally do that because of my contract."

"I'll read it, but I know that some houses can be predatory about how they deal with creatives. So they fired you because you took offense?"

"They fired me because I made two formal complaints to HR. One about not getting even secondary credit for my designs and the other because I was told in no uncertain terms the only way I was getting to Milan was on my knees."

Gemma sat back with a long sigh. "I'm going to assume he was smart enough to not do this in front of an audience."

"We were alone, and there weren't any security cams." She sniffled because she knew what Gemma was going to say. "It's a he said, she said, and HR interviewed him and decided he was credible and I was bitter over the fall line."

"Okay. What reason did they give for firing you?"

Shame poured through her. "I was fired for creating an uncomfortable work environment."

"Because you accused your boss?" Gemma perked up as though she'd seen the light at the end of the tunnel and there was actually something she could do.

"No. They said some of my coworkers complained about how I talked about my family."

"Your family?"

She nodded. "Specifically my brothers."

Gemma seemed to get the gist. "You were open about your brothers sharing a wife. They felt like your friends, so you make a couple of jokes about how weird your hometown is and suddenly they can use it against you. I would bet no one had a problem with it until after you went to HR."

"No. I thought they were all cool with it. I mean it's not exactly a prim and proper business. Everyone's creative and quirky, but they all turned on me."

"I'm so sorry, Brooke."

"I don't have grounds. Do I?"

"Oh, you have grounds," Gemma said. "So much ground, but I

will tell you that taking this to court is going to be difficult, and more important, very costly. It's better to put together a good case for them to settle. Basically, threaten a nasty suit and at the last minute you offer to settle for say a million dollars."

"I don't think it would work. I don't think they will settle," Brooke admitted. "I think they would know I'm playing chicken with them since if I actually took it to trial, my brothers and more importantly, my sister-in-law and niece and nephews get dragged in. So does this town. But he's going to blackball me. They basically said good luck finding something new."

"I can file some paperwork and we could see how they respond. We can gauge where to go from there. But if it goes anywhere, you'll need counsel in Manhattan. I don't have those connections anymore. I'm still licensed to practice there, but this was not my specialty. But I can start the initial work if you want to."

"I can give you some money."

Gemma waved her off. "No. I'll handle it pro bono, but I want you to have realistic expectations. It's going to take a couple of weeks. This is not a quick process."

Brooke wiped away a tear and swore she wasn't going to cry. "I will. I feel like I should do something. Fight for my career."

"Do you want your job back?"

"No. I could never work there again, but how can I let them get away with it?"

"Then we'll start the process, but it's an uphill fight. Have you thought about trying to find a job in LA? Or London, maybe? You know you have some impressive connections. Stef alone could get you on somewhere."

There was a reason she hadn't wanted Stef to help. "Then I'm the nepo hire or the girl whose rich uncle bought her a spot."

"And you prove yourself," Gemma countered. "Look, Brooke, I've literally been on the other side of this. I was pushed out of a job for a person who had way less talent than I had. Less education. Less work ethic. What she did have was a very wealthy dad. So I loathe people like that, but I don't know what I would have done if I had connections. You have the right to use what you have as long as you prove yourself once you're there."

"And if I need some time to think about what I want to do? I know I should find another job as quickly as possible," Brooke began.

"Or you could give yourself the summer to figure things out. What's your lease situation?"

"Oh, Ami sent me a text late last night asking if I was staying because she's got someone willing to pay three hundred more than me," Brooke explained. It was one of the many revelations waiting for her this morning.

"We'll send someone to pack you up." Gemma started making notes in a small book. "I'll call Seth. I assure you he can have someone over there by this evening. Give me a list of things, or do you trust this roommate?"

"Ami doesn't want anything I own. She'll point it all out. I can pay…"

Gemma groaned. "Stop. See, this is the independent woman trap. I'm going to tell you the secret I've learned. You can be independent and need help. Your friends and family aiding you isn't about you being weak. It's about your family being strong. So toss those thoughts right out, and now we're full circle and you've answered your own question about how you can have liked the sexual encounter and still hold your head up as a woman. Because it has nothing to do with your independence. It has to do with your needs. There is nothing stronger than being open and honest about your needs. You found two men who made you feel safe enough to let go."

Nope. She was crying. Damn it. Gemma was right. "They did. I felt free."

"Because you found something good. Do not let anyone take that from you. Don't let shame lead you. Tell your brothers what happened and why you feel like you can't fight. Let it be their choice to give you permission to move forward or to ask for you to sacrifice this for their kids. And then when you know what you want, we go to Stef or Seth and make a plan."

It felt like failure, but she wasn't going to argue with Gemma. "You came here after you got fired. How long was it before you knew it was right to stay?"

Gemma seemed to think about it for a moment. "I suppose when I looked up at the stars and I really saw them for the first time. I laid back on the grass outside of Jesse and Cade's cabin and I realized I never looked up. I never let myself be. I was so worried about the future that I had never once enjoyed the moment. The present is all we truly have. The past is sweet memories and the future, well, it comes faster and faster now, and then it's the present, and I was still moving the goal posts. I'm still ambitious, but my ambitions are about helping people more than acquiring a bunch of stuff that won't make me happy in the end. I love this town. I love my husbands. I love that my mom is healthy and happy. And I love me now in a way I did not before, and D/s helped me find all of those things. Because D/s taught me to trust not only my partners, but myself. Tell me something, and be honest about it. Even if it's only with yourself. How did it make you feel?"

"Powerful. Beautiful. Worthy." She dabbed at her eyes with her napkin. "But I don't see how I could make it work with them."

"You don't have to. Sweetie, when was the last time you weren't working toward a goal?"

You are going to college, kiddo. I do not put on that sheriff's uniform so you can work at Stella's.

Don't you worry about a thing, Brooke. Rye and I will make sure everything is okay. All you need to worry about is getting into a good school and getting a good job.

Oh, they hadn't meant to do it, but her brothers had flipped a switch inside her with the words. They were trying to let her be who she wanted to be, but in trying to do that, she'd simply wanted to make them proud, and that had become her ambition. "I don't remember."

"Then breathe, Brooke. You are in a unique position. You don't need a job right this second. You can take some time and enjoy a summer."

"I kind of have a job, not that it pays much. Cleo asked me to take over the wardrobe department for the rep theater. She's under the impression that I'll be gone in a couple of weeks, but I don't think she'd be upset if I stuck around."

"And how does that make you feel?"

Brooke shrugged. "I used to love costume design, but by the time I got into Parson's, I was set on high fashion."

"Because you loved it?"

"Because it was the best."

"The best for who?" Gemma asked, but kindly. She reached out and put a hand on Brooke's. "I have seen so many people come to Bliss to find themselves. Stop listening to the negative voices in your head. Stop listening to a society that will never serve you properly. I wanted to be the best. The best lawyer. The most successful person my family had ever produced. I figured out the only thing that matters is being the best Gemma I can be. The best friend and partner and daughter. The best me possible, and I work on it every day. And I'm still sarcastic and I still don't want kids, even though I love my friends' kids to death. I didn't fall into some small-town dream life. Bliss helped me make my own paradise, one I built from the ground up, but it started by figuring out who I really was. Who I am. Just because you grew up here doesn't mean you've ever once given in to the real magic of this place. So take the summer and see Bliss through new eyes, and maybe you'll find a new you, too."

She squeezed Gemma's hand. "Do you think I should suck it up and apologize to my brothers?"

Gemma shuddered like that was the worst plan ever. "Why would you do that? They sicced a PI on you. They need to apologize."

They weren't known for apologies. They would think they were in the right, and the fact that she was in trouble proved it. "So I can have a place to stay."

Gemma leaned forward, putting her other hand over Brooke's. "Oh, no. You have a place to stay. You have the foreman's house."

"But it's not mine, and I don't want to put Beth and Hope out."

"I need you to think about why Beth leapt on the opportunity to steal you right out from under Rachel. She didn't have to offer that house up. They use it as their playroom. I assure you they'll cut back with the three of you living there. So why would she do it?"

"To help out Shane and Bay." Oh, she was being dumb. "She knows I'll babysit."

Gemma chuckled and sat back. "And there we are. She's not planning on taking advantage, but Hope's in her last months, and they depend on each other to help with the kids. I need to emphasize that she is not bringing you in as an unpaid nanny, but I know she'll feel better if there's a competent woman she can leave her babies with if she needs to take Hope somewhere."

She actually felt better knowing she could help. "Well, I will have to split my time then because I think that's why my sister-in-law was excited to have me here. The good news is the G is a great place to hold a play group. Between that and my theater job, I'll have plenty to do." It felt good to make some choices. It felt good to get rid of that stupid timer on her relationship with Bay and Shane. "Could you please ask Seth to send someone to my old place and do the paperwork?"

"I'll need a formal interview, but not today." She closed her notebook. "Today we're going to talk about sex and kink, and how there's nothing shameful about it."

"I am here for this talk." Lucy Carson was suddenly at the table, and she hadn't come alone.

Brooke had texted her when Gemma changed the meet spot to the lodge. She couldn't walk into Lucy's workplace without at least giving her a hug. Apparently Lucy had called River Lee, because she was here, too.

Brooke got up and got those hugs. "I'm so glad to see you."

Lucy held her close. "We're happy you're home."

River got in on the affection. "So happy."

River sniffled as she stepped back. "Now Luce texted me and told me you were coming, so we're crashing your lunch. And I heard something about an engagement."

Lucy snorted. "I told you. She got caught with her hands in the ménage jar and her brothers were obnoxious, so she tossed that out thinking all the men would run, and now she's caught in her own trap." Lucy waved down a server. "Hey, Val, we're going to need some rosé."

Gemma looked them over, and a brow cocked over her intelligent eyes. "See, I told you. Threesomes. Even in friendships, and Ty doesn't count. Those two have been down a friend for a long time."

"Well, I was down to me and Ty while River here followed Jax all over the world." Lucy took a seat.

River sat down across from her. "He was on the run from a crazy lady who took all his memories. I made vows. In sickness and health and in case of supervillain trying to kill us."

"Well, I'm glad that particular villain is dead and gone." Lucy pulled her napkin over her lap. "So did you see the latest paparazzi shots of Georgia?"

Georgia Stark-Warner didn't care what the world thought. She went all over the city with her husbands, Logan and Seth. Seth being the billionaire he was, the press was fascinated.

Georgia handled it all with her usual aplomb, though Seth had upped their security since they had their first kid.

"They were all over her at the airport. Seth was pissed." She leaned over to look at River's phone and winced. "I look like the nanny. And like the really sad nanny. Yikes."

The picture was of them walking toward the airplane. Georgia was smiling and holding hands with Seth. Logan was on her other side, carrying their infant son against his chest. Brooke trailed behind carrying her sad suitcase with a backpack on her back.

Awesome. She was in the society pages and she looked like the world had kicked the hell out of her.

Because it had. She sighed and turned back. "Well, it was worth it for the free ride."

River nodded. "Now tell us everything."

The server brought the rosé, and Brooke relaxed with her friends.

* * * *

Bay looked around the place and wondered if they shouldn't make it…prettier. Even that tiny place Brooke was in last night had some decorations. Not much, but there had been flowers. Should he go get some flowers? Brooke liked pretty things.

The house was nice, had plenty of room, but it was…neutral. He didn't want her to see it as a hotel room. He wanted her to get comfortable here.

"It's fine." Shane set his pack down. "The place looks great."

"Nah, it looks like the last person who actually lived here was a man who did not give a damn about anything but comfort." Trev

McNamara chuckled as he walked through the doorway. He was a big guy, his body still evidence of his former NFL career. He'd been a famous quarterback with the world open to him, but he'd had an addiction to a bunch of stuff that wasn't good for him, and now he was a rancher.

And seemed happy about it. Oh, he still played some ball, but only with his friends and family. Bay had caught a couple of that dude's spiral passes, and the man could hit a target.

Shane looked at their boss. "Oh, it's fine. We're thankful that you're allowing us to use it. I need you to understand we know it's just while Brooke is here."

Trev studied Shane for a long moment and then gave the same scrutiny to Bay. He wondered if they were about to get a lecture about taking advantage of his wife. "How long do you suspect that's going to be?"

Yes, he should have known this was too good to be true. "I think she said she was going to be here a couple of weeks."

"And you're okay with that?" Trev asked.

"We support Brooke in whatever she wants to do," Shane said, proving he was the one with a filter.

Bay didn't have much of one. "No. We want her to stay. She thought throwing out the whole fake engagement thing would get me to run, but she doesn't know me well. Yet. Pretty soon she's going to figure out that was a mistake because I'm a tick who digs in hard."

For a second he worried he'd said the wrong thing, but then Trev pointed his way and smiled. "That's what I want to hear." He glanced out the open door. "Jamie, I was right. This is all a scam to trap Brooke."

"Thank god." Jamie Glen walked in, carrying a vase filled with red and pink roses. "I was worried they were using Brooke to fuck over Max. Not that anyone would blame you."

"Brooke would, Mr. Glen," Bay pointed out. She loved her brothers, and he and Shane needed to find a way to make up for the last several years of fucking around with them.

Jamie set the flowers on the kitchen table. "These are from Hope. She's planning on inviting Brooke over to the storage shed. There's some extra furniture and stuff we haven't gotten rid of since our last makeover."

Trev grinned. "My wife can't stop renovating. She's working with Hale Galloway on some of his projects. I swear my kids already know how to install flooring, but she's real bad about letting go of things. She's a bit of a hoarder. There's some furniture plus extra bedding. I think the kitchen is well stocked."

"Because you use it so often." Jamie leaned against the bar. "You know you're not going to be able to wander up here in the altogether to fix a couple of sandwiches during a long play session." He looked to Bay. "Trev had the brilliant idea of transforming the basement of this building into a playroom after his oldest started wandering around the house by herself. There were doors he did not want to explain why they were locked."

Trev shrugged. "The old adult playroom is now a kid's playroom. And we play here where our kids know not to go into. It helps quite a bit having someone in the place."

He hadn't even thought about that. Trev had shown off his gorgeous playroom when they'd hired on since he knew Bay and Shane were in the lifestyle. He'd offered for them to use it if they took a sub. He remembered thinking if he was a couple of years younger, he would have been all over it, but now the only person he wanted was Brooke. But the last thing he wanted to do was cause trouble for his boss. "We can clear out when you need the space."

Trev's head shook, and his expression went soft. "We don't play much right now. Three kids in, and we mostly sleep when we get the chance. It's okay. It'll be here when we're ready. I'm going to enjoy all the phases, and this phase is less sex, more kids sleeping on my chest. As Jamie here is about to discover."

Jamie smiled his way. "I'm ready. You're not the only one who's going to have wild-ass kids running all over this ranch. Those two boys of yours are getting another brother. And Miranda will have another young dumbass to dote on."

"My daughter likes to play Mommy with her baby brothers. It's the sweetest thing," Trev explained.

Bay didn't understand that, but he did know the two men were happy. "We're appreciative of the offer to stay here for a couple of weeks."

Shane stepped in beside him. "And we're well aware that neither of us is actually the foreman. That's pretty much Bo."

Trev's lips quirked up. "Bo is all about the kids right now. He's got a lot on his plate, and he's been helping out more and more in the office. We were actually thinking about how well this job is working out with you. Maybe you could handle it while Beth is working on her renovations."

"Just in a probationary way. Let's give it a month or so and see how it goes." Jamie watched them. "Unless you're planning on moving on soon. I know you don't stay in one place much."

They'd already discussed this. Bliss was their home now. He could breathe here. Work here. He would honestly miss new places and discovering new worlds to work on, but he could make Bliss his palette, his inspiration. He was sketching more, getting ready to sculpt.

Her. He wanted to sculpt her. He had drawn her a hundred times, but he hadn't drawn her forth from clay. The older he got the more he wanted hours a day to spend on his art.

"The light here is perfect. There's a room on the second floor and the light is golden."

Jamie and Trev stared like they were trying to figure out what he meant.

Luckily Shane spoke his language. "He likes the smaller bedroom upstairs because the light is right for painting, though he could be talking about sketching or sculpting. He's a jack of all art trades. He simply happens to be good with cattle, too."

"And you're good with people," Jamie pointed out. "You both have excellent skills when it comes to the job. Let's try it, and if Bay wants time in the afternoon because the light is right, Shane can take up the slack. Here's the thing. We don't care as long as the job is done and everyone is treated well. We're bringing in another couple of hands for the rest of the summer so I can concentrate on Hope and our new son. We're interviewing a few next week."

"We've got some experienced candidates," Trev added. "So you shouldn't have to train some green kid. Like I said, let's try this out. Take the weekend to spend with your girl, and if you need advice on how to handle her, we're around."

"She thinks we're just for sex. How would you handle that?" The question popped out.

Shane sighed. "He doesn't have a filter. Sorry. It's a good question, though. She views us as stress relief. According to Bay, she's in some kind of trouble. Not like danger trouble, but trouble. I don't know if she would have said yes to last night if she wasn't. She never has before, and we've tried a couple of times over the years. I think she's going to have fun with us until she figures out her future."

"She lost her job, right?" Trev asked. "That's the rumor."

"She had her job stolen from her," Bay corrected. "Not that I know everything. By the time I got her packed and in the car, all she wanted to talk about was her meeting with Gemma and the fact that she's spending the whole afternoon at the theater. She's not supposed to be back until late."

"She told us she would get a ride from the Farley brothers. She's taking that whole crazy ride share thing they have going too seriously," Shane complained. "But see, she's not even talking to us about that, and now we're living together."

He was worried they might not be if they let her find her own way home. She might not remember they had a new temporary home. She might decide to go back to her brothers'.

"Are they rehearsing tonight?" Jamie asked. "I thought they were taking weekends off right now."

"They're rehearsing this afternoon but clearing out before dinner. That's why she's working late." She'd explained it to them as they'd driven her out to the Elk Creek Lodge so she could meet with Gemma Wells. "The theater is going to be quiet, and she's basically coming in and trying to work with what they have."

"Well, let her know if she needs fabric, Beth went through a sewing period when she couldn't sledgehammer walls," Trev replied with a chuckle.

"Yeah, she and Hope decided they were going to make all of Miranda's clothes," Jamie continued. "I think they made a hat."

"Oh, they made a lot of things. None of them actually resembled clothes. Our wives are excellent at many things, but sewing isn't one of them," Trev concluded. "So there's a lot of stuff in the storage if Brooke wants to use it."

Oh, he liked the sound of that. He'd been walking around this house trying to envision how they could use it to tempt Brooke to think of them as something more than sexual stress relief. What if he split that room with her? "Is there a sewing machine?"

Trev nodded. "Two. And at least one basket of all the accessories. Are you thinking about setting up a room for her? I thought she wasn't staying long."

"Maybe she stays longer if she likes the theater gig." Shane sounded surprisingly positive. "I don't like the idea of her coming home with the Farley brothers. I think we should pick her up."

Jamie sighed. "We're going to have to walk them through this, aren't we?"

"I told you," Trev replied with a shake of his head. "They know how to get a woman in bed, but I don't think they've ever tried to get a woman to stay with them outside it."

He wasn't saying anything untrue. "We never wanted one until we met her."

Trev put a hand on his shoulder. "Then let's make sure you know how to tempt her to open up and view you as something more than a fun time. It starts with not letting her sit up at the theater alone. She's got to eat dinner, right?"

"She said she would get something from Stella… We should take her dinner," Bay said, finally getting the point.

Shane smiled at him like he was a toddler learning to use his words. "That's good. We should take a whole picnic, and while we're waiting, we should set up a place for her to work here. We can split the upstairs room. I bet she would like that light, too. If someone will give me the code to the storage locker, I'll get started. My stepmom used to sew, and I think I remember a little about how her room was set up."

Not that Shane had been allowed in there. "I'll help. And I'll call the bee lady. I hear she does picnic baskets now."

Jamie pointed his way. "Now you're talking. But you should also know that how you handle sex is going to be important."

Trev snorted. "Yeah, listen to him. He thought it would be better to hold out, and his brother got in there first. He never lets Noah hear the end of it."

"Oh, we did her at the same time." Bay frowned. That sounded bad and not at all like the passionate intimacy they'd shared. "That didn't come out right."

"We began as we mean to go," Shane corrected. "She knows we're a packaged deal, and I feel like most of our intimacy should be the three of us for now."

"Good." Trev nodded as though he approved. "Then it seems like you know what you're doing. Now let's talk about how you can pay us back for giving you this lovely house to live in and access to a ridiculous amount of toys. You see we haven't been on a date alone in six months."

"We can watch the kids." Bay wasn't going to pretend to not understand. He liked Miranda, and honestly, he was good with kids. They tended to think he was a weirdo, but kids were way more tolerant than adults. Would Brooke think it was a good thing that he probably fit better with kids than normal adults who didn't view the world as one big art project?

He could feel the sculpture that had been playing in his head. Feel the wetness on his hands as he smoothed the clay, running over and over until he got her curves right. Until he could see in a piece of art what he felt the night before. Love and lust, and an odd sense of peace he'd never had before.

"I promise we won't abuse it," Trev said solemnly. "Normally we switch off."

"But Hope's been so sick. This kid might be an only," Jamie said with clear worry in his eyes.

"We don't mind helping out. Brooke likes kids. She's got so many pictures of her niece and nephews on her socials," Shane said.

Trev winced. "You have to stop that, son. You sound like a stalker."

Shane shrugged. "Well, how else am I supposed to keep up with her? I can't call her up and ask how the designs on the fall line are going. Though apparently someone should have because that went south."

"Yeah, I'd like her to tell us something more than it all went to hell," Bay admitted. "How can we help solve the problem if we don't know the extent of it?"

Jamie's head shook. "Nope. Don't you put it like that. Have you spent a lot of time around women like Brooke? I suspect not. They don't want you to solve their problems. They want you to listen to them. To be sympathetic and then feed them chocolate or whatever their preferred sweet of the week is. They definitely don't want you making reasonable suggestions."

"You told a pregnant woman you thought the tea she was drinking was upsetting her stomach," Trev shot back. "Rookie move, my man. Because she came right back with 'oh, it's the green tea and not the eight pound baby.'"

Jamie's face flushed. "I was trying to help. She won't listen to Noah because apparently the pregnant dogs and cows he's handled over the last decade aren't the same. She barely listens to Caleb. She says she'll talk to him when he pushes a baby out of his dick. She treats Rachel like a wisewoman. I don't think her inability to make birth control work should be more important than Caleb's medical degree."

"So don't offer to help?" He wasn't getting into the pregnancy stuff. They were far from that. He just wanted her to acknowledge she liked him in an I'm-not-trying-to-piss-my-brothers-off way. "Because I was mostly going to kick the shit out of the asshole who stole her designs and then told her if she wanted to move up in the company, she should blow him."

"What?" Shane sounded outraged.

"Yeah, I probably should have led with that," Bay replied. "But I didn't want to upset her."

"I want a name," Shane demanded.

Trev stood up straighter. "All right, now this is where you can't fix the problem for her. You have to listen to her and accept her feelings and tell her how much you sympathize with her."

He had not expected that reaction from his boss. Trev seemed so protective. Not only of his kids and Beth. He was protective of Bo and everyone on the G. "I shouldn't defend her? I'm going to be honest. That'll be hard for me. I'm not sure what we're here for if we can't handle that situation."

Jamie shook his head. "Not what he's saying."

Trev continued. "You listen and hold her and then we quietly take a trip to the city and that fucker gets jumped. Now the key to this is to not take credit. You will want to say something like 'this is for Brooke' or 'don't touch my woman again.' Do not. You take him down in the form of a dude in a back alley whose features he can't remember. But you never tell her. If she sees a news report, you nod and say yeah, baby, we always knew karma would get him. She doesn't need to know that you were karma."

"But we're going to need a name, and I think maybe the way to get her to open up is to show her how nice it can be to have two boyfriends." Shane pulled out their cell. "I'll call and order some dinner, and then we can work on her room."

"You boys let me know when you need to take that trip. I'm sure there's something we can do in New York," Trev said, heading for the door.

"Yeah, like hiding because my wife might kill me." Jamie followed him, talking as they both walked out the door. "I really was worried about her ankles."

"I told you. You say nothing but 'yes, baby' and 'damn, you look pretty.'" Trev's voice cut off.

Shane was quiet for a moment, his eyes on the door that had just closed. "You sure this is what you want?"

"Brooke? I thought we talked about this."

"No, I mean the whole foreman thing," Shane replied. "Of course we want Brooke, but we have to figure out what to do when she inevitably wants to go back to the city. You've never been able to work in a city."

"Then I won't work." He knew it in his bones. "Or I'll find a way. She's everything. I know you don't understand this impulse of mine."

"It's called genius. It's called a gift. It's not an impulse. It's who you are and what you do." Shane's stare nearly burned through him. "You have a damn calling, Bay."

"She's more important." He didn't want to think about this right now. "We'll figure it out."

"I don't think we should go into this thing without a plan."

"Or you can chill." His brother could be over the top when it came to staying in control. "Look, let's take it one day at a time."

Shane started for the door. "Those days are going to go real fast, and she'll be walking out the door before we know it if we don't figure out what we can offer her that competes with her career. Not a lot of fashion designers here in Bliss. Anyway, I'll order the food and get things ready for the picnic. If you need me, I'll be out at the storage shed."

"Shane," he began.

His brother turned and gave him a slight smile. "No worries, right? We go with the flow."

"That's not what…" Bay began. But his brother was gone.

He stared at the door for a moment. What had he missed? He didn't usually miss cues from Shane because Shane always explained it to him. Or did he? Did Bay roll through life expecting his brother would be there? What was in his brother's head?

He took a long breath and banished the thought. He had some time.

He pulled out his sketchbook, the one he'd been working in for the last couple of months. It had been fresh and clean when they'd taken the jobs at the Kingman Ranch, and now he was down to four or five pages left. It made him oddly anxious. When he got this deep in a sketchbook, he kind of wanted to start a new one. To feel fresh and new. This one chronicled the last year of their lives. There were sketches of Kale Kingman lording over his land like some Greek statue. A drawing of one of the only female hands he'd worked with there. He studied it for a moment. She was walking away from the main house with the saddest look on her face. He'd taken a mental picture and thought he'd done a good job capturing all the chaos going on as the woman was walking toward the truck that would take her to the bus stop.

The later pictures were of Bliss. There was one of everyone sitting in Stella's in the early morning light. One of Trev and Bo on their horses, riding out to work. One of Beth and her children in the sunlight.

One of Shane standing alone in the bunkhouse. It had been a question of light at the time. He'd liked how the sun lit his brother up like a halo, but now that he was looking at it there was a loneliness to the drawing, an ache for something. For a home.

How hard had all the wandering been on his brother? He'd never thought about it but had Shane ever had a real home? One where he was welcome and loved simply for who he was and not what he could do?

What if Brooke could give him that love?

What if he couldn't handle living in the city? What if he couldn't breathe?

Well, he was here now. He wasn't thinking about that. He pulled out his pencil and started to draw his perfect future.

Chapter Seven

Brooke stared at the sketches the last designer left behind and decided Cleo was the luckiest director in the history of time. "None of this works. I understand you're modernizing *Three Sisters*, but did she even read the play?"

Cleo sat back in the makeup chair. The Bliss Rep Theater didn't have a ton of office space, so she was working in the large dressing room the cast shared. "I won't lie to you. We fought about it. A lot. I think it's one of the reasons she left. She was, as she put it, an artiste. I think the whole guy thing was just an excuse."

"Well, I like to think I'm an artist, but I also have to serve the customer. In this case the play itself is the customer." She'd watched the rehearsal and thought she'd gotten the vibes Cleo was throwing out. Though they'd modernized Chekhov's play, Cleo still had the heart of it in the production. What if she could do the same? At first it had been a simple way to get her mind off her trouble. A way to justify being here and staying for a couple of weeks. She had a job to do. It wasn't about Shane and Bay. She was just hanging with them while she was here. That's all.

She wasn't sure her friends were buying that but at lunch they'd all nodded and agreed that it was good to take a sabbatical.

Could she call it a sabbatical when it hadn't been her choice?

"So what are you thinking? Usually you would have months and months, but we're running short on time. It's why I decided to not do it as a period piece. This way we can order the things we need that we don't have," Cleo offered. "Not that I have much of a budget."

She wasn't sure she needed much of one. She'd worked with very little before. "I'll figure it out. I want to take a look at what we have. Is it all here?"

"Yes, though the older pieces are kept upstairs. I'll leave you a key so you can come and go as you please." Cleo stood and grabbed her crossbody bag. "I can't tell you how much I appreciate this. I know it's kind of beneath you."

She looked up. "It's not, you know. I can't believe you haven't heard the rumors by now. Everyone else has."

Cleo sobered. "Yeah, you didn't mention that the other night. You know it's okay. We've all been there."

"We've all had our work stolen from us by a sexual harassing asshole?"

Cleo sent her a sympathetic look. "Unfortunately, yeah. I work in the creative world, too, though it's not just us. It's kind of what it means to be a woman. I wish it wasn't true and maybe some of us come out of it without ever having to see the harsh side of life, but I know what happened to me. I was straight out of college with a degree in theater. I got on at a really great theater group in LA and quickly became an assistant director. I was told how amazing I was. How they couldn't live without me. When the play moved to Broadway, they cut me. I staged three quarters of that play because the director was working on a TV show at the same time. But let me tell you, he took all the credit and didn't change a thing when the show had its Broadway run. He didn't bother to mention me in his Tony speech."

Her heart ached for her friend. "I'm so sorry."

Cleo nodded. "Me, too, because I loved that show but what I learned was no one is coming to save me. I have to save myself. We work in a field where the goal posts are different for men and women. From directing to acting. Everyone loves an ingenue. A twenty-something is an it girl. A forty-something is lucky to play someone's mom. So actresses learned that they had to become producers if they wanted anything to change. I'm done playing by their rules. I'm taking the money from this gig and borrowing some more and I'm shooting a couple of short films. I'll see where I go from there, but I know one thing. I won't let them drag me down. I won't let them take my dreams. If I'm not welcome in their world, then I'll build another."

Tears pierced Brooke's eyes because she understood. "It feels overwhelming. Gemma explained suing the company probably won't do anything but cost me money and my family a lot of trouble. I can't exactly start my own line."

Cleo pointed to the slouchy comfy top Brooke had put on this morning. It was a lightly woven fabric that managed to be roomy and also cling where she wanted it to because she'd tailored it. It looked nice with jeans. "I don't know. I would buy one of those. Did you make the jeans, too?"

Brooke shrugged. "I like to work with denim but I'll be honest, I've gotten bored lately. It's why I went off script and designed the ski and leisure line my asshole boss stole."

Cleo started for the door. "Well, think about what I said. If you ever decide to roll the dice on costume design and you want to work for very little money, I'm your girl. What I will promise is credit for every design, every stitch you make. I guess what I would promise is to be a real team. To make art together. To entertain the people like the family I hope we all become. Good night, Brooke, and thank you again. Lock up when you're done. Not that anyone would come in, but Mel claims there's an intergalactic war going on and this would be a good place to hide. I would love to live in that man's head for a day. I wonder if he would let me do a documentary?"

Oh, she would bet no. "It would have to be classified."

Cleo grinned. "And that's what would be fun about it. 'Night." She turned back. "Uhm, apparently you have visitors. Oooo, and they brought dinner. Again don't do anything I wouldn't do with two gorgeous men."

She sat up straight as Shane strode through, giving Cleo a nod. He had a big basket in his hand and Bay followed him. Nope. They hadn't gotten less attractive. She'd kind of hoped in the stark light of day she would have a different reaction to the two men she meant to use and lose and now was fake engaged to, though no one actually believed it. She was kind of the worst and they were…here. Here and big and masculine, and they smelled good. Her stomach grumbled a little because she'd ordered grilled fish for lunch. It was excellent but it wasn't very filling and she'd walked all over town because Fuber didn't run during school hours. She could only catch a ride between when the Farley brothers were out of school and when the devil decided to wake up. So four to ten was her only spot.

She needed a car.

Or she needed to ask for help.

It smelled so good. Why had she picked the fish when she'd wanted a burger? She knew. She still had that voice in her head telling her if she was thinner, they would take her more seriously. Not that any male designer had to look like a model. "What are you doing here? I told you I would be working late."

"You have to eat." Shane set the basket on the table.

Bay stared down at the big book of design sketches the former designer had left. He frowned. "Is this a new line you're working on?"

She shuddered at the thought. "No. I love an eighties influence, but I wouldn't do this to any woman. It's like she took all the bad things about the eighties and put them into one outfit." She turned the page. "She seemed to be trying to represent nostalgia in each of the three sisters. I don't hate the idea, but I don't think she thought it through enough. Olga is Alexis from *Dynasty*. I'm worried she took her inspiration for Irina from watching nineties music videos. And Masha is wearing mom jeans. It's a big old mess."

"Good. Those didn't look like you," Bay replied, stepping back.

She was curious. There was a lot they hadn't gone over the night before. "What do I look like? Design wise, I mean. You're an artist, right? I'd like your opinion."

"He's really good," Shane said.

"It's not the same. My job is easier. All I have to do is follow my eyes and instinct. I draw or paint or sculpt the things that speak to me. You have to make something functional beautiful. Those designs are neither," Bay explained. "If I had to describe your aesthetic, it would be clean lines and classic vibes, but with a nod to the future and functionality. Your clothes are wearable."

Yes, he had her down, and that was the problem. "I design the clothes I like to wear, and apparently that means I'm not high fashion."

"Very few people wear high fashion," Bay said with a shake of his head as though he didn't understand the problem. "I mean I know some people like to see pictures of stars on the red carpet, but I would think you would make way more from designing something a lot of people are going to wear."

"Well, you would be wrong." She watched as Shane set the basket on one of the makeup tables. "I'm also into tailoring clothes. Like the shirt Shane's wearing. If I took it in slightly at the waist, it would create a better silhouette. I suppose that's not so important to you, but for a woman going into the office, how the shirt wears can be important. It can make the difference between looking professional or slightly messy. But try to explain to an haute couture company that we need to consider how our blouses will fit larger breasts and they laugh because our sizes don't go larger than a twelve. If you're bigger than that, they don't want you."

"Is that why your clothes always look so good?" Shane sank down to the chair Cleo had recently occupied. "Do you tailor them yourself?"

"Yes, and I know it's not possible in mass market clothes, but it's what I love. It's why I adore designing wedding gowns." She loved working with actual people instead of simply designing and pulling in some wafer-thin model who wouldn't ever wear it. "I designed Jen Talbot's gown and did all the bridesmaid's dresses. Callie still wears hers."

"I heard Lucy was getting married." Bay's hands went to the back of her neck, and she sighed as he started to rub her shoulders. That felt amazing. "Are you going to design hers?"

She let her eyes drift closed. She'd thought she needed this quiet time to contemplate how to handle them. What if she just went with it? What if she did exactly what Gemma told her to do and took this time to rest and explore the possibilities and enjoy herself for once? She'd already disappointed her brothers. She wasn't sure how she could make things worse, although they had that dinner coming up. "Lucy's wearing Ty's mother's dress. It's lovely and looks good on her. I'll tailor it. I'll have a harder time with the boys because they'll want to rent tuxes, and I can't fix those." She would use temporary means if she had to so Lucy got the absolute best photos. "I'm going to help Sabrina and her sister shop for dresses. We either have to go into Alamosa or Colorado Springs, or buy one off the Internet and hope for the best. If we were in New York, we would have all the choices."

Bay seemed to think about that for a moment. "I know a lot of choices sounds good, but I can get overwhelmed."

Shane nodded. "He can. They put Netflix in the bunkhouse and Bay keeps shuffling through but never actually watches anything."

Bay shrugged. "What if there's a better movie?"

"It's not always about what's better. It's about how we make use of the experience, but I get what you're saying. I've lived in the city for the last couple of years, and I don't understand how fast the world is going until I come home and smell the pine and hear the wind rustle through the grass in the back field."

"Is it home?" Shane asked. "Because for me home is your place. The place you always want to be."

"I suppose Bliss is the place I will always come back to. It's my touchstone, where I know I belong." Even if her brothers were mad at her. Even if Rachel had been in on the whole PI debacle. She knew she was being stubborn, but she needed time. And she wanted to know these guys a little better. If she was staying with them for a couple of weeks, she might as well talk to them. She would probably hear a bunch of stories about how they were high school superheroes and moved on to rodeo superheroes, where all the buckle bunnies fawned over them. "Where's home for you?"

Shane shrugged. "Don't really have one."

"Our parents died a couple of years back." Bay seemed to think about it for a moment. "Well, over a decade, I guess. We were in our teens and went into the system because we didn't have more family."

"Your parents," Shane corrected quietly.

"He was your dad, too." Bay's hands kept moving on her shoulders and up her neck. Gentle but firm.

"He was my biological dad. He didn't do much for me beyond that." Shane opened the basket and pulled out a bottle of wine. A familiar bottle.

"Oh, that's my favorite," she said.

"I know." There was a smile on his face as he used the corkscrew to open it. "The good thing about a small town having few choices is every shopkeeper knows what their customers like. The liquor store always brings some in when they know you're coming."

"How would they know? It was a…" She sighed. "My brothers. I would bet they keep a couple of bottles, too."

"Probably. I was also told you like cheese and this one… What did she say?" Shane asked, passing her a glass and then taking out some plates.

"It pairs well with the wine. That's what the beekeeper lady said," Bay replied, his thumbs rubbing over her skin.

She was relaxing but more than that, she was getting aroused. She took a sip of the wine and it was utter perfection. Crisp and cold, with notes of green apple and pineapple. Delicious.

What had Shane said? She opened her eyes and watched him unwrap the cheese and crackers. "You said you were half brothers and you shared a dad. But you're close in age."

Shane nodded. "When my mother realized Dad wasn't going to leave Bay's mom, she dumped me on their doorstep and never looked back."

"She left you?" Brooke sat up.

Shane put the cheese plate where she could get to it and then sat back down, pulling her feet on his lap. "I don't love talking about this so if we're going to, you have to let me do something I do like doing."

He pulled her shoes off and then she groaned as his strong hands moved across her aching feet.

This was dangerous. The night before had been about passion and crazy lust. This was something different. This was caring. She should set boundaries. She should tell them she was going to the Movie Motel or let Lucy get her a room at the lodge. The last thing she should do was let them surround her with sweetness and allow their stories to touch her.

"She left you?" She couldn't do it. The truth of the matter was she wanted this time with them. No matter what the outcome would eventually be.

"She did." Shane seemed intent on making her bonelessly relaxed. She hadn't realized how much walking today had affected her. Or maybe some of it was the ruthlessly athletic sex she'd had with them. "I was a kid. I don't remember much about her, though my stepmom did like to talk about her a lot. According to her, my biological mother's professions included whore, homewrecker, and certified gold digger."

Bay snorted. "Our father never had any gold to dig. I still haven't figured out how that hypocritical jackass managed to get two women to sleep with him."

She was confused and a little horrified at the thought of a baby being left behind by his mother. Her own mother had died and her dad had taken off, but she knew her mom loved her, and she'd had her brothers. They hadn't left her on someone's doorstep, and it would have been easy to. "They took you in? I mean you were a kid. You didn't cause the situation."

"I think a psychologist would say the situation was complex," Shane replied like they were simply talking about what he'd done with his day and not how awful his childhood had been.

"What he means is dear old dad was a deacon at the fundamentalist church we were forced to attend," Bay continued. "The preacher and his wife found out about Shane and basically informed my mother that she couldn't consider herself a woman of God if she didn't take Shane in and forgive her husband. She had to stand in front of the congregation and forgive him and ask for his forgiveness since a man didn't sin if he didn't have reason. You know what they didn't make her do? Ask for forgiveness for beating a kid because she couldn't hurt anyone else."

Her heart threatened to break. She thought they'd likely left behind a nice home so they could party and live the cowboy life. She knew men who did. They worked for a while and then played until they needed more cash. They had a woman in every city. Sometimes two or three.

"You didn't start in this life because you wanted to, did you? If no one took you in, you aged out of the system." She knew a bit about foster care. It wasn't great for the eighteen-year-old.

"My father's family ran a small cattle ranch. My dad didn't work it. He was a salesman. Mom was a stay at home, but they would send us both out to the ranch on weekends and summers, and Grandad would teach us. He was an old man and bitter because he missed our grandmother so much, but he did what he could," Bay explained.

"Teaching us how to work the ranch was how he showed he loved us. I don't claim my father, but I loved my grandfather," Shane admitted. "The time we spent at the ranch was heaven for me."

"Why didn't you stay?"

"He was too old to handle a kid, and by the time I wasn't a handful, I realized I needed to stay home." Shane's voice was so steady.

Bay's fingers found her hair, and he moved them along her scalp. "He didn't go live with our grandfather because he thought if he did, my mother would take out her rage on me. And he was probably right. I know I'm the artistic one, but Shane knew how hard it would be on me when he was ten years old. He made the choice to take the abuse so I didn't have to."

"Stop," she said, unable to simply sit there. Did they think they could tell her all of this and she would just… Emotion threatened to overwhelm her.

They weren't party boys. They might tease her brothers and be assholes from time to time, but wasn't everyone? They were real men with real problems, and so far they had treated her like she was made of gold.

They treated her like she was the one who got all the affection and comfort, and she didn't have to give it back unless it was sexually.

Both their hands came off her like the well-trained Doms they were. Even though they hadn't gone over their limits or set hard rules, she knew she could trust them.

It was herself she didn't trust, but that didn't mean a thing right now. What mattered was what they'd gone through.

What Shane had done for his brother.

Sometimes words failed and all a person had was touch. She stood and she saw Shane's face fall as though he thought she was rejecting them.

She moved to him, putting her hands on both his shoulders and then lowering herself onto his lap so she was straddling him.

His expression relaxed, and his hands found her hips. "You're not disgusted by my childhood."

"By how you were treated? Absolutely." She studied him for a moment. He looked a lot like his brother, but there were stark lines in his face that seemed softer on Bay. Like life had carved him up in a way it hadn't Bay. She ran her hands over his hair and watched him. She couldn't imagine how sweet he would have looked as a child, how vulnerable. How he'd been forced to grow up quickly, and even at a young age he'd made choices to sacrifice for the brother he loved. He was a good man. She leaned over and kissed him, bringing their mouths together in the connection she didn't even know she'd been looking for.

This time it wasn't lust that moved her body. It was something more, something infinitely dangerous, but she couldn't stop herself.

"Tell me you came here for this," she whispered on his lips before running her tongue there.

He shuddered under her, fingers tightening on her hips, and she could feel his cock come to life. "We came here for you. We wanted to make sure you got dinner and had company if you wanted."

"And we came here for this." Bay pushed back her hair and kissed the nape of her neck, sending shivers down her spine. "We came because we can't stay away now that we've had you, now that we know how fucking right this feels. Shane was nervous about telling you how we grew up. I told him you would never think less of him. I told him I was the one who should be worried. I was his older brother."

This was the way to talk. With their hands on her, with knowledge that they were together and connected, at least for now. For now she wasn't alone. She wasn't fighting some good fight she couldn't win. She was riding a wave of feeling, and they were right there with her.

She didn't have to think about the future, but she had some things to say about their past. "You were a kid, too. Did you ignore what your mom did?"

"He fought for me. He put himself on the line for me," Shane confessed as he ran his hands under her shirt. "When he was old enough, he explained to her that if she kept hitting me, he would act out. He would do terrible things, and everyone would know what an awful mother she was. Not because she hit me. Not because she couldn't love me."

"I told her I'd make sure I got myself arrested. I would drink and steal and do whatever I could to make her look as bad as possible. I told her I would make shit up." He licked the shell of her ear. "She believed me. Up until then I was her shining light, and my only rebellion was to share my room with my brother."

They had protected each other even when they were kids.

What would they do for a lover? Would they let a lover into their secret world, or would she just be a distraction for a time?

In that moment, it didn't matter. "I want you to play with me. I want to know what it means to be yours."

Bay's hand twisted in her hair, sending a thrill along her spine and straight to her pussy. "You want us to top you. You want a couple of hours where you don't have to think about anything but what we can do to your body?"

She was worried it was way more than her body that was engaged. "Yes."

Shane grinned. "Now you've done it."

Bay picked her up. He hauled her right out of his brother's arms and lifted her up in the air. She gasped as he clutched her to his chest. "Then we should take this to the main stage."

* * * *

Shane watched as his brother carried Brooke up the stairs.

He liked this theater, though it could use some work. Mostly cosmetic, but there were a couple of places where he could make things safer than they were.

What didn't need any work at all was Brooke Harper. She was stunning, but then she always took his breath away.

They'd set the stage. Apparently they were in early rehearsals since there wasn't a bunch of set pieces on the stage. Just a bunch of tape. Blocking. He thought that was what they called it. Blocking rehearsals. No matter what the technical term, it gave them a lot of space to work with. There was a desk backstage that moved easily because it was on wheels. It was exactly the right height. He pulled it along and placed it center stage, where the light would hit her perfectly. He took the kit from his brother.

"Take off your clothes." Bay stepped back and frowned. "I want to see her tied up. I didn't bring much more than a basic kit because we were going to be good boys tonight. I don't have any rope. We spent the afternoon making sure her room was ready instead of prepping our kits."

They'd only made sure to bring one specific toy. One that would prepare her for what they all wanted.

That had been a mistake because Brooke seemed to like their bad-boy sides. They'd been so busy trying to make things perfect for her that they'd forgotten to be prepared. Luckily he rather thought this place would be a treasure trove. "Where are the props, Brooke? And will Cleo be pissed if she finds out how we're using her props?"

The last thing he wanted to do was get her in trouble with the new boss.

Brooke's eyes had gone wide as she stood there in the spotlight. "You set up a room for me? We're not sharing?"

Bay frowned like he didn't understand.

Shane moved in and loomed over her. She came to his chin, and he loved the way her head tilted up to look at him. "We are absolutely sharing a room, and your things are already in the closet. There are two in the primary. Bay and I will share one. No, he's talking about the sewing room we set up. Beth and Hope tried their hand and didn't like it, but they still had all the equipment."

Her jaw dropped slightly. "A sewing machine?"

"All kinds of things, and there's more in storage if you need it. This way you don't have to be here to work." Or maybe she would want the escape. "Not if you don't want to."

Her mouth curved in the sweetest smile. "I want to. I miss my machine. It's getting shipped to me, but it'll be a while before it gets here." She looked to Bay as she reached for Shane's hand. "Thank you. I'm sure I'll love it. Did Cleo lock the door?"

"I'll check." Bay started down the stairs. "You get undressed."

Shane kissed her forehead. "I'm going to find some rope if you think it's okay."

"I think Cleo would find it amusing," Brooke replied and then sobered. "I had a rough day, Shane. I would like to forget for a while."

This was what they could offer her. Respite. Calm. A place where she didn't have to worry.

"Do you want it soft and sweet?" Shane asked.

She shook her head. "I want to play. I want what we started last night. I know you have a lot of experience…"

Shane stared down at her. "We're with you, Brooke. For as long as you'll let us be, we're yours. No other women and no other subs. We do have experience, but sharing it with you makes me so fucking happy. We started this because Stef offered us training. Well, he offered Bay training, and I came along for the ride."

"He offered us both training," Bay said, walking back up the stairs. "He might have liked my art, but he saw something in you, too."

"He saw I needed to find some control," Shane conceded. "I'll be honest, at first all I cared about was having sex. And kinky sex. Meeting women who didn't pretend, who were upfront and honest about what they wanted. It felt like a whole new world, and I reveled in it, but the last couple of years, I've wanted something more. I don't want to walk in a club and select a partner for the night like I'm picking out a treat. I want a woman who walks in there with us every time. Who we can get to know so well it's second nature to please her. So I don't want to hear about how inexperienced you are. I want our experiences for now to be together, and that means you have to tell us what you want."

"I want you to be rough with me. I want it hard and kinky. I don't want to feel like myself."

"What do you think you are, Brooke?"

Her expression went stubborn. "Weak. I feel useless. I feel like I wasted my brothers' time and money. I feel like a failure, and I want to feel…wanted."

Bay had gone still beside him, and he knew what his brother was thinking. If she wanted some discipline, this was absolutely the way to get it.

But Shane was the one who would talk first and then spank. The last thing she needed was to think she was right and that she was being punished for it. "You think you're weak because you got fired?"

She nodded.

"You tried to fight." He knew a little about it. "You went to HR."

"Yes, but…" she began.

"Did you shrug and cry and walk away? Or did you meet with Gemma this afternoon for something other than catching up?"

"She told me how hard it would be." Brooke sniffled but seemed to fight off the emotion. "I can't put my family through it."

"So let me get this straight," Shane began. "You were so talented that some asshole stole your designs and the company stood behind him. That's not about you being weak. That's about them being corrupt. Do you know how many times I've seen people fired because the boss wanted to cover up his own mistakes? Hell, if I go by your standards, I'm the weakest man in the world because I took all of my stepmother's abuse."

"You were a child," she argued.

"And you were an employee they took advantage of," Shane replied.

"I signed the contract."

"You were naïve, not fucking weak." Bay sounded grumpier than usual.

Probably because he wanted to get straight to the sex, and now they had to get creative.

The good news was dinner would wait, and while Shane might not be known for his artistry, he could get real creative about this.

"I need you to understand that what we're about to do to you has nothing to do with you being weak and everything to do with you being rough on yourself. I would never allow anyone to say those things about you," Shane said in a quiet but firm voice. "You are so lucky we're not home because I suspect I could find a hundred torture devices there. But don't worry. I'll come up with something."

She bit her bottom lip. "Torture?"

"Discipline," Bay corrected. "Punishment. I do have one thing. I was planning to plug you while we're here. Since it's going to take a while and I don't want to wait forever. I intended to ask you to wear it while you're working and then take it out later tonight. Now I wish I'd brought the exotic lube."

"I'll be good with the regular lube, Bay." She looked slightly panicked, but Shane would bet she wasn't thinking about how weak she was now. "I want the plug. I want to be able to have you both. I'm sorry. I'm still reeling. I'm very strong."

Brat. "Not what I heard a few minutes ago. Now strip and stand directly in the spotlight. I'll be back, and I better see a lot of skin."

He went backstage and sure enough, there was some rope. A lot of it, actually. He selected the thinnest of the set and placed it on that rolling desk. He moved it out to where Brooke stood, settling it behind her and locking the wheels down. The wheels that needed something. He would oil them up, but only after he'd handled her.

She'd been a good girl. She stood there, her clothes tossed to the side. Bay was being an asshole, standing outside the light where she couldn't see him.

Shane approved.

It was time for some role-playing.

"Good evening," Shane said to the non-existent audience. "I have an offering tonight. A pretty virgin who needs a good fuck to make her a woman."

Brooke's eyes went wide. "We're going that route?"

"She talks too much," Bay said from the shadows. "You're going to have to convince me to spend my hard-earned money on her. She's lovely, but I suspect she's trouble."

"Trouble?" Brooke asked.

It was time to show her how they were playing tonight. "Give me your hands. It's obvious to me you don't know how to behave at an auction. Do you understand that I'm selling you tonight? To the highest bidder."

She giggled. "There's only one bidder, and I don't think he's got a lot."

He could correct this behavior. "Turn and place your hands palms down on the desk. If you say another snarky thing to me, I can find a ball gag."

She stared for a moment and then turned. "I did say I wanted it kinky, and we are on a stage, so I suppose role-playing is par for the course here."

"So is discipline. Bend over further. Ass in the air. I want him to see it," Shane commanded. "You're a disrespectful brat who insults a woman I happen to think highly of."

"Uhm, I think that was me so shouldn't that…"

He wasn't listening. He swatted her ass, and not in an erotic fashion. He meant for her to feel it for hours. They'd played with it last night, but she seemed to need more now, and he was going to give it to her. He heard her gasp but she didn't move, merely curled her hands around the desk. He gave her a hard ten and then stepped back.

"She handles discipline well," Bay said, his voice deep.

"She's not well trained, but she's instinctively good at giving a man what he needs. And you can't possibly complain about how lovely she is. Look at that ass." Shane smacked it again. "It pinkens up beautifully, and you'll find she needs a bite of pain, as I'll demonstrate. Spread your legs wider."

She complied, and he could see how her nipples were hard, and he would bet she was already getting wet.

"You said she was a virgin."

"That doesn't mean I haven't trained her," Shane replied. He liked role-play. It was another thing Stef had introduced them to, though they hadn't played this scenario before. He had participated in many a chase scenario. He had a vision of Brooke running through one of the clubs. She would be naked, and they would chase her down and have their way with her.

He was so hard he could barely breathe.

He'd done a lot of kinky things during his time in clubs, and the truth was it had become dull to him. The idea of introducing her to this lifestyle, to get to experience it all with her, made him feel alive in a way he hadn't in a long time.

"You've trained her to pleasure you?" Bay asked the question in a throaty tone that let Shane know he wasn't unaffected.

Oh, he knew where this was going. "I did. She's too beautiful to keep all to myself, and I knew how much she would bring at an auction like this."

"Every man here is watching her," Bay said. "They're all desperate to be the man who has her, but I need to be sure. I want to see what she knows. I want a skilled woman. What can she do to you after you tie her up and she can't use those soft hands? I personally have specific tastes. I'd like to know if she's been prepared for anal sex."

His cock twitched in his jeans. He wanted nothing more than to play with her ass, to get her ready. If he was right, no one had even played with it before. She'd had boyfriends, but it seemed like his sub hadn't been adventurous up to this point.

Then they could fuck her with the plug securely in her pretty hole.

After he tied her up and made his present look stunning.

He fucking loved rope. He loved spending time trussing up a sub, but even that had lost its appeal lately.

Not with her. "Stand up. Turn around. I want them all to watch."

She did as he asked, and he could see how deeply affected she'd been by the spanking and the playing. Her nipples were tight, her skin flushed. Her eyes were softer now, filled with a sweet lust he intended to appreciate to the fullest.

She stood there and let him wrap his ropes around her body, let him twist and pull and form a rope dress of sorts. The ropes emphasized her breasts and waist. Another bound her hands together. It would make it easy to hang her on a hook, leaving her on her toes while he and Bay played with her.

They didn't have a hook here, and that was an oversight.

Her hair caressed the tops of her breasts as he eased her to a kneeling position.

"Yes, she's quite lovely like that." Bay stayed in the shadows, keeping the illusion up. "Every man watching her has his hand wrapped around his own cock right now."

He bet his brother did. He opened the kit and brought out the small plug they'd bought specifically for her. They'd been feeling optimistic when they'd gotten the whole set. It wasn't like they talked about it, but they'd both known it was all for her. Now that he thought about it, they'd spent quite a bit of their non-hefty incomes replacing their kits so everything would be new for Brooke.

And that was before she'd said yes to even having coffee with them.

If she only knew how far he'd go for her…

"Ass in the air again. The man wants to see how your asshole takes a plug," Shane commanded.

A shudder went through Brooke's body, but it was easy to see it had nothing to do with distaste. She was into it. She liked the role-play. "But shouldn't I get to see him? Shouldn't I see the man who's going to take my innocence?"

Oh, they could play so hard. He was going to get her a nun's habit and play Viking raiders with her. Right now, though, he was playing the hard-ass brothel owner. He gripped her gently by the neck. He would put a collar on her one of these days. A pretty signal that they were together. "You don't have any rights here. You're my possession to be used and sold at my whim. You are a gorgeous sex toy, and it's time to put you to use."

Her eyes narrowed. "I should hate that."

He grinned. He wasn't the dude who didn't break character. It was all fun. All games to play with the woman in his life. "Because you know it's not really true. It's okay. We can play like this and you'll go back to bossing us around when it's done." He leaned over and kissed her nose. "Did I mention we brought fried chicken and pots of banana pudding? I'm going to properly feed and worship my sex toy. I thought about you all day, baby. This is nothing but play, and you can stop it anytime you like."

"And you're going to share me with your brother," she whispered as though she had to make sure.

"I am. Are you okay? We also don't have to play at all. We can stay at your acceptable level of kink."

She held up her tied hands. "I think you can push my boundaries a bit." Her chin came up. "And what if I don't want to be sold to the highest bidder?"

Oh, she definitely wanted to play, and she apparently wanted more discipline. He reached out and tweaked her nipple, giving it a hard twist. She gasped, the sound sending another wave of arousal through him. "Put your ass in the air. You fuck who I tell you to fuck, baby. You're mine and I decide how and when to share you."

He heard a growl from the shadows.

He snorted. "Yeah, you're going to have to soothe him. He sometimes takes things way too seriously. Now do as I asked and get ready for the plug. I think I have a serious buyer, and he wants to make sure you're up to his standards."

Bay was usually extremely patient. He was happy to be the guy in the background when it came to role-playing. The fact that he didn't want to stand back and watch was a revelation.

Brooke bit her bottom lip and assumed the position, turning her head to look up at him. "Master Shane, is this how you want me?"

He wanted her bratty and sweet and irritating in the best way because in a single day she'd given him more purpose than he'd had in years.

She was leaning on the table, her forearms flat. He considered her form as his brother joined them.

"I think I'd like her spine a bit straighter." Bay's eyes were hot, taking in every inch of her gorgeous flesh. "And legs a bit further apart. That's right. I want to watch as your little asshole puckers around my plug. You're going to fight me, but I'll win. You'll take it and then later you'll have my cock. I'm going to fuck you every way I can. I assure you I'm going to get my money's worth."

Another shuddering sigh came from her. She loved the dirty talk, the play. He was sure there was some psychology behind it, but all that mattered to him was it worked for her.

Bay slid his hand between her legs, and Shane caught the whimper that came from Brooke's lips. She tilted her pelvis back as though trying to get Bay's exploring fingers right where she wanted them.

And that gave him the perfect opportunity to slap her ass a couple more times.

"You will not steal an orgasm," he commanded and then brought his hand down on her cheeks, one and then the other, alternating back and forth until he heard her cry out.

He stepped back, worried he hurt her.

Bay shook his head. "She's into it. Trust me. Her pussy is so fucking wet. I would give her what she needs, but not until she proves what a good purchase she's going to be. I won't have an untrained sex toy in my home. She'll prove she can take the plug or I'll put a clamp on her clit and see how she likes it. Do you understand, Brooke?"

She replied quickly, her fingers curling around the desk as

though she had to hold on to be still. "I do. I'll be good. I won't move again. I'll take what my Masters give me."

Oh, that word went straight to his cock. He knew she was the smart one, the talented one, but he could serve her here and earn that name.

"Once I pay your price, you'll be mine." Bay said the words with a dark tone, but he shrugged Shane's way. "I can learn."

So could he. They had her trussed up and bent over, and she did seem to want the whole ménage experience. Shane shucked off his clothes. "Oh, Mr. Kent, I'm only selling half of her. No one man could possibly please her. She needs two."

Bay chuckled and picked up the plug and lube. "I suspect you're going to show me how we can share this piece of heaven between us."

He knew exactly how he intended to do it. He was glad the desk looked sturdy and someone had thought to put brakes on the wheels because it didn't move as he hopped on it and positioned himself. Brooke's head came up and she licked at her lips as she obviously figured out what he wanted from her.

"But my hands are tied," she said quietly.

He palmed his cock and noticed Bay was prepping the plug.

She was going to need a distraction. "I don't care about your hands. Open your mouth. You said you would take what we wanted to give you. You'll take my cock and then you'll take the plug and then I suspect your partial new owner is going to give you a little cock, too."

"Big cock," she said with a grin. "I suspect New Master has a big, gorgeous dick. Like yours."

"I'm glad you like them, baby." He intended to make sure she didn't want another for the rest of her life. "Open up. Take me inside. I'm going to fuck your mouth while he gets you ready for what we really want."

To share her. To give her everything they had and make her the center of their world.

Shane let go of all his worries as her tongue stroked over his cock.

He was right where he needed to be.

Chapter Eight

Bay stared at her backside and thanked the universe that Shane was such an overly prepared asshole. It was something they'd argued about all his life since Bay didn't see the need to plan every second and his brother had list after list. Bay knew he was kind of a weirdo and that Shane got most of the charm, but he was also the uptight one.

Of course, Shane was also the one who thought to pack more than a couple of sandwiches and some beer. He'd been smart enough to throw one of their kits in the truck so they could keep this thing moving along. After last night, his brother had known to be prepared to throw down with her wherever they happened to be.

Brooke wanted sex, wanted to feel wild for once. They could help with that, but it was a delicate dance because the last thing he wanted was for her to consider him a fuck buddy.

He had her brothers to thank for this opportunity. He had weeks with her, and he wasn't going to waste them.

"That's right. That's what I want," Shane moaned, and his fingers tangled in her hair, gripping her and showing her how he wanted her to move.

He stood there as Brooke started to suck Shane's cock. He watched for a moment, enjoying the way she moaned and her body moved. It was awkward because her hands were tied in front of her, but she didn't complain. She simply accommodated them. She let her body flow to the rhythm Shane set.

His own cock was hard and trying desperately to get out of his pants, but he was taking his time. He wanted to make this moment last.

She was so fucking gorgeous. He could practically see her as a painting. A sculpture. Simply drawn.

He had the most insistent urge to sit back and draw, memorialize the moment.

Instead, he concentrated on the task at hand. If he was caught between his artistic urges and the needs of his cock, his cock was winning this time.

He slicked up the plug with the lube his brother had thoughtfully packed. It was a starter plug. They would need some time to get her ready for them.

How long did they have? How long until she decided to go back to the city and pursue her real life? Until she left the dumbass cowboys behind to find a husband who fit into her version of society.

He let the thought go because he'd always known they only had the now. The future was something that could be ripped away from a person. All he could count on was the present and that everything would inevitably change, and he had no choice in the matter.

But the now included her, so he would revel in it.

"This might be cold, baby," he warned before parting her cheeks. Pretty hole. His whole body tightened at the thought of having her there. "Don't tense up on me or I'll have to spank you again."

He heard her gasp as he dribbled the lube where he needed it.

She did exactly what he'd known she would do, and that was why he'd told her what the punishment would be. He wanted to spank her. Wanted that pink sheen to her cheeks to be partially from him. Shane couldn't have all the fun.

He slapped her ass, measuring the pressure. He didn't want to leave marks beyond the sheen. He wanted to leave her with a nice ache she would feel for hours, but nothing that would make her truly uncomfortable. They would find the balance between pleasure and pain that best suited her.

Shane hissed, but it was a pleasurable sound. "Don't you let him distract you. You're mine right now. Until he puts his money down, he's only playing with you. You're still mine."

His brother liked role-playing way too much. Bay had to remind himself that play was all it was, and it was for Brooke's benefit. She seemed to like it. He'd played like this with subs before, but Shane always took the lead. But damn, his inner caveman wanted to argue with Shane that she was his right here and now, and nothing was going to change it.

"Yes, Master Shane." That voice was sex and submission, and it went straight to his dick. "I know I belong to you, but I have to please Master Bay, too. He's going to pay good money for me. He's going to own me, too."

Okay, inner caveman calmed. All it took was a few sweet words from her and he was at peace and able to function properly again. He leaned over and kissed the small of her back. "This is one purchase I would never return. I'll keep this one forever, if I can."

Probably too much, but he was being honest in the moment. It was sappy, but then he was about to shove a plug up her butt, so he could soften it with some sweetness.

Shane actually gave him a damn thumbs-up. While he was getting a blow job.

There was a reason people thought they were weird. Of course weird was the kindest thing most people called them. Perverse was more common. Though not here in Bliss.

They would be perverse in New York.

He needed to stop thinking about it and concentrate on her. He had a job to do and then he got to have his time with her. Though it wasn't like he hated this job. No, playing with her was kind of what he wanted to do every day. He pressed the plug to her, gently at first, and then with a little more pressure. He watched the way her spine went straight, and it was obvious she was trying to focus on the task at hand. Excellent. He wanted her focused, but no job she was doing would completely distract her. She would be feeling the pressure as he rimmed her with the tip before pressing in and gaining ground.

"That's right, baby. I'm almost there," Shane urged, his hands in her hair.

He was almost there, too. She was opening for him. He rimmed her again and again before starting to fuck her with the plug. He watched as it disappeared and reappeared. She was steady at first and then her hips started to move, trying to find a rhythm with him even as she moved with Shane.

His brother groaned as the plug slid in fully. It was sexy as hell peeking from between her cheeks.

And it was his time. Finally. He breathed a long sigh of relief and chucked his pants as his brother finished up.

"You taste so good, Master," Brooke whispered as her tongue moved over Shane's cock, licking up every ounce.

"You're going to feel like heaven." Bay stroked his cock before rolling the condom on and taking his place behind her. Her ass wriggled as though inviting him in. Brat. He was falling so hard for her, harder than he ever thought he would. She was rapidly becoming the most important part of his world.

He lined up his cock and started to press inside.

Brooke gasped, and then she was wiggling for another reason. "It feels… I can feel the plug. It's making me so full."

"That's how it's going to be, baby," Shane whispered. He ran a hand over her hair and kissed the top of her head. "You'll feel us both, know how much we both want you. You'll know how gorgeous you are. You are so much woman, baby. You need two men to please you."

Bay pressed his cock inside, her pussy squeezing him in the most pleasurable way. This was what he'd needed all day. To be with her. To have the other half of him with them and know she accepted them both.

He let go of everything except the sensation of being inside her. The plug made her tight, dragging on his dick in the most erotic way possible. He gripped her hips and fucked her over and over. She tilted her pelvis and moaned, her pussy spasming around him. She held onto Shane as she rode out her orgasm.

And Bay found his own, pleasure causing his spine to bow, and he held on to her, giving up everything he had.

He slumped over, his cheek to her back.

"I hope you enjoy your purchase, Master Bay," Brooke said with a chuckle. "I think I'm going to like being a sex toy."

He meant to make her see they could be so much more.

* * * *

Brooke laid back, her belly pleasantly full and body still humming with the pleasure she'd gotten out of the play. How long had it been since she'd indulged the way she had tonight? In sex. In food. In being lazy, lying around with her lovers and talking about everything from their favorite foods to how many broken bones they had from years of rodeoing.

Mexican. And too many to count.

She made good enchiladas. It would be fun to cook for them. It had been a long time since she'd done that, too. She typically downed a protein shake in the morning, sucked down another for lunch, and ruined the whole thing by getting takeout on her way home because she still had work to do.

Back at House of Bianchi, she never had gorgeous men bring her fried chicken and then fuck her and feed her and lay around naked with her. It was probably a good thing since she wouldn't have gotten anything done.

"I only broke a bone once," she said, staring up at the dark ceiling. They'd turned off the spotlights and brought out a big blanket they laid out on the stage for their kinky picnic. It was kinky because she was still naked. So were they. Everyone was naked, and they'd taken turns feeding her like she was a sweet pet who needed a treat.

It shouldn't feel this good to be with them. There should be some awkwardness. It shouldn't feel so right to have her head on Bay's thigh like it was a pillow, while Shane stared down at her with the sweetest smile on his face. He held a grape to her lips, and she enjoyed the sweetness for once.

"What happened?" Bay asked.

Memory washed over her. It was easy to forget she hadn't always been such a city girl. She'd grown up in the country. "I took the dirt bike I wasn't supposed to ride. I wanted to go to my friend's house, but Max didn't have time to drive me. Normally I would have taken the four-wheeler. My brothers taught me how to drive that, and I would go all over our property and sometimes even into town since the sheriff at the time liked to look the other way. The dirt bike was a leftover from when Max and Rye were kids, but it worked so I took off myself, and turns out it's not the same as a bicycle. I wiped out right in front of Mel's place. Naturally he was on patrol and found me and took me to the hospital in Monte Vista. We didn't have a clinic back then. Mel was surprisingly good at field dressing a wound."

"How did Max handle that?" Shane asked as though waiting for her to tell a story of epic rage.

Her brother had been mad, but mostly she remembered how he'd hugged her, his hands shaking. He might be known for his temper, but Max tended to be a flashfire when it came to irritation. He could be quite understanding about a lot of things, and he'd been far more scared than angry with her. "Well, he didn't realize I was gone until he called me in for dinner. Mel was excellent at getting me help. He was not so great at calling my brothers and letting them know what happened to me, so Rye was a deputy at the time and he had the entire police force looking for me. Oh, also, did I mention that I was in a lot of pain? Yeah, Mel had something for that."

Shane's eyes went wide. "His tonic?"

It was infamous around these parts. Mel's tonic was brewed to keep aliens away. Apparently only some of the bad aliens were driven off with beets. The rest required rot gut whiskey. There were probably more alien home cures, but she only knew about the two. "He didn't know what else to do," Brooke admitted. "I was sixteen. It wasn't like I hadn't had a nip or two, and it helped. Compound fractures hurt. And that is why I don't ever ride motorcycles."

She could remember how worried her brothers had been. How Rye looked pale, and Max's eyes had been red rimmed.

"What are you thinking right now?" Bay had a hand on her head, stroking her hair.

"I was thinking about how close I came to going into the system," she said quietly. "It wasn't good for you. I wouldn't have even had a sibling. You know I never really thought about what could have happened after our dad walked away and didn't leave a forwarding address."

"I'm still shocked that he walked out after your mom died." Bay sounded outraged.

It was funny, but that was the least worst thing that happened at that time. "It wasn't like he was around much anyway. By that time he mostly drank and complained about whatever we were doing. I don't remember a lot about him. Just that I used to call him the angry man instead of Dad."

When she thought about her bio dad, all she remembered was how angry he was. With her for being a kid. With her brothers for not doing enough. With her mother for not being enough. Her father leaving was nothing but an afterthought in her mother's death.

"Wow. I can't imagine taking on a kid at eighteen," Shane said with a shake of his head.

She glanced up at him, loving the way his longish hair curled slightly at the ends and how broad his shoulders were. He was a beautiful man, and his sweet smile belied his history. Would she still smile like that if she'd been through what he'd been through? "No, sweetie, you were literally tossed out into the cold at eighteen and forced to find your way with nothing."

They were remarkable men. The truth was they'd survived a lot. Survived and stuck together, and Bay was having his first big art show and Shane… Shane held everything together. He didn't understand how important he was.

Shane leaned over and kissed her forehead. "We had each other, at least."

"They gave us some money and offered to help us find jobs, but we had already decided to rodeo," Bay said. "Shane was an excellent rider, and he was everyone's favorite because he would go around fixing things for them. He's always been handy and able to organize things. Shane's always found a way to make us somewhat comfortable."

Because he had to make himself valuable. Her heart constricted because he'd done it today. He'd spent his day off organizing a house for them to live in, a room for her to work in. He was offering her everything he could.

This was so not what she'd expected, but she had to go with it. All she could think about was how Gemma had found herself when she let go, when she lost the world she thought she wanted and found a place to call home.

"How did your brothers make it work?" Shane asked. "I can imagine it would be hard to survive. They were kids and you were practically a baby."

He wasn't exactly wrong. She'd been so young, and she'd clung to them. Instead of resenting her, they'd changed their lives so they could keep her with them. "Rye took a job as a deputy, and Max did odd jobs while trying to keep the business running. He'd worked as a trainer for years by that time, but our dad had never taught him how to keep the books."

"Who did?" Bay shook his head. "I bet it was Stella."

"Marie," Brooke replied. When she thought about it, raising her had been a town project. "Stella came out a couple of times a week with food, and she would clean and teach us how to run a house. She would make sure I had everything I needed. Since my dad wasn't dead, CPS assumed he was taking care of me. The whole town got together and pitched in. The man who was our mayor for a long time was basically my grandfather, though we didn't share an ounce of blood. He taught me how to fish and took me and some of the other kids camping. He came to all my school events and cheered at my volleyball games. For the first couple of years, Mel posed as my father. That was fun. Then one of my teachers turned out to be from a planetary system we're at war with. That was when CPS got called in but…" She grimaced. "Stef took care of it. Damn it. I want to stay mad at him."

But it was hard when her body felt so good, when her soul felt oddly at peace.

Something about a naked picnic did it for her.

Or it was about the men she was with.

Either way, she didn't want to wreck it by being angry.

Shane's expression went soft. "You don't have to be mad at anyone. I want you to know that we're on your side and we'll stand by you. You want us to fuck with someone, we can do it."

Bay kept up his stroking, seeming to enjoy lying around on a blanket in the middle of a stage with her. "I'm going to explain to him that the show is off. I'm not working with someone who doesn't respect my… Who doesn't respect you."

She looked up at him. She knew it should be weird because his dick was right there, but it felt oddly normal to be like this with them. "I'm their kid sister. They put a lot into me. And I'm not merely talking about Max and Rye. Stef and Callie, too. Stella and Mel and Hiram and Teeny and Marie. Logan was practically my brother growing up. You know he calls me at least once a week to see if I'll have lunch with him or come to dinner with his family, and I always turn him down."

"Why?" Shane asked. "You live in the same city."

She huffed out a laugh. "No, I lived in an apartment that barely qualifies as a two bedroom, and Logan lives in a penthouse on the Upper East Side. We were in two different worlds. Logan is going to have a thriving practice when he graduates. I don't have a job or an apartment anymore."

"I don't understand why that means you shouldn't spend time with a guy you grew up with," Shane replied quietly. "Look, Brooke, I grew up with a woman who constantly told me what a failure I was."

Again, not the same. "You were a kid. I'm a whole, grown-ass adult who had everything she could want handed to her."

"I don't know about that. I think you probably would have liked to have a dad who loved you, a mom who lived," Bay pointed out.

"I had my brothers," she said with a sigh.

"That doesn't give them a pass to spy on you and make you feel small," Shane replied with quiet surety. "Even if they gave you everything." He frowned for a moment. "Baby, are you worried they're going to be disappointed in you?"

She sniffled and found herself being dragged into Shane's arms. He tugged her until she was sitting on his lap, his arms wrapped around her. "How can they not be? My degree wasn't cheap, and they didn't have to pay for it."

"Of course they did. You're their sister." Bay shifted so he could lean against her back.

She loved how warm she felt when she was caught between them. Safe. She felt safe with them and that wasn't what she was supposed to be looking for. Especially not when she would have to leave them. But she wasn't thinking about that now. "They could have easily turned me over to Teeny and Marie. I know they offered to take me in. Marie went so far as to look for a bigger cabin. Stella said I could live with her. My brothers wouldn't hear of it. There was a whole town hall and everything. I remember Logan and I sitting together playing Uno and drinking root beer. There was popcorn, too. And Rye stood up and said if anyone tried to take his sister away, he would leave the town and never look back. Max said he would go, too. He would leave everything he knew behind so we could stay together as a family, and I yelled at him this morning."

Shane held her tighter. "Baby, families fight. At least I think they do. I think part of what makes a good family is being able to disagree and still love each other. No one's perfect. I think that phrase was invented for Max."

She could feel Bay shrug behind her. "Max is obnoxious, but he's actually reasonable. Rye seems reasonable, but he's a hard-ass. She's way more worried about what Rye thinks. Max is fine as long as the people he loves are happy and someone gives him bacon his wife doesn't know about. Rye is trickier. He'll hide what he feels. I've always known we can handle Max. It's Rye who might take real offense to us dating his sister."

"Rye is a sweetheart," she countered.

"Rye wants you to think that. Believe me. I know how sibling relationships work. Especially when you have to bond the way me and Shane did. I know for your brothers it's in their DNA, but Shane and I had to do something similar in order to survive our childhood."

"You would have been fine without me," Shane insisted.

"No, I wouldn't, and you know it. You think I don't know all the things you've done for me over the years, but you're wrong. I don't think the way other people think. My brain is always running, but not on the everyday things," Bay admitted.

"Because you're an artist." Brooke turned so she could get her hands on Bay, too.

"Or maybe I'm an artist because I can't be anything else. Maybe my brain is why I have to do these things," Bay replied.

Brooke understood. "You make it sound like it's hard. I feel like I need to work, too. I always have. Even as a kid I would make clothes for my dolls and later for myself."

"It's not exactly the same. I would bet you can write down your ideas and come back to them later," Shane explained. "Bay's mind doesn't work that way. If he sees something that sparks him, he has to sit down. Mostly right then. It's why he carries a small sketchpad at all times. Well, when he's not on top of a horse working he does."

"And Shane makes sure to replace it when I'm getting close to it being full." Bay sighed. "I don't function well on my own. I sometimes wonder what my life would have been like if I hadn't had Shane. If he'd been my full brother and there had been some years between us. He likes to talk about how he's the one who doesn't have talent, but my talent means nothing without Shane around to balance me. I just… You should know I'm not whole."

Her heart constricted. They were both broken and yet there was something so sweet about them. Had they survived because they had each other? Her brothers had been born as halves of a whole. They were those twins who could sense what the other felt, could finish each other's sentences, couldn't be apart for long.

Bay and Shane weren't twins, but they functioned a lot like Max and Rye.

Was that why she was so deeply attracted to them? Because they reminded her of the men who raised her? Because they offered the possibility of the odd stability she had as a kid?

"You are whole," she whispered, touching Bay's face. "And so is Shane. I am, too, but I feel like there's a hole in my life."

"Because you lost your job?" Shane asked.

She thought about it for a moment. Honesty. How could she figure out what was wrong with her life if she wasn't honest? "I don't think I've been happy for a long time. It's more than the job. I feel adrift. I like the city but I miss being here. When I'm here I miss the city. I loathed so much about my job. Not the design part but the work part. The company. And yet when I lost the job I felt like I lost part of myself. I think I'm a little fucked up."

"I feel that way all the time." Shane's hands moved on her skin, like he needed the contact. "I think what you're trying to do is find your place."

No. That would be ridiculous because she'd gone to college and did grad work at Parsons and lived in the greatest city in the world. She knew who she was and what she wanted.

Didn't she? It wasn't like she was a teen anymore. She'd made decisions a long time ago. She'd set herself on a path. This whole thing with the firing was nothing more than a speedbump. She would find another job and go back to New York and back to working fifty plus hours a week in a too-small apartment she wouldn't be able to afford. She would design fast fashion T-shirts that would end up in a landfill.

"Hey, it's okay." Shane drew her back. "You don't have to know everything right now. You should just be glad you don't have his brain."

She realized Bay had gotten up. She glanced around and he had grabbed a small sketch book from his kit and had a pencil in his hand. He moved it across the page.

"What's he doing?" she asked.

"He found something interesting in the way you look. I told you sometimes he can't help it and he needs to work. It gets hard when he's out on the range or driving somewhere. It's why I have to make sure I'm around him most of the time," Shane admitted. "I would bet that book is getting another not-safe-for-work drawing."

"He's drawing me?" Brooke sat up. It felt weird. Like he was taking a picture of her naked. "I don't know that I like that idea. I don't want naked pictures of me."

"Could you show her? I know you're in the middle of a flash, but your genius can wait for a second so she'll feel comfortable," Shane requested. She noticed he'd sat back. He didn't cover himself but there was a definite withdrawal.

Bay frowned but passed her the book. "It's kind of new. I started it right before we left the last job, so it's not quite full yet."

Brooke took the book and flipped through the pages.

There were drawings of dogs and horses, a ranch she didn't recognize. A young woman with tears in her eyes and a man watching her from the shadows. There was an odd menace to the work at the beginning of the notebook. Like no matter how sweet the subject was, there was a darkness surrounding it. And then it changed. There was a picture of Jennifer Talbot standing in front of an easel, little Logan playing with toy cars at her feet. Somehow he brought light to a black and white pencil drawing. There was a drawing of the Christmas trees at the town hall where they'd had the annual holiday party. She recognized her niece. Mel was holding her up and letting Paige put the star on the beet tree.

Tears pierced her eyes because there was so much sweetness in the drawing.

He was a master. He brought more than simple pictures to life. He'd caught Paige's grin, her shining light. He captured Mel's softness, his willingness to open his heart to all kids.

She turned the page and stopped.

It was her. She stood in the middle of town hall, a glass of wine in her hand and a brilliant smile on her face and yet…she felt her aloneness. She was beautiful, but a little lost. Lovely but damaged.

He saw her. He knew her. Somehow without spending hours and hours, he saw the basic truths of her life.

She turned the page again, and now every other picture was of her.

"Uhm, some of those obviously didn't happen. They were in my mind or sometimes I sketched the pictures you posted on social media." Bay sounded embarrassed.

But the pictures were gorgeous. There were pictures of her staring at him like she wanted to eat him alive, desire stamped on her features. She held out two hands, seeming to offer herself to them both. There was a picture of her lying back on a bed with big hands on her body. One of her with her head thrown back at the moment of orgasm.

He had a vivid imagination.

Then she'd obviously come to this point in the timeline of his book because it was her sitting in the booth at Stella's, the sun on her face as she studied the menu.

The loneliness was back, the feeling that the subject of the drawing was hiding something.

He saw way too much.

She stared at that last picture. Odd how she was far more disturbed by that piece of art. And yet he'd made her beautiful. He'd made her warm, her softness a base for the work. It was the sorrow he managed to capture. And… "Max does not have fangs."

Bay grinned. "Of course he doesn't. That's Rye, baby." He sobered. "I can try to not draw you if you don't like it. Or I can at least promise no one will ever see them."

Did she want to hide such gorgeous artwork? Was she so

horrified that someone had seen her, acknowledged her pain, and still thought she was beautiful and worthy of drawing?

The truth of the matter was she kind of liked the version of herself that Bay caught. She looked back at a couple of the ones he'd drawn from her socials. In the photograph version, she'd carefully controlled the image, putting filters on and cleaning up the imperfections. He'd somehow put them back. Like he knew her face well enough to give her back her laugh lines and the wrinkle she got on her forehead when she smiled.

"Are you okay?" Shane asked, and she noticed he hadn't moved.

He was worried. He thought she would think it was weird.

It was. It was weird and wonderful and Bay had the kind of talent that echoed past the artist's own age. She looked up at him. "Am I your muse?"

Bay's expression tightened as if he was trying to control the emotion he felt. "I've never drawn anyone the way I do you. You should understand that I've painted a couple of those, and I have the deepest desire to sculpt you. You take up space in my head and in my hands."

"You take up space in my soul," Shane said quietly.

Could she ask for more? It was overwhelming because she wasn't sure she could give them what they needed. Not long term, but she could be what Bay wanted tonight. She closed the sketchbook and handed it back to him. "Where do you want me?"

Bay's eyes widened. "What do you mean?"

She leaned back against Shane's chest, letting her arm drift up. "Draw me like one of your French girls."

She felt Shane relax behind her, his lips kissing her head. "That's our girl. You might be his muse, but you're mine, too."

His to take care of, to think about, to center his life around.

It wasn't so bad.

"I don't think I drew any..." Bay stopped and flushed slightly. "Is this a random pop culture reference that I don't get?"

Shane chuckled, and she felt his cock against the small of her back. "It's only one of the most popular films of all time. It's okay, baby. I'll watch all the things with you. She's telling you she wants to be your muse. She liked the drawings."

"I liked how he saw me," she admitted.

"Then lay back against him." Bay changed positions, his pencil in hand. "I wish I had charcoal, but this will do. Give me a minute. Shane, wrap your arm under her breasts."

She laid back and let Bay do his work.

Chapter Nine

Monday

Brooke liked living at the G. The first couple of days had been peaceful. She'd met with Cleo and gone over the designs for the play—which were terrible. She wasn't even sure what the other designer had been thinking, but she was glad they hadn't gotten to the actual sewing stage. Cleo was kind of the luckiest director in the history of time. If Brooke hadn't come along, Cleo would be forced to pull from the existing wardrobe, and that would have been a disaster. Brooke understood the concept of modernizing *Three Sisters*, but did the other designer even read the play? She made Olga look like she was from an 80's soap opera, while Irina was just... She knew she shouldn't use the word slutty, but putting her in micro minis didn't modernize the character. It merely let her know the other chick didn't understand her.

Three Sisters. It was about being stuck and having no way out. She understood that all too well.

The problem was she was starting to feel...not stuck. Comfortable. A bit excited some days.

"Hey, you need some coffee, baby?" Shane walked into the sewing room he'd put together for her with a mug in his hand.

"You're up early."

Oh, he said the room was a gift from him and Bay, but she'd figured them out over the course of a couple of days, and Shane was the one who took care of the everyday things. Shane kept things moving, and it was fucking delightful.

A few days of living with them and she was already addicted to having them around. It went way beyond the way they fucked her—which was often and with great enthusiasm. They'd even sort of tried the playroom, though they hadn't found their groove there yet.

She smiled at him and accepted the coffee and the kiss he offered her. "I had an idea for the first act, but I want to see how this lace is going to work on the fabric I have. It's weird to be working with a budget."

"Did you not have one at the New York job? What's the name…" Shane began.

She turned and frowned his way. "Seriously? We're pretending to not know?"

Bay chuckled from the hallway. He was so big and broad he made her sigh. He was dressed for work in well-worn jeans and a Western shirt, his cowboy hat already on his head. He was such a contradiction. So like the cowboys she'd known all her life, but with a thirst for culture and art. "It's the House of Bianchi. Brother, we know which pieces she designed for the spring line."

Shane shrugged like he'd tried. "I was hoping she'd forget the stalker stuff."

She'd actually thought about this and talked about it with Lucy and River when they met for drinks at Hell on Wheels. Sawyer naturally listened in and came down firmly on the "those boys are creepy and she should move in with cats" side, but then Sawyer hated mostly everyone. Lucy and River pointed out that she didn't have to view it as creepy behavior. More like they were fans of hers and wanted to follow her and maybe fall into her bed and give her multiple orgasms and save her from her brothers and bring her coffee and make sure she had a place in their home to work in.

She stood and gave Shane a real kiss. "I'm choosing to look at it as pre-relationship research. After all, I wouldn't have this lovely room if you didn't know an awful lot about me. And to answer your question, not really. I mean I didn't ask for Mulberry silk or baby cashmere, but for the most part anything I wanted was either in-house or we had an account at several fabric stores."

"But sometimes it's fun to see what you can do with what you have," Bay said. "I think my favorite piece of work I've ever done is a sculpture of Shane riding a bronc that I made out of scrap metal and aluminum cans."

She'd seen it. How had she not realized it was Shane on that powerful horse? "It's at Stef's, right? He keeps it in his foyer. I hope you know how much it means to him to keep it there."

If there was one thing she was feeling bad about it was the rift between her and her family, and that included Stefan Talbot. She hadn't talked to her brothers in days. She'd seen Rachel when she brought the kids by to say hello and dropped them off for some babysitting. She'd been working in the theater, and Paige had given her the rundown on everything that happened during last summer's kid production of *The Little Mermaid*. Apparently Poppy thought Ursula was misunderstood and probably disturbed by the amount of pollution in the ocean, and Charlie and Zander had told Paige that the actor who played Prince Eric was a poopy face, but only after Paige said he was cute. And Sierra Kincaid-Briggs had cried during the part where Ariel lost her voice so loudly they shut the show down because they were worried she hurt herself.

Rachel had looked sad even as she smiled. Tired. She looked tired and a bit lost, and that made Brooke feel infinitely guilty.

Bay leaned against the doorframe. "Well, I would have left it wherever we were. I can haul my sketchbooks around, but there's not a lot of places to put a one-and-a-half-foot sculpture when you're working ranches and staying in bunkhouses. We were outside of Denver at the time, and Shane insisted on calling up a gallery."

"Four, actually," Shane explained. "I called the first one and they hung up on me. That was when I realized I needed a good story. So I made up a bunch of crap about being a dealer from back East who'd found this amazing modern Western artist to rival Remington and Dixon. It took me a while but once they actually let us in, they agreed to sell it. Well, once they agreed to let Bay in."

He did not take enough credit. "You were right the first time.

How did you meet Stef?"

"The gallery owner called him," Bay took up the story. "Apparently he has several gallery owners on the lookout for interesting contemporary Western artists. Stef went up to Denver the next day, bought it, and got our number from the owner. He showed up at the ranch we were working at and had a laugh that my high-powered East Coast agent was my kid brother who was knee deep in cow shit the first time they met. That was when he offered to mentor us. Me in art and Shane in the business of art."

She knew it was more than that. "And both of you in the art of Dominance and submission?"

Bay's lips curled up, his eyes heating. "Yeah. That, too. He got us memberships to a club in Denver, and we stayed close for a while. He would have us come out to his place and I would work, and then at night he would open his playroom. This was all before Jennifer."

"Yes," she replied with a wrinkled nose. "It was around the time you hit on my sister-in-law."

Bay moved in, putting his hands on her hips. "She wasn't your sister-in-law at the time." He leaned over and brushed those generous lips against her own, and she felt Shane move in behind her. "What did we ask that day, brother?"

"We asked your brothers if they had a sister," Shane whispered.

She had to laugh. "I'm sure they took that well."

They still weren't taking it well, but Bay kissed her and Shane's hands found her breasts.

The world could wait. And so could work.

Tuesday

Shane held the goat gently as Noah Bennett showed Henry how to prime the needle that held the vaccine.

Noah was the town vet and happy to help teach Nell and Henry how to take care of the animals they were planning on welcoming at their new animal sanctuary.

Shane had been in the kitchen when Noah walked through and announced he could use help.

Some days it was all about where a person happened to be. The right place—since he'd been grabbing some coffee filters—and the wrong time because now he was spending the whole afternoon here with the Flanders clan and thirty-two traumatized goats. Bay probably finished up early and was already fucking their girl.

It was something they'd both gotten used to. Only yesterday Bay had a meeting with the gallery owner and Shane had gone to the theater to bring Brooke a late lunch and ended up fucking her backstage during a rehearsal. It had been hot as hell.

And then he'd gotten roped into doing a bunch of work on the set. He liked working on the set and it happened more and more. Once Cleo figured out he was handy, she'd been more than happy to give him a to-do list.

Damn, but he liked living with her. He liked everything about it, from waking up with her all sweet and sleepy in his arms, to getting her coffee because the sweet part didn't last long and she needed caffeine, to having dinner with her. Simple things like she'd made spaghetti and garlic bread and a salad. Sitting and talking about their days, knowing he would sleep with her… It felt too good to be true.

"You're sure it doesn't hurt them?" Nell sat on a camp chair ten feet away from them, her hand on her belly.

She looked like she probably should have had that kid a couple of weeks ago, but everyone swore she still had some time.

What would Brooke look like? Did she want kids? How many? They would be lovely, like their momma.

He would love them. Whether they were biologically his or not, he would be their dad and he would never, ever leave them or make them think for a moment they weren't loved and welcome. He would never treat them like trash someone left behind.

Yeah, he had some issues to work out.

"It doesn't bother them at all," Noah replied. "But then it didn't bother Poppy either, did it, big girl? Doc Caleb said you were a champ."

Poppy stood with her father, petting the goats. She'd been calm and patient with all of them, and even the nastiest of the group seemed to chill out around the girl.

Maybe she could talk to them. He could believe it. After all, it was Bliss, and weird shit happened here.

"It hurt, but the doctor told me it was like a little sting. It was a big sting," Poppy replied and wound her arms around the goat's neck as though she could protect him.

Nell stood and made her way to Poppy, putting a hand on her child but looking Noah's way. "Are you sure this is necessary? I've been thinking about vaccines…"

Henry cleared his throat, and his gaze narrowed.

Nell sighed. "I do believe in science, but is it necessary since the goats are all adults? How can we know they need this?"

"Because all goats need to be vaccinated for tetanus and Clostridium," Noah said as he handed Henry the syringe. "It's safe, Nell. I know you don't like to think about putting chemicals into the animals, but there's a reason we no longer lose whole herds. It's not going to hurt him. It's going to ensure he has a good long life."

"But what if he's already had it?" Nell asked with uncertainty.

Shane held the goat as Henry carefully cleaned the spot he was going to use the needle on. "Ma'am, these goats were all neglected. The owner didn't feed them. I seriously doubt they kept to a careful vaccination schedule. They didn't love these goats like you obviously love Poppy there."

Nell's eyes filled with tears, and he worried he'd said something wrong. Then she nodded and leaned over. "What did you say the dosage was, Noah?"

Noah started talking to her while Henry expertly filled the syringe. Poppy and her mom were suddenly invested in the lesson, while Henry got on with the job.

"Thank you." Henry pinched the skin and slid the needle in, administering the dose. The goat barely moved. "That was exactly the right thing to say to her. My wife is a loving woman, and sometimes she worries she's doing it wrong. Sometimes she needs to be reminded that love is the most important part, and she does that spectacularly."

"She's a kind woman." From what he could tell Nell tried to help everyone she could.

"She is." Henry petted the goat and nodded at Shane to let him go. The little thing happily ran into the meadow. "Brooke seems to be settling in at the G. I saw her yesterday with Beth and the kids."

The Flanders family was spending a lot of time out at the G while they were setting up their sanctuary. "She seems to like it, but it's only temporary. She's looking for a new job."

It was a lie, but one he kind of needed to tell himself. She wasn't looking, from what he could tell. For days she'd seemed perfectly happy to go to the theater and work with Cleo and her group and come home and work a bit more before she started dinner. She read while they cleaned the kitchen, and then they went to bed. For hours.

It was heaven.

It wasn't going to last.

"Do you think so?" Henry mused as he looked over to where Noah was showing Nell how to measure the dosage.

"I mean she's not going to stay. She needs to work, and the theater is only open in the summer. Besides, I can't see her staying. Sometimes I wonder how she grew up in this place."

Henry looked at him, the glasses making the man seem very intellectual. "Why do you say that?"

He shrugged. "I don't know. She's very…what's the word…chic. I see her in fancy hotels. Not here."

Henry seemed to think about that. "Are you sure you're seeing the real her? Because I assure you Brooke Harper has vaccinated some horses in her time. She used to work the farm on her summers off and on the weekends. I know she worked the sheriff's dispatch when she was younger and Callie needed time off. She's also taken her turn on alien watches and worked many festivals with me and Nell, selling organic cider and crafts. You think she doesn't fit in here?"

Shane shook his head. "No. I know everyone loves her. I just can't see her leaving the city."

"You know I would have said the same thing about Logan Green. I would have told you that kid was never getting further from Bliss than Alamosa," Henry admitted. "And I was wrong. The world is bigger and smaller than we think it is. I've seen most of it. I've seen the good and the bad. The beautiful places of this earth and the war-torn ones. I lived in DC for a long time. I don't ever want to live anywhere but here. I'm glad my Nell doesn't want to go anywhere else because this is my home."

He had some questions since Henry seemed so open in the moment. "Is it true you worked for the Central Intelligence Agency? You don't have to tell me. I can mind my own business."

"I get the feeling you do that a lot, and what's the fun in that? One of the things I love about this place is how no one minds their business."

Oh, he got a bad feeling that he'd opened a door better left closed. "I mean some people do."

"Nah," Henry said. "And yes, it's true. In another life I was a man named John Bishop. I worked intelligence, and not in some ivory tower. I was an operative, and a deadly one. And then I found this place and I discovered another part of me. We don't have to stay the people we are when we're younger. We don't have to be who they told us to be. In my case I didn't stay who the Agency said I was. Cold. Unfeeling. Unable to care about real people because of abandonment issues."

That cut close. "I get the feeling you're trying to tell me something. You should be clear. I'm not real smart."

Henry's lips tugged up in a rueful grin. "Oh, there it is. You see, you are smart. You're good at solving problems. You're excellent at a lot of things, but you downplay everything good about yourself. In another life, I would have recruited you, Shane Kent. I would have taken you under my very deadly wing and taught you how to play the game."

Shane laughed at the thought. "I would be a terrible spy."

"Not after I trained you," Henry said in all seriousness. "I've noticed you're organized and you see mechanical problems easily. You also hide your need for praise. I would have become the father figure you so desperately needed, and you would have found yourself in my debt and later in my pocket."

Okay, Henry was kind of scary. "I thought about going into the military, but Bay didn't want to."

"Bay saved you," Henry said quietly. "I assure you if you'd gone into the military, you would be on a Special Forces team very quickly, and then someone like John Bishop would have come knocking on your door. All I'm saying is it's become apparent to me that you're hiding a lot out of fear. You might not even realize it's fear. For you it seems like a logical thing to do, but I've learned when we close ourselves off to possibilities, it's always fear that drives us. Fear. Shame. It's all the same. You're looking at Brooke through a pair of glasses someone else put on your face. Like I did once. I saw Nell the way I'd been taught to see. With cynicism and a belief that all people are basically the same. It took falling for that magnificent woman to get me to take them off. It's hard when you think it's the only way you *can* see."

"You think I'm seeing Brooke wrong?" He knew the question sounded simple, but he got the complexity Henry was talking about. He hid his intelligence because anything he had when he was a child was something to be taken away. He qualified for AP classes and honor classes and his stepmother decided if he was so smart, he could get a part-time job that took up all his time to study. And then he had some money, so she made him pay rent.

That woman had fucked up his life.

"I think you're protecting yourself and you think you might be protecting her. You're wrong. Brooke is smart, and I believe she's already figuring out that getting fired might have been a blessing in disguise. It's hard to let go of something you've told yourself you wanted all your life. It's damn near impossible to admit what you truly want is smaller and yet infinitely more. That what you want isn't a job or a level of financial security. That what you want is a feeling."

To be loved and appreciated. To know the work he did served the people he loved, and he had an unassailable place among them.

Henry was right. He wasn't fucking dumb. He'd been excellent at school, and when there was no more school and no way to go to college, he'd read. He'd taken shit from everyone for enjoying a book. Bay had too, though it never seemed to bother him. There was a deep well of certainty in his brother that he didn't possess.

Or was he wearing the wrong glasses?

"I can't work at the G forever. Even if she stayed, she would need more than I can provide," he heard himself saying.

"But she doesn't." Henry put a hand on his shoulder. "Another thing you've had placed in your head. I know Brooke. She wants a teammate. Probably two, given how she grew up. She's a unicorn, you know."

He realized how often he played down his own intelligence since his first instinct was to ask Henry what he meant. But he knew. "Because where else would we find a woman we don't have to convince that the relationship we want can work. She's unique."

"She is indeed. Stop coming up with all the reasons why you don't deserve this. Start enjoying what you have. You want to know what will keep her by your side? Build something with her. Help her. Grow with her. Or you can let the people who hurt you win. It's as simple as that. Poppy, sweetie, I don't think the goat wants you to ride him."

But it kind of looked like the goat did. That goat was bowing down and letting the girl climb all over it. It was weird, but then everything about the Flanders family was weird. And true.

He watched Henry scoop up his daughter and wondered if his stepmother's cruelty would haunt him forever.

Wednesday

"But I already took the beet." Bay had done a double dose because apparently there was a certain part of the ranch that attracted aliens, and he'd worked there for a couple of days. So Cassidy had shown up with her monthly dose for all the ranch hands.

He'd had to brush hard so his teeth weren't purple.

Brooke gave him a stare as she downed her own. "The worst that can happen is you don't get hypertension. You know beets are a superfood."

"No, honey, the worst that can happen is one of the spores the Jelan males leave behind gets under his skin and worms it's way to his lower intestine where it takes root and grows into a baby in roughly three months," Cass pointed out.

"Hey, don't you have that red spot on your leg?" Shane asked. He'd already downed his. "What if it wasn't poison ivy?"

"Cass," Bay said, "we're going to need to make that a triple."

Thursday

"You're sure you don't want to order something? Or bring in a famous designer?" Brooke sat in the big cabin Seth Stark had built years before. This monstrosity of comfort had been designed with a family in mind, and like all things Seth Stark wanted, he'd made it happen.

Georgia shrugged. "Why would I do that when I have you? Unless you don't want to do it." Georgia was a gorgeous woman with blonde hair and a sweet face. "I'm reluctant to go with most of the famous designers. You know they don't like to design for larger women."

Larger? Brooke barely managed to not roll her eyes, but she understood. Georgia was a whole size ten instead of a zero. She was stunning and sexy and had two men panting after her, but the fashion world could be cruel to anyone with hips and breasts.

The theater was different. She designed for the character, not some standard few people could ever meet. She had to think about the character, how they would dress, how clothes would make them feel. If clothing was armor or an outward expression of who they were inside.

She was remembering why she liked it so much. And it didn't hurt that Cleo praised her as a goddess every day.

And then Bay and Shane worshipped her like one at night.

"I think they'll make an exception for Georgia Stark-Warner. You're kind of the coolest woman in the city right now," Brooke pointed out. "And I don't know if you've noticed, but there are a whole bunch of ladies in Manhattan who follow your every move and dress exactly like you."

"Because she's the most gorgeous girl in the world," Seth said, walking through, carrying a bundle of the cutest chunk ever. Wesley Stark-Warner looked like his mom, with a mop of blonde hair and a wide smile showing the beginnings of his first tooth. The baby drooled and hung onto his father.

"There are plenty of people in Manhattan who think I'm a gold-digging moron threatening to upend their society," Georgia pointed out.

Seth leaned over and kissed her forehead. "And we don't give a fuck about those people. Is this about the Met Gala? I told you, if you don't want to go you don't have to."

"She's going." Logan walked in from the back. "This is something she's dreamed about all of her life, and she's not going to allow a bunch of societal assholes to hold her back. She's on the board of the museum and has more than every right to be there on the big night."

Which was why she should have a famous designer doing her dress. The Met Gala was one of fashion's big shows. It was one of the most anticipated and photographed and talked about events in her world.

"Oh, I'm going. They're not going to stop me, but I need the right dress. Something dramatic," Georgia said with a smile. "Honestly, I wouldn't hate something that played to the stereotypes they put me in. So I need something gold and stripper-like."

Seth laughed. "And I'm putting Wes down for his nap. Let me know what I'm wearing, baby. You know I never have to wear a tux to the annual heritage festival here in Bliss."

"Or to Woo Woo Fest," Logan pointed out. "Brooke, how's the engagement going to two men you barely knew a week ago?"

She could always count on Logan to point out the obvious flaws in her plans.

She'd never had him out to her apartment because she was ashamed of how small it was. How little she'd been able to achieve.

Brooke stood up and gave Logan a hug since she hadn't seen him in a couple of days. Logan squeezed her tight and whispered. "She's nervous about having a gown custom designed. She only trusts you. Please."

She wasn't big enough to design for the Met.

Or she was, and it was time to prove it. She didn't want to let her family down, but maybe it was time to figure out if what she thought she wanted at eighteen was what she wanted at twenty-eight.

What would her eighteen-year-old self say? Now that she thought about it, her eighteen-year-old self had been kind of kick ass.

She took a deep breath and stepped back before turning to Georgia. If Georgia could walk out in front of that crowd proud and steadfast in who she was, then Brooke could design the clothes she would make a stand in. "Gold, then. I'm thinking flashy on the surface but deep and complex underneath. How do you feel about a gown that transforms?"

She was thinking about starting out with a gown that looked hard and metallic and then revealed itself to be soft and lovely under the outer coat.

Georgia's eyes lit up. "I feel amazing."

Brooke settled in and got to work.

Friday

"I don't know." Trev stood outside the bunkhouse, a mug of coffee in his hands. "How the hell would they get in?"

The bunkhouse had been… Bay wouldn't say vandalized. Not exactly. It wasn't like there was a bunch of broken stuff, but it was obvious someone had been through it and they'd taken the small safe where they were supposed to keep valuables when they needed a place to put them.

"We were all hands on deck this afternoon," Shane pointed out. "No one would have been in here, and we had a bunch of people over for the inspections. I don't think we would have noticed extra cars, and the inspectors have free rein."

It was probably Trev's most stressful day of the year. In order to keep their organic status, the ranch had to allow inspections, and this time it coincided with regular USDA inspections. It had been a day, and now that it was done they had to deal with the fact that someone had been in the bunkhouse.

"Boss, I don't think they got anything." Jeff had been around far longer than Bay and Shane. He was a bit older and handled a lot of the day-to-day operations when Bo and Trev were traveling or dealing with their families.

Bay was almost certain he was pissed he and Shane were staying in the foreman's house. He'd overheard Jeff talking to some of the other hands about how he thought it was bullshit he and Shane got the foreman's house, and if one of them is named the new foreman he'll quit. Someone tried to explain that it was more about Brooke than he and Shane, but Jeff wasn't listening.

It didn't matter since Brooke was already talking about heading back to New York in a few weeks. Oh, she claimed it was so she could find some fabric or something for Georgia Stark-Warner's museum party, but he didn't understand why Teeny couldn't order some.

She'd casually mentioned they could come with her.

The idea of being with all those people sent a damn chill up his spine.

He hadn't been able to handle Denver. He damn straight couldn't do New York City.

He was going to fuck this up for all of them.

"They got the safe." Trev walked over to the place where the small safe had been. "The whole damn thing. I thought it was in there better than that."

He ran a hand over the place where the safe had been. They'd done a good job of extracting it.

"No one uses it except for Bay," Shane pointed out. "He sometimes puts his sketchbooks in it so none of the perverts around here can see he likes to draw our girlfriend."

Jeff sighed and shook his head. "Yeah, we're the perverts."

"Excuse me?" Trev's tone went icy.

Jeff's hands came up. "I was talking about the porn drawings, boss. Sorry. I suppose they're art."

He did use the safe sometimes, and yes, it was about the drawings of Brooke. Of course now he kept his sketchbook either with him or in the foreman's house.

He was damn straight glad it wasn't in the now-missing safe.

"Why would someone take a safe in a bunkhouse? No one here has anything to steal," Bay said.

Trev shrugged. "I think it's going to be a mystery."

Bay sighed and let it go because he had way bigger fish to fry.

But at least that red spot on his leg was gone, and he was almost sure he wasn't pregnant by aliens.

Beets for the win. Now he had to figure out a way to keep their girl because he was certain they were both in love with her.

Chapter Ten

"So I was thinking about the set." Shane held the door open for Brooke, allowing her to go before him. It was late and he'd spent the evening watching the rehearsal and then working on the light board while Brooke finished up her fittings and Bay sat and drew. He had some nice sketches of the cast now. "Everything is on wheels."

The last few weeks had been damn near perfect except that Brooke was still not talking to her brothers. It apparently had made the shower her sister-in-law had thrown the day before the slightest bit awkward. Well, not any more awkward than Nell protesting it since she was one of the guests of honor and he'd been told all of the babies had been blessed by the beet, as Cass called it. Still, Brooke seemed to be in a good mood, and he couldn't wait to get her home.

"Yes," Brooke replied, moving out onto the walkway that ran all the way up Main Street, connecting the stores and restaurants. Though the actual buildings were mostly modern, there was an old-school Western flair to the center of Bliss. The theater was at the end of the street, and the parking lot across the way. It was one of the only parking lots in the town, and at this time of night it was fairly empty with the exception of their truck and a couple of SUVs. The only other lot was on the opposite end of Main behind the Sheriff's Department.

He hoped that one had better lighting.

The streetlamps had come on, but it looked like the ones in the parking lot were out.

Bay seemed to see the same thing and moved to get in front of Brooke.

Not that anything dangerous would happen in…

He reached for her hand, so she didn't walk ahead. If there was something going on, he wanted either him or his brother to find out first. But it was most likely a burned-out bulb.

"It's so they can move the set around quickly during set changes. I think they're keeping it fairly simple," Brooke explained. "Kind of like my wardrobe."

He was fascinated by her and by the job she was doing, and that included the set. He liked the theater, though he hadn't had many chances to go. In high school the drama class had put on a production of *Our Town* and he'd gone to every performance since he volunteered to help with the props. He liked the camaraderie of the theater.

He'd kind of liked that no one compared him to Bay there since his brother fell asleep during the performances.

But he'd stayed so Shane didn't have to walk back to the group home in the dark alone.

He looked up and down the street. It was quiet, with only the lights from Stella's at the other end and Trio illuminating the night. "I saw they had some artwork on wheels."

She nodded, her fingers threading through his like they were made to be together. She followed him as they began to cross the street. "Yes. Several of the sets revolve around a drawing room. Originally it takes place in turn-of-the-century Russia. Cleo wants to set it in the modern era with a Western twist. So the location is outside an Army base here in the States, but the house where the three sisters live needs to have touches of their former life in Moscow. Though in this case Denver is substituted. Hence the nice tea set and the artwork. It's to show a longing for something they lost."

There was a problem. "The desk hides the wheels well, but the artwork looks like it's on a chalkboard," he pointed out.

Brooke winced. "Yeah, I thought it was clunky, too. I understand the need to move things quickly and in the dark, but the paintings look weird."

He had a solution. "But the pulley system is right there. And it's in layers to accommodate four rows of curtains. Why not use one for the artwork and the mirror? Then it would look like it was hung on the walls."

She stopped in the middle of the street, her expression going to what he'd come to think of as her thinking face.

He let her stop because it wasn't like there were cars coming.

"I like it, Shane." She nodded as though she could see the thing in her head. "You could hang them by strings so they're fragile and could break easily. Like the sisters. It's a good idea, and it would move just as quickly."

"More." A thrill of pride went through him, the kind he always got when he solved a problem. "Because you move it from back-stage."

Brooke smiled, sending another kind of thrill through him. "That is smart. You should talk to Cleo about it in the morning. I know she's got some issues with the set design. Is it weird that I'm kind of excited to be working for very little money? I think I'm being paid in popcorn and free passes."

He squeezed her hand. "I think it's wonderful that you're helping out."

"Hey, guys." Bay stood on the sidewalk opposite them. "We seem to have a problem."

Brooke's expression fell. "What?"

Shane started to lead her toward Bay. "What's happening?"

"Someone slashed our tires." Bay frowned. "You know, I don't expect that here. We're not even into high tourist season. Who's going around slashing the tires of a shitty old truck?"

A chill crept along Shane's spine. He let go of Brooke's hand and went back to inspect the truck himself. Sure enough, all four tires were done in, and someone had smashed the passenger's side window and rifled through the cab. Not that they had anything to steal.

"Hey, Elisa." Brooke had her cell to her ear as she and Bay joined him. "We've had our truck vandalized. We're in the parking lot across from the theater. Yes. We want to file a report at least. Sure. See you in a couple of minutes." She hung up. "Elisa's coming. She won't be long."

"Why would..." Bay's head shook. "Never mind. I know why.

People are assholes. Unless this is the work of the Sasquatches. Mel warned me."

"It wasn't a Sasquatch." Shane was worried it was something else. Something tied to their past. It had been months and they hadn't heard anything. He thought they'd left it all behind when they fled in the night. "Do you think there's any way this is Kingman?"

Brooke's head turned, like she'd scented an excellent story. "Kingman? Like Kale Kingman, the rancher who owns a big portion of Wyoming? Why would he slash your tires?"

"Well, I don't think he would do it himself." Shane's gut was in a knot. Had it taken the man this long to find them? They hadn't talked a lot during their short stay on the ranch, so it was definitely possible no one knew about their connections here in Bliss.

Bay's head shook. "Nah, he has people for that."

"He has people to do crimes?" Brooke asked, her eyes wide. "And you've seen this? You saw Kale Kingman's ranch hands commit crimes for him? I knew they got that show from somewhere."

"I never watched the show. I have to deal with ranch shit all day. I'm not going to sit around and watch it at night." It was precisely why he liked shows about other times in history. And action shows. And science fiction. And anything but damn Westerns where they usually got shit wrong. Ranch work was boring. Well, for the most part. Apparently not so much if the rancher was Kale Kingman.

"We never saw that," Bay countered, and there was something about his sigh that raised Shane's hackles. He sounded dismissive. "Of course there were rumors, and Shane once thought he saw something, but it wasn't anything. There were always jokes about how if you found yourself on the wrong end of Kingman, there was a nice canyon you would spend eternity in, but that's not real. Shane overheard some talk, but again, it was only talk. It was more of an excuse to get us out of there."

Brooke turned Shane's way. "Bay said you saw something."

He was surprised his brother didn't believe him. "I overheard something the night we left. They talked about handling the new guys. We were the new guys."

"See, I know he's saying he doesn't watch *Yellowstone*, but I assure you everyone in the bunkhouse did, and I think that got into

Shane's head and when he heard something about the new guys, his imagination went a little nutsy," Bay offered. "He was unhappy there. Hell, I was unhappy there, but they paid well. He woke me up in the middle of the night and we took off. It's been more than five months. It's not like anyone has come after us."

"What if he didn't know where you were?" Brooke seemed to get into the mystery.

He was annoyed by his brother and the fact that he would bring this up in front of Brooke. "I wouldn't make that shit up."

Bay sighed. "I didn't say you made it up. I said you blew a small thing out of proportion. Don't make the same mistake now. I'm not calling you a liar. Brooke, baby, this is a random thing. Probably done by kids who were looking for money or something to sell, and when they realized they tried to rob the shittiest truck in the county, they got upset and slashed the tires."

"Which kids would that be?" Brooke asked. "Because my niece is all about shins. She is not into tires. The only young people who could do it wouldn't." Her head tilted. "Unless they saw it as a way to force us to Fuber."

"Fuber?" Shane asked.

"Yeah, I've decided it's what I'm calling their business, and I've got a design logo in mind. Not that it'll go anywhere. The Farley brothers are headed to college soon. So see, there's not even a financial reason for them to fuck with the truck." She checked her watch. "Also, it's almost ten, so they are probably off the clock and safe from the devil. Which begs the question of how we're getting home. Because it's not going to be in that truck."

The only truck they had. Damn. They probably had the money to replace the tires, but it was going to be tight. He still had to buy Bay a suit for the gallery show and shoes that had never stepped in cow shit.

"I guess I can call Trev," Bay offered. "He can send one of the other hands out to pick us up. I hate waking everyone up. The main houses are both lights out by nine o'clock."

Because they had young families, and at least Trev and Bo and Beth would be up and down with the babies all night. Hope needed more sleep and peace now that she was getting close to her own due date.

There weren't a bunch of crazy teens running around. Oh, they could come in from other places, but that seemed like a stretch to Shane. "Maybe Elisa can give us a ride. I would hate to wake up the house, and the hands are mostly in bed since we start work early."

"We are three whole-ass adults, and now we don't have a single car between us." Brooke resettled her bag over her shoulder. "Well, I know I should call my brothers but I…"

"Brooke? Brooke? Are you okay?" Max rounded the corner at the fastest speed his well-worn boots would take him. "Hal walked out and announced there was a slasher and you were dead in the parking lot."

Shane was confused. Why the hell was Max here?

"How does Hal know?" Bay asked, seemingly as confused as Shane was.

Brooke took that one. "Oh, he listens to the police radio like most people do podcasts. He gets bored late at night, and I'm afraid he can do the telephone thing all on his own."

"Telephone?" Shane asked. He didn't like any of this. Moments before he'd been feeling so good about the world, and now he was a mess of anxiety and Brooke's brother was here.

Max was looking her over as though trying to assess her injuries. Which she had none.

"You know the game. You start with one story and then the person who heard it first has to tell the next, and so on and so on, and that's how we end up with aliens invading," Brooke replied. "Hal doesn't need a bunch of people to filter through to get to an outrageous story. He's good to go right off the bat. Max, someone slashed the tires on Shane and Bay's truck. I was working late at the theater, and they came to pick me up."

Max's eyes narrowed. "That better be all you were doing."

Brooke's eyes narrowed right back, and her hands made fists on her hips. She reminded him of her niece in that moment. "In fact, it wasn't. They also brought me dinner."

"Well, you wouldn't need dinner if you were at home where you belong," another voice said. Rye rounded the corner, and he wasn't alone.

Rachel rushed over to Brooke. "Are you okay?"

The fam was all here. Well, except for the kids, and that was a blessing because Paige would probably try to defend her beloved aunt. He could only imagine what the Harper twins were saying about him and Bay.

Brooke waved off her worry. "It was tires. No one threatened me except my own brothers."

Rachel looked back at her husbands. "You threatened her? You know I've been quiet in this thing, but I would like some explanations as to why my sister-in-law is now living with Beth McNamara-O'Malley."

"Who's with the kids?" Brooke asked and winced. "I'm so sorry, Rach. I promised I would watch them tonight and I completely forgot. I got this job offer."

"Yeah, I heard about that," Rye countered. "What's Cleo paying you? I would bet it's next to nothing. Does she know you design for a living? You're not supposed to be working in some rundown theater."

Oh, this was going to turn into a Harper family smackdown.

All of Brooke's relaxed air was gone, and she was stiff again. "It's not rundown."

"Rye, I thought we were going to back off," Max began, looking uncertain for once.

"I have backed off for two weeks, and she's still with them. I don't want anyone taking advantage of my sister," Rye shot back. "She's naïve and not used to saying no. Like she should to these two. And you did flake out on us tonight, Brooke. Henry and Nell came over so Poppy could play with the kids and we could go out to our very non-sexy anniversary dinner."

"Whose fault is that?" Rachel asked, indignation clear in her tone. "Not Brooke's. She's not the reason we're not having sex."

"No, obviously that's Max's fault because he was afraid to get his balls snipped," Rye argued. "But it was Brooke's fault for throwing a hissy fit when she found out we were trying to take care of her."

"By siccing a private investigator on her." Shane couldn't stay quiet, especially when he'd seen Brooke turn in on herself. "She's not naïve. She's sweet natured, but she's worked in a cutthroat business for a whole lot of years."

"And look where it got her," Rye pronounced.

Rachel sighed. "I told you this is not the way to handle it. Brooke, I knew about the PI. They were so worried about you. When you came home at Christmas there was obviously something off, but you wouldn't talk about it. It was wrong, but in their heads you're still six and you need them to protect you from the world. You're an innocent virgin and they have to make sure you someday marry well."

"I told you it's like *Bridgerton*," Shane whispered to his brother who'd come over to stand beside him while they watched the throwdown.

"What's like *Bridgerton*?" Elisa Leal joined them. It was obvious she'd walked down from the station. She had a tablet in her hand and was dressed for her job. Which was deputy of Bliss. She was Nate Wright's second in command since Cameron Briggs had left to work with his partners. She took in the Harper family fight as though it was no big deal. She was used to Bliss drama.

"Max and Rye are pissed that Brooke is choosing to spend time with men they don't approve of," Bay supplied. "Us. I'm pretty sure he's going to tell us if we want to marry her we have to come up with… What's it called? Like a downy?"

His brother was the smart one? The genius? "Downy is a fabric softener. You're talking about a dowry, and we wouldn't pay it. They would."

"Wait? What? We would get to marry her and they would have to pay us?" Bay asked. "And this was bad for us how?"

Shane bit back a groan. This was not going to end well.

* * * *

"Rye, you know I'm not a virgin, right?" Brooke was saying.

Bay was confused, but he was used to that. Sometimes he didn't pick up on social cues the way he should. He was almost sure her brothers should know the answer to that since they'd caught him with his pants down that first morning. Not literally. He'd had pants on, but there was zero way he hadn't spent the night in Brooke's bed. Since there wasn't any other place to sleep.

Was his brother pissed at him?

He shouldn't have made that crack about what happened at Kingman Ranch, but he also didn't want Shane's anxiety to get Brooke all riled up. No one was after them. All the talk about the weird things that happened on the ranch was just that. Talk. Ranch hands liked to mythologize everything.

"I do not need to know anything like that." Rye sounded awfully prim.

"Oh, but you did need to know everything a private investigator could find out," Brooke accused.

"He was worried about you, sweetie." Rachel seemed determined to keep the peace.

Max chose to turn on the deputy. "Why the hell would you put out that there was a slasher after my sister? I ran all the way here thinking I would have to fight Jason or that *Halloween* guy."

Elisa's lips curled up. "Because sometimes chaos is fun, and I know Hal is listening even when the sheriff asked him to stop. I didn't exactly put it like that when I called Nate to let him know what's going on, but I did know where Hal would take it. So here we are. Now I'd like to figure out what happened and why that light is out."

"Because it needs to be changed," Rye replied, obviously ready to get back to the fight with his sister.

"It was on earlier." Mel Hughes stepped into the parking lot, and Bay realized their truck wasn't the last vehicle left. There were two. Mel's Chevy from like the eighties or something and a big SUV he would bet was Stef Talbot's. "The lot was well lit when I parked here an hour ago. I had to meet with my friend, Ash. He's having some trouble with portals opening and needed some advice. Hey, sweetie. I was about to come down and see if you needed some coffee. I hate that Nate has you on nights. You know that's when the worst alien sightings happen. Ash is worried about an invasion."

Lord. This was about to take a turn.

"My guys brought me dinner and a big thermos of coffee since I can't figure out Gemma's monstrosity. Ash? I haven't met him. Does he work for the government?" Elisa grinned her father's way.

Rachel was arguing with her husbands, completely ignoring the deputy and Mel. Brooke was standing beside her sister-in-law.

He wondered where Stef was. That was his Navigator. Had it gotten hit, too?

"Ash and his boy do some work for the government. They're super soldiers, created and bred for war, but when their galaxy was finally peaceful, the public decided they were too dangerous to live," Mel explained like all of this was perfectly normal. "He managed to get out with his whole creche, and they've been here on Earth for the last several years. Good man. Blends in real well and is always helpful when I need him. Now why are Max and Rye acting like assholes? Beyond Max's normal level. I heard they kicked Brooke out because they didn't like her new boyfriends."

"Not her boyfriends," Rye said quickly, turning from his wife's lecture. "They are nothing more than an act of desperation."

"Desperation?" Brooke asked, her eyes narrowing.

Mel gave him a pat on the shoulder as the Harpers started in again. "Don't take that unkindly. They've been more like Brooke's daddy than her brothers. You two seem real nice."

"You had no right," Brooke declared.

There was a lot going on around him.

"I didn't notice the lights," Shane was saying to Elisa. "We got here when it was still light, so they wouldn't have been on. There were a bunch of cars here then."

Elisa made a note on her tablet. "It was on earlier when I did a drive-by on my way in. It's actually two lights, if you notice. They were both fine earlier. We don't have a big civic workforce taking care of things like streetlights, so whoever's on duty checks every couple of days. I find it highly suspicious that they stopped working at the same time and right before an act of vandalism."

"Tell me something, Rye." The Harper clan ignored the whole police report thing, preferring to do their form of family therapy here and now. Brooke had her hands on her hips and a frown on her face. She was always pretty, even when she was cutting a man down to size. "Why didn't you get me a chastity belt when I was a kid if you're so determined I'm going to marry the right person and need to be ready to hand my virginity to him."

Rye's jaw straightened, and a stubborn look hit his face. "You didn't need a chastity belt. Not when we made sure everyone in this town was watching you. Don't you remember how Teeny and Marie happened to be at the movie theater in Alamosa whenever you were on a date? Or at the Chili's you thought was too far out for me or Max to follow you?"

That was not going to go the way Rye thought it would. Although Bay would admit he had no idea what Rye thought he was going to get out of this beyond pissing his sister off. He needed to get this thing done so he could figure out how to get them back home. Because the way this was going Brooke might marry them tonight just to piss her brothers off.

"Was anything stolen out of the truck?" Elisa asked as her dad went over to check on his own truck.

Bay had looked through the cab before he'd gone back for Brooke and his brother. "Not that I can find. We didn't have much in there. We keep our tools in the bunkhouse since we tend to use horses or four wheelers at work."

"I'm going to go take some pictures and make sure they didn't hit the other cars," Elisa said, taking out her phone.

"You had people follow me?" Brooke kind of screeched the question.

"We had people looking out for you, sweetie." When had Max become the nice one?

"Do you think I made it up?" Shane kept his voice low, his eyes still on Brooke. "Do you honestly believe that I would make shit up to get out of a place I didn't want to be in?"

Bay knew he'd fucked up the minute the words left his mouth. "I think you thought you saw something and it made an excellent excuse to get out of a place you weren't comfortable with."

"Brooke, you were a teenager, and you were driving off to meet boys an hour away from home." Rachel seemed to be the voice of reason. "They didn't have experience as parents then. They took things a little too far, but can you blame them?"

"I know what I saw," Shane said stubbornly.

"I thought you saw a glint of metal," Bay reminded him. "You didn't come back and say you saw a bunch of guns. You said the crate lid came slightly off and you saw something metallic."

"Well, they wouldn't have been talking about offing us if I saw fencing materials," Shane insisted.

"Oh, I can blame them." Brooke ignored everything but her family. "I can blame them because the last time it happened I was twenty-four. I had come home for vacation and met a nice tourist, and guess who was at the Chili's? Mel and Cass. I got to have skillet queso while discussing the mating habits of aliens, and guess who didn't get to mate that day?"

Elisa was still filling out her report even as she walked back to them. "Are you sure nothing was stolen? Because they did a number on the cab. It looks like they went through everything."

"I actually think they did steal something." Bay nodded with a frown. Damn. He'd kind of hidden it from his brother so he didn't have to share or be told he was getting pudgy. "I had a whole Snickers bar in the glove box and now it's gone."

He'd been looking forward to that Snickers.

Shane rolled his eyes. "I fed it to Maurice. No one stole it. Could we pay attention to the real problem we have?"

"You gave Maurice candy?" Maurice was the legendary moose who walked the woods around Bliss and made frequent appearances in town. There were a bunch of myths and legends about the big guy, including the one about how if someone offered Maurice food and he accepted it, that meant the person would become part of the town.

Now he had to get another Snickers bar and hunt down the moose because he wasn't getting left out.

"He looked hungry," Shane admitted. "Can we focus now?"

"I'm trying to help by getting the police report out of the way," Bay argued.

"Why? So we can get insurance to fix the tires?" Shane asked with a long-suffering sigh. "In case you forgot, we don't have insurance."

"Twenty-four? She was twenty-four years old?" Rachel rounded on Rye. "You told me you only did it when she was a teenager and you didn't want her taken advantage of."

"Well, I still don't want her taken advantage of. You don't know how guys are, Rach. If you fall in bed with them too soon, they treat you like a…" Rye stopped, and his mouth went closed.

"Like a what?" Rachel's tone had gone icy. "You should finish that sentence and then give me a timeline on how long it is before it's okay to sleep with a man. I slept with Max on our first date. It wasn't much of a date. He caught me swimming in the pond in the back field and we did it right then and there. Did that make me a whatever you were about to call your sister?"

"I didn't mean it like that." Rye lost his cold, calm demeanor, and his hands were out as though he could stave off the attack. "I just think she's a bit naïve and needs someone to look out for her. You know she is practically a nun in New York. She doesn't like the same things you do."

"Like sex?" Rachel asked. "It's okay for you and Max to knock me up about a hundred times, but your saintly sister is to be kept pure and innocent." She sniffled and turned to Brooke. "Sweetie, I'm sorry. I don't mean to…"

Brooke waved her off and then reached for her hand. "I know you're not saying anything bad about me, but my brothers are. It's okay for them to have a sex life but I should keep myself virginal or some shit until they find a good man for me to marry. And don't think I didn't figure out Stef was sending men you all approved of my way. Did he think I wanted to date some banker?"

"Yeah, but he was doing that because Brooke asked to be set up," a new voice said. "I told him we needed to find someone a bit more artistic."

And there was the owner of the last vehicle in the lot. Stef and Jen Talbot were here, and his humiliation was probably complete. Unless Trev or Jamie showed up.

Jennifer Talbot dropped her husband's hand and rushed to her friend. "Rachel, are you okay?"

Max frowned and turned their way. "What do you mean you don't have insurance?"

"She didn't ask you to set her up," Rachel answered Jen. "I would bet she didn't know they've had a private firm doing background workups on all the men she's dated."

"She doesn't date much." Rye stepped closer to Stef, who had a deeply constipated look on his face.

Probably because his date night had now turned into Family

Fight Night.

"Stef, when you parked, were the overhead lights on?" Elisa looked down at her notes.

"You sicced PIs on the guys I dated in the city?" Brooke asked.

"I think both lights were on or I would have called it in," Stef told Elisa. "I would at least have made a note for someone to come out and fix it."

Stef was the town engineer. Architect. Something that meant he took care of shit for the town along with the mayor and council.

"Again, it wasn't like there were many men, but yes, I had the ones you dated checked out," Rye replied. "Brooke, we have done everything we did to protect you from men like the ones you're getting dangerously close to right now. Do you know they both have records?"

"For bar fighting." Stef was dressed in jeans and a T-shirt, expensive boots on his feet. "I've gone over this with you before. They're good men. You know Max has a record that's way longer than Bay and Shane."

"At least Max has insurance, and I stand by all my false arrests. Nate is prejudiced against me because he knows his wife once had a crush on me and he was a second choice. Or maybe third, since I think Callie only took him on because of Zane," Max announced.

Yeah, Bay had figured out those relationships quickly. Max was a mouthy asshole who pushed the sheriff way too hard and got taken in on a regular basis, while Zane poured him beers and didn't tell about Max's hot wing addiction.

Jen gasped. "I can't believe he said that."

Rachel wiped her eyes and put a stoic expression on her face. "I should get home. I would bet Nell's having a hell of a time with Paige. Getting her to eat vegetables is a real trial these days, and the boys are a handful. This was a bad idea. We don't need to go out anymore. We have too much to handle at home."

"We can't afford more than liability. And honestly, we would end up paying more than the truck is worth." There was something wrong with this scenario. If there were three cars in this lot, then two of them were absolutely more break-in worthy than theirs. "Uhm, why would they break into our truck when Stef's car is over there? Did they not see it?"

Elisa sighed. "That's why I'm trying to establish a timeline."

"There is nothing wrong with Bay and Shane. I know I joked about Brooke breaking them, but that was a long time ago. I kind of think they might be good for her now," Stef announced and turned Brooke's way. "Brooke, I'm sorry for the part I've had in this. You should know the only reason I agreed to pay for the PI was I knew they would do it if I didn't, and they don't need to be spending money right now. They're expanding the business and have a new kid on the way, and they're stubborn about what they consider charity. I didn't want them to have more pressure than they have right now. They were worried about you. You weren't yourself the last time you were here."

"Well, now we know for sure she's not herself since she's decided to take up with those two," Rye accused. "And Max is just annoying. Those two have serious time on their records."

"I don't have any time." Shane was confused. "I mean I did spend a night in the Amarillo jail because I got caught in a bar fight. But I pled out and did thirty days' worth of community service. Bay, too."

"Bay shouldn't be getting into damn fights because he could damage his hands," Stef said with a shake of his head.

"I jumped in so he didn't hurt his hands," Shane admitted. "I remembered what you said. It doesn't matter if my hands get broke."

Wow, that sounded bad, and it wasn't at all what Stef had said. He had told them they were too old to pull this crap anymore and asked if Bay had thought about what he would do if he couldn't paint or sculpt anymore because he got his hands crushed at a honky-tonk.

"Shane." Brooke turned to him. "Of course it matters, and Stef is an asshole if he told you that."

"I did not say that." Stef defended himself.

"Yes, Sheriff." Elisa was on her radio. "He totally said that. I think Max still thinks you were Callie's second choice and that's why you jail him so often."

"Hey." Even in the dim light, he could see how pale Max had gone. "I didn't put it like that. Nate, I was kidding, man. Your deputy is mean."

Shane leaned toward the radio. "He absolutely said that, Sheriff. He said it like he was proud. And his wife is standing right here. Also, could you weigh in on who has the worse criminal record? Because he's using that as an excuse to make Brooke feel bad for dating us."

All true, but Bay wasn't sure Rachel needed to hear that right now. Something was up with her. Tears caressed her cheeks, and she put a hand to her stomach. He suddenly remembered one of the only smart things his father ever said to him.

You got to use the things you have. Everything you own is an asset, and if it isn't you should probably throw it away.

Sometimes he wondered if his father had been talking about him.

But tonight he at least had something he could offer. "Miss Rachel, I'm sorry we interrupted your dinner at Stella's. I have some leftover cookies. Brooke likes it when we bring her a picnic for dinner."

He didn't mention what they liked to do after.

Rachel sniffled. "From the bee lady?"

"Oh, Rach loves those charcuterie boards they make there. You know I didn't get to finish my dinner either," Max pointed out. "By now those waitresses will have thrown it all out, and I was looking forward to that peach pie."

Brooke's head shook. "You are such an asshole. Look, both of you. I am leaving with Bay and Shane and there's not a damn thing you can do about it. And I would back off right now if you know what's good for you."

Max's head shook. "Rye, we're going home. Rach needs a break. Stef, will you make sure Brooke and those two can get back to the G?"

Stef pulled out his keys and offered them to Shane. "I'll do one better. Take it. Mel can drop us off on his way home, and we'll drive Jen's until we can get your tires replaced. And do not fight me on this, Bailey Kent. You need transportation and so does she."

"And I want to finish my report," Elisa announced. "I checked my dad's truck. It was fine."

"Also, I definitely remember seeing Bay and Shane's truck when I came in," Mel offered. "Been worried about them getting stuck out on the alien highway because that truck is on its last legs. You know the greys have been working that highway lately."

He'd been taught that little green men were actually little gray men. He tried to stay away from Mel's world. Nice guy. Weird world. "The whole cast was here earlier and the crew. They left a couple of hours ago."

"So you were bugging my sister at work," Rye said under his breath.

"You can't help yourself, can you?" Rachel sounded dull, her head shaking. "Is this the way you're going to treat Paige?"

"Are you asking if I'm going to protect our daughter?" Rye asked.

"Protect her from what? From enjoying herself? From having good sex." She looked to Brooke. "Unless the sex isn't good."

"I'm not wearing a butt plug for my health," Brooke replied.

Max winced and his head hung low. "Too much information."

"She's doing it to rebel. She's feeling bad because she got fired and she's acting out," Rye replied.

"She is not a child," Rachel announced, and her shoulders squared.

Shane took the keys. "Elisa, can we do this tomorrow morning? I think we should get Brooke out of here. It's not a good environment for her."

His brother was right, but those probably weren't the words he would have used. Or rather they're exactly the words he would have used, and Shane was supposed to be better at this than he was.

"Good environment? You think keeping her out at Trev's sex palace is a better environment?" Rye started to get in Shane's face.

Elisa stepped in. "Do I need to call in some backup, Rye?"

"I think you might. I think maybe you should take these two in and see what they're truly after," Rye said, giving them both a really good stink eye.

"I'm pretty sure they're after Brooke," Max said. "Because you're being ridiculous if you think they're after like our money or something. Or they want to take over our horse farm. I'm trying to figure out what they could be after other than sex."

Bay could answer that question. "We could want to be with her.

We're after her because she's the single most beautiful woman we ever laid eyes on, and I think she might be the one woman who can make us feel whole."

Shit. He'd said that. Out loud. With words and stuff. Him. The quiet one. He was quiet because when he talked, he tended to get in trouble and say weird shit like the stuff about the koala bears.

Everyone was quiet for a moment, and then Elisa put her radio away. "That's sweet, Bay. And Rye, I was talking about you. I was wondering if I was going to need help keeping you from making a fool of yourself for no reason I can see. Also, I was joking about needing help. I assure you I can put you on your ass myself if you push this any further. Your wife is in tears, and your sister is probably feeling humiliated right now."

Brooke shrugged. "I don't know. What Bay said kind of took the sting out, and honestly, the sex is fabulous. I'm more irritated that he made me feel like a whore."

Rye seemed taken aback by everything. His hands came down and his eyes closed for a moment before he opened them again. "I didn't say that, Brooke. I'm sorry if I made you feel that way. I'm worried about you. I'm worried about the world eating you up and spitting you out and not doing anything to protect you. Obviously, no, you don't need to call anyone, and I'll give Stef a ride. I'll move some car seats. We're parked on the other end of Main."

"Might I suggest some family therapy," Elisa offered. Then her dad was whispering in her ear, and she nodded. "I'll take the Talbots back."

"Max, Rye, let's go to Trio and get a drink and have a talk." Mel tipped his hat Brooke's way. "Are you going to take care of her? She needs a break."

Rachel? He thought Mel was talking about Rachel.

Rachel sniffled and put her arm through Brooke's. "I can use a break. Is it okay?"

Brooke nodded. "Of course."

"Rach," Rye began.

Max put a hand out. "No. You are going to let her have a night. Maybe a couple of nights. Baby, we'll take care of the kids. You relax, and maybe we should do that talky thing Alexei wants us too because we've got a lot on our plates and we're not expressing ourselves properly." He put a hand to his gut. "Wow. Words can make you nauseous."

"I'll call Nell and Henry," Jen promised. "See if they need any help."

"I'll process the truck and have Long-Haired Roger tow it back to his shop," Elisa announced. "I might need to talk some more, though. I don't like how this feels. But it can wait until morning."

Everyone was breaking up. Rye was looking at Rachel like he was losing her, but Max made him walk away with Mel.

What was happening?

"Uhm, can I drop you off somewhere?" He was still feeling weird about basically telling Brooke he was crazy about her in front of everyone. How would she handle it? They were supposed to be playing it cool.

Shane leaned over. "I think she's coming with us."

Brooke's chin tilted up. "She *is* coming with us."

Rachel was coming with them. To the place where he'd planned to fuck her sister-in-law all night.

Well, at least Rye was going to get what he wanted.

Bay sighed and followed his brother and hoped he hadn't fucked everything up.

Chapter Eleven

Brooke set the coffee down in front of her sister-in-law and wondered if Bay and Shane were already riding the fences. They'd been out of bed before she woke up, and the night before had been weirdly tense when they'd gotten home and settled Rachel into the guest bedroom.

Bay and Shane had been weird. Not with her. They were sweet and affectionate and made sure Rachel had everything she needed. But she'd felt the tension.

They hadn't even tried to get in her pants, and she worried it had something to do with what was said the night before. Did Shane not feel the same way Bay did? When Bay said what he had about how they felt about her, had Shane been upset?

Rachel looked down at the coffee. "Do you know how long it's been since I sat in the quiet and enjoyed a cup of coffee?"

She felt for her sister-in-law. She settled in across from her. The foreman's house was cozy, with three bedrooms and a nice-sized kitchen. "Well, I think this coffee is excellent. Beth stocks it for Trev, and she sent some over. You know Trev is made of caffeine, right? At least that's what Beth says. So this coffee is truly fine."

Rachel's lips turned up faintly, and she brought it to her lips. She took a sip and her eyes closed. "Yes, it is."

Brooke tasted the rich roast and sighed. "It's ready before I wake up. Did you get any sleep?"

"Is it wrong to say I slept better than I have in a long time?" Her sister-in-law sat back, and her gaze went to the big windows that showed the expansive ranch. "Ethan is teething, and Max and Rye are trying to expand the business, which means they're gone a lot of the time. They've been making excellent money with breeding, but it requires them to be on the road a lot. Paige is about to be out of school for the summer, so I'm going to have three kids and this pregnancy to deal with, and now I wonder who the hell your brother is."

She knew who Rachel was talking about, and for once it wasn't Max. "Rye feels the need to be in control. He has to be the respon-sible one. Not that Max isn't, but he can let things go that maybe he shouldn't. Rye can't do that. When our mom died and our dad walked away, Rye took on the task of getting a job that had hourly requirements while Max took care of the business. Do you think Rye wouldn't have preferred the other? I assure you he did, but when times got tough, Rye was the one who stepped up. And Max took care of all the stuff like making sure both Rye and I were ready for work or school. I often wonder if we would have survived if one of my brothers hadn't stayed. They're not capable of functioning without each other."

Rachel nodded. "Oh, I know. They're halves of a whole."

Bay and Shane were the same. Did Shane understand how important he was? Or did he think he was nothing more than the guy who did the mundane tasks? Did Bay understand that he brought more to the table than artistic genius? "How do you handle it?"

"I don't know that I am right now." Rachel put her coffee down. "I'm tired. I'm frustrated. I'm anxious. I'm also feeling shame because I know they're trying. I'm going to love this baby, but I thought we were done, and I don't blame Max. I knew he was scared about the procedure and I still slept with him, still let myself get lost and didn't think about anything but feeling sexy and young again. You know when I talked about the pond last night?"

"Yep. It was too much information, but then there was a lot of that, and some of it was from me, so I think we should go with it," Brooke replied.

Rachel put a hand on her barely-there belly. "I know where this one was conceived and exactly who his bio dad is. I went out to that pond for some peace and quiet and then Max showed up and it was like that first time all over. I didn't think. I only wanted to feel that way again."

"Rachel, you're not old."

"Maybe not," her sister-in-law allowed. "I guess the better way to put it was I wanted to feel like something other than a mom. I sound terrible. I love my kids."

"Of course you do." Tears pierced her eyes, and she reached out for her sister. "Have you talked to them about it? How you feel?"

"Have I told my husbands how unhappy I am with the current state of affairs? No. I don't want them to know. I'm supposed to be happy. Everything is supposed to work. We love each other. That's supposed to be enough."

Brooke squeezed her hand. "Damn, I think I've been around Logan enough that I know what to say to you. Rachel, the story didn't end when you said *I do*. It started there. You can't have four kids in seven years without a whole lot of change, and change requires one thing. Communication. What if Max and Rye are feeling the same thing but it's coming out in different ways?"

Rachel's brows rose. "What do you mean?"

"I mean for you it's anxiety. You feel the disconnect. You feel like you've become nothing more than a mom, and the wife part is about service instead of intimacy. I bet they feel it, too." Brooke groaned as a couple of hard revelations hit her. "Damn it. When Rye feels anxious, he tries to control things. He feels like if he's in control, he can handle it. But he won't ask for help. And what is something he can try to control?"

"You. Or at least the world around you," Rachel said. "Max is worried about money. I told him I didn't think we needed to worry, but we can't always go to Stef."

"Yes, you can. I assure you, you can." Stef had more money than he would ever know how to spend. His money made money at this point, and her brothers and Callie were Stef's family. No one would question Stef investing in his brothers' business. Any more than they asked why he sponsored artists from time to time. Stef might never have been a starving artist himself, but he cared about them.

Would Stef be interested if she started her own business? Or maybe wanted to invest in helping her change things up?

"They're worried about paying for college for four kids." Rachel sighed and sat back. "I'm worried about having four kids under the age of eight. I need to admit something to you."

Brooke already knew. "You were excited I was coming because I would babysit for you, and having me in a tiny house of my own on the property would make that super easy. Especially since I didn't have a boyfriend and my job was in shambles."

"I didn't know about the job. I thought you would come for a nice long visit."

"I'm not upset about that. I love my niece and my nephews, and I will help you out. I'm pretty sure that's why Beth offered up this place."

Rachel's eyes narrowed. "Yes, I believe so."

Oh, she did not want to start a range war between those two. Beth wouldn't be able to handle it. She was sweet, and while she had grown in confidence, she wasn't ready for Rachel's fury. "She's got three kids, too, and Hope is having a hard time with nausea."

Rachel's expression softened. "Damn, I didn't think about that. See, I'm being selfish."

"Admitting how you feel isn't selfish. You're under a lot of pressure, and you think you're letting Max and Rye down by not being happy about the current arrangements. But they're worried, too. My brothers love you. You are the sun in the sky to them, and they would never want to hurt you. Talk to them. I can watch the kids for a night or two."

"Maybe you could even switch houses." That had come from the window. The open window. Beth McNamara-O'Malley stopped in front of it, and she was holding a big basket. "Rachel, you have a delivery, and I apparently should make an apology."

She moved to the front door, and Brooke went to greet her, Rachel following behind. Now she could see there was a basket and a lovely bouquet. A dozen red roses. It looked like her brothers were going all out.

Beth was a petite woman with long brown and gold hair and a sweet face. "I think they included every snack food known to man."

Rachel sniffled and took the basket as Beth set the flowers on the bar. "That's so sweet of them. I'm surprised they're not on the doorstep demanding I come home."

"Max dropped it off and asked me to look out for you while you rest. He said there's a note in the basket," Beth explained. "Rachel, I'm so sorry. I didn't realize you were struggling, but I should have. With Nell pregnant and Callie taking fertility treatments, you can't count on them the way you could. I know Jen's been working on the school and trying to convince Stef to have another kid. I was thinking of myself, though you should know I love the hell out of those boys and I always would have offered them the house."

Rachel wiped a couple of tears and offered Beth a hug. "I'm glad they have you because I think Brooke needs this place for a little while."

Her work here was at least halfway done. Though it sucked that she probably had to forgive her brother.

Beth stepped back. She was dressed in overalls and looked ready for a day of installing dry wall or chinking a cabin. "She's welcome for however long she needs. Honestly, I know Trev and Jamie were kind of hoping they would take a bigger role here. Bo is the nominal foreman, but he wants to have more time to spend with the kids and us. I guess offering this place is kind of an incentive to stay around. I know they like to roam."

But did they? Oh, now that she thought about it, maybe Shane wasn't irritated with Bay's declaration of…longing, wanting? Bay had kind of accused him of lying about the reasons they left Kingman Ranch.

Had he liked it there? Had a girl there? Had Bay been irritated at having to leave her behind? What if it had started to get serious and that was why Shane had decided to escape in the middle of the night.

She let that thought go. If Bay had a girl there, he would have mentioned it because he didn't lie well. He tended to say whatever was on his mind, and that meant she took what he said at face value.

Shane would have gently explained to her that he didn't feel the same way as Bay.

So this might be about leaving their last job.

"What do you know about why they ended up here at the G?"

Brooke asked. "Also, would you like some coffee? I don't actually think the boys drink it much. They left me a full pot this morning."

"I would love a cup," Beth said as she followed them back into the kitchen. She sat down beside Rachel as Brooke poured the coffee. It was kind of nice to have a place where her friends and family could come in and have a cup of coffee and talk and not have to deal with the fact that there were only two chairs because nothing else fit. "I know they left their last ranch pretty quickly. The way Shane told it, they weren't comfortable there."

"This is Kale Kingman's ranch, right?" Rachel picked up her mug. "Haven't there always been rumors around him?"

Beth nodded. "Trev met him once and said he wouldn't do any business with him. He talked Jamie out of a couple of ventures Kingman offered us. I don't think any of our business partners chose to work with him."

The Circle G was a part of a ranching cooperative with a couple of ranches in Texas. They used organic principles and worked on the idea of quality over quantity. The Barnes-Fleetwood Collective had become a major source of beef for upscale restaurants and hotels.

She was so curious. Kingman was a flamboyant figure, though he likely wouldn't appreciate the title. He was known for doing things up big, and he often admitted to playing around in politics if it helped his business. "Why? Was there something shady about him?"

"Not on the surface, but Trev has a bit of an instinct for people who hide their darkness well. Not that I think Kingman's trying. He doesn't mind admitting to screwing people over, though he says it makes him the smarter businessman," Beth continued. "Bo would have fallen for it immediately because my man only sees the best in people, but that's why Trev's the Dom and we are his happy, well-loved and protected subs. Bay and Shane had done some seasonal work here before and they'd been reliable, so when Stef asked if there were positions, we made a couple. I worried they wouldn't stay after the beginning of the year, but they've seemed intent on hanging around. I'm hoping this relationship with Brooke seals the deal."

Brooke shrugged. "Well, it's not like I have anything better to do. Maybe I should chuck it all, move back to Bliss, open a daycare, and live out my life here."

"Okay, I know that sounds bad right now…" Rachel began.

Beth snorted and took the coffee Brooke offered her. "She is not going to do that, but you and I need to sit down and find a solution to our childcare problems. School only lasts nine months out of the year. We still need breaks in the summer. I say we call a meeting. No one's shot a son of a bitch recently."

Ah, the women's meeting. It usually involved tea and cakes and discussions of what to do the next time an outlaw MC came to town or a serial killer or the mafia. It often also was about the women of the town figuring out how to help when problems arose. "We're going to have more and more kids in the next couple of years. River told me she and Jax are trying. Nell and Rachel and Hope are about to add to the baby boom."

"Laura and Rafe and Cam are looking to adopt again," Rachel added. "And I truly believe Stef is going to come around. I talked to Seth at Stella's last night and with Logan finishing up his doctorate, they want to come out more, and Georgia is merely waiting until her body heals before trying again."

She'd heard all about Georgia's plans on the plane trip. "She wants like six kids. Logan goes a little pale when she talks about it. Seth wants to compromise on three at most. But my point is the only reason we haven't had big kids' group activities available right here in Bliss was because there weren't many kids. And Mel's alien camp does not count."

"But now we're going to have enough for it to be good business to offer summer programs," Rachel mused.

Beth took a long sip of coffee and glanced down at her watch. "I have to get going. Hale is picking me up. We're meeting with Jesse and Cade about adding on a room to their cabin. But it's a surprise, so don't tell Gemma. They've saved up and they're basically going to make their old bedroom their office and Hale and I are putting in a new primary bedroom and a bath to die for. With extra closet space. It's going to make me want to renovate."

If there was one thing she knew about Beth McNamara-O'Malley, it was this. "Everything makes you want to renovate."

"That sounds like fun," Rachel said with a watery smile.

Beth looked thoughtful for a moment. "Why don't you come

with us? I'm considering all the options and I'm going to be honest, I'm worried I'll have to hold their hands and talk them out of some things. Jesse and Cade have spent a lot of time in mechanic shops. Their tastes tend to be limited."

"Oh, they have to get that right. Gemma has very specific tastes," Rachel agreed. "Jesse thinks putting gold on everything makes it designer. It could be fun if you don't mind. Want to come along, Brooke? You have the best taste here."

She was sure Beth and Rachel could handle it, and it would be good for Rachel to get out. But she had things to do. "I need to get to town. I need to get dressed and call a Fuber. Unless they're in school, but I think they finished up early. I'll check the app."

"Oh, you don't have to do that. The Navigator is still here," Beth announced. "Shane had to go into town for some parts, but he got a ride."

"I noticed the keys on the counter," Rachel added. "I think they left it for you. There are enough vehicles and people here that they can easily get a ride. That's what's great about living in a place like this. You have so many people around to help."

And Rachel was feeling isolated.

She was surprised they'd left her the SUV, but she would take it. She needed to run to the theater. "I'll try to return before they get back. Bay wants to go out to Stef's and get some work done. I heard him on the phone earlier, and he said something about a materials delivery. I think it was clay."

"Everyone's getting ready for his show at the end of summer. Stef thinks it could be his big break." Rachel hugged her. "Thank you for letting me stay the night. I'll have Beth drop me at the house."

"You can stay," Brooke said, hugging her.

Rachel stepped back. "I know I can. I know my husbands are patient and understand, but my kids won't. I'm heading home after I spend a nice day out and Max and Rye and I are going to sit down and talk. Maybe we could use some time at the clinic."

Alexei Markov had formed a mental health clinic that serviced the valley and the small towns around Bliss. He offered triples therapy as one of his specialties. The Bliss Wellness Center also offered help to those affected by alien abduction. Mel and Cass held special sessions.

She missed Bliss.

"It's never bad to give your marriage a tune up," Beth said with a smile. "We've been. We went after the boys were born because I was feeling too focused on nothing but Miranda and the boys, and it was hurting my marriage. Alexei helped me see that letting Bo and Trev be hands-on dads helped us all. I was very much in the mindset of where I came from instead of where I want to be. I thought the mom should do it all. Now we split the load pretty equally, and I get to do a job that feeds my soul."

Rachel nodded. "Yeah, I feel that. I love my life, but I might need something more. I might need some work outside my house."

"Let's talk about it." Beth gave her the biggest smile. "If you want to learn about home repairs, I'm your girl. You could start trying some stuff out and see what fills your soul."

"I would like that." Rachel smiled back, the first time Brooke had seen her sister-in-law smile in days. "And I'll give you some recipes for Hope. Nell taught me how to make some ginger candy that helped with nausea. Brooke, I'll see you later."

"And I'll make sure you get all your presents. I'll drop the basket and flowers off at your place."

Beth's head shook. "Oh, I'm sorry. The flowers are for you. I should have mentioned that. See, the guys are trying."

"Oh, they're trying. Let me tell you what happened last night," Rachel was saying as the door closed behind her.

They sent her flowers? It was odd. When had they had time to go down to The Trading Post and get some flowers? She reached for the card. Sure enough, her name was on it but there wasn't an address.

They shouldn't spend money on flowers. They had a truck to repair. She hoped this wasn't what put that distance between them. She opened the card and felt her whole body flush.

I'm at the Lodge. We need to talk. We can make all of this right and you can take your place at Bianchi. Call me. You've been keeping secrets.

Mark

Her old boss was here and her peace was completely shaken.

* * * *

Shane was still thinking about Bay's accusations even as he sat in the cab of a truck that would either take him to his doom or maybe drop him off in the middle of nowhere and leave him to rot.

"Was she okay last night?" Max Harper had been at the front door of the main house when Shane had been walking through. He'd been planning on asking Noah Bennett if he could catch a ride into town, but the vet was closed off with his wife. Hope was having a hard time.

Did he need a credit card to call a Fuber? Or did those kids take cash? That was what he'd been thinking when Max had shown up, shoved a bunch of stuff for his wife Shane's way, and then asked if they could talk.

Shane decided they could kill two birds with one stone and offered himself up as a sacrifice. He'd passed the basket to Beth, who it looked like already had some flowers, and gotten into Max Harper's truck.

Somewhere out there his brother was fixing fences and probably still thinking Shane was a moron who didn't know what he saw. Or heard.

Shane watched the acres fly by as Max started toward the town. "Rachel seemed sad, but I think she was comfortable. I think she's just… I don't know. I don't have a lot of experience with moms. I think she loves her kids and she loves you, but she's overwhelmed."

He was a bit overwhelmed, too. Last night when Bay had made his statement of intent, Shane had frozen. It had come to such crystal clarity. Bay could find a way to fit with Brooke's world. Eccentric, renowned artist was kind of the dream for a woman like Brooke.

"Well, that's what happens when you think you're finally done with kids and suddenly your asshole husband gets you pregnant again." Max stared out, too. The man seemed different this morning. More serious. Like sleeping without his wife in bed had made him more solemn. "I fixed it, though. At least I hope I did. I have to go back in a week and make sure none of my swimmers survived. Gotta make sure Doc drowned them real good. You using a condom when you fuck my sister?"

"You could push me out here," Shane offered. It looked like there were some soft places to land. If he waited until they were closer to town, he could push him over an edge and into a chasm.

Like what they planned to do to him and Bay in Wyoming. You know it would serve Bay fucking right to find his murdered body in a ditch somewhere. See if that asshole could get along without him.

"Been pushed out of a lot of moving vehicles, have you?" Max asked.

"Just the one." Shane wasn't going to play scared around Max Harper. He either would try to hurt him or he wouldn't. He rather thought this whole trip was about telling Shane how he wasn't worthy of Brooke.

He wasn't traditionally educated.

He didn't have a family to offer her.

He had a job that didn't pay much and was often transitory.

His brother thought he was a liar.

"Who the hell pushed you out of a car?" Max sounded shocked for once.

He hadn't thought anything could shock Max Harper. Well, he would probably laugh. "Let's just say the supposed maternal figure in my life did not want to take me to a family wedding but my cousin insisted, so she accidently took a curve too fast on the golf cart she used to take people around to look at apartments. She was a property manager for the complex we lived at for a couple of years. This was after my dad lost all our money gambling. They had to sell the house her parents left them and my grandfather's ranch. To say she was unhappy would be an understatement. Naturally she blamed me. She then tried to sue the complex saying the seatbelt was faulty, but she told me not to wear it. So it was a win win for her. I broke my arm, and she didn't have to explain my presence at the wedding. I stayed home alone. I was nine. They were gone for three days. They left food for the dog at least."

Max's hands eased, and he slowed the truck to the normal speed limit. "Your own momma did that to you and Bay?"

He didn't know? He wasn't surprised. Everyone thought they were fraternal twins. "She was my stepmother. My mom had an affair with her husband and while she tried her hardest to prove I wasn't his, DNA didn't lie. When my momma left me on her doorstep, she decided I would make a fine whipping boy."

"I thought you and…"

It was what most people thought. "We're a couple of months apart, though I don't remember a lot before I went to live with Bay's family. She hated me but she couldn't let me go into the system because that would make her look bad. The good news was she also couldn't starve me because that made her look bad, too. She wouldn't let me eat at the dinner table with her family. I learned how to make simple food when I was young because if I didn't, she would give me a couple of pieces of bread and that would be dinner. Going to school did me a world of good because there were suddenly eyes on me wondering why I weighed half what my brother weighed."

"Holy shit. I thought I had a bad parent."

Just because his stepmom had been worse didn't mean Max hadn't had it bad. And it was obvious the Harper boys had taken a bad situation and made it work. "You did. He left you. Your mother died and while you were mourning her, he left you alone to raise a young girl. He was a shitty parent, Max. You were a good one."

Max stilled at the words and seemed to get emotional. "I don't know that Brooke would say that right now."

If there was one thing he knew, it was that Brooke loved her brothers. She would forgive them eventually. "Brooke is hurt that you don't trust her. She's feeling guilty because she thinks she wasted all the time and money you spent on her."

"That's such bullshit. We never said that."

"The trusting her part or the wasted money and time part?"

Max's head turned, and his expression was oddly calm. "Both, and you're excellent at deflecting, but then I suspect you would have to be. It's hard to be the one who always fucks up, isn't it? Even though you never fucked up. It was just put on you. I've been thinking all this time that you and your brother were somewhat like me and mine. And you are. I keep trying to figure out which one is me and which one is Rye. You see, Rye is the one who always does the right thing and I'm the one who fucks up."

At least Max saw him. He supposed it was inevitable that someone would see through his arrogance and bravado. "Well, then I guess I'm the fuck-up."

"I'm sure your stepmother made you feel that way." Max's tone softened. "Why are you still with Bay? I know your parents died, but I can't imagine wanting to stay with the brother who sat by and watched you be abused."

"He didn't." A single memory washed over him, a moment that formed so much of the core of his being. "When my mom left me on the doorstep, my father wasn't home. My stepmom left me outside. She told me I should run away. That no one wanted me. I didn't know where to go. I had a SpongeBob suitcase and a backpack my mom had packed for me. I remember it was raining and I was cold and she hadn't fed me lunch. She said my new mom would, but it was obvious my new mom didn't want me. It was getting dark and then Bay showed up. He'd come from around the back since his mom was in the living room calling everyone she could trying to figure out how to get rid of me."

"How old were you?" Max asked.

Brooke's brother was going to truly understand how imperfect he was for his sister. "I was five and so was Bay. Dad was doing well at the time. I mean not well enough to pay child support or anything, but they had a nice house and a treehouse in the backyard. Bay took me up there and told me we were brothers and that it didn't matter what his mother said, he was my big brother and he would take care of me. And he did. I spent that first night in a sleeping bag in the treehouse, and then Dad got home and the pastor came and suddenly I had a little space in Bay's room. When he was old enough he told her he would run away if I couldn't do the things he could."

A long moment passed before Max spoke again. "And how did you adapt?"

Shane shrugged. He supposed he had in a lot of ways. Ways he was trying to unlearn. "I learned to not like anything. Or at least to never express I liked something."

"Because she would take it away?"

"Yeah," Shane admitted. "I know everyone says foster care sucks, but it was better for me than being home. It was hard for Bay, though. Despite everything he still had some love for our parents. His mom saw how talented he was. She gave him everything he could want when it came to art. She tried to make it so he didn't have to do a thing but work on his portfolio. She had dreams of him going to art school in Paris. I don't know that would ever have worked out, but one day he had a future and the next he didn't."

Max seemed to think about that. "You never had one so it didn't bother you."

It was nothing less than the truth. "The group home felt like freedom to me."

Max's head shook. "Was there any money? I know that's a stupid question. If there had been money, someone would have come forward and taken you and Bay in. So she wanted Bay to go to art school but she didn't save any money?"

His stepmother had been a complex woman. "In her defense there was never any real money. My father blew it the minute it was in his hands. She thought Bay's talent would save her."

"So you decided to rodeo and make some money that way," Max surmised. "Let me guess—you got tired of making the money and then it all going to pay for your next broken bone."

So he knew the circuit. "By then we knew some ranchers and they hired us on, and that's what we do."

"That's what you do. Bay makes art. According to Stef he's incredibly good, and Stef isn't wrong about those things. What happened to the grant? Stef told me all the money from the auction that day you and your brother tried to buy my wife went to Bay."

"It was ten grand, and we coasted on it for a long time."

"Why doesn't Bay hang out here and work on his art?" Max asked. "Stef would get you a cabin. He's real high on what Bay does."

They'd talked about it, and Shane knew he couldn't do it. He couldn't freeload off his brother. "We liked to move around a lot when we were younger."

"And now?"

How much should he tell this man? "I like Bliss. Bay, too."

"What made you decide on Bliss?"

Shane sighed and turned. "Do you want me to tell you how much I love your sister?"

Max nodded. "Yes. I think it's time for you to say those words to me so I can start dealing with the situation. I'm damn tired of sitting around and pretending everything is going to work out and that all we need is time."

He got the feeling Max was talking about more than Brooke. "I love Brooke. I've loved her from the minute I met her. But I don't know that I'm good enough for her."

"No one is good enough for Brooke." Max's lips curled up in a sad sort of smile. "Sorry, but I remember her as a kid who looked up to me and asked me to tuck her into bed and look for monsters under her bed, and now she's got to deal with the fact that the world can grind you down, and she's doing it all alone. We built that house because we hoped she would come home one day. But not like this."

"I think she feels that. I know you're not saying you're disappointed with her, but you are disappointed, and she can feel it. And I'm saying this knowing it'll probably hurt me in the end because you fighting means she spends more time with us, but the truth of the matter is I want her to be happy more than I want her to be with me." There was a hole in his gut when he said the words. If she left, he wasn't sure that hole would ever fill again. And there was a reason he'd never pushed Bay to take Stef up on all his offers. "I think Bay's going to hit it big someday. I think he'll fit into Brooke's world."

"But you won't."

"I don't think I bring much to the table. I think she probably likes having two men around, but I worry I'll drag them down."

"Shane, that is the voices in your head talking." Max made the turn onto Main Street and quickly pulled into The Trading Post parking lot. "That is what your stepmom taught you at a young age. Bay is perfect, and you're a pain in everyone's ass. I would bet you feel the need to organize everything and take care of the people you think are important in your life. I would bet you handle things for Bay that he doesn't even think about, and you're probably already taking care of Brooke."

"Why would you say that?" He was confused because it almost sounded like Max was trying to convince him he wasn't an asshole who should stay away from his precious family.

"Because Bay is way too caught up in his own shit. He doesn't mean to be, and I'm sure when it's pointed out to him, he wants to make things right, but you two are what I like to call a symbiotic relationship. There's nothing wrong with that. Rye and I wouldn't know what to do without the other. I don't think we were born whole.

Something split, and we had to make sure we survived. Now we have to make sure we properly love and take care of our family. We're failing."

He was being hard on himself. "I think Rachel needs a break."

"I think Rachel needs to be reminded that those kids exist because we love her. She needs to remember that she's the center of the world and Rye and I need to stop being so stubborn and let our family help us out," Max admitted. "Look, the truth of the matter is I'm more like Bay. I sometimes get lost in what I'm doing, what I want. For Bay, it's his art. For me, it's horses and this business. I'm sure Alexei will tell me a big part of my drive to make it all work is to prove to my father that I'm better than he was. He's never come back. Never looked for us."

"My mom has another family. I found her last year. I guess I was curious." A light rain started, gently tapping on the windows and the top of the cab. The good news was he'd put a rain poncho in Bay's pack this morning. "She's in Nebraska. She married a grocery store manager and has two kids. I suppose they're my half siblings. She's got some socials. In her bio she calls herself happy wife and mother of two. Like I never existed. Like I was a mistake she left behind."

Max took a long breath and huffed it out. "So you found your way here. Shane, this can't work if you don't value yourself."

He was surprised at the words. "I thought you didn't want it to work."

"I want my sister happy, and the truth is I'm learning the older I get the more I feel for young men like you. You come by your assholery honestly. I would probably be more freaked out if you weren't on the assholish side. I don't think going back to New York will make Brooke happy."

"You think she should stay here?"

"I think she needs a change. I was always worried about her living in New York. Not because of the city. Because of the industry. She's not ruthless. She's going to be taken advantage of, and quite frankly, she will never like being told what to do. She needs to pick her projects. That's what I want for her. I want to have given her an education and training that makes it possible for her to not get stuck. I love working for us. Really working for my family in a way that maybe one day they'll want to join me. I like building something for us. In our name. Brooke needs to do the same."

"I think she's kind of happy with the job at the theater. I know it doesn't pay much."

"She doesn't have to make much. She doesn't need to be high powered," Max explained. "She's got it in her head that she needs to make something of herself to pay back me and Rye. We only want her happy and fulfilled. Honestly, right now I would just take her talking to us. I was thinking about having all three of you out to dinner."

He wasn't sure he could handle it. "Maybe she could bring Bay. I'm not real good with kids."

"I suspect you're excellent with them," Max countered. "Tell me what's happening. Up until real recently you and Bay wouldn't take a crap alone."

"Of course we… Look, I think Bay is giving this art show thing a go, and when he does, I don't have a place there. Especially…"

"Especially what?"

"He doesn't believe me about why we left our last job. He thinks I made it all up."

"Is this the Kale Kingman stuff?"

He shouldn't be surprised that Max knew. He was sure everyone knew and thought he was a lying asshole. "Yeah."

"You think he was going to take you and your brother out because you caught him doing something criminal?" Max asked.

"I know it sounds…" Shane began.

"It sounds like that fucker finally might get caught. I would believe anything about that man. Why don't you tell me what happened."

Max believed him? There was suspicion in the back of his mind, but he was trying to be more open. Not everyone was out to get him. But Kale Kingman sure as hell was.

Before he could start, there was a knock on the cab. He glanced over and Nate Wright stood there.

Max rolled down the window. "Now, Nate, I know what I said sounds bad…"

"Max, we have trouble," the sheriff said. He eyed Shane. "And I would like to have a talk with that one."

His day had definitely taken a nose dive.

Chapter Twelve

Bay nodded to Trev as he closed the door to the cab. "Thanks for the ride. I wanted to make sure Brooke could get to the theater on time. They're starting dress rehearsals in a couple of days, and that means Brooke's got to work a lot. I don't know what happened with Shane. I'm surprised he hasn't called."

"Yeah, I'm worried, too," his boss admitted. "Beth said she saw him but didn't know he was leaving the ranch. He'll turn up. He seemed upset this morning. Anything happen?"

Bay was at a loss. Shane had been cold and distant. Was he that upset that Rachel was staying with them?

A voice in Bay's head told him it was definitely his fault. He'd called his brother out in front of Brooke, and worse in front of Max and Rye and Rachel. "I might have mentioned I thought that Shane might have fibbed about why we left our last job. I don't think he took it well. I didn't mean to insult him. I left when he wanted to."

Trev joined him on the sidewalk that led to the Feed Store Church. They were picking up a shipment of organic feed. One for the ranch and another they would deliver out at the sanctuary. Trev seemed real high on Nell and Henry's newest venture. He'd said something about every creature deserving a second chance. "This is about Kingman?"

"It's about something Shane claims he saw and then something he heard," Bay admitted. "Shane watches a lot of TV. And he reads a lot of fiction. Sometimes I think he should be a writer."

Trev's expression went serious. "What does he think he saw?"

He shouldn't have said a word, but Trev was starting to be a man he looked up to, and he could use some advice. "He saw some metal when he was unloading something and thought it might be guns."

"We all have guns on a ranch. They're necessary," Trev pointed out.

"Not like rifles or even pistols. I think Shane got it in his head that maybe Kingman was running guns." He waved the thought off. "I shouldn't have said anything but last night I mentioned I thought he made up the story to get us out of there. He wasn't happy on that ranch. I wasn't either, but I can ride things out in a way Shane can't."

When times got tough, he sank into his work. It was why he drew so much when he was out at the Kingman Ranch.

Trev's head shook. "Shane has ridden out things in a way most people can't. He chooses not to now that he's an adult and he can decide what he will and won't put up with."

"I didn't realize you knew that much about our childhood." It made Bay a bit antsy.

"I don't bring men into my home who I don't vet. Well, *I* didn't vet you at all. My partners use a firm in Dallas. I'm sorry if it makes you uncomfortable, but I have a file on you both. My process is to interview potential employees and then have McKay-Taggart run a trace on them. You did what you could for your brother, you know."

Sometimes he didn't. Sometimes he remembered all the times he sat at the dinner table while Shane was stuck in their room. He'd done his best to steal and hide food to supplement what his mother would give Shane, but there were nights his brother went to sleep hungry. Damn it. It didn't matter whether or not he lied. He owed it to Shane to leave when he wanted to.

And if Shane wanted to let Brooke go? What the hell would he do?

"Did I? Sometimes I wonder." He needed to man up and talk to his brother about what went down the night before. He needed to figure out if he was pissed at him for calling him a liar or if he was worried about what Bay had said about how he felt for Brooke.

He'd been so damn sure they were on the same page.

"You were a kid and she was your mom. You did what you could. You need to let that go, but what you shouldn't underestimate is what Kale Kingman is capable of. You don't get that much money and power without being willing to play dirty."

Trev was being hypocritical. "I don't think you would say the same of Stef Talbot."

Trev's head shook. "Stef inherited that money. He didn't make it himself. And I would bet he would tell you his father was pretty ruthless when he was younger. Also, it's not the same. Kale Kingman runs a good portion of Wyoming. He's not happy simply having his ranch. He wants power, and to get that he needs way more money than a ranch can provide. I've always wondered where he got it."

Well, that was a reaction he hadn't expected. "I don't want you to think we know anything for certain, Trev. We know Shane thinks he saw something and then he overheard the foreman and one of the veteran guys talking about taking care of the newbies."

"There have been several accidents on Kingman Ranch," Trev mused. "And I happen to know Kingman likes to hire people without ties to family. That would make them easier to handle if he needed to."

"I don't know exactly what they said." Because he hadn't really listened to his brother that night and then they'd come to Bliss and put it behind them, but one way or another it looked like it was coming back to bite them in the ass. "I find it hard to believe they were going to kill us."

Trev held up a hand. "Well, it seems I have more of an imagination than you do. I think I'd like to talk to Shane."

Maybe Trev taking him seriously would help. Though it still might be a problem. "If he'll talk. I said some things last night that he's mad about."

"You mentioned that," Trev allowed. "He told you he was upset?"

"He's not talking, and that's the problem. I can't tell if he's mad about that or mad because Rachel is staying with us or mad because I basically told the Harper brothers last night that we're going to marry their sister."

Trev snorted at the thought. "It's the first one. Shane wouldn't be angry about Rachel needing a break. He's a damn sweet kid. He'll do everything he can to make her comfortable. And he obviously wants to marry Brooke, though I worry he doesn't think he's worthy. He's absolutely pissed that you made him look like a liar."

"I didn't mean to." But there was something soothing about Trev's certainty. He could handle apologizing to his brother. He didn't know what he would do if Shane didn't feel the same way about Brooke.

She was the one. He would have told anyone in the world who asked that he didn't believe in *the one*, until he laid eyes on her. He was struggling to think about her leaving, to think about what she might need that he couldn't give.

"I'm sure you didn't, but I can bet he feels embarrassed. Especially if he wasn't fudging the truth and he honestly believes he saw something." Trev seemed to think for a moment. "Has anything odd happened to you lately? Any new people coming around asking questions?"

"No," Bay admitted. "The only people I talk to are the other hands, and now we talk to the cast and crew at the theater. They ask a lot of questions, but nothing too weird."

Mostly about ranch life, though a couple had figured out he was an artist and asked about his work. Honestly, they talked to Shane more because he walked in and started helping fix things. His brother had learned a lot of skills along the way. He'd fixed some of the lights and rewired the sound board. He'd repaired the wooden stairs that led to the stage.

Shane was comfortable in this world.

Bay didn't want to screw it up for him.

"I'm probably being paranoid, but that's what happens when your wife buys a house that used to be the home base for a drug dealer and the cartel shows up when you least expect it," Trev admitted. "I'm sure it's nothing, though I don't like the fact that we had a break in and your truck was rifled through. What if someone's looking for something?"

"Like what? I don't know what they would be looking for if this is about Shane seeing something. I would think they would come after Shane." He didn't like that thought, but none of this made sense. Shane couldn't put a memory in a safe.

Trev sighed. "Like I said, I'm being paranoid. But I'll talk to him, try to figure out exactly what he saw. Until then we need to get that feed. Did Long-Haired Roger say when he would get the tires in?"

Long-Haired Roger told him the whole damn thing was falling apart. "It could be a week or two. We have a little more damage than we originally thought. Have to get a new alternator. That didn't have anything to do with the vandalism, but it still has to be fixed."

"Or you could bite the bullet and get a new one." Trev started walking toward Stella's. "I know it's pricey, but Stef keeps talking about how much money you're going to make off this gallery showing. Apparently he's got some big spenders coming out, including the guy who runs the collective the G belongs to. Not that Jack Barnes cares much about art, but his wife does."

Yeah, he was getting nervous about that, too. What if nothing happened? At one point he wouldn't have cared. It wasn't like he sold his work often. Every now and then he had a piece that Shane decided would catch someone's eye and they would sell it or show it to Stef. Otherwise, he gifted most of his bigger pieces and didn't think much about it. It was a compulsion, a deep-seated need to make the art. He didn't need it to hang around.

Except the pictures of Brooke.

But now he needed the money, and Shane was acting like it was all nothing more than a waiting game. What if Brooke came and no one bought a thing and he had to deal with the fact that all her expectations were shattered?

Shit. This was how Shane felt the night before. Embarrassed. Ashamed.

He needed to talk to his brother.

Wait. Where were they going? "I thought we were picking up feed."

"I texted Pastor Dennis and he'll put it in the trailer. I'm picking up some lunch for Nell. Hal's making her favorite corn and black bean burritos today, and Henry asked if I wouldn't mind bringing a couple in since they can't make it to town." Trev stopped in front of the door, and Bay's heart sank. Trev had to stop because Rye Harper was standing there.

He nodded Trev's way. "I saw you walking up the street. Thought we might talk."

Trev looked from Bay and back to Rye. "Everything okay?"

Rye shook his head. "Everything sucks, Trev, but that's not your fault. I appreciate you taking care of Rach. She needs breathing room, and it seems Max and I needed a kick in the pants. I'm not going to beat up your ranch hand."

"Like you could." Shit. He was supposed to stop that.

Rye's lips curled in a smirk. "Oh, I could. You might be younger, but I assure you I'm meaner than you can imagine. But I think my sister would take exception, and I'm pretty sure my wife would, too. Also, Stef tells me your hands are a world of imagination or some shit."

"That's terrible." Bay felt his nose wrinkle like he'd smelled something bad—which was Stef Talbot's choice of metaphors. "Tell me he doesn't actually say that."

One big shoulder shrugged. "Stef can be a pretentious ass, but he's practically my brother, so what am I going to do about it?"

Trev opened the door to the café, caution clear in his expression. "I'm going to order Nell's food. Do not kill each other."

"If I was going to kill him, I would be sneaky about it," Rye vowed. "I would do it in a way no one could figure out it was me."

That sounded like a threat. "Well, I would prefer to not be killed. Also, I wouldn't kill Rye because I don't want to piss off Brooke or Rachel. I think they're plotting the downfall of man right now."

"I'm feeling good about this." Trev's words didn't match his frown. "You two work it out."

The door closed behind him.

"I'm not sorry about what happened last night," Bay began.

"Is she okay?" Rye asked, ignoring his hard tone. Rye's voice had gone soft, as though even asking about his wife made him more serious.

"She's fine. I mean physically. I don't know what's going on and it's none of my business, but I do know she loves you and probably everything can be settled down if you would look at the workload and figure out how to take your fair share."

Rye's head tilted, like those were the last words he expected. "What the hell would you know about that?"

"I know that most of the women I've ever known just want some fairness when it comes to the workload. I watched my mom do everything. My father worked and she stayed home at first, so she did all the cooking and cleaning and childcare. Funny thing, though. When she had to go back to work so we would have a roof over our head, she still had to do everything. My father was useless at anything but cheating on his wife and gambling away every dollar they made. Same with my aunts. I was taught at every family gathering that women served men. They made dinner and we watched football. And my brother sat alone in our room so he didn't disturb anyone with his presence. I wonder if I would have thought about the inequity of the division of labor if I hadn't been thinking about how unfair it was for my brother to miss out on holidays. Would I be like my dad? Thinking women owed me because I was a man?"

"Bay," Rye began.

But Bay wasn't finished. It was time for this man to know him. "So the funny part is Shane had to learn how to do everything for himself. How to cook and keep things clean and wash his laundry. And I decided that made him strong, not weak. I started looking at my dad differently. My father was fairly helpless. That wasn't something for him to be proud of. When I was around twelve or thirteen, I started to help… I don't like that word. Not when you're living in a place. I started pulling my weight. I did the dishes with Shane. I learned to do some rudimentary cooking when we were in high school. By the time our parents died, we were both not lost when it came to the work we do on an everyday basis. The work that is almost exclusively done by the women in our lives. So that's what I mean by if she needs a break, look at the division of your labor."

Rye seemed to take that in. "Max and I have been on the road a lot. I don't mean to leave her with the whole load. We've been trying to make sure we can afford what the kids are going to need."

"Balance that with what she needs now and you'll be okay. That woman loves you. She has to because she puts up with Max," Bay said and then winced. "I'm sorry. I'm going to be better about that. Look, Rye, I want to be honest with you. I intend to marry your sister, and that means we need to start figuring out if we can be family."

Rye's jaw tightened. "You might not be as bad as I thought. So you take that whole division of labor thing seriously? You're not planning on turning Brooke into your housekeeper?"

Did the man know his sister? "She would be terrible. Do you know how lost she gets in her work? I think she's worse than me. Look, I'm not perfect. I can forget a lot of things when I'm deep into a project. Shane picks up the slack, and when we get to the other side I try to make it up to him. What we need is to find his passion because I do worry that he'll get lost between me and Brooke, and I don't want that for him."

Rye's eyes rolled and a long huff came from his chest. "Damn it. All right, then. Let's do this thing. I don't want to lose my sister over this, and I have no intentions of my wife needing a longer stay. Max has your brother."

Shit. Bay felt his eyes go wide. Max kidnapped Shane? "Where is he? I don't have any money."

"What? Dumbass. Max was out at the G and Shane needed a ride. What did you think he was going to do?"

Bay shrugged. "There are plenty of silver mines where you could hide a body."

Which was exactly what Shane thought was going to happen to them in Wyoming, although it would have been a lonely gulch.

Was it so wild an idea that Kale Kingman would protect his empire with a little murder?

Rye's head shook, and he reached out and put a hand on Bay's shoulder. "How about we start with lunch? You can tell me what your plans are. I can drive you back out to the G when we're done."

He wasn't sure he had plans beyond making Brooke happy and apologizing to his brother and hopefully selling some of his best work. "All right. And I won't even tell your wife if you get fries."

Rye chuckled and opened the door. "Nah. I think I'll stick to the dietary plan. The last thing my wife needs to worry about is losing a husband. Come on. I have to pick up the kids from Stef's in a couple of hours. I want to know how my sister is doing."

Bay walked through the door and realized how Brooke was doing.

And that was when he saw red and started charging like a bull.

* * * *

"You know you could have come out to the lodge." Mark Hallway looked decidedly out of place sitting in one of the red booths in Stella's. He wore a designer suit and loafers that likely cost more than most people in town made in a month. Or two.

Not that Mark would have paid for them. Oh, no. Other designers gave him samples or he stole them from whoever did get them. Mark was also considered an influencer since his socials had thousands of followers waiting for him to tell them what was hot and what was not.

"It's surprisingly nice for…where we are. I guess the skiing is good so the wealthy likely visit, but I was surprised there wasn't more. I should have known it wouldn't be like Aspen."

It didn't surprise her that Mark was disdainful of her hometown. He wouldn't see the beauty in either the land or the amazing people.

"My new job is a couple of stores down and I have to be there in—" she glanced down at her watch "—an hour and a half. So if you have something to say, you should say it."

"I was unaware you had a new job." Mark's face probably would have frowned if it moved. He used way too much Botox. She knew some people who used it perfectly, but Mark went over the top. "Where on earth would you work out here? I mean beyond doing some private consulting or design. You're obviously doing some of that."

She wasn't sure how what she was doing was private. "I'm working with the local rep theater. I used to do costume work before Parsons. I'm kind of getting back into it."

Mark's brows came together in seeming consternation or they tried to. "Costumes? You've worked at a major house. Don't you know costume design is beneath you?"

It wasn't. It was fun, and it was a strangely intellectual exercise. Instead of hoping to please some influencer on social media, she had to please a character, represent them. It was fulfilling in a way she hadn't been in a long time.

Was she seriously starting to think about Cleo's proposal?

"Hey, Brooke." Stella brought over a carafe of coffee and pulled Brooke out of her thoughts. "How's it going out on the G?"

Mark's nose wrinkled like he was offended by Stella's presence.

Well, she wasn't going to tell that asshole that the woman currently serving them coffee was married to a billionaire, and her stepson was one of the most influential people in the art world. Nah. Way more fun to watch him hang himself. "It's great. Oddly peaceful for having all those kiddos around."

Would she be here when Hope's baby came? When Nell's? Whatever happened she would fly home for Rachel's due date and stay in her spinster house and she and Paige could have sleepovers and take care of the younger boys while her brother's bonded with the new baby.

Of course that would be hard to do if she had Bay and Shane with her. Or would it? It would only be weird if Paige kept taking out their shins. It was a nice place, if crowded, but they all fit on the bed, and that was the important part.

Stella poured coffee into Brooke's cup. "Well, Miranda is a sweetie, but those boys are a handful. I heard Hope's having a boy. There's going to be a whole pack of them on the G running wild."

She turned and started to pour some into Mark's cup, but before she could, he put a hand over it.

"I'll take a seven-pump vanilla soy with twelve scoops of matcha green tea latte, and make sure it's exactly 180 degrees," Mark ordered. "Not a hundred and seventy-nine. Not a hundred and eighty-one."

Stella sighed and looked Brooke's way.

Brooke yawned. "Stella, this is my former boss. You know, the one who stole my designs and fired me, but not before asking for a blow job."

Stella's brows rose in surprise. "Any particular reason you're sitting here with him?"

Brooke shrugged. "Curiosity."

"Ah," Stella said. "He can fuck himself then. I'll get you the usual. You let me know if you want to graduate your membership to a real one, baby girl. You know I'm always ready."

Brooke gave her a thumbs-up.

"What did that woman mean about membership?" Mark watched warily as Stella walked away.

"Oh, just a woman's club." She didn't mention that Stella was talking about her membership in the I Shot a Son of a Bitch Club. Not that she'd actually like blown a dude who deserved it away, but she had hit one with a water gun when she was eight because he was complaining that The Trading Post was terrible and Marie should be fired. So Brooke tried to take him out, and then she'd been made a provisional member of the club. Mostly because Marie thought it was cute and Teeny thought she needed to learn gun safety.

Mark didn't need to know that charming story from her childhood.

"Well, she was rude and so were you," Mark complained. "You know some things should be kept private. Also, I thought you signed an NDA."

"I would have to have been offered compensation to sign an NDA," she pointed out. "I can say whatever I like. Tell all of my truths to anyone who would like to know. Now why am I here?"

Mark frowned. "You know I have some truths of my own. Do these people know how your brothers live?"

She managed to not emit an entirely unladylike snort. She leaned over. Caleb Burke was sitting at the counter with a plate of bacon and eggs in front of him. "Hey, Doc. Did you know my brothers are married to the same woman?"

Caleb's head turned and he frowned her way. "Of course I do. Who do you think did their vasectomies? Not in time to spare the world another of Max's spawn, though. I'm pretty sure those two quiet boys in the middle are Rye's, but Paige is pure Max."

He went right back to his breakfast.

"No one cares here." Brooke was finding it kind of satisfying to see this man so out of his element.

"I'm sure no one who matters cares," Mark replied. "We're in the middle of nowhere and some random man doesn't care. I assure you there are people who will. She's going to get my order wrong, isn't she?"

Oh, Stella would have already forgotten he existed. "You won't be getting any orders here. Stella hates you."

"Who is Stella?" Mark asked, glancing around.

"She owns the café, and her husband owns a company called Talbot Industries," she explained.

"Any relation to Stefan Talbot? The painter? I thought he was the heir to Talbot Industries." Mark always did know who the rich and powerful people of the world were.

"She's his stepmom. Now Stef is actually married to one woman."

"Jennifer Talbot. She did the series of watercolors that took the New York art world by storm. That's his stepmother? What was his father thinking?"

"Uhm, that he loved her. Also, the guy at the counter who doesn't matter is Dr. Caleb Burke, but he goes by his mother's maiden name. Sommerville is his real last name. The Chicago Sommervilles. His brother is a sitting senator. Oh, and he's married to a woman named Holly and has a partner who's a former Russian mobster. Now Alexei is fully reformed and has a deep belief in nonviolence, but I bet he would be willing to take a trip down memory lane if you want to insult his wife and partner."

Mark's head shook as though it needed clearing. "I'm confused, Brooke. You never mentioned you had ties to such interesting people. I knew you were from this tiny town in Colorado. I would have assumed if you knew anyone important, you met them in the city."

She had no doubt he wasn't talking about Denver. In Mark's mind there was only one American city. "I have a couple of friends who live part time in Manhattan. They're my family and friends. They don't have anything to do with my work beyond helping to pay for my education. Stef ponied up the cash for Parson's. Should I have put that on my résumé?"

"Well, I do admit to wondering how a girl from such a tiny, poor town managed to go to Parson's for her graduate work. You have to admit you're not the usual."

She wasn't from a wealthy family. She wasn't from a city with the best schools. "I never wanted to be usual."

But hadn't that been what she kind of strove for in New York? She tried so hard to fit in, and until she'd gone to work at Bianchi, she'd never wanted to do that. She'd enjoyed standing out. No one in Bliss would ever tell her she needed to wear the right clothes or speak in a certain way. They celebrated her weirdness and loved her for her unique soul.

Had she been so worried about failing she let those people in the city grind her down?

It was a revelation. One that kind of smacked her hard.

Why would talking about her brothers' relationship create a hostile work environment? It was New York City. One of the women who complained to HR talked about how she had three guys on her string and none of them knew.

What about the dude in accounting who told all kinds of stories about how he managed to get women in bed because they thought he could get them free shoes? He couldn't and he ghosted them the next day.

Why should she let them take everything from her? Her brothers would stand beside her. So would Rachel. So would…

Her niece would offer to kick all their shins and bring Charlie and Zander Hollister-Wright into the battle.

They had no idea what the world could do to them.

Sometimes the fight was worth it. Sometimes the cost was far too great.

"No, I'm not usual. I suppose that's why I never fit in at Bianchi," she admitted. It was an admission to herself as much as to Mark.

Mark's expression took on that pained, slightly constipated look he got when he was trying to seem compassionate. He reached across the table and put a hand on hers. "Brooke, that's simply not true. I don't think anyone understood how important you are. I came here to apologize."

She pulled her hand away and wished she could put more space between them. "For stealing my work or sexually harassing me?"

Caleb stood and turned.

Damn the doc and his excellent hearing. And for a man who claimed a certain level of misanthropy, Doc liked to listen in. A lot.

"Caleb, I can handle him," Brooke said in a firm tone because Caleb liked to handle things for people from time to time.

She'd heard Alexei started a group for citizens with anger issues. Caleb would be their poster child. Not that he belonged to it. He'd told his partner that he was fine with his own rage. No issues involved.

Though she had heard Marie was doing well.

Maybe she could get Paige in early.

Caleb gave her a perfectly feral smile. "But why when I could stick a fork in his neck, collapse his jugular, and then refuse treatment on the grounds that I don't wanna."

"Sit down, Doc," Stella ordered in a soothing tone. "Your wife is walking up the street with Amelia. You don't want your baby girl seeing you murder someone. Even if they deserve it."

Mark had moved to the window side of the booth. As though that could save him. When Caleb sat back down, Mark leaned over, whispering. "He does not seem like a Sommerville at all. I don't think they're violent."

"He's not. He's literally a doctor, and I've watched him save the lives of people over and over," Brooke explained.

"Yeah, well, today's a new day," Caleb vowed, but he refocused on his breakfast.

Mark seemed to gather his courage around him and sat up straight again. "As to your question, it's both. Brooke, you're a gorgeous, unbelievably talented designer, and I am both attracted to you and jealous of you. It's what I should have admitted in the first place. I should have offered what I'm going to offer now. A partnership."

If he had before, she would have jumped at the offer and never looked back.

Would that have been a mistake?

She wanted to throw it back in his face and tell him to go to hell. She didn't need his partnership. But she also shouldn't toss out the offer. Not that she would work with him. She couldn't trust him in any way, but if he was her way back to the life she had before, she had to hear him out.

Did she want that life back?

She couldn't even contemplate the answer to the question

without talking to him. If she tossed him out right now, she would never have the chance to make the choice.

"What would that look like?" She was curious about how far he would go. And what prompted this visit since she knew damn well it wasn't because he was sorry. The man had no shame, so this was about something else and she wanted to know the whys.

Mark's eyes lit like he thought he had her now. "Well, I've talked to Gianna and she's agreed to put your name on the line along with mine, and she wants us to design a fabulous gown as the final look, something that will wow on the runway."

Curiouser and curiouser. "My line was ski and resort wear."

It was chic but fairly casual. She'd done plenty of evening gowns but mostly in a wedding sense or as costumes. She'd never been allowed to work on the high-end gowns at Bianchi. That was for the Marks of the company.

She glanced over and saw Trev McNamara walk through the door, the bell jingling as he approached the counter.

Her heart squeezed because seeing that cowboy walk in made her think of her own. It made her wonder if Shane had run his errands and was back on the G with his brother. Hopefully talking about whatever went wrong the night before.

Trev nodded a greeting her way and then started talking to Stella.

Mark huffed, getting her attention again. "Yes, I know, and I see such great potential in them. It's why I fought for you with Gianna. She's impressed, too."

Gianna Bianchi wasn't impressed with anything. Also, Brooke would be shocked if the woman knew her name. She spent all her time in Europe. She came to the New York offices for Fashion Week and left as soon as she could. "That's nice. So she wants me to design a gown to close a show?"

Mark put up a hand. "She wants us to design a gown to close the F/W show. But she's going to give an early preview. A salon show in Milan. You'll be in the room with some of the most influential people in fashion. You understand what a salon show can do for you?"

Fall/Winter show and a salon show? F/W would be a showing during Fashion Week, and having her name on an actual show would be unimaginable at this stage. But a salon show… Fashion Week was always dizzying with so much going on it could be hard to stand out. A small salon show at Bianchi HQ in Italy would be all about her. She had no doubt Gianna could bring in some heavy hitters from the fashion world. And they would leave knowing the name Brooke Harper.

Was she willing to put her pride on the shelf for that opportunity?

"I still don't understand the change of heart." She didn't trust it at all.

Mark stood and moved to her side of the booth. He didn't give her a chance to protest, simply sat beside her, crowding her. "Brooke, you don't understand why I want to make things right with the most talented designer I have? Baby, there's a reason I wanted my name on your work. First, though, we should acknowledge that while I didn't do it in a particularly nice way, I had every right to take credit. You worked under me. It's common practice."

She didn't like being so close to him. Did Caleb still have his fork? She looked over and he had Amelia in his arms, the little girl wrapped around her loving father while her mom had a cup of coffee. Alexei had found his way in, too. He'd probably parked the car while Holly had walked down the street.

They looked so happy together, and once no one thought it was possible for Caleb to be happy.

Could she have that with Shane and Bay? Could she find a way to make it work?

What did she want more? Her career back or something new?

"Sure," she said absently. Trev usually came into town with someone. Likely because he was running errands, and that often involved lifting heavy objects like feed and manure, and that should make her wrinkle her nose but all she could think about was the fact that it was getting warm and sometimes Shane would take off his shirt when he was hauling stuff and his chest would be on display. Only a few days before the men had been replacing one of the barn doors and Beth had brought out lemonade and cookies. The kids had played, and she and Beth and Hope had sipped lemonade and watched all those pretty men.

When Bay realized she was drooling over Shane's abs, he'd tossed his own shirt off, and she swore that man figured out a way to make his jeans hang super low on his hips. Trev had even commented on it.

Beth told him to stop messing with her show, and that was when Brooke found herself watching some kids while Beth got to go to the playroom.

Hope had sighed and wished someone would spank her, too.

She never got to do that in New York, much less watch two gorgeous men who claimed to want her. Or sit around and boldly talk about spankings and which flogger was the best, and no one blinked when she complained about the plug her men made her wear.

She felt Mark put a hand on her wrist. "Good, then you understand that I'm offering you something real. Brooke, I went about this all wrong. I should have asked you to dinner and discussed how we could move forward. I should never have said what I said to you, but I was jealous. You seemed to be flirting with everyone but the one man who really wanted you."

"I don't flirt." Much. She wasn't some outrageous flirt, drawing men into her web. What had he said about someone wanting her? "Who are you talking about? Please tell me it isn't Ronnie from reception because you know he's teasing, right? If he doesn't know he's into men, someone should tell him."

He brought her hand to his mouth and laid a kiss on it. "I was talking about me, Brooke. I think we can build something beautiful together."

She was horrified when he started leaning toward her.

"Hey, you two stay calm," Trev was saying.

And then Mark was ripped from the booth.

Bay and her brother were here, and she was going to need bail money.

Chapter Thirteen

"All right, we've had a rash of vandalism around the town and I wanted to talk to a couple of people who've been affected to see if there are any threads I can start weaving together," the sheriff said as he sat back in his chair.

Shane felt anxious but then he was in the sheriff's office and Max Harper was next to him. It was kind of his nightmare scenario with the exception of the fact that Rye wasn't here and Bay wasn't about to be tossed in jail beside him.

"I told Deputy Leal everything I know." Shane had been given a cup of coffee as he walked in. Actually, he'd been given what Gemma claimed to be the greatest latte ever made, but he hadn't touched it because it might be one of those police trick things. Give him a bunch of coffee and then not let him go to the bathroom.

"Which was not much," Max proclaimed. "See, I was thinking maybe the boys pissed someone off. They both got big mouths."

Nathan Wright's blue eyes narrowed on Max. "Really? You want to talk to a certain pot, Mr. Kettle?"

Max simply shrugged. "Game knows game, man. The Kent boys are annoying as fuck, and it is no surprise that someone decided to take a knife to their tires. Or someone decided to finally put that old truck of theirs out of its misery. It was a kindness, I tell you."

"It's not that old."

Max stared at him for a moment.

It was older than he or Bay. "Well, it's not as old as you."

Max nodded as though he'd made his point. "See, that's what I'm talking about."

"Okay. Then why did someone break into the tiny house you put on your property?" Nate asked. "You know the one you intended to lock Brooke in so she could never lose her innocence."

Max paled. "Shit. Is that what they're saying? Because that is not… What do you mean someone broke in?"

Shane leaned in. "Was anyone there? The kids weren't there, right?"

Max put a hand on his arm, and the expression on his face was softer for a moment. "The kids are with Stef. They're fine. I appreciate that being your first thought, though."

"Stef called it in," Nate explained. "He had to get Ethan's stuffed whale, and he went in the back way. He saw the door was open and stopped to check. I'm surprised he didn't text you."

Max pulled his cell out. "I was busy talking to Shane. I didn't notice it rang. Why would anyone break into the tiny house? Did they steal anything? I bought some of those things brand new, and let me tell you Marie thinks the products she sells are precious. I would go to Walmart in Pagosa if I had the time."

"Don't let Marie hear you say that," Shane grumbled. He'd already gotten the *Buy Bliss* speech. Although it wasn't like he could get to Pagosa Springs even if he wanted to since he didn't have a car.

Max couldn't be too impressed. He might have a job, but he didn't have much else, and everyone knew *cowboy* wasn't a great thing to put on a résumé. He couldn't even say he was an expert at anything beyond handyman.

This was where it all fell apart, but then he'd always known it would.

In a few weeks Bay would be a celebrated artist, a master of the modern Western movement. Shane would be Shane. Brooke's brothers would start asking her what he brought to the table, and what would she be able to say? He brought multiple orgasms? Her brothers definitely didn't want to hear that.

"The place was trashed," Nate said with a rueful sigh. "We already processed the scene. We documented everything, but I hope you'll be able to tell me if anything's gone."

He passed a tablet with a set of pictures on the screen. Shane got a good look at them and his stomach knotted. "They tore up the whole place."

Max studied the pictures. "No, they didn't tear anything up, but they were definitely looking for something." He looked at Shane. "Did you take anything from Kingman?"

Shane was at a loss. "I didn't take anything. I saw something. I was helping some of the senior hands move what I thought was equipment into the barn where he stores heavy tools."

"I'm not sure I understand how a new backhoe means Kingman wants to kill you," Nate observed. "Was he trying to keep it undercover?"

"It wasn't a backhoe, dummy," Max said with a frown. "It was guns, and a lot of them."

Well, he didn't know about the "a lot of them" part, but it was oddly soothing to have Max accept the story as truth. "I'm almost certain I saw one of those guns the Army uses. He was bringing in a whole bunch of wooden crates and they had writing on the side, but it was in a foreign language."

Now he had Nate's attention. "Did you see a country name on it?"

"Yes." He had told Bay all of this and thought Bay believed him. Now it felt like he was telling the story for the first time. "Belgium. There was another word that looked like it was maybe a point of origin or a person's name. FN Herstal."

Max nodded. "We need to find this Herstal person."

"It's not a person." Nate stood up. "Gemma, come in here. I need your big brain to check my foggy one." He looked back at Shane. "That woman should go on *Jeopardy*. She knows everything."

"Not how to spot a douchebag," Max quipped.

Gemma growled his way as she entered the room. "I knew my ex was a douchebag. He was exactly what I was looking for at the time. It was New York. I didn't have a lot of choices if I didn't want an overly ambitious douchebag. Good news is I came to Bliss and found a couple of superhot, completely unambitious dudes who can fix my car and cook my dinner and rock my world. I think your sister is finding the same thing. Especially the getting her world rocked by two hot cowboys without a bank account between them."

Gemma could also be a little mean. "We have one. It doesn't have much, but we do have an account."

Nate ignored him. "Gemma, where are P90s produced?"

Her eyes rolled. "I researched all of this for Nell because she said she didn't want Henry to be sad. Apparently he had a P90 he loved, and she doesn't want to stir the John Bishop in him. It's Belgium. The main manufacturer is Fabrique Nationale Herstal. Publicly traded as FN Herstal. Give me a hard one."

"Is a P90 a gun? Like the Army uses?" Shane asked.

"Not the US Army. Only Navy SEALs use them regularly. They're used by a lot of elite units around the world," Gemma explained.

"Would they have any use when it came to ranching?" Maybe there was an explanation.

Nate had been fiddling with a tablet, and he turned it around and showed it to Shane. "Only if they needed a submachine gun to take care of critters. Is this it? Or did it have a longer barrel?"

Gemma looked over his shoulder. "The standard P90 is restricted in the US. Only law enforcement, military, and people who hold special licenses can buy them. We can look that up, though I can't think of a reason why a rancher would need one. Otherwise, it would have to be a PS90."

Nate shook his head. "Do I want to know what Nell's doing with that information?"

"Writing a magnificent romance about an arms dealer who falls madly in love with a gun control activist. It's actually kinda dark. I liked it," Gemma said and pointed at the picture. "Do you remember if the barrel was long or short?"

He'd gotten such a quick glance before the foreman had whisked the big box away and sent Shane back to the bunkhouse. "I think it was short, but it was a quick glance, but I did see the markings on the boxes and it was FN Herstal."

"Then it's almost certainly a P90 and nothing that you would need on a ranch." Nate sat back.

"It would explain why he's flush with cash when every other ranch in the States is getting creative." Gemma was more than an office manager. Nate relied on her to do research and as a sounding board when he needed an opinion. She was super smart and well educated and happy here in Bliss.

Could Brooke be, too?

Hell, could Bay be happy in one place?

"I've heard rumors he's got ties to one-percenter clubs in California," Nate mused.

Max's hand came out, slapping Shane on the shoulder. "Dummy. Don't you know you're not supposed to get involved in illegal gunrunning? I'm going to work on him, Nate. We cannot have another one of those people who walk into crazy situations all the time. We already have Mel. And Callie. And poor Lucy. I swear that girl is like a walking *Dateline* episode."

"Hey, I didn't mean to," Shane protested. "And I got out as soon as I could."

Nate's brows rose. "Yes. Five months ago, so why are you only now sitting down in my office? I had to call you here. You didn't come forward on your own. It makes me wonder what else you were doing for Kingman."

Oh, that was a turn he wasn't ready for. "I wasn't sure. I only knew it felt wrong, and they were talking about dealing with the new guys."

Max pointed his way. "And they were the new guys. Nate, what the hell did you expect him to do? Walk into your office with zero proof and accuse one of the biggest ranchers in the country of gun running? He followed his instincts and got the hell out of there and got his brother out, too. Don't you try to intimidate him." He looked to Gemma. "Hey, I need you to represent Shane here so Nate doesn't throw him in jail. You know how much he enjoys tossing a man in jail for no reason at all. Especially men from my family."

"Only you," Nate replied.

"I'm going to need a retainer," Gemma began. "And it can't be pecan pie or horseback riding lessons."

"How about free babysitting?" Max offered.

"Am I the babysitter or are you offering to watch Cade and Jesse when I stay out at the G next month to help Hope?"

Max frowned. "Obviously the first since I'm not changing Cade and Jesse's diapers. They're going to have to do that on their own."

"I don't need a lawyer." He was so deeply confused. Gemma and Max were still arguing over what constituted a retainer, but Shane leaned toward the sheriff. "Sir, where I come from you don't accuse a man unless you have proof."

Nate sighed and studied him for a moment while Max extolled the virtues of his children and Gemma the same about cold hard cash. "I'm sorry. I have a suspicious mind. It goes with the territory. So you think they were going to off you and Bay because of something you saw for a couple of seconds?"

"I don't know." He was as confused as everyone else, and he was finding it hard to believe that Max Harper, of all people, seemed to believe him when his own brother didn't. "I only know it's the weirdest thing that's happened in years."

Gemma put a hand out to stop Max's arguing. "You left five months ago. Why wait until now?"

"They didn't know where we went," Shane offered. "And for the first couple of months Trev and Jamie paid in cash because we didn't know if we would stay on."

"So Trev finally did your paperwork," Nate mused.

"It wouldn't be hard for a PI to run a trace, probably several over the last couple of months." Gemma leaned against Nate's desk. "I assume Kingman had your information."

Shane shook his head. "Nah. He paid in cash and under the table. Said he didn't bother getting to know a cowpoke until they'd been on his team and tested. I wasn't sure what the test was, but he hadn't given it to us yet."

"If he's running guns, then I suspect the test would have been helping with the delivery or something else that would have been a major criminal offense. It's often how they bring people in. They would be more open about it when it comes to the MCs. You would have been in a probationary period until you proved yourself, but this feels sneakier," Nate admitted.

"But none of this explains why we have a sudden rash of vandalism," Gemma pointed out. "If they want to make sure Shane keeps his mouth shut, why would they blow the tires on his car? Why wouldn't they simply go right to him and let the threats begin? Or kill him and hide his body so they know he can't talk. There are a lot of places to hide a body here in the West. Hell, Kingman Ranch is huge. If they buried you out there, I can't imagine anyone finding you. It's what I would do. I mean if I was a hardened criminal and stuff."

"You are a scary person, Gemma," Max said with a frown. "But I do get your point. The vandalism feels petty."

"Or someone's looking for something." Shane couldn't come up with anything else. "I get the truck. They might be looking to make us more vulnerable. Being without a way to move around could do it."

Nate sighed, fingers drumming along his desk. "All right, that's a possibility. They could be trying to herd you into a place you can't get out of, but I don't buy it. It would be way too easy to pick you up. You usually work with Bay, right? Trev and Jamie send their guys out in pairs mostly."

Shane nodded. "Unless it's a real easy job, yes, but the G is still big. Unless they have someone on the inside, they won't know where we are, and Trev's got wildlife cams all over the place. They're not monitored all the time, but he likes to keep eyes on everything."

"And it doesn't explain why they trashed my sister's lovely house that is far too small for large men, and I'm going to have to add on to," Max complained. "At least I've now got two young, strong backs to work the land. You and Bay need to understand that marrying Brooke means you work at Harper Stables."

"You have to pay them, Max," Gemma began.

"I'm paying them with my sister," Max insisted.

Gemma's shoulders squared. "You know this isn't the seventeenth century, right?"

"He's fucking with you." He was starting to understand Max. "When he gets worried he gets even more obnoxious than usual. He's worried because while we put together the truck getting vandalized and even the theft of the safe out at the G, it's hard to…" Shit. He figured it out. "Right after we made things official with Brooke, a woman hit on me at The Trading Post."

"We all know that." Max waved him off. "Teeny said you looked like a deer in the headlights, and if Nell hadn't come along, she would have sent Marie in to save you. You had zero interest in that tourist."

Max was missing the point. "What if she wasn't a tourist?"

Nate picked up his phone. "How long does Teeny keep those tapes? We might be able to ID her on facial rec. I'm going to assume she asked some very specific questions."

"Oh." Max seemed to catch on. "You think she was sent in by Kingman to figure out where you would be. Well, that makes way more sense. I was sitting around trying to figure out how all these beautiful women decided to hit on you and Bay. I do not get it."

Nate seemed immune to Max's sarcasm. "She asked where you worked?"

"She asked a lot of questions, but she specifically wanted to know where we were staying. I'm going to admit I didn't want to start a relationship with the woman of my dreams by having to explain why I was flirting, but I was also trying to not be rude. I was surprised she still wanted to talk to me after I told her I had a girlfriend."

"Because she didn't care about that. She wanted to know where to look," Gemma surmised. "And then you weren't there and you were at the G. I wonder…" Gemma pulled out her phone, and her thumbs worked the small keyboard. She nodded as she stared at the screen. "Kingman was in DC last week. There's talk about him running for Senate. He's planning to primary the sitting senator. I mean it's a great time to clear up all those loose ends."

"Then maybe we should think about stashing all three of them." Max seemed to focus, going serious. "I'll talk to Stef about hiring a bodyguard. Maybe we should think about sending them down to Dallas."

"Whoa. I don't think I need to be sent anywhere. Brooke can't leave. She's got the play." It was moving fast for him. "We aren't even sure the incidents are related."

"They all involve the three of you, and while I'm confused about how he's going about it, I think he's either looking for a way to make it seem like an accident or waiting for the right time. I would rather be safe than sorry." Nate stood. "Do we have any idea where Brooke and Bay are?"

Shane stood, too. “I have to get back to the G. We’ve got a bunch of stuff planned with Nell and Henry this afternoon. Trev expects me back to help. I think Lucy’s coming out, too. Noah’s teaching them about cattle today.”

He didn’t want to leave Bliss. He didn’t want Brooke to have to leave. She was just settling in.

Would Bay even believe him, or would he think this was another way to get out of town?

Damn it. He wasn’t like that. Bay was the one who felt the deep need to roam around. Shane wanted a home, wanted roots. He didn’t mind travel, but he wanted a place that was his. Someplace where no one could toss him out like trash or forbid him entry.

“Hey, Shane.” Max sounded more than serious now. He stood and put a hand on Shane’s shoulder. “This is going to be okay. You and Bay are going to be fine, and we’ll figure out how to protect you. Well, Nate and likely Stef will. Maybe we could bring a couple of guards out here. We’ll tell that Taggart fellow to send some cute ones since I know the new waitress they hired down at Trio is looking.”

“Also, Del at the school. Sabrina promised her she could get two men as her signing bonus,” Gemma quipped. “And I wouldn’t worry about Shane going back to the G this afternoon if Henry’s going to be there. How about we call Stef and see about a couple of bodyguards? Until then we can take turns watching them. At night they can hole up at Stef’s or stay with Seth. Both have excellent security, and that way Brooke can finish her work.”

Max snorted and started to say something.

Shane pointed a finger his way. “Don’t you dare make less of Brooke’s work.”

Max sighed. “Sorry. Force of habit. I wish she’d become something I can understand.”

He wasn’t going to argue with his future brother-in-law. “I need a ride back to the G. I should talk to them before they come into town. Brooke’s going to be at the theater soon if I don’t catch her.”

There was the squawking sound of the radio and Gemma hustled to pick it up. “Go ahead, Tate.”

“Hey, Gemma. We’re bringing in two men suspected of assault and battery at Stella’s. The alleged victim is being looked at by Doc, but I'm not so sure I trust him to actually fix what those cowboys broke. Apparently he was flirting with one of their girlfriends. I would say both because of where we are, but one of them is already married, so I don't think she belongs to both of them. It would be a weird trio since one of them is old."

"I am not old, asshole," a familiar voice said.

"Rye?" Max had the biggest grin on his face. "Hey, Nate, is your new twelve-year-old deputy hauling my brother in?"

"He is not twelve but apparently yes," Nate growled. "Tate, what happened? Did you say Rye Harper got caught fighting? Tell me he didn't beat the crap out of Bay Kent."

Shane's gut went tight. "Is Bay all right?"

"He did not beat the crap out of me," Bay complained over the line. "Though I did have to protect him from a guy who practically crapped his pants."

"Hey, he got a couple of good hits in," Rye replied.

The deputy was back. "Uh, no, Sheriff. Apparently they fought the guy from New York City together. We're about three minutes out. Could someone get a cell ready for me?"

Well, at least they were getting along.

* * * *

Bay didn't like handcuffs or getting his ass hauled away via police vehicle no matter how comfy said vehicle was. It sucked.

But nothing sucked more than the look Brooke had given him. Like she was disgusted.

"Stop it, Bailey Kent. You stop it right now," she'd yelled.

He hadn't listened. He'd seen red when he'd caught that man with his hands on her. The fucker had her backed up against the window, and there had been nowhere for her to go. He had no idea who the asshole was, and he didn't care. No one laid hands on her. No one.

When the deputy had come in and hauled him off the guy, Brooke had stood there with tears streaking down her face as though she'd lost her last friend.

"Okay. We need to figure out how we're going to play this

because Brooke will not be far behind." Rye sat beside him. "Honestly, if this deputy had an ounce of experience in his adolescent body, he would have walked us to the station. It's literally at the end of the block. This is stupid."

"This is protocol, Mr. Harper," the deputy explained. "And I am twenty years old and have an associate's degree in criminal justice."

"Whoop-de-do, buddy. Look, son, I used to be the sheriff of this town and if you're a slave to protocol, you're going to have a tough time. What the hell are you going to do when the next alien invasion happens?"

Tate stopped at the only light in town.

Bailey could see Trev and Brooke gaining on and then passing them. Brooke followed his boss, her arms crossed under her breasts and tears still clinging to her cheeks.

"I will enact protocol forty-seven in accordance with the intergalactic treaty of solar year 4750.7," Tate replied simply.

He would give it to the deputy. The kid seemed unflappable.

Bailey tried to get Brooke's attention, but it wasn't like he could knock on the window. Well, he had his head. He kind of tapped it against the window. "Brooke!"

"Mr. Kent, those windows are bulletproof," Tate advised. "I assure you no matter how hardheaded you are, you're not going to break them. They are also compliant with safety protocols set forth by the Earth Council Against Hostile Aliens. ECAHA knows how to make unbreakable glass. That sucker will hold a damn Noxil spawn, and those fuckers can emit acid when they feel like they're in danger."

Rye groaned, and his head fell back. "You're Cassidy's nephew. I forgot. I don't know whether to praise Nate for being smart or call him intensely crazy."

"Why not both?" Tate replied. "And protocol is what separates us from chaos. I'm sorry I didn't recognize you, Old Sheriff. I haven't been on the job long, and I'm living out at my aunt's place for now. I'm going to be honest. I'm surprised at you. I was told you were a good sheriff. I didn't expect you to be in a… I can't call it a bar fight. Diner fight? Is that a thing here?"

She wouldn't look at him. She stood beside Trev until the *Walk* sign changed and then followed him.

"Everything is a thing here, Deputy, and it wasn't a fight. Not really. It was setting boundaries," Rye explained.

Had she been happy to be with that asshole? Had he interrupted something she wanted? It hadn't looked like it at the time. She'd pushed at him, but maybe she'd done that because she was trying to keep their relationship on the down low.

His heart ached at the thought.

Had she been using them all along?

"All right. So you saw red and couldn't stop because you thought he was hurting Brooke," Rye said.

"Well, that's the truth," Bay replied, watching Brooke walk away with Trev. She was going to get to the Sheriff's Department before they did.

Shane was there, apparently, and so was Max, according to the call the deputy made after shoving them both in the squad car. He'd been kind of shocked at the time, but now he wondered why the hell his brother was at the sheriff's.

Would she walk right into Shane's arms or ignore them both? Had he fucked this up for all of them?

At least she was going and not calling a Fuber and heading home to clean out her stuff.

"Of course it is, but you have to finesse things," Rye encouraged. "You have to make sure to put the emphasis on her safety and not on your caveman-like possessiveness, even though that is hard wired into you, brother. Women do not understand. If you want my sister to take your balls, you mention the words *he had his hands on my woman*."

"But she is my woman. I'm literally supposed to protect her." Bay didn't see the problem.

"I think I'm with Old Sheriff on this one. Women don't like to be thought of as possessions. Unless they come from other planes. You see, there's this fairy plane and the women there…" Tate began.

Bay turned to Rye. "Can we get him fired? Like can't the town vote?"

"Hey, I just got hired," Tate protested, and the light finally turned green.

"We're stuck with him for now," Rye replied with a sigh. "But the good news is at some point he'll get the shit kicked out of him by either the mafia or an MC club or… We haven't had a serial killer in a while. We're due for one of those. The point is the young, shiny deputy is always the one who ends up getting his ass tortured. It's practically a rite of passage."

"What?" Tate asked, seemingly alarmed. "My auntie told me it would be a cushy job."

Rye grinned fiercely. "Your auntie lied, son."

Tate turned his attention back to the road and slowly started making his way to the sheriff's.

"Do you know who that was?" Bay asked. "I've never seen him around here."

Rye sat back. "I think that was her boss. I've never met him because we've never gone to New York." Rye glanced out the window. "We've always made excuses, and they usually are about the kids. Damn it. I've let my sister have a whole life in a city thousands of miles away and I never visited her even though Logan has invited us to stay with them. Why?"

He kind of thought he knew the reason. "Is it because you're worried your wife is going to get to a big city and remember everything she loved about it and wonder why she's stuck here with two whiny-ass men and all their babies?"

Rye went pale. "Holy shit. I think that's it."

"Rachel loves Bliss. She doesn't want to leave it, but I would bet she would enjoy traveling a bit and showing the world to her kiddos. I grew up never going anywhere. I didn't get out of New Mexico until Shane and I started rodeoing, and once we hit the road, it was hard to stop. We became nomadic, and I think it's because as children our world was so small. It felt good to bust out of it."

"Brooke didn't leave this part of Colorado until she went to college, and then it was Denver and then New York, and Max and I have been waiting for her to come home."

"And that made her feel like you thought she would fail. Or hoped she would. I'm not sure which is worse," Bay commented.

"They're both terrible," Tate said, judgmental eyes looking at them through the rearview. "I feel sorry for your poor sister, and then you beat up her boss. He's probably going to press all the charges he can."

So he was looking at time, maybe. Fuck.

"I'll make sure he doesn't," Rye promised. "Trust me. It's not the first time we've dealt with something like this. He was assaulting her."

"She didn't mention that, but I'll talk to her when I make my report," Tate offered as he turned the vehicle into the parking lot.

Nate Wright stood out front looking twelve kinds of authoritative. Shane looked worried.

Max was laughing his ass off.

Nate stalked over and opened the door. "Rye, you know I expect this…"

Rye managed to get out of the car. "From Max. I know. But that asshole had his hands on my sister." He looked back in and winked Bay's way with a conspiratorial gleam. When he stood up, Rye had a serious expression on his face. "I wasn't about to let some asshole manhandle my sister in the middle of a café. How the hell would that look?"

Max stopped laughing, and his eyes widened. "Really?"

Brooke's whole body went on alert. "Excuse me?"

Bay got out of the car and Nate had his hands out of the cuffs quickly.

"Tate, did you need to cuff the former sheriff and our local artist?" Nate asked.

Tate shrugged. "It's protocol. Sir, we need to talk about serial killers. I think they were joking, but I'd like to have the conversation."

"Oh, I'll let you read the files, buddy," Nate promised. "Now go to the clinic and get the city guy's version of events. Elisa's coming in, and she'll handle the rest."

Tate nodded. "Yes, sir."

"I am not a piece of property, Ryan Harper," Brooke announced. "Do you have any idea what that stunt might have cost me?" She strode over as Nate was getting around to uncuffing Rye. "Don't you dare, Nathan Wright. You would totally toss Max in jail for the night. Rye should get the same treatment, and I'll make sure the only thing he can get from Stella's for lunch and dinner is a cabbage and beet salad."

Rye went pale. "Hey, we should talk about this."

Rye was trying to give him cover. The trouble was he wasn't sure where all the land mines were.

"I think that guy's version of events is that those two kicked his ass," Tate said, though he was already walking back to his vehicle. "My auntie told me Logan is the great man he is today because of what happened to him here in this office. I thought that was about training and stuff."

"You're going to love that beet salad, Rye," Max taunted.

Shane moved into his space. "What the hell happened?"

"Did you think for two seconds about what we'll do if he decides to press charges?" Brooke asked. "How is that going to affect Rachel and your kids? Do you know how much stress she's under? I could have handled it."

"Oh, it was what happened to him here, but it definitely wasn't training." Gemma watched as Tate got in his car. "It was about fourteen hours of being tortured by the Russian mob, but you should know nothing bad has happened since I took over. I'm really careful since before I came, someone drugged Nate's coffee. Now that wasn't the mob. That was the serial killer."

"He was here to offer me my job back," Brooke announced.

Shane's jaw tightened.

Bay felt his stomach drop.

"So nothing bad has happened at the Sheriff's Department since Gemma came on board?" Tate asked as he started his engine again.

"Now that I think about it, it's all happened out in the field," Nate mused, completely ignoring the fight going on around him. "Let's see, Henry got kidnapped by a drug cartel, but that was on his own land. Lucy did nearly get murdered."

"But that was up at the lodge," Gemma pointed out.

"What do you mean he offered you a job?" Rye asked.

"She's going back." Shane whispered the words, sounding like he was already defeated. "She's leaving."

His brother could be pessimistic at times. He often wondered what he brought to the table beyond pretty art. Shane was the one who managed their day-to-day lives, but Bay was the one who slapped him upside the head when he wanted to quit. Bay was the one who could see there was hope. Shane was always trying to find the dark side. Likely because he'd lived there most of his life. "She said he offered. She didn't accept."

"How was he offering you a job? Did you have to look for the offer down his throat?" Rye asked.

"Dummy. She wanted to figure out why he was asking," Max argued.

Bay pointed Max's way. "What he said."

"And that man who was trying to kill Hale was thoughtful enough to do it outside of town," Nate reflected.

Brooke whirled on Bay. "No. You don't get to have a say in this. I know exactly why you charged into the fray. You didn't like his hands on me."

"Of course he didn't." Shane stepped up. "You should know I would have done the same. Brooke, we love you. We're never going to stand by while some asshole who's already cost you so much tries to drag you back into his hell."

Shane trusted him. Shane didn't have to hear his side of the story.

Damn it. He'd done his brother wrong.

"Uhm, is that it? Because that's a hell of a lot." Tate rolled down the window. "Auntie told me it would be an easy job and I can help out with the alien hunting. I'm not sure how I'm supposed to protect Earth from invading Reticulan Greys if I'm always stopping some murderer."

"You would have done the same damn thing." Brooke pointed that well-manicured finger Shane's way. He had to wonder if in addition to the gel, it was also coated in righteous judgment. "You both think you own me. Well, guess what. He's going to sue, and none of you will be able to talk him out of it."

"Well, then you'll sue him right back. He harassed you," Rye replied. "I don't understand why you're taking this lying down. This is not the Brooke I know."

She went still, and he knew this was going to be bad. Rye was pushing her in a way Bay never would have. He would have silently taken all her worry and bile and offered to get her a glass of wine and agreed with everything she said because she was processing. She would come back in an hour or two and be reasonable.

Or he would fuck her until she wasn't mad at him anymore.

Rye only had the one option, and he'd chosen poorly.

"Well, we did have to deal with a bunch of dead MCer's, but they had the courtesy to die at Hell on Wheels," Nate replied, though he was warily watching the Harpers now. "Also, they burned down a good portion of the bar, but Sawyer got that fixed up real quick."

"The Brooke you know?" Brooke's eyes were red as she stared at her brother.

"He didn't mean that, sweetie." Max was all kinds of serious now. "You know how he gets when he's under stress. He's worried about you and Rach and everything."

"No, I'm worried that my sister won't fight for herself," Rye insisted. "She ran back here like a dog with her tail between her legs."

Brooke looked down at her watch before sniffling and wiping at her eyes. "I'm due at the theater. Rye, don't worry about me. I'll be leaving soon, and you won't have to see me again. I'm sorry I was such a disappointment."

Rye's shoulders dropped. "I didn't mean it that way. I'm confused."

Brooke turned and started back toward the sidewalk. "It doesn't matter. Like I said, I'll be leaving soon. There's nothing here for me anymore."

"But you got two boyfriends," Max called out. "And we kind of like them now."

"Not the right time, dude," Bay said.

Brooke stopped and stared at them. "It wouldn't have worked anyway. I think I'm going to work with Cleo on her new films, and we all know those two wouldn't change their plans to follow a woman around."

"What the fuck is that supposed to mean?" Shane asked.

But she was walking away.

"Go after her," Bay said.

Shane simply watched her.

Max looked to Nate. "Come on, man. We need to go talk to our sister. Look, I'm usually the one in the cell. Can't we pretend you think I'm Rye? If you'll turn away for a second, we'll change shirts and no one will be the wiser."

"She didn't fight it because she was protecting you." Gemma's eyes had gone hard as she stared at Rye. "Also, I don't think Rye should be the one talking to her at this point."

"What do you mean she was protecting me? I don't need protection from that little asshole, as he so recently learned," Rye shot back.

"Because they threatened her with a counter suit. Creating a hostile work environment by talking about her brothers and their unusual marriage," Gemma explained.

"We don't care about that." Max's head shook. "Like we care what a couple of people in New York City think of us."

He wasn't thinking at all. "And Paige? How about your kids when the press gets wind of a weird and juicy story? You're connected to some powerful people. Brooke wasn't thinking about you. She was thinking about your wife and kids and was willing to sacrifice her dream job to keep them safe. Do you think she didn't want to fight? The first thing she did when she came home was consult with Gemma."

Shane stood tall next to him. "She was doing it out of love, and you called her a coward. Rye Harper, if this was a hundred years earlier, I would challenge you to a duel."

Gemma frowned Shane's way. "Dude, that would be the 1920s. No duels then. Knife him in a back alley. It's the smartest way to get revenge."

Rye sighed and looked haggard. "I didn't think about that. Damn it. I have to go talk to her."

Nate's head shook. "No. You have to hop in that cell until I get this sorted. Bay, you, too. Just because I took those cuffs off doesn't mean you're not spending some time in the cell. Unless this guy doesn't press charges, I'm going to have to book you both."

Trev had been standing silently in the background. He hadn't even seen the man. It was good to know his boss had witnessed his descent. "I'll bail Bay out."

"Trev, I…" Bay began.

Trev shook his head. "No. I get it, man. I don't think I would be able to stay calm if someone was putting hands on my wife. Hell, even Bo. I'd have lost it, too. Shane, stay here and deal with your girl. I don't need you until late this afternoon anyway. I'm meeting with Nell and Henry over lunch, and then they're working with Noah. I have to interview the new guys. Try to be back around four."

Shane shook his head. "I'll come with you now. I don't have a way to get back, and honestly, I don't think there's anything to deal with. I always knew if she had to pick between us and her dream job, we were going to lose. Maybe she can talk him in to not pressing charges if he wants her back so bad."

Max's hands fisted. "You want to send her back to the man who tried to harass her and apparently wanted to do it again today?"

"Of course I fucking don't." Shane sounded tortured. "I love her. I love her so much it's killing me, but I can't give her that life, and I don't think I can live it with her. What the hell am I supposed to do when her rich friends come for dinner? At least Bay's an artist, and he's about to go real big. I'm nothing."

He'd done this to his brother. He'd done it. Bay got in his brother's space, putting a hand on his neck and looking him directly in the eyes. "You are everything, Shane. Me and Brooke depend on you for fucking everything. If you want to tell some truths about your life, start there. Start with how you taught yourself to take care of the people around you when there was nothing in your life that told you it was a good idea."

Shane softened. "But there was. There was my brother."

Bay heard a sniffling sound and worried they were making Gemma emotional. "And you make our world work. The same as you do for Brooke. If we have to live in damn New York City because it's the only way she can be happy, then you're going to figure that out, too. We don't work without you, Shane."

"But I…"

He shook his head. "No fucking buts. She's it. She's the one. I know she's pissed that I lost my shit, but she'll get over it because we're good for her, too. I understand her and give her space to be who she wants to be. You make it possible for both Brooke and I to do what we love. No more roaming. All that time, all that searching, and it was for this. Home isn't this place. Home isn't some building we can buy. It's her. It's always been her."

"That was beautiful." Nope, not Gemma. Max was the one wiping away tears, and Rye didn't look all that far behind him. He put a hand on his twin's shoulder. "I'll pick up the kids and I'll take care of them tonight. You know how much Rach loves a jailhouse quickie."

"Absolutely not," Nate was saying. "Bay, come on. I think Shane needs to handle this. If he can't handle this, then you're both in trouble."

Rye looked to his brother and nodded. "You have to both be able to talk to her. You have to figure out how to give her what she needs even if the other isn't around. Which is why we're either going solo on our business trips from now on or one of us is staying home with the kids and Rachel can help with clients. I think she would make a hell of a salesperson for our farm."

Max got the most peaceful smile on his face. "I agree. I don't want our daughter thinking her place is at home with kids. Not when she's probably going to have two husbands who can handle their share of the load. Shane, talk to her. Please let her know we love her."

"I think Shane can handle this nicely," Trev said with a nod. "We'll sort all of this out. I promise. And if things work out, we'll have another couple of hands. Hopefully you can train them before Brooke decides she wants to roam the country with film crews. You know it's not unlike cowboying except the cattle are way more dramatic."

"Costume design." Max said the word as though tasting it. "I like it."

Rye nodded, a little choked up. "Our baby sister is going to win an Oscar one day."

Bay took a long breath. She needed her brothers. She needed her family. They all needed Bliss as a homebase. The rest was negotiable.

If she didn't kick them to the curb simply because she could. If she felt what they did. If she'd been telling the whole truth about living in the moment because her future wasn't here, wasn't with them.

Shane seemed to think for a moment and then pointed a finger Bay's way. "You are going to take the art show seriously. You're going to listen to everything Stef says, and you'll wear whatever

Brooke puts on you. I'll handle the legal stuff. Well, I'll bring Gemma coffee and do what she tells me to do."

"Throw in some cash and you're my best client," Gemma agreed.

"If I'm taking charge of this household, then I won't sit around and hope things work out. I'll be proactive, and I'm not always going to sit down and have a long chat with you. The first thing we're doing is taking our savings and buying a reliable vehicle," Shane announced. "We can't borrow from Stef long term. It's time to figure out how to make this work with two artistic careers and me in the middle managing everything."

"And we're going to figure out what's happening with Kale Kingman," Bay replied.

Shane stilled.

"I'm sorry. You know I don't like to deal with the bad shit, but I was wrong to question you. I won't ever do it again. You say you saw something, you saw it. You would never make shit up." Bay held out a hand. "I'm so sorry, brother, and when I make bail, I'll clear things up with our girl, too. As for the rest of it, I'll follow your lead. I might have talent, but talent means little without discipline and drive, and both of those things are housed in you. We need you. Brooke and I need you. It doesn't work without you, brother."

Max and Rye started arguing about who was the talented one and who was the one with discipline and drive between them. Bay ignored them.

Shane took his hand. "All right, then our path is set, and I need to figure out what's going on in Brooke's head. Try to stay out of trouble."

Bay shrugged. "I will. I don't actually think I'll have much of a choice."

"I'll see you at home, brother," Shane promised and he stood taller, seemed far more confident since they'd properly defined his job and his place.

He watched as his brother walked away a more secure man than he'd been before.

Hopefully it would be enough to convince Brooke to forgive him.

Chapter Fourteen

Brooke stood in the shadows of the catwalk of the theater, watching as the actors moved with ease through the set. Shane had worked on that set. The set designer hadn't stuck around to make changes or adjustments. He was already back in LA working on another project, so Cleo had to deal with everything on her own. Except Cleo had started to treat Shane like a stage manager, which was good since the stage manager they had was barely eighteen and way more interested in picking up women than doing his job.

But his grandma was on the board, so Shane was taking one for the team.

The team. Were they a team? It felt like it, and then it felt like they were assholes who thought women were possessions.

What would she have done if she'd walked in on a woman basically trying to molest one of her men? Bay would tell the woman no and mean it and deal with it if she didn't give up. Shane would struggle to not offend her.

How would she have handled it?

She took a long breath and tried to focus on the costumes. The actors were moving well. Cleo had reset the play in Colorado, with the three sisters having moved from Denver and missing their old cosmopolitan lifestyle. They were stuck in a tiny mountain town.

They couldn't seem to find the beauty, and that was the part of the tragedy of the play.

Was she making the same mistakes?

The actress who played the youngest of the sisters settled on her spot. "I've never been in love before. I've dreamt of it, day and night, but my heart is like a fine piano no one can play because a key is lost."

Longing. The whole play was about longing for something they no longer had. About feeling as though they don't fit in. The whole play was about how dreams didn't often mesh properly with reality.

Was she making the same mistakes? Not being willing to accept the reality in front of her? Would she always long for something that hadn't been great in the first place? Time and distance might paint a patina over that time in New York, and she might always wonder.

Her cell rang and she sighed as she looked down at it.

Mark. Asshole. Still, she picked up. She was in the top part of the theater where they accessed the lights. She was far enough away she shouldn't disturb the rehearsal, but she kept her voice low anyway. "Mark, are you doing okay?"

"No thanks to those overly muscled meatheads. Also, the doctor here is terrible. He wouldn't even prescribe me some valium to get through the day. I'm going to go back to the lodge and hopefully they have someone better," Mark complained.

Nope. They had Ty Davis, who handled small emergencies as an EMT, and if they needed more they called in Doc Burke. "I wanted to talk to you about what happened in the café."

"What happened in that café was I got brutalized."

"Mark, you were sexually harassing me," Brooke said in no uncertain terms. She'd thought about it on her way over and decided this was how she would handle it. No matter what he'd done, she couldn't leave Bay to face Mark's wrath. She knew her ex-boss, knew how he loved to sue. Anyone. For anything. It was like a game to him, which was one of the reasons she knew he would absolutely use her brothers' family against her. She was bluffing, but she had to do something.

"I was being affectionate," he countered. "I'm an affectionate guy. Hey, I don't think I need… What the fuck, man. I didn't get bitten. Brooke, that asshole doctor shoved a needle in my arm without even asking."

"It's an antibiotic." She could hear Caleb in the distance. "I would let my nurse give it to you but she's currently taking care of a billionaire dumbass who got in a car accident and stole my best employee."

"Naomi is his only employee," Brooke corrected. "Well, at least she was. I've seen the billionaire in question, and he's hot. He's a friend's brother. Really, it's better when Naomi is around."

"Which friend?" She could hear him moving. "Are you talking about Georgia Stark?"

It wasn't surprising he knew who she was. Georgia was a force of nature. She wasn't the shy, retiring type, though she absolutely was kind and empathetic to everyone she met. But Georgia was unapologetically Georgia, and that included being upfront and brazen about her nontraditional marriage. "Georgia Stark-Warner. Yes, she's a friend of mine."

"No one gives a fuck about the other guy," Mark dismissed. "Stark is one of the biggest tech giants in the world. Georgia is rapidly becoming an icon." He paused, and she could hear him thinking. Manipulating. Coming up with the best way to get what he wanted. "I heard you're working on a project for her."

Well, that had gotten out fast. And now she knew why he'd had a change of heart. He'd seen the pictures in the society pages. The one where she was getting on the plane with the Stark-Warner family. She would bet Georgia had been talking to friends about their new project. The news would be all over town now. "This was never about how good I am at my job."

"Of course it is. If you're designing the Met Gala gown for one of New York's most interesting residents, you're good." He sighed. "But you lack experience. You wouldn't want to send your friend out in a dress that's guaranteed to be mocked by the press, would you?"

Fucker. "Let me guess. All I have to do to get my job back is let you take credit for designing the gown."

"It's about more than credit. I would need to take a guiding hand, and I'll definitely want to sit in on your next session with Georgia. I'm here for however long it takes, and when we're done, we can head back to New York together, but first we'll stop in Milan."

"Hey, Brooke. This guy is trying to manipulate you." Caleb must have been practically shouting because she could hear him loud and clear.

"You will hear from my attorney, sir," Mark announced, and she heard the jingle of the bell that announced someone was coming into the clinic. "Now I need my Uber. Shouldn't they be here already?"

"I think your Fuber driver is probably finishing up math tutoring," Brooke admitted. "He'll get there. Eventually. So all I have to do is give you access to my wealthy friends."

A low chuckle came over the line. "Well, not the doctor, though I'll be happy to sue him."

"I'm sure his brother will be thrilled." Georgia could handle him. She handled assholes all the time. It was a wave through her head, the idea that if she couldn't trust Bay and Shane to behave like normal humans, that she should go back to New York. After the Met, she could likely find another job and tell them all to fuck off.

Georgia had to deal with so many people wanting everything from her. She couldn't be another person who used Georgia's sweet nature for her own betterment.

"Here's how it's going to go, Mark. I'm not coming back. I'm going to be making Georgia's gown, and it will be my name on it. I'll rise or fall being Brooke Harper, but the honest truth is I don't want to do fashion. It bores me. I stayed because my family spent so much money on it and I hated the idea that I could fail." The truth of the matter was the worst had happened. Rye was absolutely ashamed of her. Max would never say it, but then his standards weren't as high as Rye's. For all his obnoxiousness, Max had always been the softer touch of her brothers. Rye was the one who had to deal with the day-to-day stuff.

A bit like Shane.

She was sure he would show up and try to cover for his brother. He would accuse her of overreacting.

Had she? Again, what the hell would she have done if she'd walked in and found some woman all over Bay? Or Shane? Would she have stood there and watched, or would she have gotten down and dirty and saved her man?

"Listen to me, you little bitch, I have a plan and I'm not going to let you fuck it up," Mark snarled over the line.

Oh, she was not done. "And if you do decide to press charges against my boyfriend, I'll press charges against you for assault. I said no. I said it loud enough for people to hear it."

"No, you didn't. You didn't say a damn thing," Mark replied. "It's going to be he said/she said, and we all know how that goes. Now that I think about it, you might have tricked me. I think you set it up so your boyfriend would hurt me. Now why would you do that, Brooke?"

She sighed. "I'm certain this would work in New York, but buddy, we're in my hometown, and I assure you Dr. Burke heard me say no. So did Stella. Hell, I'm pretty sure Stef Talbot happened to be walking by, and he heard me, too. Also, I'll talk to our local judge. He's like ninety, and he and his wife used to babysit me. That's what happens when you're one of four kids in the whole town. They become a village. You're not going to get my village to turn against me."

"You small-town folks sure don't mind using corruption when it serves you," Mark said bitterly.

"Not at all. I've learned that there's no fighting fair with a person like you. You put me in a corner. You should expect me to fight my way out and not to give you a whole bunch of consideration about how I do it. Call the Sheriff's Department. Tell him you made a mis-take or this is going to go poorly for you. I can probably get Georgia to talk about how the House of Bianchi seems to be in a downward spiral."

He paused for a moment as though trying to find any kind of way out. "But she would be talking about your line. It's the next one out. It's the one everyone is going to be talking about. You would be hurting yourself."

"Oh, that line? It doesn't have my name on it, asshole," she shot back. "No one outside of Bianchi knows it's mine, and if you try to say it is, I'll explain to the press that I have no knowledge of that line. Do not assume that I work off the same principles that you do. Right now the only thing I care about is fucking you over as thoroughly as possible."

"Fine. I think the deputy's here." There was a deep bitterness to Mark's tone. "I'll let him know it was all a misunderstanding, and I'll be out of here as soon as possible. Shitty town. And you know what? I didn't want to dress that cow anyway. I have no idea why the press is fascinated with that overweight bimbo. Good luck. If it works, maybe you'll get more of the fatties to try to design for."

There was a click over the line. Rage bubbled inside Brooke. How many times had she heard that? Fashion was supposed to be for everyone, but the truth of the matter was if you weren't a sample size then you were a token.

She had what she wanted. She should let it go.

She pushed the number to connect her to an old friend.

"Hey, Brooke." Logan's calm voice came over the line. "I heard you got attacked."

Even through her anger, she was amused by how fast the Bliss grapevine worked. "Has he morphed into Sasquatch yet? Or an alien? I've heard we're crawling with them lately."

"No, some city asshole. Maybe your old boss," Logan replied. "I mean of course by the time it got to me you were absolutely in the hands of aliens from the Faraxis system. Apparently they like our females. But I speak Bliss, so I know it's probably your ex-boss, who happens to be irritating the shit out of everyone at the lodge. I talked to Lucy earlier. Pretty sure that was the guy she was complaining about. I caught up with her at my moms' store."

It was good Logan remembered how things worked here. He would understand exactly what to do. If there was one thing beyond tolerance and acceptance that Bliss was good at, it was revenge. "He offered me my job back but only if I introduce him to Georgia."

Logan paused as though thinking about it. "I'm sure she wouldn't mind him coming over for a couple of drinks."

"Fuck that." See, Logan had spent too much time in the city. He was getting soft. "I'm not letting that lowlife in the same room as my friends. That's not what I'm calling about. I'm going to need you to tell Seth that in six months he needs to purchase House of Bianchi outright and burn it to the ground and explain to every other design house that the same will happen to them if they hire Mark Hallway. I need time because I don't want him turning around and pressing charges against Bay. He's got a show soon, and I don't want this hanging over his head."

Getting him into a suit would be hard enough.

Damn it. She'd been a bitch to him. He might have already written her off. She'd let her emotions get the better of her, and it might honestly be for the best. What could she offer them?

"Do I want to know what he said about my wife?" Each word out of Logan's mouth was coated in ice. "I ask because you would never take this kind of revenge for yourself, so this is about Georgia."

"You do not. Just know she should never be let around anyone from that company," Brooke replied. "They're all snakes."

"So you're not going back?" Logan asked. "You want me to talk to Seth? Look, I think you'll find Georgia would love it if you would design for her and her alone. You know moneybags will open up his wallet."

"I would love to sit down and talk to Georgia about designing some clothes for her, but I think I'm going to give costume design a real shot. Cleo is starting to direct some films, and I think it's a challenge I would like to take on." Even as she said the words, her heart ached because she knew Bay and Shane likely wouldn't come with her.

Logan's voice went low over the line. "And what about the Kent brothers? I've heard you're getting married. And yes, I also know a fuck-you sibling move when I hear it. Rye push you too hard?"

"He's been a wildly massive overprotective asshole, but he has his reasons." No matter how sad she felt that her brother was ashamed of her, she wouldn't throw him under a bus with Logan. "As for Bay and Shane, well, maybe they'll still be willing to see me when I'm in town."

"We won't," a deep voice said.

From below she could hear Cleo correcting something the actors were doing, but all of her focus was suddenly on the man at the top of the stairs. Shane stood there looking stern in his jeans and T-shirt.

Damn, she was about to get her heart ripped out. "Logan, I need to call you back."

"Okay, but you might want to talk to Lucy since she's been dealing with the guy. She's going out to the G to help Nell and Henry. They've got some kind of lesson with Noah today, but Henry's worried because she's been having Braxton-Hicks contractions, and damn I can't believe that not only do I know what those are, I can speak competently about the effects on the mental health of the mother. Who the hell am I? Do you think I can get my comic books back?"

She loved Logan, loved how far he'd come. "I think you can read all the comics you like. You're still going to be Dr. Logan Green, therapist to all. I'll talk to you later."

She hung up and pulled all her strength around her. She had to get through the next couple of minutes. She slid the cell into her jeans. "Hello, Shane. I'll be out of the house before tonight. Tell Bay I'm sorry he felt like he had to deal with Mark. I've made certain Mark is going to drop all charges, so he should be out in an hour or two."

"What is that supposed to mean?" Shane asked.

She pointed to the stage. "They're rehearsing. Keep your voice down, please. I won't cause any trouble. Like I said I'll be out tonight, this afternoon if I have to, and I'll arrange with Bobby to get a pickup out there so I can leave you Stef's car."

Shane stared at her, his eyes nearly glowing in the light cast from the stage. "Just like that?"

What did he expect her to do? "Like I said, I'm not going to cause trouble."

"Oh, my love, but I will." He stalked across the narrow hall, and she took a step back. It didn't matter since he wasn't giving her space. His hand came around her neck, and he gently brought her up on her toes. His mouth hovered over hers, and despite all the crap of the day, a thrill went through her as he spoke. "You have no idea the amount of trouble I'm going to cause if you step foot off the G without one of us with you. Something is going on and it's not about your former boss, though you should know I would have done the same damn thing as Bay."

"I was going to handle it." He was so close, and he was giving off some serious Dom vibes.

He stared at her for a moment as though deciding how to handle her. If it had been Bay staring down at her with intense eyes, she could have gone on her toes and kissed him and distracted him, but Shane was far more intense about some things. "If some woman had her hands on me, what would you have done?"

She could lie. "I would have trusted you to handle it."

His eyes narrowed, and she felt the hand on her neck tighten slightly. "Some woman is making me uncomfortable and you're fine with that. I'm on my own?"

She let loose a low groan of frustration. "Damn it, Shane. That's not fair."

"Tell me why you freaked out. Did you want your job back?" His jaw tightened. "If that's the truth, then I'll talk to Bay about apologizing, though I would bet that asshole will be nasty about it."

"I handled it."

"How did you handle it, Brooke?"

"I told him he could either leave Bay and Rye alone or I would press my own charges and make sure everyone in the world knew exactly who he was," she replied with some fire of her own.

"There's my girl," he said, his mouth hovering above her own. "Now tell me what you would have done in his place. No fucking lies, Brooke."

Such an ass. "Fine. I would have pulled her off you by the hair, and I wouldn't have thought twice about it."

"Again, my girl." There was a wealth of satisfaction coming off the man. "Now tell me why you're so pissed off about losing a job you didn't want back in the first place that you're willing to leave both of us behind. I'm suspecting you weren't planning on asking us to go with you wherever it is you think you're going."

Put like that it didn't sound great. "I'm going with Cleo when she leaves town."

He took a step back as though he needed to consider her decision. After a long moment he nodded. "Will she stick around after opening night? I read some directors hand things over to the assistant or the stage manager."

He sounded so calm it made her heart ache. She'd kind of thought he would fight her. Still, it was better if they could be civil. "She'll stay for a couple of weeks. We're going to hole up somewhere and start talking about design for the film. There's not a ton of money attached, but we'll make do. I expect to stay at her place in LA for a couple of weeks until I can figure something out."

"I'll start looking. Is there a particular area you're interested in?"

"What?"

"I know the marriage thing was fake for you, but it wasn't for us. If you go to LA, we go to LA. Bay will make some money off the showing, and even if it's not a lot, I'm going to apply for some art grants that should keep us afloat until he does. He won't like it, but he can start doing some commissions."

She shook her head. That wasn't how Bay worked. "He needs to feel inspired. You can't count on that when you're doing commissions."

She should know. It was what she did every day. She could handle it, could find the artistry in giving the client what they wanted, but what she and Bay did was different.

"All he needs is you," Shane announced quietly. "We'll let Trev know we need to put in two weeks' notice. It'll be okay because he's interviewing a couple of new hands. We'll have some time to train them."

She was floored. "You have to talk to Bay about that."

His head shook. "No, I don't. If there's one thing I know it's where our priorities are, and they're with you. We love you. We've waited all of our miserable lives for you. If you think we're going to let you walk away, you're wrong."

"You can't do this." She couldn't believe what she was hearing. "You haven't known me long enough to chuck your job for me. How would we even handle that financially?"

"I'll get a job. Bay will work on commissions, and I'll let Stef know he's off the leash when it comes to promoting Bay. Up until now he's wanted to stay out of the spotlight, but he'll do what it takes to take care of his family."

It was overwhelming. Could she ask them to do this for her? It didn't make any sense.

Shane's expression softened, and he stepped back into her space. He lowered his lips and kissed her forehead. "Hey, calm down, baby. You don't have to do anything today. You need to take a deep breath, and when Bay gets back, we'll sit down and talk. Or better yet we'll get naked and talk because I think you'll be more honest with me if my hands are on you."

"It's too soon," she whispered. "But I can't let this chance go. Do you understand what I'm saying to you? It's not fair, but I have to pick myself this time."

He seemed to consider her words. "Brooke, if you don't want us, it's okay. I mean it's not and my fucking heart will break, but I won't bother you anymore."

This was her out.

And she should want it. She should keep them right where they were. A good time. A couple of wild weeks.

But it hadn't been. Sure, the sex was crazy, but most of the moments she would remember had been sweet. Quiet and loving. She felt safe with them. She didn't honestly feel the wild anxiety she sometimes got when she decided she was in love.

And yet she knew she was in love with them.

"I can't be the reason you leave again," she said quietly. "I don't know when I'll be back."

"That wasn't an answer."

"I don't know that I can give you one." She was overwhelmed. Once again it felt like her life had flipped on a dime and she was left trying to pick which way to go.

She wanted them, but she wasn't sure she should.

Why?

Tears filled her eyes because she didn't want to make this decision. She wanted to float for a while, to be with them without having to think about changing their lives along with her own.

"Hush, baby." He kissed her again. "Calm down. I can see your brain working, and it's been too much. Do you want me to leave? I can give you time, but I can't let you walk away unless you tell me it's over."

"I don't want it to be over." She wrapped her arms around him. "Maybe I don't know what I want at all."

But she did. She didn't know if she should want it.

The fight with her brother weighed heavily on her. What Mark had said. Was moving to LA the right thing? She loved it here. She missed seeing Rachel and the kids, and she seemed so far from the brothers who had raised her.

She could breathe when his arms were around her.

"Baby, let me take you home. We can help Nell and Henry with the goats, and I'll make us dinner and you and me and Bay will go to the playroom and you'll feel so good. We'll go to dinner at your brothers' place this weekend and you'll see that Rye didn't mean shit. He loves you. He's scared, and the world is changing."

"It's too fast." Tears pierced her eyes, but she held on to him.

"I know, so we're going to slow it all down and bring it back to you and me and Bay. No decisions. Just being together," he promised. "We don't have to talk about the future. We have some time before opening night. We won't talk about the future at all until then. If you don't want me to say it, I won't. I won't pressure you."

She knew what he was offering. "I don't want you to not say it."

"Good," he whispered. "Because I love you and not saying it doesn't make that go away. I'm going to love you for the rest of my life. But we don't have to deal with that today. All we have to do today is breathe and maybe deal with the dental health of goats."

She laughed. He was so good at making her laugh, at making her let go of all the bad shit because she was safe with him and Bay.

"Okay," she said quietly. "Let's go back. But we'll have to deal with it eventually."

"And we will," he vowed. "We'll deal with it together."

She took his hand and let him lead her away.

* * * *

Shane pulled the SUV into the drive as Trev was hustling out of the big house, Bo running right behind him. There was a definite harried look in Trev's eyes. Bo had one of the kids' bags over his shoulder, and while he moved a bit more slowly than his partner, there was no way to miss his tension.

"That doesn't look good." Brooke unhooked her seatbelt before he got the car slowed down.

He noticed there were two young men standing on the porch. They looked to be in their early twenties, and they were wearing standard cowboy gear. Jeans, Western shirt. They had bolo ties on and belts neatly wrapped around trim waists that let Shane know they were dressed to impress.

Trev paid them no mind, simply ran to his truck, but Bo stopped.

"Hey, Shane," Bo said and tipped his hat toward Brooke. "Beth took the kids into town today after her consultation with Hale, and Miranda fell off the monkey bars at the playground. Her arm might be broken. I would ask Jamie to take over the interviews, but he took Hope into Alamosa to shop for baby stuff, and Noah's in the barn with Nell and Henry and Lucy."

"Bo!" Trev yelled.

"He's overstimulated." Bo was cool under pressure. "Beth already told us she's going to be fine, but Trev can't stand the thought of our baby girl bumping her knee, much less breaking a limb. I happen to know our boys are going to do a lot of that. Talk to the new guys for us, Shane. They seem okay, but Trev is acting like he doesn't trust them. He's been standoffish since they walked in, and we need some help, so figure out how much experience they have."

The truck honked and Bo stepped back.

"I'll handle it," Shane told him.

"Do you need help? Does Beth have the boys?" Brooke got out and walked around as Bo got into the truck. "Is my sister-in-law here?"

Bo's grin kicked up. "Your sister-in-law found out one of her husbands was in jail and made a beeline for town. Apparently Rye's asking the sheriff to leave them alone in the cell for a half an hour."

Shane could guess what would happen then. "You need one of us to come help with the younger kiddos?"

Those boys could be a handful.

"Thanks, but we've got it," Trev promised. "I'm sorry to leave you with the new guys. And those dumbasses brought a girlfriend, though she's done nothing but sit in the living room and play around on her phone."

Shane got out of the SUV. "We'll be fine. Maybe Brooke can make some cookies. Miranda loves her peanut butter cookies."

"I'm sure she would love that. By the way, Max is bringing Bay back," Trev said, his eyes grim. "The guy declined to press charges. Nate's finishing up paperwork and then Bay will be back. We're supposed to…"

"Move the herd. Clean out the back barn. Get the new fencing ready for Friday. I'll get it all done. Go." Shane waved him off. It was nothing he couldn't handle. In the last couple of months he'd noticed

Damn, Bliss had chilled him out on so many things. "That is none of your business, and if you have a problem with outside-the-norm relationships, then this is probably not the place for you."

Bull Rider held his hands up. "No problems. Just curiosity, which we will check. Sorry about the questions. We heard you worked with your brother, and since this is Bliss and she's gorgeous…"

Well, they weren't wrong about that. He started walking toward the main house. In this part of the ranch there were two big houses and what they liked to call the front barn. It was where they kept the horses and smaller livestock. There was a second barn they kept out in the fields with emergency supplies and space to keep sick animals. The house the McNamara-O'Malleys lived in also included a couple of rooms they considered the business offices of the G. Shane started moving toward those. Trev would have left notes and such on the desk, including their résumés. "I'm Shane Kent. I suppose I'm the foreman when Bo's not around."

"I'm Billy and this is my friend Ned." The tall one kept up with him.

Shane noticed that Ned had stopped a ways back, seeming to check his phone. "Well, welcome to the G. I'm sure Trev's already gone over some things with you. How far did you get?"

He opened the door for Billy as Ned slid his phone in his pocket and strode confidently toward them. "Not too far. I'll be honest, we were surprised at how few people were around. The ranches we've worked at are filled to the brim most of the time."

He noticed Noah walking up. The veterinarian jogged in from the barn. Shane held the door for him since he appeared to be coming his way and not heading to the other family home, the one he shared with his brother and their wife. "Well, most of our hands are out working. This is a big ranch, and getting to the remote parts can take some time. Not all our land is flat and reachable with a four by four. Sometimes we have to do it the old-fashioned way. Don't worry. There are dorms out there."

There were a couple of small buildings in the far fields that offered food and water and protection from the weather. There were cots he'd spent some time on when he got caught out there way after dark.

"I wouldn't call them dorms." Noah gave him a smile. "They're more like basic shelters, but with halfway decent snacks. Hope makes sure those get changed out every now and then. She didn't like the fact that some of them had cans of beans from the last century. Sorry. I need to grab some towels, and Trev's place is closer."

He disappeared down the hall.

"Who is that?" Billy asked.

"One of the owners, though he doesn't do a ton of actual ranch work. He's a vet," Shane explained. "Normally Noah works at his office in town, but it's nice to have him around."

"Why isn't he there now?" Ned asked. "I thought we met everyone."

It was such an odd thing to say. Why did he care that Noah was hanging around? "Like you said, it takes a lot of people to run a ranch this size. Why don't you two take a seat and I'll be right with you. I'm going to grab a water."

He moved to the kitchen where Beth kept two things eternally available. A pot of coffee was always on, and she had a case of water waiting for anyone who needed it. Shane pulled his cell as he entered the kitchen.

No bars.

Damn it. He was going to call Bay and see when he could get his ass home. Brooke needed some cuddle time and some rub her feet and prove she's a goddess time.

But he'd heard the newbies on their phones. They'd definitely made at least one call, and Ned had seemed to be actively texting someone.

That was when he heard it.

A loud bang crashed through the air.

Gunshot. There was no way to mistake it. Pistol. Not rifle, and it came from inside the house.

He had to get to Brooke.

He started to push out of the door when Billy stood there, a gun pointed directly at Shane's head. "Why don't you sit down and we'll have a talk. My boss should be here any minute."

He could guess exactly who was coming. Kale Kingman. And they were all in trouble now.

Chapter Fifteen

Brooke slipped inside the big barn and heard a low groan.

"Baby?" Henry stood beside Noah, holding a small goat in his arms.

Noah was carefully inspecting another goat's hooves. They were set up with Noah's veterinary kit, and it looked like someone had been taking notes on the care of hooves, specifically in horses, goats, and cattle.

"It's Braxton-Hicks." Nell wore a long skirt and a matching shirt, her brown hair up in a ponytail that was only slightly messy. Her hands were on the small of her back as she turned to her husband. "It's nothing to worry about. I still have a couple of weeks."

"I'm not sure. Caleb says the baby is getting big." Lucy occupied one of the camp chairs they'd set up around the barn. She glanced down at her watch. Nell and Henry weren't the only ones learning new talents. "I think we should start timing them."

Oh, she was walking in on some serious drama. "Everything okay? Can I get you anything, Nell?"

She'd been around her sister-in-law enough to know this was a delicate stage of pregnancy. Nell was huge and having trouble moving, and everything could feel like a train was coming to hit her. At least that was how Rachel described it. There was a lot of worry and anxiety surrounding the last couple of weeks.

Nell glanced over and gave her a smile. "I'm fine. Henry's being a worrywart."

Lucy held up a hand. "I am, too. Not the fine part. The worry-wart part."

Brooke gave her friend a smile. "I thought you were moving into management at the inn. Why are you suddenly studying midwifery?"

Lucy stood and moved closer to her. "You know everyone in Bliss has a couple of jobs. Like Gemma's a lawyer but she works most of the time running the sheriff's office. Which could be a serious conflict of interest anywhere else. Callie works at Trio, but she also teaches part time with the nursery school kids. The Farley brothers have like ten jobs."

"You do not need another job. You literally have three incomes," Brooke pointed out. Her guys had good jobs. Ty was an EMT, and Michael worked for the US Marshals.

"I think it's wonderful that Lucy wants to help out." Nell's smile was bright but slightly strained.

"I want to get to know a little of what Ty does," Lucy admitted. "Let's face facts. If I'm going to help one of my guys out at his job, it's going to be Ty. I'm done fighting criminals. Also, everyone's worried that Naomi isn't coming back from Dallas. That Dawson guy kind of stole her. I don't know if she'll fall for him or just take the big wad of cash he offered and enjoy the rest of her life when the job is done. That means a new nurse, and finding one who's willing to work with Doc might be harder than we think. With all the pregnancies around the town, I want to be able to pitch in. We had a woman give birth out at the lodge, and I helped Ty. It made an impression on me, and I want to know more."

Lucy had her dream job.

Lucy worked hard to get where she was. And she wasn't stopping there. The job wasn't the destination. It was part of the road, and the road kept going. She kept trying to find a place to stop, but life didn't stop. What if she was looking at it all wrong? What if the job wasn't the most important thing? What if the road was? The journey itself. What if some power position wasn't the destination at all, and the place she was looking for all her life was right here in front of her?

"Hey, are you okay?" Lucy put a hand on her arm. "I tried to call you when I figured out who our annoying guest was. I'm sorry he surprised you. He's an ass, by the way."

Brooke felt something wet on her cheek and wiped away a tear. Damn men were making her feel too much. "He doesn't matter but I do want to talk to you. Would you leave the lodge if you decided you wanted to be a nurse?"

The men were talking in the background and the baby goat was braying, but Brooke found herself completely focused on Lucy.

"I love what I do." Lucy seemed to understand this was serious for Brooke. Her tone gentled, and she gave her friend a squeeze. "But yes, I would if I decided I wanted something else."

"But you worked so hard. People helped you along the way."

"And I'll pay that forward." Lucy sighed. "Sweetie, you get to change your mind. No matter what the world has given you, you can change course. I know what you're thinking because we've been friends for a long time. You think your brothers will be disappointed."

"Rye said he was." She could still see him staring at her.

A gasp came from Nell's mouth. "He said that? Henry, we're protesting Rye."

Henry gave his wife a thumbs-up even as he scrambled with the baby goat. "Sure thing, babe. Are we protesting his business practices?"

"No, his human ones," Nell replied primly.

Henry nodded. "I've got signs for that, too."

"Don't protest my brother." She appreciated the gesture since protesting was definitely Nell's love language. "He's trying to catch up. I can see where he might be upset about me abruptly changing what I want from my career. After all, he spent years doing a job he didn't love so I could have this chance."

Nell rubbed her lower back as she spoke. "Sweetie, your brother loves you, and whatever he actually said, he is not ashamed of you. No one is. You're our girl. We watched you grow up. I remember you graduating from high school. The whole town came out."

Lucy got a little teary. "They did."

"They always do. For everyone." Brooke didn't want Lucy to

feel left out.

"Of course they do, and I can't tell you how much I wished I'd been living here at the time. I didn't make it to my own graduation. I had to watch my siblings." Lucy wiped away a tear but there was a smile on her face. "I did for my younger siblings what Rye did for you, and I need you to understand if they decided not to use their degrees or the training classes I paid for, if it turned out they could be happier with something else, I wouldn't care. I would be thrilled for them. Brooke, are you hurting anyone?"

She hadn't realized how much she needed this. "No. I think I might be finding myself again. I think I got lost somewhere in trying to be successful."

Nell was crying, too. Not that it took much these days. "The only real success in life is to love and be loved. It's to leave this world a better place, to experience the human range of emotions."

Lucy laughed. "Don't talk like that around Mel."

Nell frowned, but it was an amused expression. "Mel knows my stance on interstellar visitors. We should talk to them. The galaxy is our home. Though I do take the beet regularly because beets are an excellent health food."

"Don't let her fool you," Henry called out. "She took extra because Cass told her there's a group of non-corporeal aliens who sometimes zip into the unborn."

Nell put a hand to her belly. "Well, one can't be too careful, but what I'm really saying is the world is a big place and you deciding you want to change your mind about something, well, that's normal. Open your heart and ask yourself what you truly want."

That was oddly easy. "I want to work with Cleo for a while and see how I like costume design, but more than that, I want them. I want Bay and Shane, and it's too early to ask them to follow me. It's too early for me to give up my career for them and start working at the Stop 'n' Shop."

"Nah." Henry joined them. The goat he previously held was happily running around the barn now. "Those two won't mind. Shane will find his way. That boy can make a home out of almost anything, and Bay has his art. He can create anywhere. Those boys know what they want. Don't break their hearts and yours because you think it's too soon to know. I'm the one who knows that. I cost us months and months because I didn't think I could change. I'd already changed. I changed the minute I met Nell. I became a different person, but I fought it because I thought I owed other people. You don't, Brooke. Not Stef or the town. Not your brothers. Yes, they sacrificed for you. Pay it forward. Help out others because once they helped you."

"Love your niece and your nephews," Lucy advised. "Come home when you can and be with your family. That's all your brothers are ever going to want. I think that's why Rye is so touchy right now. You've been gone a long time."

She loved her family so much. What if she could have the best of both worlds? A career and her men, new places to see and worlds to design, and the comfort of knowing she could always come back here. To her physical home, where the door was always open and she was always wanted.

She'd been so wrong this morning. She absolutely should have yelled at Bay because his hands were far more valuable than the joy she got from Mark taking a punch to the face. But she should have hugged him and been kinder.

She was going to have to make up for that, but somehow she thought it would all be okay.

Nell gasped and stepped back. "Oh, shit. Oh, no. I said shit. I don't know why I said that. I don't curse."

Lucy's eyes had gone wide. "Because your water broke."

Oh, shit. Brooke did curse and often. She took a deep breath. "Hey, Noah. We're about to have way more than baby goats in here. Nell's in active labor."

Henry had gone pale. "Oh, no. She's been having the pains for a couple of hours now. We need to get her into town."

Nell clutched her husband. "I'm not due for another two weeks."

Noah put his bag down and started for the barn door. "You're fine, Nell. It's always an estimate, and you're well within a safe time to deliver. I'm more worried because your last delivery was a c-section."

"Caleb said I could try," Nell informed him. "Poppy was late, and she was too big for me to deliver naturally. He said this one might be okay."

"I want you in the clinic no matter what." Henry's hands were shaking slightly.

"I'll grab some towels and I'll bring my SUV around." Noah moved to the door, opening it. "Someone call Caleb and let him know we're coming in. Lucy, monitor her contractions, please."

"On it." Lucy pulled a notepad out of her pocket and wrote down the time.

"What can I do?" Despite the craziness of the situation, Brooke felt so much relief.

It was going to be okay. Bay would be back soon and she would apologize and they would take her to bed and they would talk all of this out.

And she would get to meet another Bliss baby. She bet this kid would be as calm and peaceful as her sister.

Nell let out a long groan. "Oh, that was a rough one."

Henry frowned. "How many have been rough ones?"

She shrugged. "A couple. Maybe the last hour or so. But I didn't want to stop the lesson. We only have babysitting for another few hours."

Brooke pulled her phone and started to dial the number for the clinic. "Who has Poppy? I'll call them, too."

"Laura has her. She's playing with Sierra this afternoon." Nell hissed as she tried to straighten up. "They're having a tea party."

"I'll call her after I talk to Caleb," Brooke said.

"Let's get outside and wait for Noah." Lucy ran back and grabbed Nell's purse.

"I can drive her," Henry offered.

Lucy's head shook. "Nope. You are going to sit in the back and hold her hand and help me keep track of her vitals. You shouldn't be driving while she's in labor. Let Noah handle it."

Henry nodded.

"This is the Bliss Clinic. Are you shot?"

The town was going to miss Naomi so much. "No one is shot, Doc. Nell's in labor. We're on our way in."

Nothing. The line went dead. She wasn't sure if he'd heard her or not.

She glanced down at her phone, ready to try to reconnect the call.

No bars. But they'd put a tower fairly close so the major parts of the ranch had cellular coverage. Shane had told her if he was out in the far reaches of the ranch, coverage could come in and out, but it should always be available here.

What was going on?

She looked back at Henry, who was gently herding his wife to the doors, helping her around the goats. "Henry, do you have bars?"

Henry stopped and slipped his cell out of his pocket. "No. I don't. The call connected?"

She nodded. "Yes. I got him on the line but…"

There was the sound of something going off in the distance.

Gunfire.

"Ladies, I need you to move to the far corner of the barn." Henry's tone had gone icy cold. Like something had washed over him and all the hugginess was gone.

"Did Noah's car backfire?" Lucy moved to the door.

Henry blocked her. "No. That's not how modern cars sound. That was gunfire, and it's coming from one of the houses. Lucy, please take my wife to one of the back stalls and make her as comfortable as you can while I figure out what's going on."

"Henry," Nell began.

He seemed to take control of himself. A long, deep breath and his expression cleared and he was Henry again. "I know, baby. I'll be careful. I'll be gentle."

Nell's hands shook as she reached up and cupped her husband's face. "I'm sorry. I called the wrong name. I need you, John Bishop. This baby needs you. Our baby."

Whoa. Okay, now if she didn't sort of know the story, she would think Henry had a double personality disorder. John Bishop was the name he'd gone by when he'd worked for the CIA in black ops. When he'd been a deadly operative.

"Nell," he began.

She shook her head. "Do what you need to do, John. Whatever you need to do. You are off the leash, my love."

His eyes hardened at the words, but he kissed her tenderly. "Stay safe. I'll be back."

Brooke's heart rate tripled because she heard the sound of large vehicles pulling up to the driveway. "I think that might be Bay."

She started for the door but Henry moved in front of her. He eased the door open slightly, and his frown told her most of what she needed to know. The low growl of his words told her the rest. "Not Bay. It's two trucks. Maybe ten men, and they all have weapons, which will be helpful to me."

A chill snaked along her spine. Shane had been worried about something happening. Bay hadn't believed him, but it looked like Bay was going to eat those words. Shane was still out there. "Shane and Bay had some trouble with a rancher a few months back."

"I know. I actually started looking into the man months ago when Trev was worried about him joining the ranching collective the G belongs to. I will say the man is good at covering his tracks. I can show you where his books don't align, but I can't prove where the money is coming from," Henry admitted. "I suspect he runs his ranch like a mafia head, including getting rid of disloyal employees."

"How is them having guns helpful?" Lucy stood by Nell. "I think they're going to try to kill us all."

She would give it to her friend. Lucy was calm under pressure. She took Nell's wrist in hand and took her pulse, watching the timer on her cell.

"They won't have the guns when John is through." Nell also sounded almost preternaturally calm. "He'll have them, and normally I would ask him to be as earth friendly as he can when dealing with persons of this nature, but I'm about to push a baby through my vagina and I want him to be fast."

Henry's brows rose as if he was thoroughly surprised. "I can use the guns?"

Nell's expression turned fierce as Lucy let her wrist go and she faced her husband. Even Brooke could see the way her belly tightened. The woman was not merely in active labor. She was close. "Guns, knives, I don't care, John. Deal with this and get back to me because our daughter is on her way. I swear she heard that gunshot and took it as a sign she should come into this world right now."

Henry nodded.

Brooke could hear the men outside whooping it up. Like this was a party.

Who had they shot? Shane didn't carry around a gun. He was beyond competent when it came to rifles and shotguns, but he didn't walk around with one on his person at all times.

Was Shane dead? Had she spent all of their time together making him feel like he couldn't give her what she needed?

Why did it take a gunshot to get such perfect clarity?

All she needed was them. They would figure it out. Happiness wasn't ever based around one single choice, but a never-ending string of them that could be confused by circumstance and guilt and fear.

They would never ask her to choose them over her career. They would adapt to her because those men loved her in a way she'd hoped to be loved. Unconditionally. Wholly. Without fear on their part.

"I need to help Shane." Resolve began to flow through her. She wasn't some whiny baby who hid when her man was in trouble.

Henry put his hands on her shoulders. "I need you to protect Nell and our baby. I'll get Shane out. One way or another."

"I've heard the rumors, Henry, but I also know Bliss likes to make mountains out of molehills. I should come with you," she replied.

"Go check the barn," a deep voice commanded. "According to Billy there's a couple of people out there. Take 'em out. Don't you leave any witnesses. You know what's at stake. Find the other Kent kid. Ned says they have Shane. We can use him to get Bay to talk."

Shane was alive. She could breathe.

This was about Bay?

The boss wasn't finished. "I want to get out of here before McNamara and his boys get back, though you should know killing that asshole would have been fun."

"Should I leave the bodies, boss?" another voice asked.

Brooke could barely hear them, but every word made her nauseous.

Henry kept his voice low. "He told him to prep the bodies. I think they're planning on dumping all the bodies somewhere. This man has no idea where he is. He probably thinks Nate Wright is some small-town sheriff who'll investigate a little and then let it go."

Nate wouldn't. Nate would go to the ends of the earth to figure out who hurt his people, and he would have a lot of help.

Lucy was getting Nell to the corner of the barn. As far from the door as they could get. She dragged a couple of horse blankets down and set Nell up in one of the empty stalls.

How was this happening?

"What do we do?" Brooke asked. "We don't have any weapons."

"We will," Nell replied, her words calm even as she grunted through a contraction.

"Brooke, I need you to stand in the middle where he can see you when he walks in. I need to be able to come up behind him," Henry commanded. "I won't let anything happen to you."

How could he say that? He was a nice guy who sold homemade cider at Woo Woo Fest and protested with hand-done signs. The man was wearing Birkenstocks and socks. He was not…

She didn't have time for this. Nell and Lucy needed her. Shane needed her. She moved into position. "All right. But I'm going with you. You need backup."

Henry's brows rose but he didn't say anything because the barn door was opening. Henry moved into the shadows.

"Hello to the house. Or the barn, as it is." The cowboy standing there wore dark jeans and a black T-shirt. She could see the brand on his forearm.

She would bet that was the same brand Kingman used on his cattle.

The cowboy had a shotgun in his hand, but his eyes were on her. On her breasts, checking her out, likely to see if it would be worth it to risk having some fun with her. "Now see, they didn't tell me there would be a pretty lady in here. Where are your friends, sweetheart?"

Nell let out a low moan, and the guy took his eyes off her.

Brooke was about to make a run at him. She could fight and hopefully get the gun. She would sacrifice if she had to. The whole scene played out in her head, but then Henry stepped out of the shadows and one minute the guy was trying to figure out what was happening and then next there was a cracking sound and his ass fell to the floor.

Henry picked the gun up and stepped over the dead body.

Well, that had been way easier than it should have been.

"I can stay in the barn," Brooke said. No lies there. Henry was everything they said he was.

"My love, I'm sorry about the noise. Brooke, if you could scream, please," Henry apologized, and then the sound of a shotgun going off exploded through the air.

The goats brayed and ran in circles.

"Brooke," Henry prompted. "I need to make this sound real or he'll send someone else. One shot for each of us because I don't know how good their intel is."

Brooke screamed at the top of her lungs. It felt good, actually, because it was so fucking unfair. How dare they walk in here and expect…what? They were walking in and murdering people who'd done absolutely nothing to them, and she included Shane in that.

Another shot and another, and those poor baby goats were terrified. She screamed again because she was pissed about the goats. They were in their home. They should be safe.

Henry fired again, and Brooke could hear Nell's long groan.

This baby was coming faster than she could believe.

Henry came back and held the shotgun out to her. "Now they'll think he's prepping the bodies. They've been careful. They made sure the ranch was as empty as possible. I'm going to hope that means they think they've got time. I need you to watch over my wife. If anyone walks through that door, you shoot. Do you understand, Brooke?"

He was so cold, so unlike the Henry she knew, but he was also deeply competent and she trusted him. The Henry who always helped, who'd read her college history papers and edited them for her, was still in there. "I do. Please help Shane. I know they said they have him, but I can't help but wonder if he's been shot."

The barn door came open and Brooke held the shotgun up, but Henry quickly deflected it before she could fire.

Noah Bennett stumbled in, blood pouring from his left side. "Henry, you have to get Nell out."

Brooke rushed to help him. "Noah, what happened?"

Henry glanced out the barn door. "Brooke, I need a shot. Someone saw Noah and they're coming to check on him. We might be able to deflect."

Brooke quietly apologized to the goats and blasted a shot toward the back of the barn.

"Everything okay in there?" a deep voice asked.

"Is now," Henry replied, his voice equally deep. "Tell the boss I got it handled."

He did an excellent laconic Western accent.

Henry turned. "He's going back. Noah, what am I dealing with?"

Noah was pale, and he gritted his teeth as he moved. "I'm not sure, man. I walked into Trev's place to grab some towels for the ride. Birth is messy. And then this woman stepped out of the living room and shot me. I went down, and luckily she didn't look too closely. She assumed I would die. She's a terrible shot and doesn't know anatomy. I've got a while before I bleed out. How is Nell?"

"She's great if we want to have a baby in a barn in the middle of some kind of range war," Lucy replied. "And among a bunch of goats."

Brooke noticed a couple of the babies were huddled against Nell. Like they knew she would protect them even when she was at her most vulnerable. One of the little suckers rested his head on her belly. Nell simply petted the animal as though she got comfort from it, too.

"I pretended to be dead, and when I was alone, I made my way here," Noah continued as he allowed Brooke to help him to the back where Nell was currently fighting through a contraction. "I counted at least seven men, but I suspect the interviewees were sent in to tell Kingman when it was a good time to murder us all. So nine men and one woman, give or take."

"And they're in the big house?" Henry asked the question blandly, as though all his emotion and anxiety had been shoved deep.

"Yes. I heard some as I was lying there," Noah managed. "They have Shane. I think they want something from him."

"He saw something he shouldn't have," Brooke said but then why… "If that's true, then they would have killed him. Why all the drama? Why risk this? There's something more here than silencing a witness. That man said they could use him against Bay."

It made no sense that Kingman would put himself in this position when it would be so easy to arrange an accident for Shane. For Bay, too. Why risk becoming a *Dateline* special when he could keep this quiet?

"It doesn't matter," Henry said. "Not now. I'm going to get to the radio Trev keeps in the office. I'm fairly certain Kingman is the reason we don't have cell service, but I bet he hasn't taken the radio offline. Nell, I love you."

"I love you, too, Henry," she said as she held Lucy's hand and her whole body seized.

Henry disappeared like a wraith. Brooke took her eyes off him for one second and he was gone.

He left the dead body behind. It was dead, right? "Should I check and make sure he's dead?"

Nell groaned. "I assure you my husband doesn't make mistakes when it comes to this. He's dead. You should barricade the door."

"After she helps me," Noah replied. "I need to be closer. Lucy hasn't actually delivered a baby on her own yet."

He was covered in blood. Brooke moved in beside him and lent him her strength. She walked him into the stall where Nell was… open and on display.

Lucy knelt between her legs. "You're doing great, Nell. Noah, I think she's fully dilated. I'm not great with the centimeters' thing yet, but I can see the baby's head."

Noah nodded Brooke's way, and she helped him down to the ground, back to the wall. He sat behind Lucy so he could see a bit of what was going on. "How close are her contractions?"

Brooke ran to the door, shotgun in hand. She quickly found a pitchfork and slid it through the handles. The doors opened out. It wouldn't hold forever, but it would at least give them a fighting chance.

"Two minutes," Lucy said. She had her bag open and pulled out antibac. "I know I should wash my hands, but this is going to have to do."

"Brooke, there's a hose in the back. Could you fill a couple of pails?" Noah asked.

She went back to where he directed her and was so grateful that whoever was in charge of this place believed in organization and cleanliness. The metal pails used to feed and water the barn animals looked like they'd been cleaned and dried. She located soap and carried that back, too, along with the big roll of duct tape she found.

Nell wasn't the only one who needed medical help. She had to keep Noah alive until Doc could get here.

Huh, someone *had* been shot. Doc knew what he was doing.

If he'd heard anything she'd said, Doc was likely trying to figure out what was happening. The first thing he would do would be to call Nate Wright.

She prayed Bay was still at the sheriff's office.

"I need to put pressure on that wound," she explained.

Noah hissed as he shifted but allowed her to do what she needed to do.

After she'd duct taped Noah together, she sat down for a moment and held Nell's hand. "Just breathe, Nell. We'll get through this. Tell me what you're naming this baby girl we're about to be blessed with."

Lucy had Noah's kit out, the two of them deciding what she could and couldn't use.

"I was going to name her Justice Heart Flanders," Nell said, sweat dripping from her forehead. Her face was red but she was handling it all with such grace. She laughed before her whole body went tense. "Henry hates it. I think I might change it if we survive." She gritted her teeth and squeezed Brooke's hand tight. "Noah, how is this possible? It took so long with Poppy."

"All pregnancies are different," Noah said, his voice a bit strained. "Often the second comes on much quicker than the first. Like your body knows what to do. Or baby Justice there really wants to be here."

"Lucy," Nell whispered. "I'm naming her Lucy. Lucy Brooke Flanders. She's going to be my fierce warrior girl. I don't know how I know this, but I won't understand her all the time. She'll be like her father. I dream about her. Poppy is mine but this one is…"

Brooke held her as she suffered another long contraction. "I speak for both of us when I say I'll be honored and I'll always help her. Always."

"Me, too," Lucy said, getting into position.

Nell sank back, her words coming out in a breathless sigh. "My mother always said we came from another place. From a faery world. I know. A little on the odd side she was, but maybe she wasn't lying. She claimed I had a bit of what she called the sight. I never believed her until I started dreaming of my children. When I close my eyes at night, I see Lucy with a sword in her hand, and Poppy tends the gardens. My girls. In my dreams we live by a shining river like the one we do now, but we're in a brilliant white palace with my kin from there. My girls are princesses of the realm. They have more power than anyone knows." She touched her belly, stroking it. "She likes this name better. I can feel it. She's Lucy Brooke, and she's ready to be here. She won't be a princess in this world, but she will move mountains."

Lucy took a long breath and Brooke watched her calm herself, settling herself to take on the herculean task in front of her with grace and competence. "She is definitely ready. She's crowning. All right. Brooke, make sure no one gets in. Let's have a baby."

Brooke gave Nell's hand one last squeeze. "I won't let anyone get in."

Nell clenched her teeth as another contraction hit.

"All right, let's do this," Noah said. "Lucy, I'll walk you through it. Nell, it's going to be okay."

Brooke moved into position, staring at the barn door.

She was ready to defend her people.

She prayed Henry saved Shane and that Bay stayed far away.

Chapter Sixteen

Bay sat next to Max as his old but beautifully kept Ford rolled toward the ranch.

"See, I should have punched Nate or something." Max's head shook as they approached the drive that would take them to the big house. "I could be having jailhouse sex right now."

Nate had told Gemma that it was time to take a break the minute Rachel showed up and started yelling at her husband. Apparently she'd been having a lovely day when she'd been told her husband was in jail.

"Uh, she seemed real upset," Bay pointed out. Rather like Brooke, who was having none of him when it came to jailhouse sex. That could be fun. He and Shane could pretend like they were prisoners and she was the prize in some kind of wicked game. He could come up with some fun scenarios.

If she ever forgave him.

He was going to lose her because he hadn't proven himself. She was still wary, still worried he wouldn't do what it took to make her happy.

"See, that's where you don't understand women. Rach was pissed off, but we made a deal a long time ago. When I do something to upset her, I owe her sexual servitude. Usually that's my place because it's hard to be the charming, funny one all the time. Some of my adventures don't go the way I want them to, and I end up hanging out with Nate. Rye doesn't usually get into the same kind of trouble, but I have to give him this one. Those two need to reconnect. I'm actually happy she walked in yelling. It means she's coming back to us. My baby has some anger issues. I can handle those. What I can't handle is her being sad all the time. Especially when we're the cause. We've been parents and not spouses, and being her husband is my favorite thing on earth to be. We have to remind her of that."

He didn't hate the sound of Max's reasoning. "So you're saying if I want to get Brooke back, I should make her happy in bed?"

Max winced. "No. I am not saying that. Not saying that at all." His hands tightened on the wheel, and he let out a long sigh. "But I'm also not not saying that, damn it. Where is your daddy?"

"Well, he's dead, but if you're asking why I'm not talking to him about this instead of you, it wouldn't matter if he was still alive. I wouldn't be talking to him. My dad was pretty pathetic. I always talk to Shane."

"Son, that is the dumb leading the even dumber," Max quipped. "Well, I guess the only thing to do is take you both in hand and under my tender care."

"What is that supposed to mean?"

"It means I think my sister is in love with you, and while I wish like hell I could blame you for all of this, we might be looking at a problem of my own making. Or rather my other half's. Hell, I'm involved too because I never wanted Brooke to leave at all. I would have been perfectly happy with her coming home and staying in that house we built and being auntie to all our kids. It's hard when you have to deal with the fact that the people you love, the ones you watched grow, turn into actual adults who need to make their own way in the world. We handled it poorly with Brooke. We made her think she owed us something. We didn't try to but that's what happened."

"She loves you."

"Which is why she's hurting. We haven't been communicating well. See, this is the funny thing about a great love story. Which is what I have with Rach. She and Rye have a regular old love story, but the outcome is the same."

He wasn't going to debate with Max about whether Rye had the better love story. It was ridiculous because they both loved her. It was all their story. But he was curious. "What outcome?"

"See, when you get married you think it's all settled, but here's the hard part. You still grow, and you have to make the choice to do that together. You have to watch the woman you love more than life itself become a mother and give herself to those babies you made together. You have to watch them become their own people and know that one day they're going to leave and you won't be able to protect them anymore. They want their own stories, and your story never stopped. If you aren't careful, you'll forget that love is an active choice you make. And you start using the kind of words I just did."

Bay felt a deep well of emotion open inside him, and his childhood spilled out. His parents hadn't loved each other. They'd gotten married because it was time and they were dating. There had been no grand love story for them. He'd grown up in a house where they didn't even like each other. They stayed together because someone told them they had to in order to be good human beings. They hadn't chosen each other. They hadn't chosen themselves. They had chosen misery.

He knew the words Max was talking about. "You don't have to. You get to. You said that was the bad part, but it's the good part. You get to watch the woman you love become more. You get to hold her hand. You get to have a partner to watch your kids grow, and no matter what happens you stand beside her. Those kids are there because of you and her and the love you have. It isn't an obligation. It isn't a sacrifice. It's the whole reason we're alive."

"You're going to be all right, Bay," Max said quietly. "And so are we. We're going to be family. I know you've been the big brother all your life…"

Bay chuckled even as his heart felt so damn full. "Was I? I don't know about that, but I understand what you're saying. Be careful. I think you might find me and Shane would welcome a couple of older brothers to advise us. Max, I love her. Shane loves her. She needs to roam for a while. She needs to figure out what to do with all her talent. It's not designing jeans for some snobby fashion house."

"You take care of her and you bring her home from time to time." Max was the one who sounded emotional now.

"She'll always come home, and someday she'll want to put down roots," Bay said. "My vote will be for here, but she's got to have her work."

Max's head shook. "Damn cowboys. Knew you would be trouble the minute I saw you."

"We were being paid to annoy you," Bay admitted. "I would probably take that back if I could. Especially if I'd seen Brooke first."

"Little asshole," Max said under his breath and then he started to turn and stopped in front of the gates. Which should be open. "What's going on? The G's gates are always open during the day."

They were open most of the time since the owners never discouraged visitors. He'd heard Jamie and Trev joke about never spending money on the gate since they didn't use it.

It was the first time he'd seen it shut.

Max pulled up to the reception box. "What's the code?"

He didn't know there was a code. "No idea, man."

Something was wrong. Trev wasn't here. He'd called and asked Max to bring Bay back because he and Bo were going to help Beth. He wouldn't have locked the place up because Jamie was taking Hope into Alamosa. None of this made sense, and every instinct he had was flaring up.

Max started to reach for the button on the call box.

It would alert the house that someone was trying to get in.

"Stop." Bay's heart rate ticked up as adrenaline started pumping. "Let's call Trev."

Max put the truck in park. "You worried? Didn't you think your brother was overreacting?"

"I might have to eat those words." He glanced at his cell. "Why don't I have any bars?"

Max looked at his phone, too. "Yeah, I got nothing. Let's head back. This feels like a Nate problem. We can find service and tell Brooke and Shane to stay where they are."

Bay's gut took a deep dive. "He texted me over an hour ago. He was bringing her back to the ranch."

"My sister's in there?" Max asked.

Bay's whole fucking life was locked behind those gates. Shane and Brooke were in there, and he had no idea what was going on.

"Open the glove box. I keep binoculars in there. Paige is crazy about bird watching right now." Max opened the driver's side door. "What kind of cameras do Trev and Jamie have on this place?"

Bay found the binoculars and handed them over, getting out of his side. "There's one here, but it's not on. It would have a light, and it would move." He'd read enough thrillers to ponder what had happened. "I suspect when they took out the cell signal it locked the camera. If someone's here, they damn straight wouldn't want to get caught on tape."

"So if someone's in there, they won't know we're here," Max mused, looking through the binoculars.

Bay needed to be clear. "Not someone. Kale Kingman, or at least his crew, and I'm betting I was entirely wrong and my brother was right. They're deadly, Max. If the rumors are true, it wouldn't be the first time they got rid of someone inconvenient."

A single image passed over his brain. A young woman walking out of the main house, a bag in her hand and a look of desolation on her face.

He'd drawn her because the emotion on her face had called to him. It had been one of those moments when he'd known he had to draw. The vision seared into his brain and late that night, he'd taken his sketchpad and drawn the scene. Now he remembered Kale Kingman had been in the background. He'd been holding something. A tool of some kind. Maybe a hammer, which was weird because it wasn't like the man did his own work.

He'd still been holding it when he'd gotten into the truck and driven her off. To go back home, he'd told everyone.

Except she'd told Bay she didn't have a home.

Was she alive?

It was insane, but was this about him? Was this about the drawing he'd made? It wasn't a photograph. It wasn't evidence of anything.

But it might make people think, might lead some to ask questions.

"I think this is about a drawing I did," Bay said quietly.

Max hopped on the hood of his truck. Well, hopped was a strong word to use for the awkward maneuver, but then the guy was getting up there in years. "I thought Shane was the one who saw something."

"But if it was Shane, they would simply kill him. They wouldn't need to do all this. It's easy enough to send someone in and then eventually the guy they sent in is alone with Shane and oops, accidents happen on ranches. Shit. That's why they stole the damn safe."

It was all falling into place, and he was on the edge of panic. He wanted to get back in the truck and plow through. That gate wouldn't hold if they hit it hard enough. He needed to get to them. He would give Kingman everything if it meant Brooke was safe. If it meant his brother survived.

"What the hell do they want with a drawing?" Max asked, somehow staying calm. "Can you give it to them?"

"If it's the one I think it is, then it's in my sketchpad in the foreman's house. I usually take it with me, but we weren't supposed to be long," Bay admitted. "I left it on the bar in the kitchen. I think a couple of Brooke's books are on top of it. I thought about that because I like it when Brooke's on top, so I liked her books being on top of mine."

"Too much information," Max gritted out. "Why would they care about your drawings? I mean I can see Stef trying to steal them since he's certain you're some sort of brilliant artist person, but Kingman doesn't give a crap about art."

There, Max would be wrong. Kingman actually had some lovely examples of contemporary Southwestern art, including a couple of pieces that should have been in Native American museums. But that was all about showing off. Kingman's art gallery was like his mansion. Meant to intimidate and bring glory to Kale Kingman.

"There was this woman. She'd been on the ranch for a couple of years," Bay said, his anxiety growing. "Kingman didn't have many women on the team, but she seemed close to him. And then one day she was leaving. I was working near the house that day and I saw her getting ready to leave. There was something about the whole scene, some deep emotion I didn't understand but I had to catch. I know that sounds weird…"

"Stef Talbot has been my brother for my whole life. You think I don't get the weirdo art stuff? Trust me. I've had to sit while Stef tried to capture some shit I didn't understand. It's a damn tree. There are thousands of them around here, but Stef's got to paint that one. All right, but how did Kingman even know you had it?"

Oh, he remembered now. "It was right before Thanksgiving, and one of the guys was being an asshole. He got hold of my sketchpad and started looking through it. When I walked in they were all making fun of me for my drawings of Brooke. Saying I was a pervert but hey, could I introduce them to that girl?"

"They were talking about my sister? Bay, I don't care what anyone tells you, it's your job to kick the ass of any man who looks her way."

He wasn't sure he'd be able to handle any man since she was gorgeous and every man with eyes would look at her, but he would take care of the ones who touched her. "Anyway, they were all joking about me sitting around drawing women I could never have, but one of them pointed to the picture of Meli Smith. I didn't think anything of it at the time, but now I wonder."

"You wonder?" Max put the binoculars to his face. This part of the G was in the valley surrounded by mountains, but the land where they had the houses and the barns was fairly flat. Max should have a decent view if the binoculars were powerful enough. Even from Bay's place he could see the houses and the barn, at the least the roofs. Max was higher. "What does Kingman drive?"

"A black Escalade when he's showing off, but he's got several cars. A couple of Jeeps. A tricked-out F-150 when he's working," Bay replied. "But it's been a couple of months. He trades them in pretty fast."

"There are three vehicles I don't recognize. Two trucks, and there is that Escalade," Max confirmed. "It looks like they're mostly in Trev's house. He's going to lose his shit on those boys when he gets back here. Bay, they're all armed."

Bay's gut clenched. "Can you see Brooke? Shane?"

"No," Max informed him. "I've got two men on the porch. They look like they're guards. Probably the lookouts. One just walked out. He's heading for the barn."

"Henry and Nell are in that barn, along with Noah and Lucy."

What the hell was about to happen? Where was Brooke? Did they already have her? Had Shane already tried to defend her? Nell was pregnant. She couldn't get killed for his mistake. He would never fucking survive being the reason the town mourned. He could jump that fence. "I'm going in."

"Don't. Not if Henry's there."

Yes, Henry Flanders, the dude who ate tofu and claimed to be some kind of badass. Except he didn't actually make the claim. It was a town legend. "I need to go make sure he doesn't get hurt."

Max snorted. "Yeah, you need to help Henry. Get up here. I assure you Henry already knows what's happening. Maybe not the whys, but he knows they're here. I hope like hell Brooke and Shane went out to that barn to say hello and they're with him now."

Bay climbed onto the truck and took the binoculars from Max.

He heard the sound of a gunshot. At least he thought it was. It came from the barn, maybe. It was muffled from the distance. The man who'd been stalking to the building stopped and he said something. It was only a second later before he turned and walked back toward the house.

A shot. He'd walked away because he was confident whoever was in the barn was dead. "I think someone was in there and they finished off the people in the barn. I think I'm going to be…"

"Yeah, wait for it," Max advised.

He was getting ready to jump that gate and run like a madman when he saw the barn door open slightly and a familiar figure slip out.

Henry Flanders moved with the grace of a true predator.

"There he is," Max said with what seemed like a sigh of relief. "We need to get in. He might need help. There are a lot of them. The least we can do is lock down the barn, though I assure you Henry's left strict instructions to shoot anyone who tries to get in, so we'll have to be careful."

It was like he was watching a nature documentary. Henry was the lion stalking the gazelle who should have been way more careful. Bay felt his breath hitch as Henry easily moved in behind the man before he could reach the part of the yard where the guards would see him. One swift move and the man's body crumpled to the ground.

"You see, Henry likes to do this thing where he internally decapitates a son of a bitch. It's quiet and neat and why I no longer have any desire to see a chiropractor." Max jumped down with far more grace than he'd gotten on. "I was going to try to send you back to get Nate, but I think Henry's got this. We should go and check on the people in the barn. Figure out exactly where everyone is."

Max had an enormous amount of faith in Henry.

Max reached inside his truck and came back with a shotgun.

In the distance, Henry already had the dead man's pistol and was moving around the house, away from the porch. He moved toward the back where there were windows and a way to get into the basement. From there he could carefully move through the rest of the building.

He looked like he knew what he was doing.

Bay needed to see them, needed to know they were still alive.

"I'm going to turn myself in," Bay announced. "Me walking into that house will distract everyone from where you're going. And if my brother's alive, it might buy me some time."

"If you're right about what they want," Max handed him a small pistol. "Put it in your boot. They're less likely to find it there. I'll check on the people in the barn and see if I can get them out. You stay safe and trust Henry. He knows what he's doing. If I can get them back here and Brooke is with me…"

"Get her into town and bring the sheriff," Bay replied, carefully putting the pistol in his boot. His heart was in his throat, but a sort of calm came over him. This was the thing to do. He had to give his brother and Brooke every chance to live.

And if it came down to one of them or Brooke, he knew what they would both do. She was their love, the woman who completed them in a way they wouldn't be had they never met her. They might have found some form of happiness, but they wouldn't have been whole. They would lay down their lives to ensure her safety.

Max brought out a big set of wire cutters. He had it in his tool kit in the back of his truck since Harper Stables also had to deal with fencing. He walked to the side. "I'm not going to risk alerting them by busting through the gate. We'll have better luck sneaking up like this."

He would have to fix that fence later, but he followed Max, ready to save his family.

* * * *

Shane was fairly certain he was going to die. And he wasn't even sure why.

It was clear now that this had little to do with him since Kale Kingman was pissed as hell that he wasn't Bay.

"Well, they look a lot alike," Ned said, watching the boss with a wary frown. "How was I supposed to know?"

The girl he'd met at The Trading Post a few weeks ago rolled her eyes. "Well, you were supposed to let me be the one to call the boss. Also, I think I heard McNamara call him Shane, so that should have been a sign that he wasn't the asshole we were looking for."

Billy sighed. "Okay, I'm going to admit I might not have heard that. I was busy dealing with the fact that we had an almost empty place. I didn't think we would get a better shot since the boss was waiting." He turned to face Kale Kingman. "You go back to Wyoming tomorrow. I thought you would want to be in on this."

The young woman sneered Billy's way. "You just didn't want to get stuck here working for those perverted assholes. They're all over this town. Threesomes. It's disgusting. These people are having kids and exposing them to all their filthy habits."

"Says the woman who's sleeping with the married man," one of the others said under his breath.

She simply shrugged. "I'm only sleeping with one man. The women around here are disgusting."

"I don't care what anyone thinks. I want to deal with the situation, and the sooner the better. I know the original plan was to find that safe, but it wasn't in there, and I don't know that I have months for Ned and Billy to spend looking for it when McNamara and Glen aren't watching them. Her parents are causing a ruckus," Kingman admitted. "If Bay talks about what he saw or if someone else gets an eye on that piece of art he made, there are going to be questions. I've got a documentary filmmaker doing research and making inquiries. Dirty whore lied about not having anyone. And I did want to be here to ensure this is over, but it's not because this isn't Bailey Kent."

"Don't you think his brother knows where that drawing is?" He recognized his old foreman's voice, though Dennis hadn't stepped into the room.

Shane had three guns on him, so he didn't turn to make sure he was right. It didn't matter.

"Yeah, the way I remember it those two couldn't take a shit without each other." That was Andy.

They absolutely could and did one hundred percent of the time. "I don't know where my brother is."

"You should keep your mouth shut unless you want to tell me what I want to hear," Kingman snarled.

"I don't know what you want to hear." His gut was twisted as he sat at the kitchen table.

Where was Brooke? He had to pray Henry heard the first gunshot and either locked down the barn or had gotten them all out. Had there been enough time?

Noah. He'd figured out that the first shot had been to stop Noah from leaving.

Noah was dead. His whole soul ached for Jamie and Hope. How would they go on?

Kingman got to one knee in front of him, his eyes narrow slits. "I want to know where your brother keeps his frilly drawings. Son of a bitch apparently drew a shitty picture of the last time anyone saw Meli Smith."

Andy shook his head. "It was a pretty good picture, Boss. That's what I was telling you. He even got you in the background holding the hammer you used."

Why were they talking about a drawing? "I thought this was about the guns I saw."

Kingman slapped Andy upside the back of his head before returning his attention to Shane. "What guns? What are you talking about?"

Dennis stepped back as though he knew he would be the next to get a slap from the boss. "Uhm, it was the shipment the MC ordered. The P90s. I needed help storing them, and Shane was around. In my defense, we had talked about bringing them in."

"I told you I would bring this dipshit in but not Bay, and I then explained he would never leave his brother behind," Kingman argued. He sighed. "It's why I was planning on letting them go before they saw too much, but you needed help. It doesn't matter. The fact is we killed a bunch of people in that barn, and we're not going to get another shot. I need that drawing. She told me her parents kicked her out, but damn they're determined to find the whore."

"What do you mean you killed them?" Shane's whole body had gone cold. Brooke had been in the barn.

Kingman snorted. "Killed as in shot and dead, and now we gotta haul them all the way back home because I've got a place no one will ever find. My own killing ground, which is where you should be right now, but you somehow figured out we were on to you. Mostly I like to do the killing right there, but we'll transport the bodies and the cops won't have any clue."

"I assure you they will, and if you killed everyone in that barn, I won't help you. I won't save you. If you killed everyone in that barn, I'm already dead and nothing you do to me will make me talk." Shane felt something hollow open in his gut. Brooke. She couldn't be dead. He couldn't have brought this to her.

In the distance, he heard another crack of gunfire.

Was that her? Had she managed to hide and now she'd been found and everything that was glorious and amazing about her was gone?

Kingman got in his face, taking his jaw in one hand and forcing him to look up. "We'll see about that. Let's see how much pain you can take, you little shit. You and your brother think you can take me down."

"We weren't thinking about you at all until you pulled this stunt, you dickhead." Shane wasn't afraid of pain. He'd had enough of it to know it was simply one more thing to get through. But what this fucker had taken from him was more than pain. It was his whole heart ripped out and shredded on the ground in front of him. His soul would go with hers.

Kingman slapped him. Like bitch slapped him hard, making his head turn, but Shane didn't make a sound.

If Brooke was dead, he wanted to go with her, but he was going to take Kingman with him.

Kingman stood, and Shane felt his whole body tense.

"This is a clusterfuck," Kingman announced. "Someone go and see if Jones needs help. I'm serious about getting those bodies out of here. I don't know who was in that barn, but I don't want to leave evidence behind."

One of the men started outside. There had been nine in here at one point, including the three who had come out for the interviews, but Shane had figured out Kingman had sent one to murder everyone in the barn.

The barn where Noah had been teaching Henry and Nell.

Where Brooke and Lucy had been with Henry and Nell.

Nell, who was a do-gooder pacifist pregnant with her second child.

Henry… Henry, who had once been a killer trained and paid for by the Central Intelligence Agency. Bay didn't believe the hype about Henry. He thought it was all Bliss antics. Brooke, too. They'd talked about it one night while they laid in bed and Brooke told stories about the Bliss of her childhood. She thought he'd likely been an analyst or some sort of consultant. But that's not what Shane heard.

Henry was a ruthless protector, trained in a way very few people ever were.

Henry might be smart enough to figure out what was happening and turn it back on his attacker.

Shane felt a surge of hope as Kingman railed on about how they might as well burn the place to the ground and then they wouldn't have to worry about Bay's drawings. Someone mentioned he might have it on him and they were debating that when Shane saw the hint of movement outside the window. It was nothing more than a flash of brown hair as someone moved past the kitchen, obviously toward the basement walkout. He could access the house from there.

Henry fucking Flanders.

If Henry was alive, there was a shot that Brooke was, too, and that she needed him.

"I know where it is," Shane said quietly. "You could burn down both houses and the barn and the dorm and not find it."

Kingman stopped yelling and turned his way. "All right, where is it?"

He had to buy Henry time. If it was Henry. No. It was Henry. It had to be Henry, and he would get them out of this situation.

If Brooke was alive, he had to buy her time, and he had to believe that at least someone else in that barn was alive or Henry would go about this entirely differently. He wouldn't sneak in while his wife and child were lying cold on the ground. He would torch the place and not care. So if he was being careful…there was a chance.

Shane had learned a bit about acting in his weeks helping Brooke at the theater. You sold a scene with more than words. He let his jaw go tight and hoped he looked like he was thinking things through. "I think I saw him working on it this morning. We're out in the foreman's house. We haven't been in the dorms for days, which is why it wasn't in the safe."

Kingman nodded, and two of his guys took off.

"And tell Jones to get his ass back here when he's done bagging those bodies," Kingman called out.

Shane needed to thin the herd. Maybe send some guys for Henry to handle. He wondered if Jones had already been dealt with.

Shane cursed under his breath.

"What?" The girl who'd come along was the same one who'd questioned him at The Trading Post the night after they'd made things official with Brooke. If he'd caught sight of her, he would have known something was wrong, but now she stood by Kingman. She was at least forty years the man's junior, but she slid an arm possessively through his. "I think he remembered something."

Denial might help him. "Nah, it's fine. I'm sure it's in the foreman's house." He gave her a once-over. "You know he'll toss you into that ravine when he's done with you, too, right?"

Her eyes rolled. "He ain't going to be done with me. I'm the one who gives him what he needs. Ain't that right, Kale?"

"Shut up." Kingman stepped away from her. "Where else could it be? I'm not joking, Shane. I want that sketchbook. I can kill you slow or we can do this easy."

But they wouldn't kill him until they had what they needed. Nope. They needed him alive, and he could send them off on wild-goose chases because Bay took that sketchbook with him almost everywhere.

Shane let his expression go stubborn. He wasn't worried about getting hurt. He could handle it, but he needed to keep them thinking he wasn't a problem. They hadn't even tied him up. They thought the threat of guns would keep him in line.

Kingman slapped him again.

Shane spat blood and decided it was time to give him another little something. "Fine. We were here last night for dinner, but Bay wanted to work in quiet. He might have left it in the basement. But probably not. I can't remember. He leaves the damn thing lying around. He's always losing it."

He didn't. He kept that fucker close most of the time.

"Ned, go check," Kingman ordered.

He hoped he was helping Henry and not hurting him, but it seemed safer for Henry to deal with them on a one-by-one basis.

He knew if he could get the numbers down in here, he might be able to make a move. He wasn't ex-military like some of these guys, but he'd had plenty of self-defense training. Enough to know that sometimes surprise beat out training. And that there was no such thing as a fair fight. If he had the chance, he would stab these fuckers in the back and never think twice about it.

But he was still at five in the kitchen. He wouldn't discount the young woman since it appeared she was the one who shot Noah. Killed Noah. If Henry had done what he thought he'd done, then two were already dead. Kingman sent three more out, two to the foreman's house and one to the basement.

There was the sound of banging coming from the west end of the house.

Kingman frowned. "Go check on Ned, Billy. If that asshole fell down the stairs, I'll kill him myself."

Billy hesitated but went anyway.

Four. It was Kingman and the woman and Dennis and Andy.

He just needed to wait for the right moment.

Well, he also needed a weapon of some kind, but he could try.

Brooke. He had to think about Brooke and seeing her again.

"I don't like this. Something feels wrong." Kingman proved he had some instincts.

"Nothing's wrong. I told you. I checked and James Glen is with his wife and they're all the way in Alamosa," the woman explained. "And from what I overheard on the phone, McNamara's girl got hurt on the playground and he and the other one took off running. You've got hours."

Kingman's eyes narrowed on her. "And the hands who are out in the field? What do I do when they show up? You know they don't work twenty-four seven. They do come in every now and then."

She sighed and shrugged. "Kill them."

They started arguing about how every extra body was another problem, but Shane didn't care. He was fairly close to the butcher block of knives Beth kept, though he probably shouldn't say they were Beth's. Both Bo and Trev cooked meals for their family. They spread out the work so it wasn't piled on Beth.

Like he and Bay wanted to do with Brooke. They'd learned from their parents. The workload was a thing to manage, not to dump on the human with female genitalia. He and Bay had talked about setting up a schedule. Laundry and cleaning and cooking. They would all participate.

He prayed he still had a chance.

Or that Bay and Brooke could carry on without him. Bay would find his way. He leaned on Shane as much as Shane leaned on him, but his brother was strong. He would honor Shane by taking care of the woman they loved.

"That girl is going to get us all killed." Dennis stared at Shane. "You're fucking with us. It won't work. The boss can't leave it. I wish we could because the truth of the matter is I liked you, Shane. I wanted to bring you and Bay in, though I agree with the boss that Bay is the lesser of the two of you when it comes to being solid enough to be one of us."

Awesome. So he was the better brother when it came to potentially being a criminal. Bay had his savant-like art skills and Shane had…blind obedience? Well, turned out he wasn't good at that either. "I would never have joined. I wanted out a week after we hired on. I knew something was wrong."

Now that was a better way to look at it. He had way better

instincts than his brother. He had known something was wrong with the Kingman Ranch. The same way he'd taken one look at that magnificent woman and known she would complete their family.

Dennis sighed as Kingman and his mistress yelled at each other. "Well, I thought you handled seeing the guns pretty well. You didn't run until a few weeks later. What made you do it?"

He could be honest. He was close to the knives. He couldn't make a move yet, but it was coming. "I heard you and Andy talk about getting rid of us. I knew enough by then to think it wasn't going to be a firing."

Dennis chuckled. "I wondered if someone was in the barn with us that night. I thought that might have been the reason you took off but I didn't say anything because the boss sometimes loses perspective, as Dinah is about to find out."

Kingman slapped the shit out of her. "Shut the fuck up. You need to learn your place. Get outside and wait in the truck."

Dinah held her hand to her cheek. "But I did good, King. I killed that asshole when he was going to leave. I killed him right in the living room."

Dennis frowned. "Where did you move the body?"

The room seemed to stop. Dinah shook her head. "What do you mean? I didn't move no body. That's man's work. I shot him. That was my job."

"That was not your fucking job, Dinah," Kingman said between clenched teeth. "Your job was to ID where they would keep the sketchbook. You failed at your job or we wouldn't be here."

"How was I supposed to know they moved?" Dinah returned.

"Well, my dear, you were supposed to get into his bed and find it for me." Kingman's face was a mottled red.

Dinah sniffled, the first crack in her bitch-of-the-world armor. "He didn't want me. I don't even think it registered that I was flirting with him."

Dennis stood. "Look, I don't care about y'all's relationship drama, but we have a problem if she says she killed a man who got up and walked away. Have you thought about that?"

Noah wasn't dead? If Noah wasn't dead, then they had more hope. Noah would try to find a way to call in Nate.

"He's dead. I killed him," Dinah shouted.

"I walked through there, and while there was a lot of blood, there wasn't a body on the floor," Dennis replied.

Kingman's eyes closed. "Fuck. We need to burn the whole place down. Dennis, go tell Jones to forget the barn and get the gasoline ready. We torch the place and pray for the fucking best, and while we're at it, I should solve another of my problems."

He turned to Dinah and calmly raised his pistol and shot.

Shane's whole body went stiff. He certainly hadn't liked the woman, but no one deserved to go like that. And it all fell into place. "Meli was your mistress."

Kingman's expression was bland. As though murdering his lover was simply another task. "Bitch said she was on birth control but then she showed up pregnant. Wanted a piece of my fortune. That night I told her we were going to my lawyer's. I couldn't let her stay around or my wife would find out."

"Now see, she actually could take a big old piece of his fortune," Dennis explained. "No prenup."

"Why the fuck would I have a prenup? We got married in high school. We had nothing to protect," Kingman argued. "And I love her. But she's old and doesn't get my dick hard anymore. Trust me. My wife would have pulled that trigger, too. Now let's get moving. First thing to do is take care of that asshole."

And he was out of time. Shane moved as Kingman raised his gun again. They should have tied him up. He kicked the table over to give himself some cover and reached for the knives as the first shot blasted.

Cover. He had some. All he had to do was get to the next room. Trev's office had heavy oak doors.

"Like that's going to keep you safe," Kingman said and picked up the table and tossed it to the side.

Fuck. He was going to die. He was going to die right here and now. He stood and started to rush at Kingman when he heard a loud blast.

Time seemed to slow, and Shane realized getting shot didn't feel as bad as it should. He reached for his gut, trying to stop the overflow of blood that would come.

Except it didn't.

Kingman's eyes had gone wide, and that was when Shane realized he wasn't alone.

Bay stood behind Kingman, and he had a gun.

Shane's heart thudded as Kingman clutched the hole in his chest and dropped to the floor beside his mistress.

Bay's skin was a pasty white but his voice was steady. "You okay?"

"Where did Dennis go? He has a gun, too." Shane had never been so fucking happy to see his brother. And there were plenty of times when Bay walking in a room had saved him from something terrible in their childhood.

"The older gentleman?" Henry Flanders walked in the room, and he was covered in blood. "He's dead. I caught him a few seconds ago. I got the others before that." He seemed to realize they were all staring at him in horror. "Oh, this? Not mine. The one in the basement found a knife. I got it away from him. Then I used it on him and his friend, and then the older guy. I took out the guards the old-fashioned way. It's been too long, and even though my wife told me I could use the guns, I find them loud and impersonal. The knife was better."

He was scared of Henry freaking Flanders, who looked very Dexteresque in that moment. "Brooke?"

Bay stepped over Kingman's body and took a place by Shane, helping him move around the wrecked table. "Is she okay?"

Henry's manner was detached and cold. He wiped the big knife on his already coated jeans. "She's protecting the barn for me. We need to get the radio working. Nell needs an ambulance. Are there any other men I should take care of? I handled the one in the basement and the one who came to check on him."

Just then the door opened and Shane heard a voice call out. "Hey, boss. Everything okay in here? We didn't find…"

The knife hit the man in the center of the neck with a deep, thudding sound as it sank in. Instinctively the man pulled it out and blood gushed forth.

He was dead before he hit the ground. Henry calmly picked up the knife.

Bay's head shook. "Uh, I think I saw two of them walking out to the foreman's house. This one and a tall, dark-haired guy. It might have been Mike."

Shane nodded. "It was Mike. They were looking for Bay's sketchbook. We need to get to Brooke."

He heard the sound of a gunshot and couldn't handle it a second longer. He took off running.

Chapter Seventeen

Brooke stared at the door even as Nell somehow managed to keep it all together, despite the fact that she had just expelled a baby out of her body.

"She's here," Lucy said reverently, and Brooke heard Nell gasp and sigh as she fell back. The labor had been rushed and furious, as though the child knew something was happening and she didn't want to miss a minute of it.

"Brooke, I hear someone," Noah said, his voice still steady. He'd been a rock all through the last terrifying moments. "They're coming in the back."

"Hey, sister, don't shoot," a familiar voice said.

Max. Her brother was here, and he was coming in through the back door. She hadn't even realized there was a back door, but then Max had spent a lot of time out here with Jamie and Noah growing up. By the time she was a kid, they were all working so she hadn't had the same experience. She breathed a deep sigh of relief and ran to him.

Max wrapped his arms around her. "You okay?"

She sniffled and hugged her brother, still holding the shotgun Henry had given her. "Shane is in the house and I don't know where Bay is, and Nell had her baby."

more myself when I come back. Should I bring you anything?"

Oh, she wasn't the only one feeling the press of the day. It wasn't that Henry didn't care. He didn't trust himself, didn't want his wife to see him covered in blood. Nell was a pacifist.

But she was also his wife, and he'd saved them all.

"John Bishop," Nell called out. "I said it wrong. I'm sorry. John Bishop, you get over here right now and you meet your daughter."

He stopped and if she hadn't been looking so closely, she wouldn't have seen the slight tremble in his shoulders. "I need a minute, love. I can be Henry again."

"I never said it." Nell held her baby to her chest and forced herself to sit up. Her hair clung to her shoulders and cheeks, drenched in sweat, but she was clear in what she wanted. "I never said the words to you. I love you, John. I love you when you're Henry and when you're John and any other name you want to call yourself. You are my soul's mate. All of you, not just the parts I find comfortable. I love you and this is your child. You come and meet your child, John."

Henry turned, and those cold eyes were suddenly glassy with unshed tears. "I'm covered in…"

"I don't care," Nell replied in a firm tone. "I do not care. I want my husband. I want John Bishop and Henry Flanders, and throw in the former Mr. Black if you want to, but get over here and hold your baby. You didn't get to hold Poppy for long. I expect you to do your part with this baby."

That got Henry moving. John. He was both. He was his past and his present and his future, and in each he would love Nell. The dark side of Henry loved her as much as the jovial, kind man they all knew. Henry's beast was Nell's mate, too, but he rarely got to do the tender parts of love. She was sure John Bishop showed up for all the violence and likely some of the sex, but it was obvious this was new to him.

Brooke cried as she watched John take the baby into his hands. She watched as his jaw clenched but his eyes went soft.

"She's beautiful, baby. Little Justice," he whispered. "I know I said I thought we should try some other names, but it suits her."

"I changed my mind. She's Lucy Brooke Flanders, after the woman who helped bring her into the world and the one who protected us while we did it," Nell announced.

"Uhm, am I chopped liver?" Noah asked with a grin and then he winced because he'd obviously moved too much.

Henry ignored him. "Lucy Brooke. I like it. It suits her. Hey, baby girl. I'm your dad. I'm going to be with you for everything. I won't ever let you down. I might not be perfect, but I'll try for you."

She felt Bay's arm go around her waist, pulling her back against him. Shane moved in so he was touching her, too.

She heard the sound of sirens and knew she was safe.

* * * *

Bay stared at the copy of the drawing that had gotten them into so much trouble. He'd handed the original over to Nate.

"So her name was Meli?" Brooke set a beer in front of him. They were back in the foreman's house after hours and hours of talking to Nate and Elisa. They'd called in the Creede PD to help with processing the scene since there were so many bodies.

He couldn't forget the way Caleb had walked straight up to Henry and thanked him for what he called all the atlanto-occipital dislocations. Henry had stood there with his newborn and told Caleb not to thank him until he saw what he did in the basement.

Then there had been lectures on blood and autopsies, and Brooke had been praised for her duct-taping skills and Zane had shown up with sandwiches and they'd all cleaned up the G so Miranda and her brothers wouldn't come home to a killing zone that would traumatize them for life.

"What did your brother say?" Bay looked up at Brooke. There had been that perfect moment when she'd told them she loved them, but there was something of a distance between them now. Because they hadn't finished the vows they'd made in the barn. The real world had forced them apart for a while, but he wouldn't let it much longer. He glanced over at Shane, who gave him a nod.

Which meant he'd been downstairs and everything was in place.

They had plans for their woman, their future wife.

She stopped, and a soft smile hit her face. Rye and Rachel had shown up with Nate, holding hands and breathing sighs of relief when they found Brooke. Rye and Max talked to her privately, and she seemed much calmer.

"He apologized," she explained. "He told me he loved me and he's not handling things well. He's overwhelmed, too, but the last thing he wants to do is lose his family when he's trying so hard to keep it all together. So Stef is giving them a loan for the new equipment, and they're going to sit down and figure out a solution for all the work because Rachel needs something outside the home. Even if it's volunteer work. I've heard the Farley brothers are thinking about offering nanny services. I don't think Fuber is bringing in the cash they hoped for. Now tell me about the woman. I was in Elisa's office when you went over everything. What did Nate find out?"

It had been simple in the end, though it required a couple of police departments to handle the whole thing. Once the Wyoming police found out Kingman was dead, they talked to his wife who gave the bastard up wholeheartedly because she thought she would get to keep everything.

She was about to learn.

"Her name was Meli Smith when Shane and I knew her, but her real name was Meli Greybird. She ran away from her parents at seventeen after a fight." It hadn't taken Nate long to put everything together. "She was a hand when we met her."

"Real nice," Shane chimed in. "She was sweet and caring. She was barely nineteen when he hired her and started sleeping with her. Apparently he always keeps a young mistress around."

"Why did he kill her?" Brooke asked.

"She was pregnant, and she didn't want to terminate it," Shane said flatly. "She told him she wanted to go home. Apparently the wife is saying she was there, and all her husband said was he would take her back to her parents' place after they saw a lawyer about taking care of her."

"And he killed her with a hammer?" Brooke asked.

"From what they've put together, he brought the hammer along and killed her when they got to the ravine. They already found her body and her folks have been informed," Bay said. "And I'm getting calls from some dude who says he's directing a documentary and that this is the wildest turn he's ever seen, and will I sit for an interview. I can say no, right?"

Brooke put a hand on his. "Of course, but let's see if Cleo knows him. The indie film world is small. If she says he's legit, you might think about it. This might be the first time art solved a murder. It's a crazy thing to happen."

"Bay, it's not like you caused the murder," Shane said. "You literally solved it."

Bay's head shook. "No, Kingman's paranoia caused it. I wouldn't have done anything with it. I didn't know what it meant. If he'd left us alone, no one would know."

"I'm not sure about that," Brooke mused, sinking down beside him. "You're about to have a big showing that will likely lead to an even bigger showing. Stef said he thinks one of the gallery owners he's invited is going to want to do a showing in New York. At some point that drawing would have been seen. Her parents cared about her way more than Kingman knew. They'd been looking for her since she left, and they contacted someone who produces true crime documentaries. That picture, whenever it came out, would have caused the police to look more closely at Kingman, and once they did, it would all have fallen apart."

"I won't let it get out," Bay vowed. "I told Nate I'll show her parents if they want it, but then I would like to keep it out of the public. I'm not going to make money off Meli's death."

Brooke nodded. "That's a good thing for you to do." She turned his way. "Maybe we should talk. I know we all said some things in the heat of the moment, and I need you to understand that I won't hold you to it."

Shane sat up. "Really?"

Bay saw her tense, like she hadn't expected that. "Of course. It was a lot. We should talk when we're less emotional."

Oh, she misunderstood that "really." Shane hadn't said it in an "I'm getting out of something I don't want" way. That "really" was asking how deep a hole she was going to dig for herself.

Because while she might not hold them to it, they were damn straight holding on to her words for the rest of their lives.

"I think we shouldn't talk at all." Bay stood up. It was time. She'd had dinner with her brothers and they'd all taken showers and gotten ready for rest. Except he wasn't feeling like sleeping. She'd been wearing a plug for over a week. It was time to put that training to use.

He understood her. She was worried she was putting them in a corner. She needed to understand that they were hers. Forever. There were no corners. Only the home they shared, and it was wherever the hell that girl wanted the home to be. Here in Bliss. In California. If she wanted to try the city again, he would find a way to deal with it since she was the most important part of their lives.

"Bay," Brooke began. "We need to talk about what I said. What you said."

"Why?" Shane stood, too. He was wearing pajama bottoms and had conveniently left off his shirt when he'd come downstairs from his shower. "We said everything we needed to say in the barn. It's done. It's settled, Brooke."

He watched the moment it registered Shane wasn't trying to wriggle out of it. Her shoulders relaxed and her expression was suddenly saucy. "Oh, is it? It's all settled now?

"No." Bay stepped up and had her in a fireman's hold in seconds. "It's not settled at all, and we do have something to talk about. We're going to discuss what happens the next time I attempt to save you from being assaulted and you yell at me."

He wasn't mad. He should have been calmer, but he would use any excuse to get her into that playroom.

"What are you doing?" Brooke asked, her torso coming up.

He slapped her ass. Hard. "Teaching you to give me the slightest bit of respect when I'm in jail for you."

"I did not ask you to…" she began.

He smacked those cheeks again. "To what? To stop that man from putting his hands on you?"

"Bay, he could have hurt you," she argued.

Bay snorted and so did Shane.

"Somehow I don't think that one was going to put up much of a defense when it came to another man." Shane moved ahead and opened the door that led down to the basement and the playroom Trev, Beth, and Bo were so generous with.

He walked into the space. They hadn't had a lot of time to play while they'd been here. Oh, they'd had a shit ton of sex. At least twice a day, and sometimes more since Brooke seemed happy to spend her nights with one of their mouths on her pussy. He knew the taste of that woman like nothing before. He would die thinking about it, with the taste of her on his mouth.

The dungeon Trev and Bo had built was small but stunning. He'd spared no expense. The floors were a dark wood with rolled-up soft rugs so their sweet sub wouldn't knock her knees on the hardwood.

There was a big bed to one side, with under-the-mattress restraints to hold a sub in place, a St. Andrew's Cross, a swing and a rigging setup, and the place he made a beeline for. The spanking bench. It was the Cadillac of spanking benches, with padded arms and legs and a soft place to rest her body. Shane had adjusted it to the perfect height, and Bay noted there was a tray prepared with lube and a plug and condoms.

There were plenty of paddles and whips and floggers, but he wanted to use his hands on that gorgeous ass.

He set her on her feet, and her hands immediately went to her hips, chin tilting up stubbornly. "What are you doing, Bailey Kent?"

He stared into those kick-him-in-the-gut eyes. There was so much about this woman that called to him. He could explain how he adored her intelligence and kindness. How her sassiness got his motor running. But there was some indefinable magnet that pulled him to her. It was a mystery, and he wouldn't ever question it. He would honor their connection and always be grateful for it.

She was theirs.

"I'm going to spank you for yelling at me at the jail," he announced.

Her lips kicked up. It was likely a combination of her amusement at his statement and the fact that she quite liked a spanking. And everything that came with it. "Well, it's a family tradition. I assure you my sister-in-law has yelled at my brothers in that jail often. I'm following in her footsteps. Though it's usually Max and not Rye."

He knew things she didn't. No one wanted to talk to her about her brother's sexual proclivities. "Max does it because he and Rachel have a bargain."

Shane stepped beside him, a knowing smirk on his face. "Everyone in town knows that."

Brooke's lips turned down. "I don't know that. Do I want to know?"

Probably not, but he had a point to make. He moved closer, crowding her. "When Max gets thrown in jail, he owes Rachel a certain amount of sexual servitude. It appears your sister sometimes likes to take the top spot, if you know what I mean."

Her face crinkled up and she laughed. "I can see that now. Yep, I did not want to know that." She sobered, and a calculating gleam came into her eyes. "But the sexual servitude is for Max. He's the sex slave. Ewww. I wish I hadn't said that out loud."

"Do you know what your sister-in-law does not do?" Bay wanted to make himself plain.

"If you are about to say not yell at Max, you're wrong, babe."

Such a brat. And probably right. "Well, that's not how we're going to do it. I'm going to negotiate with you. I promise to get hauled in on a regular basis, and if, perchance, something does happen, you're going to be respectful until such moment that we are in private and then I owe you."

"We both do," Shane added. "I think it's bullshit that Max gets sex because he acts out and Rye gets what? To watch the kids? We all know I'm going to be the good one, so I'm putting my foot down. If Bay gets tossed into jail, I get to serve you sexually, too."

A brilliant smile crossed her face. "You don't think we're moving too fast."

Bay groaned. "I will marry you tomorrow."

She softened and went on her toes to press a kiss to his lips and then to Shane's. "How about next year? I'm saying yes, but I would like a nice wedding. I only intend to do this once."

"But we're for real engaged now." Bay wanted to be sure.

"Yes, and I expect a pretty ring. I don't care about diamonds or how much it costs. I want you and Shane to design it and make it yourselves. I'm marrying an artist. It has some perks." She bit her bottom lip, her face flushing slightly as though she knew what was coming next.

He hadn't made jewelry before. He looked forward to learning how and the reason for it. Their wedding rings. Her engagement ring.

They would be created for her. The way he thought almost everything he created from now on would be. All for her. She was his muse. His love. The amazing woman who could handle both of them. "Deal."

Then they could get to the good stuff. "Excellent. Take off your clothes and get ready to serve your Masters."

"But I thought I was the mistress tonight," she said with a bratty pout.

They were going to be a fluid trio. He wasn't so tied up in the Dom identity that he couldn't let his sub play around with topping. He wanted to try it. He wanted to try everything with her. But not tonight. "You yelled today. So it's funishment for you, and at the end, you'll get two cocks."

It was time. Past time. He wanted them together the way they were supposed to be.

But first he had to get her naked.

He moved in, looming over her and reaching for the bottom of the tank top she wore over her tiny pajama shorts that made her legs look a mile long. She wasn't wearing a bra, and she'd taken off all her makeup and washed away the blood from earlier in the day. "You were magnificent today. You were everything they needed you to be."

Tears welled, but her shoulders came down. She clutched his forearms. "I was scared, Bay. I should have gone after Shane."

Shane moved in behind her, his hands on her hips. "No, you shouldn't have. Henry was coming. You did what we needed you to do. Brooke, there's a baby with your name now. You were a hero. You were…are my hero."

Her head fell back against Shane's shoulder. "I love you. It took everything I had not to run to you."

"I'm glad you followed that ex-secret agent's orders," Shane whispered back. "He took care of me and you took care of Nell and Lucy Brooke. I think that's what it means to be family. I might not know much, but I know that."

"You are my family. You are part of this town." She turned and kissed Shane.

Bay leaned over and kissed the back of her neck. This felt right and real. Sharing her with his best friend, his brother. They'd survived so much together, and now they were here. Now she was here and they were a family. One day, if she wanted, they would have kids and he would learn not from his own parents, but the family he'd found here in Bliss. He would learn how to be a father from Max and Rye and Henry. He would find his way because he was going to love the hell out of all of them.

He pulled her top over her head and got his hands on her breasts, her nipples hard against his palms. She needed tonight. She needed them and what they could give her. She hadn't gotten all the stress of the day out and turned the anxiety into joy.

That was his goal for the night.

He got her out of her panties. "Get on the bench. It's time to begin."

* * * *

Brooke was completely overwhelmed with emotion. It was almost too much. Almost.

They were here and alive, and Shane didn't hate her for staying in the barn. They didn't blame her for needing more time or for not being a hundred percent sure of anything but them. They weren't leaving her.

She needed this far more than she'd imagined.

The afternoon had been calm, with them taking care of her and making sure she had everything she needed. The interviews with Nate and the other officials had been nothing more than an intellectual recitation of the events she'd endured. They'd even taken her to the clinic to visit Nell and Henry and their new baby. Lucy Brooke was doing well. The baby seemed perfect, showing no signs that her traumatic birth touched her in any way.

She'd talked to her brothers, and Rachel and Paige and the boys had hugged her and told her how brave she'd been. She'd sat in their kitchen and drank iced tea and had dinner while Bay and Shane talked to her brothers.

Like being faced with a ton of dead bodies was normal.

But now Brooke realized she'd pushed it down and she needed to set that fear free or she could drown in it.

The good news was she was finally in her completely safe place.

She was finally with her men.

Right time. Right men. Right place. Bliss. She needed some of that, and now she realized she didn't have to live here full time for this place to be home. It would always be her home, and one day when they were tired of roaming and ready to build a family, they would do it here.

She lay her cheek on the padded bench, her arms and legs stretched out and her ass in the air, waiting for the first smack of a masculine hand against her skin. The air felt charged, but this time with all the sweet things of the earth. Pain that morphed into pleasure. The good release of all the fear and rage she'd felt earlier to make room for peace and love and joy. For all the things they brought her.

"Do you know how much I love you?" Bay caressed her backside with his big hand.

"We love you," Shane corrected. He stood beside his brother.

Her head was tilted so she could see them in the mirror that ran along one side of the playroom. Her men were big and muscular, and both their cocks were hard, pressed against the pants they wore. She wanted to touch them, but she also knew she needed what they were about to give her.

"You love me so much you'll leave with me if I need to go." She knew that now. The tears she was certain would only come from spanking were showing up as simple emotion.

"We go where you go, baby." Shane's fingers trailed down her spine. "Even if that means walking into New York City. Though I suspect you're going to have to upgrade our wardrobes. I've thought about this. We can go thrifting and…"

She reached up and took his hand even as she heard Bay getting into place. "No New York. We're going to LA for a while, but I think we should make Bliss our base. We'll find a cabin we can afford and set up studio space for Bay and a design room for me. Beth and Hale can help us if we need renovations. I suspect we're about to have a moneybags in our midst."

Bay snorted. "Or it can all crash and burn. We'll make it work, baby. I think Shane's going to be comfortable on film sets. I don't know how much we need to upgrade our wardrobe, but you should understand that if this thing goes well and I start making real money, you and Shane are going to have to decide what to do with it. I don't know how to invest for shit."

He would hand it over to them, trust her and Shane to watch out for him. For their family.

"I think we can handle it." She knew a couple of guys who were experts at handling money. They could have their dream cabin and get to see a whole lot of the world if she had her way. She stroked Shane's cock through the pajama bottoms he still wore. "Are you going to handle me tonight?"

He hissed but allowed her to stroke that hard cock of his. "I assure you, we can take care of you. We plotted and planned all day how to take care of you at night."

"And in the morning," Bay said. "Do you want to see what happens when I smack her ass and she's holding on to your dick, brother? It could be fun."

Shane chuckled and stepped back, his eyes warm. "No. I'll forgo that experiment. This is about her. She had a day. Baby, I think we need you to cry for us."

The first slap hit her with the force of a storm, the smack cracking through the air before the actual pain hit. When it did, it felt like heat when before she'd been so cold. The pain raced along her skin, going straight to her pussy as it settled into her muscles.

It sent shivers down her spine, lighting up her skin even in the places he didn't touch.

This wasn't about them. It was all about her. It was about giving her the safe place she needed to let it out.

"Tell me how you felt," Bay ordered. "When the trucks pulled up and you realized what was happening, how did you feel?"

"Small. I felt so small and weak," she admitted. "So scared that I was going to lose Shane and then that I wouldn't be able to do what Henry asked of me. That I would be the reason he lost Nell and their baby, and I would lose my friend Lucy."

Shane knelt down. The spanking bench was designed so her chest was supported but her breast dangled. Shane's hands went under her body, and she expected to feel him cup her but instead his fingers twisted one of her nipples, making her gasp and squirm as Bay spanked her again.

"But you didn't. You didn't lose anyone. They lost. They came for us and you stood your ground. You were everything we needed you to be," Shane said, his voice strong.

She had been strong. She had. She'd done what it took to protect the people she loved, and now she could cry it all out. Now she got to acknowledge how much she could have lost and in doing so accept all the bounty of love she was given.

The pain rained down on her as they pushed all of her boundaries. Shane continued to torture her nipples as Bay lubed up a plug and worked it inside between smacks to her cheeks and the backs of her thighs. The deeply intimate sensation of the plug fucking her ass while Bay spanked her and Shane twisted her nipples nearly fried her brain. Tears dripped from her eyes even as she could feel her pussy getting ripe and ready.

The events of the day finally came flooding out of her. She'd held it in, but she was safe now. She didn't have to be strong. Her men would hold her and make it all better. They would never leave her so she could be everything she was, keeping nothing back. The torrent of emotion was unleashed.

"That's right, baby." Shane kissed her cheek, his hands soft on her breast now. "Get it out. Don't leave that poison in your system."

Fear and anxiety were poison if left to simmer too long, if not faced and dealt with. She would likely always have dreams of that man walking in to kill them all, but when she called out, she would wake and find herself warm and safe between her men.

It was all right.

She cried as the pain turned to pleasure when Bay's hand moved between her legs and he found her clit. The plug was deep inside her body now, and she could feel the jangly sensation of it as he started to press a thumb on her clitoris, a couple of fingers entering her soaking wet pussy.

It wasn't more than a few minutes before she came, the orgasm mingling with the sweet ache in her ass and her nipples, reminders that she was alive and loved.

"You were perfect," Bay was saying. She felt him moving behind her.

Shane managed to kiss her, sending his tongue deep and stroking her own even as she came down from the high of their discipline.

Despite the recent orgasm, her whole body went on alert, ready for what they'd been promising her forever.

They were going to take her. Together.

"Relax, baby," Shane whispered between kisses. "He's going to play with you and then we'll move you to the bed. I want you to ride Bay. I want him to be your stallion."

He was her everything. Him and his brother.

She groaned as Bay rimmed her asshole, and then the plug was sliding out and in again. He did it over and over until she was certain she couldn't take another minute.

"Hold on tight, baby," Shane said before he gently turned her over and picked her up.

He carried her to the bed, and she was ready to become theirs.

Chapter Eighteen

They had game planned this night pretty much the moment they met her. Shane held her close, her hair draped over his arms.

They'd almost lost her.

Any issues he'd had with Bay not believing him had been brushed away. His brother had apologized, had made certain he knew how much he valued Shane. They were solid and would always be. And now they had their girl and no matter what happened it would be okay as long as Brooke was with them.

Bay had shucked his clothes and planted himself on the bed. As Shane moved Brooke across the room, Bay rolled a condom on his cock.

Shane stood there so Brooke could watch, too. While she stared at Bay, he watched her eyes get heated, her lower lip disappear behind her teeth. Her nipples got hard. Yeah, she liked watching Bay. It gave Shane the biggest sense of peace because he'd seen that look on her face when she'd watched him.

This was not a woman who was accepting the second husband to please the one she truly loved. She loved them both and celebrated their differences, appreciating what each brought to their marriage.

"You think it'll fit?" He whispered the question into her ear, tracing the shell with his tongue. "You think your little pussy can possibly handle that monster cock? He's going to fill you up, baby. He'll stretch you wide. Can you handle him?"

"I can handle him," she whispered back. "I can handle you both. I can take that big dick of yours splitting my asshole, and I suspect you'll love it."

Damn, but his baby didn't hold back. He adored her easy sexuality, the way she gave every bit as good as she got. She wanted him hard and hot and ready to fuck her ass. "I'll make you love it."

He was addicted to everything about this woman. His woman.

He eased her carefully down, helping her straddle Bay. His cock was dying, but he watched as she slid onto Bay's dick. She groaned and her ass wriggled as she adjusted. "Tell me how it feels."

He loved when she talked during sex, when her voice got husky and low and she spit out some truly filthy, glorious words.

"He's so big and the plug… I can feel the plug. It wants to come out but I'm clenching. I like how it feels. I like how it makes me light up with sensation, but I think it will be even better when it's you inside me. When your cock is deep in my ass and I can feel you both moving inside me."

Shane stripped off his pajama bottoms and boxers and tossed them to the side. He reached for the condoms and lube. Bay had done a good job opening her up, but Shane wanted to play more.

Her backside was a sweet shade of pink and her skin was still flushed from the spanking and the crying that came with it. Holding her while she cried was one of the most intimate experiences of his life. Knowing he and Bay were a safe place where this magnificent woman could let go made him feel ten feet tall.

"You feel so good," Bay said, his hands on her hips. "I don't need anything but this feeling, baby. Wherever you need to go, me and Shane will be there." He slid his hand around the back of Brooke's neck and dragged her head down for a kiss. "You are my muse so my work goes where you go, and Shane might start as an assistant, but he'll be running those sets before long. No one knows how to take chaos and turn it into order like my brother."

"But I like a little chaos." Shane was touched. This was his place. The trouble with what he did well was if it all ran right, no one noticed. Except the people who loved him.

Chaos was inevitable when one lived with two artists.

"I'll remind you of that when we start having kids," Brooke said before Bay took her mouth again.

Kids. He'd never dreamed he would have them, and given how he grew up, the thought probably should send him reeling. He didn't know how to be a good parent since he'd never had one, but he was going to give it his all. Seeing Henry holding that tiny girl in his arms had done something to his heart. In that moment he'd seen Brooke holding a kid, the physical proof of how their souls had melded.

"I think I'll be happy to handle it." He had a suspicion he would be a hands-on dad. "But for now we're going to concentrate on figuring out if this is what you want to do."

By the time they figured out if costume design was her passion, they would be ready. When she was established she could do a lot of work remotely, and the travel part would become something of a treat.

But he knew in his heart they would live here. They would truly build their family in Bliss.

He watched as Bay kissed their future wife, their tongues mingling. Brooke's chest was slightly up so he could see the way those gorgeous breasts moved and how tight her nipples were. He loved playing with her breasts. He could mold them with his hands and pinch her nipples and make her squirm.

"She's killing me, brother," Bay said, his head falling back with a groan. "She's so fucking tight."

"Not as tight as she's about to be." Shane moved into place, letting go of everything but the need to be with her. He parted her cheeks and tapped the plug.

Brooke's spine went straight, her body tightening.

"Asshole," Bay complained. "You're the one killing me now."

He could live with that. It would be a great way for his brother to go. He chuckled and grabbed the condom, rolling it over his ridiculously hard dick before lubing it up.

"Just that one touch," Brooke said breathlessly. "How is it so different?"

Well, the plug she had was only a bit smaller than Shane himself, and she'd never worn it while riding another cock. "I'll show you different."

He eased the plug out, watching her greedy little hole clench as though trying desperately to keep it inside.

He could give her something even better. Anticipation raced along his spine. He had to take a deep breath or he wouldn't last, and he wanted this moment to last.

"I love you, Brooke," he said, placing a kiss on the small of her back.

"I love you, Brooke," his brother echoed.

"I love you both so much," Brooke replied.

And then he wasn't thinking about anything except how to get inside her. Carefully, he placed himself at her entrance, pressing gently inside. Bay held her hips, keeping her still for Shane's invasion.

His eyes nearly rolled to the back of his head at the sensation of his cockhead breaching her. Pure pleasure swamped him. So fucking tight. She was so tight. And right. He had to be careful, had to check that primal instinct that told him to mark this woman in every way he could. He had the urge to slam inside her but she was precious to him, so he took his time. Circling her, rimming her and thrusting in short passages.

He nearly forgot how to breathe when she relaxed and he slid fully inside.

"Fuck, that feels good," Bay said, his voice shaky.

"Speak for yourself," Brooke shot back, sounding beleaguered. "I'm too full. You're both too big."

Bay laughed and Shane felt it, the low rumble moving across his cock. "We are not. We fit just right. Show her, Shane."

He carefully eased out, tilting so he rubbed every nerve.

Brooke gasped and her back bowed, coming up off Bay's chest.

"That's right, baby," Bay crooned. "That's what we want."

She clenched around him and he damn near lost it. Shane took a deep breath and gave her another thrust and then a slow retreat. She cried out, and that was all it took.

They were off, this dance between the three of them his whole world now.

All that mattered was finding the rhythm that brought them together, that melded the parts of his soul he feared he would never find, never feel slide into place like a puzzle he'd known he would never solve.

She was the solution.

She called out, her body going stiff as she rode out her orgasm.

It sparked his own, shooting pleasure through his body. The sensation seemed to last forever as he kept thrusting in and pulling out, and when he was completely spent he fell forward and the three of them were in a pile on the bed.

The moment was warm and intimate and perfect. It was everything he'd ever wanted from a woman. She was between them.

"See, that would not have worked in the tiny house," Brooke said, still dragging air into her lungs. "I don't know how my brothers make that work." She hissed. "Eww. I did not need to think about that."

Bay laughed, looking younger and more free than he ever did. He rolled over and kissed their soon-to-be wife. "Well, baby, we'll have to give you something else to think about. We should change places."

Brooke was smiling even as she argued.

Shane laid back, ready for everything the night had to offer.

* * * *

Brooke Harper soon-to-be Kent looked around the gallery and realized everything was coming together. Finally. She'd spent all of her life working slavishly toward a goal only to figure out the job wasn't the destination. They were.

"He's got such a unique perspective," one of the New York influencers was saying as he studied a big canvas Bay called *The Cowboy Retires*. It was an oil painting he'd done from a sketch he'd made while on the rodeo circuit. The painting had a haunting quality to it.

Brooke could never put a real finger on what it was about Bay's work that touched her. It was more than his masterful use of color and shadow. More than the rustic lines of his sculptures. There was somehow a glow to all of Bay's work. Like it was lit from within, as though he placed a piece of his soul in every work of art.

"It says so much." A second man stood next to the influencer.

This one was gorgeous in his brand-new suit and tie that made her kind of want to rip them off him. "This painting… I can feel the pain. The loss of a proud culture as the world moves on from it."

Shane was hyping up his brother's work, and he could lay it on thick.

But then that was what the man did. He was their greatest cheerleader, the one who hyped them up and held their hands when they were down. Shane was the center of their universe, and she was so happy for it.

The influencer nodded. Brooke seemed to remember Stef had introduced him as an art critic with a massive following online. "Yes. That's exactly it. You see both the sorrow of the man and the entire culture on this canvas. It's stunning, but then all the work is. It's been a while since I found an artist who could work across mediums like Mr. Kent."

"I believe I told you he was one of a kind." Stef wore his semblance of a suit. Slacks, dress shirt, and an elegant jacket sans tie. And he was wearing cowboy boots. His wife was a willowy beauty in a cocktail dress.

Though she noticed Jen Talbot's normally full wine glass was water this evening.

Rachel sidled up next to her. She was in a cocktail dress as well, with sky-high heels. The best part of her sister-in-law's outfit though was her smile. In the weeks since the night she'd blown up, Max and Rye and Rachel had been working on their marriage. On reconnecting as partners rather than just parents. A couple of sessions with Alexei and they were really talking.

A couple of sessions in Stef's dungeon and they were finding their groove again. She'd heard they had started using the tiny house as their own playroom. They had used the Farley brothers' babysitting service several times now, but they didn't go out. They ordered in and spent hours locked up in that tiny house together, reminding themselves of how they got to be the parents of three and a half kids. Rachel had started talking about the new baby with enthusiasm. "They're trying. Jen's excited about giving Little Logan a sibling. You know I wonder if we're always going to call him Little Logan."

"Probably. That kid will be six foot three and we'll call him LL.

Anyway, I'm happy for them," Brooke said, sipping her champagne. She'd made the rounds as the artist's fiancée. And his brother's. She had a placeholder ring for now, but Bay was learning the art of jewelry making from the strangest of places. Mel had explained that he'd spent a lot of time on the Ren Faire circuit during his active alien hunting days. Because aliens liked those big turkey legs, and apparently lute playing soothed them. His cover? He was a blacksmith who made rings as well as swords—all blessed with beet juice to keep the aliens away.

She loved her hometown so much.

"Me, too. I have no doubt she won't be far behind me. You know I will be thrilled with any baby we get, but it would be fun for all of us to have girls. Lucy Brooke and my and Jen's daughters could be a girl gang. We could do girls days. Let me tell you I wish Paige would spend more time with girls. She runs through the woods with Charlie and Zander, and I think she forgets she's a girl sometimes." Rachel took a long breath and let it out, her expression going soft. "Or I should let Paige be Paige and not worry about it. That's the hardest thing about parenting. Letting them be who they are even when you think they're headed for rough times."

Paige would handle the rough times by kicking a shin or two. Her niece was a force of nature, and she would figure out who she was. But that wasn't all Rachel was trying to say to her. "We're good. I understand. Rye and Max are more like my dads than my brothers. I think I was also an easy place to focus all their worry on. Like it was easier to worry about me than their marriage."

Rachel grinned. "Oh, you have been reading the same books as Alexei. He said the same thing. You should know how much we love you."

She glanced over and Max was holding a beer, standing next to Shane. He and Rye had become mentors to her men, and they were soaking up the big brotherly affection and advice. Sometimes too much. They were taking the jail thing seriously and looking for reasons to get locked up so they could pay her back in servitude.

Her nights were interesting.

"I love you, too. All of you, and I can't wait to meet the new baby," Brooke said. "I promise we'll be back in time to greet this one properly."

Rachel sighed, but there was a smile on her face. "I'm going to miss you. So when do you leave?"

Plans were already in motion. "Cleo has the financial backing she needs. Turns out she ended up talking to Seth at the opening night party and she coaxed a nice check out of him, so now Seth and Georgia are producers."

She'd been working on Georgia's Met gown for a solid month, and it was coming together beautifully. It was a full-on statement gown to be worn by a queen taking her rightful place in society. That gown offered no apologies for taking up space and shining the way the woman who would wear it did.

It didn't matter if some critic didn't like it. She was designing for Georgia, and only her opinion mattered.

It was deliciously freeing, and now her ideas flowed, her art like breath in her lungs again.

Rachel hugged her. "I'm going to miss you so much, but I'm excited for you. Remember you always have a place to come home to."

She hugged her sister back, a sweet sense of belonging flooding her veins.

All her friends were here. In the last month she'd spent time with Lucy and River and their families. River and Jax were trying to get pregnant, and Lucy was thinking about it. She'd gotten to know Sawyer's family. Sabrina and Wyatt were lovely, and her sister Elisa was wonderful.

She would miss this place so much, but she would always come home to it. "I will. We're going to start looking for a cabin."

Rachel's head shook. "Don't bother. You should know Stef plans to get you a place in the valley for your wedding present. When you get married."

"It won't be long." She should probably turn that cabin down. Or not. Stef wouldn't have offered without Jen's approval, and he was like another big brother. "Tell him I don't mind a fixer upper now that I know my sister-in-law is so talented."

Rachel was finding more than her groove. She was finding a passion. "I like laying tile and putting in drywall. I thought I would go and be like some designer, but what I loved was doing the work with my hands. I'm talking to the guys about adding on to our house. I think I'd like my own office and eventually we'll need another bedroom. I'm excited about it."

It was easy to see her sister-in-law was where she needed to be.

"Hey, little sis." Rye strode up and wrapped an arm around her. "What are you doing with the most beautiful woman in the world? Hello. I noticed you seem to be here without a man."

Oh, and they role-played now. A lot. Brooke managed not to roll her eyes. "Uh, she's pregnant so she's technically not alone."

"Hush," Rachel said with a grin on her face. "Well, kind sir, I'm afraid I am alone tonight, and I don't understand anything about art. Could you explain it to me?"

Oh, he would. In a broom closet somewhere. "I would like to remind you that this is Bay's professional gallery showing."

Rye didn't take his eyes off his wife. "Then Bay should have remembered that my barn is my professional space, and I shouldn't have to walk in on him and his brother molesting my sister."

She snorted. Yeah, that had happened. Her guys liked to get busy in a lot of places. "Sorry."

"Hey, I finally found a piece of art I get." Max walked up, a beer in his hand and Stef at his side. "Did you see the sculpture of the naked chick?"

Brooke worried she'd gone a bright red. One of the last-minute pieces was a lovely sculpture of…well, her torso. Bay claimed he wanted her breasts to get all the attention for once since they had to compete with the rest of her. It was white marble and could take its place with any of the master works. But it was still weird.

"Now that was a work of art. Tell Bay he should do more of that," Max said with a nod even as Rye's head fell forward and Rachel started laughing.

Stef slapped his best friend on the shoulder. "Yep. You know that's your sister, right?"

Max spat out his beer, and a pained expression came over his face. "I'm going to go wash my eyeballs. Bay, you're a freak. A pervert freak."

Bay ambled up, obviously confused but going with it. "Uh, thanks. Do I dare ask?"

Shane moved in from behind, wrapping an arm around her waist. "I think Max admired one of the works a bit too much."

Bay shrugged and went in for a kiss. "How are you doing, my muse?"

She was fabulous. "I'm excited for our trip."

To LA with Cleo. To start. To explore. To be.

"Me, too," Shane whispered. "Hey, wanna get to the broom closet before your brothers do?"

Oh, she would never say no to that. "Absolutely."

Rye frowned. "Hey…"

But they were off.

"You snooze, you lose, buddy," Shane called out.

Bay tipped his hat. "You know we're younger and faster, brother."

"I'm older and have more guns," Rye called out.

Brooke laughed and went with her men to find a little bliss.

Author's Note

I'm often asked by generous readers how they can help get the word out about a book they enjoyed. There are so many ways to help an author you like. Leave a review. If your e-reader allows you to lend a book to a friend, please share it. Go to Goodreads and connect with others. Recommend the books you love because stories are meant to be shared. Thank you so much for reading this book and for supporting all the authors you love!

The Accidental Siren

Texas Sirens: Legacy, Book 1
By Lexi Blake writing as Sophie Oak
Now Available

Joshua Barnes-Fleetwood is the prince of Willow Fork, Texas, but not all is right with his world. He's the heir to a multimillion-dollar company, has a family he adores, and his best friend at his side. He can't figure out what is missing until Nicole takes a job at Christa's Café. The pretty waitress is a mystery he needs to solve. He's never been so attracted to a woman, and after one night in her company, he's sure she can handle his needs. Unfortunately, he's also sure she's lying to him.

Jared "Grim" Burch found a home with the Barnes-Fleetwood family when he desperately needed one. With support from his newfound family, Grim beat all the odds and became a veterinarian. In Willow Fork, however, there are still people who are suspicious of him and his past. When he sees Nicole, he knows she's the perfect woman for him and Josh, but he wonders if he has the right to bring her into his sometimes dangerous circle.

For Nicole Mason, Willow Fork is nothing more than a pit stop. Once she can save up the money to fix her car, she'll do what she's been doing for the last several years. Run. Framed for her husband's murder, she can never stop looking over her shoulder. There's always someone on her trail, and she can't let them bring her back to the real killer. Getting to know Josh and Grim makes her dream of the life they could have together. If only she could trust them with her secrets.

When their past catches up to them all, they'll find out that even a small town can be big trouble.

* * * *

Josh stopped as they reached the truck, and he realized Nicole wasn't as close as she'd been before.

It was almost one in the morning, but The Barn was still rocking behind them. Neon lights split the darkness, and the thump of music formed a soundtrack.

They'd danced and talked and had a couple of drinks, but not so much he couldn't try to seduce the gorgeous woman. She'd had two margaritas and then switched to water. He and Grim had done the same but with beers. He didn't want a drunken hookup with her.

But he did want her. Like crazy want her. Like he hadn't felt in a long time. He knew damn well it was too soon, but he would make it work.

Except she looked worried now.

"Hey, you okay?" He stopped, giving her some space.

"She's worried, and probably rightfully so." Grim leaned against the truck with a sigh. "Nicole, nothing has to happen. We can take you home and drop you off. All I ask is you let me see you safely home. We probably should have sent you with Olivia."

Their sister had left half an hour before with her friends. She'd offered Nicole a ride, but the gorgeous dark-haired woman had wanted to stay.

Had she changed her mind?

It could be damn hard to be a woman in the world. "Do you have a friend you can call?"

She grimaced. "I have the number to a cab."

Josh snorted. "No, you have the number to Gwen Stapleton, who is surely asleep by this point. And honestly, she shouldn't be driving, much less pretending to be an Uber." He needed to make her comfortable. The night had been even more amazing than he'd thought it could be. Nicole hadn't preferred one over the other. She'd spent time dancing with both of them, and when she'd gotten looks, she'd simply ignored them all. When she'd been slow dancing with Grim and Josh had moved in behind her, she hadn't seemed surprised. She'd matched her movements to theirs, and he'd known this could work.

But not if she was afraid of them. Hanging out in a public place was one thing. Being alone with them was another.

"Darlin', if you're worried, we can walk right back in there and find someone to drive you home that you feel more comfortable with," Grim offered.

She bit her bottom lip, and then her head was shaking. "Who would that be? The only people I know in this town are Christa and the other waitresses, but I don't know them well enough to ask them to pick me up."

"I know Christa," Josh assured her. "She's my momma's best friend, and she will come get you. I would be all right with Christa taking you home."

"Our concern is that you get there safely. That's all," Grim assured her.

One hand went to her hip, and her sass was back. "Oh, really? So you two weren't going to try anything?"

Josh held his hands up as though to show he was harmless. "Nothing at all, if you tell me no."

Her lips formed a straight line. "And if I'm not capable of telling you no tonight?"

His cock kind of jumped in his jeans. That was what he'd been looking for. "You know what we want, right?"

She nodded slowly. "You both want me. You want to take turns."

"Not at all. There won't be any turn taking. Both of us will be with you the whole way," he vowed.

About Lexi Blake

New York Times bestselling author Lexi Blake lives in North Texas with her husband and three kids. Since starting her publishing journey in 2010, she's sold over three million copies of her books. She began writing at a young age, concentrating on plays and journalism. It wasn't until she started writing romance that she found success. She likes to find humor in the strangest places and believes in happy endings.

Connect with Lexi online:

Facebook: Lexi Blake
Twitter: AuthorLexiBlake
Website: www.LexiBlake.net
Instagram: AuthorLexiBlake

Sign up for Lexi's free newsletter at www.LexiBlake.net.

Made in the USA
Middletown, DE
08 November 2025

21097913R00209